I0702850

# UNWAVERING BRANCHES

Kelly Comiskey

Blue Dane Press

Copyright © 2024 Kelly Comiskey

Published by Blue Dane Press

All rights reserved.

This book is a work of fiction. Although some characters and incidents are based on the historical record, the work as a whole is the product of the author's imagination.

No part of this book may be reproduced, or stored in a retrieval system, or transmitted in any form or by any means, electronic, mechanical, photocopying, recording, or otherwise, without express written permission of the publisher.

ISBN 9798990268814

Cover design by: Carey Monroe

Printed in the United States of America

*To my husband, Michael, who has walked every step of this journey with me. Wherever I go, I want to be with you.*

# Katelyn
## Minneapolis, Minnesota
## July 2014

Shades of crimson crept across Jake's face, mocking the circles around his eyes and the bridge of his nose that gleamed white, forming the shape of the sunglasses he wore just hours ago. Katelyn smiled as she thought of their kiss on the dock that afternoon, so passionate that a group of children had catcalled, making her blush and him laugh. It was their third date.

Their first had been a drink that evolved into dinner. He called by noon the next day. Two days later they met for lunch and then that same night for dinner. So maybe that counted as two dates? Yes, so perhaps today was date four. Katelyn didn't know why that seemed important, but she liked the idea that this was their fourth date. After four dates you stop counting and it becomes something other than just a date. And now, after a full Saturday at the lake, she and Jake had migrated to this little restaurant and a menu boasting "Earl's Famous Chicken Spiedini."

"You've burned," she said.

Jake pushed his finger against his forearm, which turned the angry red into a brief pale blotch.

"I should've known better. I put sunscreen on this morning and meant to add more, but you were far too distracting."

"Oh sure, blame me," she laughed.

"No, I blame my family. It's my Norwegian skin," Jake sighed. "All four grandparents came straight from the land of five months of darkness, leaving me with no hope to ever tan. I'm forever cursed to be either scarlet red or pasty white."

Katelyn raised her glass.

"To your grandparents' pasty white skin, but otherwise amazing genes." She laughed at her own compliment.

"You must have been blinded by the sun," Jake teased. "But look at you. Talk about amazing genes. You certainly aren't Norwegian."

Katelyn smiled. She got that question a lot. "What ARE you?" With her pin-straight black hair, light grey-blue eyes, and olive-hued skin, she didn't fit into anyone's mold. She usually responded to such inquiries with a quip about being a mutt or lied and said she didn't know. But, for once, she didn't mind the question.

"How long do you have?" she asked.

"All night," he said.

Jake signaled for the waiter to refill their wine glasses. He looked at her expectantly, leaning back in his seat to settle in.

"Are you sure you want to hear this?"

"I want to know everything about you."

Katelyn studied him from across the table and his eyes held her gaze. She believed him. She wanted him to know. She emptied her glass and began.

# Min-He
## West of Shanghai, China
## August 1943

Min-He sat on the filthy mattress and squeezed her eyes shut, trying to drown out the affected moans coming from the wooden room next door. Her stomach churned in revulsion. Her closed eyes couldn't trap the tears now streaming down her face. Two weeks ago, she was a schoolgirl with a family and a future. Now, she could never go home. She opened her eyes to stare again at the white list posted on the splintering wooden door, all inexplicably numbered 1.

1.     Entry to this comfort station is permitted only to Army and paramilitary personnel.
1.     Visitors must pay at reception and obtain a ticket and a condom.
1.     Contact without the use of a condom is prohibited.
1.     Entry time: 10a.m.-3:30p.m. for Enlisted Men, 4pm-8pm for NCO's, 9pm-12am for Officers.

The remaining rules blurred through her tears. If she had known what awaited her on these Chinese shores, she would have leapt from the ship. But instead, she had pleaded for the opportunity to come. She had boarded the ship with the promise of a new life for her family but found instead only an unspeakable hell.

*****

The day he had come, Min-He's stomach lurched with concern when she saw the shiny black sedan by the gate of her home. Sweat trickled down her back as her black hair, just growing out from the required high school bob, clung to the back of her neck. The air permeated with the salty aroma of halibut drying on the bamboo racks by the docks of Sokcho as the balmy Korean midsummer approached.

3

Min-He swerved her bicycle to avoid colliding with her youngest brother, Jae-Sun, as he and their three cousins darted across the street to the popcorn vendor. Min-He worried; the only time her mother ever gave the children coins for popcorn was when she needed them out of the house. A sliver of annoyance crept through her worry as she got off her bike. The sedan was parked directly in front of the gate, blocking it, forcing her to lean her bike against the white stone wall encircling her home. Last year her brother Hyo left his bike in plain sight in their courtyard, and it was confiscated by a Japanese corporal. Min-He traded a month of violin lessons for this one, more rust than shiny silver metal, a bike that would bring only sneers from even the lowliest Japanese soldier. A week after the lessons ended, her violin was confiscated. But the ragtag bicycle remained. Min-He turned sideways to squeeze past the barricading car and passed through the wooden gate.

Two pairs of boots lay beside the rice paper door. One was typical of the men in her village, weathered and brown, a patch from the sole peeking up on the side. The other was unlike any removed in her home for years, shiny, polished leather, like the ones in the stores on Gwon-gil Street where only the Japanese could afford to shop. Her heartbeat quickened in her chest. Usually when a Japanese soldier entered their home, he didn't bother to remove his boots, tramping through the house like an ox, overturning and rifling through their belongings, searching for brass, metal, or other contraband they were expected to turn over to the Japanese army. Most of their belongings had gone to "serve the war effort" and "defeat the white devils", phrases her Japanese teachers loved to repeat as they droned on about their favorite subject: the war.

Since the Japanese teachers took over her Korean school, their lessons had focused almost entirely upon Japanese culture, history, and what the Koreans could do to help the Japanese win the war. Min-He had never fully understood how her family's brass spoons and silver brooches, much less her violin, were going to help shoot down American planes or destroy Russian tanks.

Expecting to see a Japanese soldier, she left the grey stone stoop and was surprised to see her mother seated at the short red oak table with two Korean men. She immediately recognized one of them as the ijang, the head of her neighborhood association. As she entered the room, Mr. Kim's wiry frame leapt from the table, knocking over a steaming cup of tea onto the plate of millet cookies in front of him. A flash of anger bolted through Min-He at the ijang's carelessness. Their food cupboards were nearly empty, and her mother had served these men a rare treat that was now ruined. In private, her father had called the ijang a "chin-il-pa", a friend of the Japanese, a traitor to the Koreans. He had never been welcomed in their home before. Min-He didn't understand why he was at their table now, being given the opportunity to defile their cookies.

Min-He had never seen the other man before. He was Mr. Kim's opposite: thick and swollen in a tailored suit. He reminded Min-He of a black bear she and Hyo had seen once while hiking near Mt. Seaorak. His flabby body merged into his pointy-nosed head, the expensive suit collar the only indication of a neck. He didn't stand when Min-He entered but offered her a slow, even toothed smile. Her mother glanced nervously at Min-He as she wiped the table, the tea turning the light blue cloth to a dull brown. The ijang, making no apologies for the spilt tea, was the first to speak. There were no introductions and no formalities.

"We've been waiting for your arrival. Mr. Park has come all the way from Seoul to provide a generous opportunity to you and your family."

Min-He stared at the man in the suit, whom she presumed to be Mr. Park. He had not risen from the table and continued to smile at her. She wondered if his cheeks hurt from all that grinning. Mr. Park spoke.

"Min-He, please sit down."

Min-He bristled at being invited by a stranger to sit at her own family's table. She looked at her mother questioningly but sat at her pleading gaze. Her mother gripped the cloth in her hands and perched on the cushion next to her.

Min-He was startled when she realized he was speaking Korean. The Korean language was forbidden in any public place. Only Japanese was allowed to be spoken and Koreans were careful to speak their native language only in their homes with family or intimate friends. He used her Korean name 'Min-He' when he addressed her. Four years before, all Korean families were forced to change their Korean names to Japanese names. Min-He Oh became Miyuki Ota.

The day the family registered their new names at the city hall was the day her father changed from her playful Abuji to the solemn, whitewashed man he had become. Her father's shame at being forced to change his name was insurmountable. That day, he took the then twelve-year-old Min-He and her brother Hyo, now to be known as Hiroshi, to the family cemetery where they prayed for the forgiveness of their ancestors.

Weeks later, the Japanese took over his fishery warehouse, which he and his own father had started twenty years before. Her father was told the gracious emperor would allow him to stay on as an assistant. Mother begged him not to quit, as the family had no other income. Each morning he walked to his father's warehouse, now run by the Japanese he hated. His back stooped lower with each step.

"Being a Korean myself," Mr. Park continued, "I know the hardships you and your family are enduring in these difficult times. Mr. Kim has shared with me the trials of your family". Mr. Park smiled at the ijang who was eating a soggy millet cookie. "I understand your uncle has run into unfortunate circumstances and your aunt and her children have moved in with your family. Your brother's conscription to Japan with the Youth Labor Corps certainly puts financial strain on a family."

Mr. Kim smiled weakly at Min-He, the crumbs from his chin falling wetly upon his yellow shirt. Min-He glared at him. It was not his place to tell her family business to this man.

"Please excuse me, Mr. Park," Min-He's mother interrupted. "I think it would be best if you spoke of these matters with my husband."

"But sometimes, as Koreans," Mr. Park replied, retaining the Korean language, "pride can get in the way of making the most rational decision in a case like this. I believe Min-He will understand the significant impact my offer can make upon the lives of her family and perhaps should decide for herself."

Min-He jolted at his words. Making decisions without her father was not the role of a daughter. She felt a twinge of pride this man thought her capable of such responsibility. Min-He could feel her mother's apprehension. Mr. Park took a sip of tea from the chipped ceramic cup.

"The Japanese army has a great need for intelligent, educated young Korean women like yourself to serve in China and Japan as nurses to our wounded Japanese soldiers. We will provide training, transportation to and from your destination, uniforms, food, and any supplies you may need. As you'll have very few personal needs during your time there, we're willing to pay your salary to your family upfront." Mr. Park paused and looked directly at Min-He. "The day you leave, your family will receive 500 yen as an advance on your salary."

Min-He gasped and turned to her mother, whose eyes widened and whose trembling hand, still holding the dirty cloth, flew to her cover her mouth. 500 yen was nearly a year's salary since her father's demotion. Visibly pleased at their reaction, Mr. Park opened a briefcase Min-He had not noticed sitting by the table. He withdrew a crisp sheet of paper and handed it across the table to Min-He's mother. He shut his briefcase and rose from the table. The wiry ijang quickly followed suit.

"I'll be leaving Sokcho in two days. Sign the contract and deliver it to Mr. Kim before tomorrow evening. Or you can refuse and continue to eat millet and weak tea."

He walked around the table, leaned in close to Min-He, brushing her ear with his lips, and said quietly,

"Remember, my child, pride must not get in the way of what's best. Your parents may resist, but it's up to you to take care of your family."

With a slight nod to Min-He's mother, the man walked out the front door with Mr. Kim scurrying behind.

When Min-He's father arrived home, the women discovered they were not the first to be approached by Mr. Park and Mr. Kim.

"Those men were not welcome in my home."

Ja-Hoon Oh pounded his fist on the clay kitchen counter, causing Min-He's young cousins to look up from their game of gong-gi and stare. In the four months they had lived in the Oh home, he had barely spoken more than a few sentences in their presence, much less shown anger.

Mi-He kneeled on the floor beside her cousins and laid several of the polished stones into sets, silently encouraging them to continue their game. Like her mother, she had learned to deal with her father's rare outbursts with calm. Pil-Ke bowed her head to her husband in acquiescence but continued to add anemic pieces of salted fish to the kimchi pot in preparation for dinner.

"They came to the fishery and showed me their offer. I told them to take their contract to another family. My daughter is a schoolgirl, not a nurse for the Japanese. They have disrespected this family by coming here and ignoring my wishes."

"Ja-Hoon," her mother's voice was so muted Min-He had to strain to hear. "The contract states the money will be paid off within a year and then Min-He will be able to return home to finish her studies. And we had already spoken about the possibility of Min-He not returning to school in the fall. The tuition...."

Her voice trailed off. Min-He seized this opportunity. "Father, this money can be used toward Jae-Sun's middle school tuition. And if I didn't attend school for a year, that money could be saved to pay for his high school. Mr. Park said I would receive special training as a nurse, which can only benefit my education. I can take my textbooks with me to keep up with the school year. I'm already ahead of my class."

Min-He knew the importance of education to her father. She and Hyo would lie outside their parents' rice paper door and listen to them negotiate what they could sacrifice that month to pay for their three children's tuition. Min-He looked over at twelve-year-old Jae-Sun, working at the table on a stick model. She knew the increase in next year's middle school tuition caused many sleepless nights for her father. Ja-Hoon Oh would forego food before he kept his youngest son out of school.

Ja-Hoon hesitated.

"A nurse for the Japanese army is not a respectable occupation. Emptying bedpans and bathing soldiers are not appropriate activities for a young woman."

Min-He started to speak but was interrupted by her brother.

"Soon-Yee Chin is going."

Everyone in the room turned to stare at Jae-Sun.

"Her brother was buying popcorn this afternoon and told me Soon-Yee is leaving in two days to be a nurse in China."

Min-He held her breath and looked back at her father, hope rising in her chest. Soon-Yee's father was an accountant in a prominent bank in Sokcho and a deacon in the community's Catholic Church. Every Saturday, her father went to the Chin family home for a prayer group. The Oh family was Methodist, not Catholic, and Min-He had long suspected the conversations involved much more than the bible but had never asked questions about her father's weekly meetings. Her father regularly quoted Mr. Chin and she knew if Mr. Chin allowed Soon-Yee to go with Mr. Park, then her own father couldn't argue it was not respectable. The room was silent as they all waited for Ja-Hoon to speak.

"I will speak with Mr. Chin and give you my answer tomorrow."

*****

Min-He and Soon-Yee leaned against the railing as they watched the Korean shoreline fade into the distance. The sunburned mountains grew smaller as the ship headed toward the coast of China. Years before these same mountains were lush and green but the Japanese army had raped the mountainside of its rich pine lumber, leaving in its place a barren, sterile skyscape. Min-He clutched her satchel to her chest in excitement.

"I just hope In-Su will have heard I left," Soon-Yee lamented.

Min-He sighed but forced a smile to her friend. This was the most adventure either of them had ever embarked upon and this is what Soon-Yee was thinking? Since leaving home two days before, Soon-Yee talked incessantly about In-Su, her fiancé. Just days after Soon-Yee's father consented to the marriage, In-Su was shipped to Japan to work in an ammunitions factory. Soon-Yee brought all his letters in her red leather bag and proceeded to read most of them to an increasingly bored Min-He on the train to Inchon. The letters consisted primarily of what In-Su ate for lunch and how much his feet hurt.

"I'll send my new address to him as soon as we arrive. I wonder if the mail takes longer from China. I hope the hospital has a post office close by."

As tedious as it was hearing about In-Su, Min-He couldn't help feeling compassion for Soon-Yee. The girls had been in elementary school together, but when Min-He went on to middle school, Soon-Yee's father ended her schooling, believing a girl doesn't need an education beyond elementary school. Other than waving hello on the streets, Min-He had seen little of Soon-Yee these past five years since Soon-Yee always seemed busy with church or housekeeping. Soon-Yee's father never allowed her to attend the parties of her old friends or go to the beach on weekends. With a wave of guilt, Min-He realized she had gradually forgotten about Soon-Yee, alone in her house or spending her days at church. It was no wonder she was so obsessed with In-Su. He was probably all she had. Min-He comforted her old friend.

"I'm sure there will be a post office nearby. In fact, I bet your father has already told him you've gone and he's waiting anxiously to hear from you." Soon-Yee brightened and the girls turned together away from the railing to inspect the ship.

Upon boarding, the girls examined their fellow passengers on the small cargo ship. They included thirty Japanese soldiers, a handful of Korean crewmen, twelve other Korean nurse trainees, and Mr. Park, who would be chaperoning them until they arrived at the hospital in China. As the girls turned to stroll the deck, narrowly avoiding being hit by a large crate hauled by massive ropes, Min-He noticed a group of the soldiers leering at the girls and laughing. A ruddy faced soldier, no older than Min-He, made a V with his fingers and jammed one of his fingers through it. The other soldiers cackled and started chanting,

"Pi, Pi, Pi...."

"What does that mean?" Soon-Yee asked, her face turning white.

Min-He had never heard the word before. "I don't know. Let's go."

This felt different than the whistles and hollers Min-He often heard from the fishermen at the docks, as she and her pack of school friends walked home from school, giggling and flirting. These young men's faces were sinister. She grasped Soon-Yee's arm and fled toward Mr. Park who was hurrying across the grey metal towards them.

"You must come below deck," he wheezed accusingly. "You girls are going to spend these three days in your cabin. You're not to engage with the soldiers."

Min-He looked at him, aghast. As if they had done something to provoke this! Mr. Park grabbed her arm and towed Min-He and Soon-Yee toward the galley's stairs. Despite fuming at Mr. Park's assumptions, she was relieved to be escaping the soldiers' leering, so she followed him obediently down the steps into a musty room. Long steel pipes extended from the ceiling to the floor. Attached to the pipes were chains holding pipe frames with grey canvas strung across them creating rows of bunks, two high. There were many more bunks than girls, but the girls had clustered in the first twelve bunks closest to the stairway.

"I will bring down your meals," Mr. Park announced to the group. "You are not to leave this room without my permission."

He disappeared into the light up the stairs.

Min-He surveyed the twelve girls they had met on the docks before boarding the ship. Most of the girls were around Min-He and Soon-Yee's age, but two, who perched on the lower bunks closest to Min-He, were at least ten years older. Three girls wore the traditional hanbok Soon-Yee's father insisted she always wear, with long high-waisted skirts paired with light long sleeved jackets and a bow in the front. But most, like Min-He, were in plain skirts and blouses. One of the girls wore a houndstooth business suit and Min-He wondered if she would survive the heat emanating from the cabin. Min-He followed Soon-Yee to two bunks just past where the other girls had settled. After placing her satchel on the top bunk, she sat next to Soon-Yee on the bottom bunk, scratching her skin on the coarse gray canvas, and watched the girls chattering easily amongst themselves.

The girls exchanged names and hometowns. Most were from tiny villages Min-He and Soon-Yee had never heard of, in the south or the far north of Korea. Light banter about schools and churches and families soon led to photographs passed around. Min-He laughed at the speed of Soon-Yee putting photos of In-Su in nearly every girl's hand. Soon-Yee was so proud. Soon, the talk turned to their destination. The girls' voices piped in from nearly every bunk.

"I heard we are going to Shanghai."

"Shanghai! Aren't there gangsters in Shanghai?"

"What's a gangster?" Soon-Yee asked.

"Shanghai is the jewel of the Orient. My uncle says there's more money in Shanghai than in all of Asia." Min-He was proud to insert her knowledge.

"I hope we can make some of that money. I'd like to send home more money to my mother."

"I hope I make a good nurse. I don't know anything about medicine."

"I hope we're not in the actual operating rooms in the hospitals. I don't think I could watch an operation," worried a pale girl in a yellow sweater.

"We're not going to be that kind of nurse," announced the girl in the houndstooth business suit, "We'll be more like nurse's assistants, changing bandages and bringing the soldiers food."

"Mr. Park told my father we're going to be giving the soldiers comfort, like keeping them company when they're missing home," claimed a long-braided girl as she took off her green rubber shoes.

A sharp voice rang out from the upper bunk across from where Min-He and Soon-Yee sat.

"What?"

A compact girl with silver wire glasses jumped down from the upper bunk and stood inches in front of the braided girl.

"What exactly did he say?"

The girl with the braid took a step back and stumbled over the green shoes. She collected herself.

"He said we'd be keeping the men company, when they needed someone to talk to or missed home. He said we would comfort them."

The room was silent, tense with unexpected confrontation. The girl with the silver glasses stood frozen for a moment. She then spoke so quietly the girls had to strain to hear her.

"A woman in my village returned last month from a job in Japan at a factory. But everyone said she didn't work in a factory. They said she kept Japanese soldiers company. And not keeping company like reading letters or talking about home. She kept them company in their beds. She comforted them. That is the exact phrase my brother used when he talked about what she did. She comforted them."

Min-He stomach began to churn with the rising of the boat. No one spoke. After an eternal silence, several girls began to speak at once.

"That's horrible but has nothing to do with us."

"That story probably isn't even true."

"My cousin once said she rode a train with a Japanese prostitute who bragged about how much money she made – it's not like she was forced."

"Stop trying to scare us." Soon-Yee spoke vehemently. "Personally, I can't believe anyone would let a dirty woman like that back into your village. What a disgrace. And you should be ashamed for even talking about filth like that. No one wants to hear anything else from you."

Soon-Yee turned her back to the girl. The girl, wide-eyed behind her glasses, met Min-He's eyes and they stared at each other for a moment. Min-He's nausea increased. The girl turned and swung herself back onto her top bunk as the girls slowly returned to empty chatter about suitcases and cosmetics. Min-He leapt from the bunk, ran to the back of the long room, and vomited. When she returned, Soon-Yee handed her a handkerchief from her satchel and stroked her short hair and she curled up in Soon-Yee's bunk.

"Soon-Yee," she whispered, asking the question she had wondered since the day in her parents' kitchen, "why would your father allow you to come on this trip? He took you out of school, he only allows you to go to the store and church and he doesn't believe in women working. Why would he allow you to go to China?"

Soon-Yee drew in a slow breath, and Min-He worried she offended her. After a moment she spoke quietly, still stroking Min-He's hair.

"Mr. Kim, the ijang, asked my father to send me to China a week ago. He refused. The next day, my father lost his job. No one outside of the family knew."

Min-He opened her eyes as she felt Soon-Yee's tears on the back of her neck.

"Two days after he was fired, Mr. Kim brought Mr. Park to our home and said he had arranged for my father to get his job back if I agreed to go. He would give him his job back and no one would know the shame of his being fired."

Min-He went cold with the realization of what Soon-Yee didn't see: intent. Mr. Park knew her father would lose his job if he refused. He had arranged it to get Mr. Chin to sign the contract. A chill ran through her. They had unwittingly been sold. But into what?

*****

The ship turned from the muddy, turbulent waters of the Yangzi to the oily waters of the Huangpu River as it eased its way to Shanghai. Brown-sailed junks and dilapidated wooden fishing boats competed with bullying Japanese cargo ships and armored cruisers in the congested river. As they churned upstream, banks holding a lone pier and vast, empty rice fields evolved into the throng of traffic-lined streets, pedestrians dotting the riverside, and hundreds of boats and ships delivering their precious wares at every wharf. Soon-Yee gasped and turned her head as two urinating fishermen waved to them from the riverside. Min-He suppressed a giggle and lifted her hand to wave back.

"Min-He! Mind yourself! That's not dignified."

Min-He put her hand back down but ignored Soon-Yee's sour glare. Shaking off her doubts from the day before, Min-He shook with excitement. Would they really live in Shanghai? Her

14

uncle, now in hiding in Manchuria, had lived in Shanghai ten years before as part of the Korean Independence Movement. Min-He had been frightened by Hyo's whispered descriptions of her uncle's plotting against the Japanese. She preferred to hear her uncle's lively stories of Shanghai, its exotic parties and massive wealth. With thousands of people from every country in the world, Shanghai had become a western city in the east filled with art, music, and movie stars.

"Look!"

The ship had turned a bend and ahead of them loomed a row of buildings more magnificent than Min-He had ever seen.

"That's the famous Bund!" she cried.

The bustle of the wharfs along the river paled in comparison to the Bund. Dozens of buildings, each different in its architecture, lined the riverside. Spires, domes, and clock towers decorated the buildings, each one more magnificent than the last. Min-He had never seen such opulence. All shapes of automobiles, trucks, and bicycle-drawn carts crowded the street in front of them. People were everywhere: walking, riding bikes, manning the boats docked at piers that jutted into the river like fingers. Min-He's excitement raced when their ship docked in front of one of these piers at the end of the mile-long Bund. She lingered with Soon-Ye against the railing, watching as the naval soldiers tied up the ship.

"Miyuki Ota! Asuka Uchida!"

The girls turned at the sound of their Japanese names. Mr. Park glared at them. Min-He and Soon-Yee joined the group of damp, skittish girls shuffling down the gangplank. They weaved their way through throngs of soldiers and peddlers to four waiting sedans. A kempei, intimidating in his Japanese military police uniform, stood erect at the front of the line of cars. Mr. Park motioned for the girls to stay where they were as he walked over and began speaking to the kempei.

The girls huddled together and nervously whispered to each other. Several tittered at the commotion around them. Soon-Yee moaned to Min-He about In-Su, but Min-He barely heard her. Her eyes were fixed on Mr. Park and the kempei, whose conversation was becoming increasingly animated. The military policeman handed Mr. Park a large, blue envelope. Mr. Park shook his head fiercely and waved his hands in the air.

Both men kept glancing over at the group of girls, occasionally pointing at one. When Mr. Park pointed toward her, Min-He kept her eyes fixed upon him, but a pit formed in her stomach. After several minutes, the kempei took a bulky brown envelope from his jacket pocket. Mr. Park, seemingly satisfied, bowed to the military policeman, and strutted toward the girls. They all silenced as he approached, waiting for his next instruction. But, instead of stopping, he walked right past. The girls gaped at each other.

"Mr. Park!" one of the girls called.

He didn't respond, his back rigid as he walked away, and the girls watched as he disappeared into the chaos of the city street.

The kempei's high black boots clicked on the pavement. A cavalry sword and a pistol hung at his side. A white armband with the characters ken (憲, "law") and hei (兵, "soldier") adorned the left arm of his crisp uniform. He motioned to the drivers of the four vehicles, who simultaneously walked around to the back doors and opened them. The kempei spoke quickly as he pointed to four girls,

"You, you, you, you" and then gestured toward a car.

They obediently piled into the backseat and the driver slammed the door. He divided the remaining girls in the same fashion until only Min-He, Soon-Yee, and Eun-Su, the outspoken girl with the silver glasses, remained. The kempei gestured toward the open door of the first car in the line and the girls got in. The driver opened the passenger door and the kempei got in. Min-He wished he had chosen one of the other cars. Eun-Su spoke.

"Are we going to the hospital now?"

The kempei made a snorting sound then paused as he cleared his throat.

"I'm taking you to the hotel where you'll be staying while in Shanghai. In a few days you'll go to a more permanent lodging. There are many officers waiting to meet you."

Soon-Yee smiled for the first time all day. She whispered in Min-He's ear,

"A hotel? I've never stayed in a hotel. I hope we can bathe. Do you think we can get clean clothes when we're there?"

"You'll be provided with everything you need."

Soon-Yee jumped at his words, surprised he heard her. Min-He looked over at Eun-Su and their eyes met. Eun-Su's eyes welled with tears, and Min-He looked away, pushing aside her increasing fear. There was no need to overreact. As she looked out the window, Min-He saw one of the cars with another group of girls turn right. Their own car didn't follow. She turned around and realized the other two cars were no longer with them either.

"Aren't the other girls going with us?" she asked the kempei.

Soon-Yee and Eun-Su whipped their heads around, realizing, too, they were alone.

He didn't answer, apparently done with his end of the conversation. No one spoke again until the black car reached the hotel.

# Marianne
## Munich, Germany
## November 1942 – May 1943

Frau Hilde Müller and Frau Ingeborg Fisk, the last members of the week's Frauenschaft meeting, were donning their coats to leave when Hans and Gunther tumbled though the door, both covered in so much that blood Marianne couldn't determine if it came from the boy or the brindle-coated boxer. Frau Müller shrieked as the dog galloped past her. A streak of crimson stained the plush tawny fur of her coat.

"Hans! Gunther! Frau Müller!" screamed Marianne.

She didn't know whether to chase the dog, scold or comfort the boy, or pacify the horrified Hilde Müller. Seeing that her son was laughing and unlikely to bleed to death, she turned to the stricken woman.

"Oh Hilde, I am so sorry. I'll pay for the coat to be cleaned. I don't know what happened. My son can get a little wild."

"My husband brought me this coat from Poland. I don't know if it can be cleaned. It is the finest mink."

Hilde Müller bent over, clutching the coat's blood-streaked hem. Marianne felt panic rising in her throat. Hilde Müller was the president of their regional Frauenschaft, the Nazi women's organization Marianne headed in her own small corner of Munich. Hilde's husband, Frederich Müller was a Standartenführer in the SS, her husband's superior. Colonel Müller would soon determine whether Eric received the promotion he coveted.

"Now Hilde," Ingeborg Fisk soothed, "a good cleaner can get anything out. Your maid can run it over to Hauptmann's in the morning."

She gestured to Marianne's son, Hans, still lurking sheepishly in the doorway, a mixture of blood and mud dripping from his Hitler Youth uniform, the smile on his red face enduring despite his mother's obvious discomfort.

"Look at him. A healthy German boy serving our Führer." Ingeborg reached out and touched the silver Mother's Cross hanging on Hilde Müller's neck. "You have six of them yourself. You know he meant no harm. If our Führer's boys can't be a little rambunctious, they'll never grow to be strong fighting men!"

Hilde narrowed her eyes at Hans then nodded in concession. She redirected her scowl to Marianne.

"I will have the bill from Hauptmann's sent to you."

Ingeborg winked at Marianne as she escorted Hilde Müller out the front door and into the waiting Mercedes. The door latched behind them as Marianne turned to her only son.

It had been a while since she really studied him, and she was surprised to find him standing at nearly exactly her height. At fourteen years old, his facial hair was starting to come in as thin baby fuzz creeping above his lip. His blond hair flopped over one eye, which was starting to swell into a conglomeration of blue, red, and black. Congealed blood gathered beneath a small gash under his left eye and the knuckles on his hands were scraped and bloody. The light tan shirt was coated in thick mud interspersed with scarlet blood stains. Hilde Müller was right. It would never come out.

"What happened to you?" she demanded.

"Nothing happened to me." He laughed, sliding off his mud caked boots onto the mat by the door. "It all happened to that mischling Jew boy."

She glared at him, waiting for an explanation.

"Albert, Karl, and I were coming home from our Hitler Youth meeting. That Jew boy, you know the one whose father used to own the jewelry store on Bunder Street, he was walking on the sidewalk and wouldn't get off when we passed."

"So?"

"So? What do you mean so? That Jewish pig wouldn't move so we could pass. He needs to learn to respect authority, so we taught him a few things. Gunther got a few bites out of him too."

"Oh, good lord. Gunther!"

Hearing his name, the boxer bounced into the kitchen, his enthusiasm only weakened by the left paw held out in front of him.

"What have you done to Gunther? This dog never hurt anyone. Hans, you can't tell me Gunther attacked that child."

"Nah, he didn't exactly attack him. I've been trying to train him to attack but he always just wants to play. That Jew kicked him a few times before we finished with him."

"I need to get Gunther to your grandfather's. We'll discuss this when I get home. Your attacking other people isn't acceptable, Hans. Your father's coming home tomorrow and won't approve of your fighting."

"Dad's coming home?" The boy brightened. "You're wrong, mom. Dad will be proud I took down a Jew. I can't wait to tell him."

The dog yelped as Marianne rolled his paw in her hands. She didn't have the time or energy to argue. She was partly relieved to have an excuse to get out of the house and end the conversation. As much as she hated to admit to herself or her son, Hans was right; Eric would likely encourage the boy.

"Get cleaned up and tell Martha to serve you children dinner without me. I'll be at your grandfather's. Ask Martha to read Christa a story if I'm not home before her bedtime."

Marianne regretted the possibility of having the housekeeper read her youngest daughter her nightly bedtime story. That was their special time together and it seemed like Christa was spending more and more time with Martha and less with her. Eric said it was the consequence of being an SS officer's wife. Frauenschaft meetings, volunteer soldier hospital visits, and dinner parties meant less time with her children. Eric frequently pointed out if they had six or eight children like many of their friends, she would have even less time. As if that made her feel grateful.

She was saddened at the reminder of her numerous miscarriages and the seven years it had been since her last pregnancy. Women like Frau Müller wore their Mother's Crosses as badges of honor, but Marianne had borne only three children. She and Eric still tried. One more child and she too could be awarded a Mother's Cross. True, it would only be the bronze medal, but then, like the other wives, she could tie it around her neck and show she was doing her part for Germany and the Führer. One more child and her family could feel complete. One more child and Eric might believe they were enough.

The blood-encrusted dog, with his injured paw hanging, pushed through the door dragging Marianne behind him. A yapping affenpinscher and an elderly dachshund sat with their owner in her father's waiting room. While waiting for her father to finish with his patients, Marianne chatted with Karin, the industrious receptionist, as she updated the day's charts. When the dachshund and affenpinscher finally departed, Marianne followed Gunther into the back room.

"Did your husband mistake him for a Jew and try to shoot him?" her father joked, crouching over Gunther's lame paw.

"Dad, shhh. That's not funny. You better not let anyone hear you," she hissed. But she dared not tell him the truth. "He just got in the middle of some of Hans' games."

Martin Bauer grunted knowingly and rolled his eyes.

Marianne sighed. At home, she had to hide her father's feelings for her husband and his politics. With her father, she had to hide what went on at home. She knew her father didn't approve when she dropped out of the Munich School of Art to marry Eric Hofmann, a charismatic, ambitious, young attorney. Eric had joined the rapidly growing Nazi party in its early years, convinced the alluring Adolf Hitler would create a new, powerful Germany. Her father believed the Nazis were dangerous and warned them both against aligning with the controversial Hitler and his extreme politics. When Hitler won the 1933 election and Eric began to rise in the Party's new ranks, he never let Martin forget his words. Marianne played peacemaker and mediator between the two men ever since.

Keeping Martin quiet about his opinions was one of Marianne's greatest burdens. When her father was a guest at one of their dinner parties last year, he had asked Obersturmbannführer Braun if he planned to send the Soviets the same way as the Jews. Eric turned so white Marianne thought he was having a heart attack. Fortunately for Martin, the Obersturmbannführer had so little a sense of humor he didn't understand Martin's sarcasm and proceeded to lecture for fifteen straight minutes about the inferiority of the Slavic race. After that, Martin was no longer welcome at their parties.

"I'll spare you and not ask for details about our little Hansi's 'games'. So that husband of yours comes home tomorrow, I believe?"

"Yes, he's on leave for two weeks. He'll be glad to get out of the Russian freeze."

"I imagine. So, what exactly is he doing out there, Marianne? He certainly isn't soldiering. Battling at the front doesn't seem like your Eric's forte."

"You know I don't talk about that with him, Dad. And even if I knew, I couldn't tell you."

"Ah yes, top secret SS business, I'm sure. Maybe you need to do a little investigating, Marianne. Open your eyes and see what your beloved Führer is up to."

"Dad, you need to be careful. If someone overheard, you could be arrested."

"I should be able to speak to my daughter about her politics. And you should be able to adequately explain to me why you believe what you believe."

"I don't believe anything, Dad, and I don't have any politics. I'm just supporting my husband and trying to raise my children."

Gunther licked Martin's hand as he began to wrap his paw. Marianne tried to change the subject.

"I got a letter from Mother's cousin Annett last week."

Marianne's mother, the only woman her father had ever loved, died from pneumonia when Marianne was ten. Marianne exchanged letters with her mother's relatives in Vienna several times a year. She continued,

"Annett's daughter, Brigitte, died in the institution last month. She had pneumonia, just like Mother. Annett is having a terrible time. I feel just awful for her. When her husband insisted the little girl go there, Annett fought it, but he convinced her they had better techniques to care for the mentally retarded. I know she regrets it now."

Martin stopped wrapping the bandage and stared at his daughter.

"She died in a mental institution from pneumonia?"

"That's what she said."

Martin shook his head and held his daughter's bewildered gaze.

"What, Dad?"

"That little girl didn't die from pneumonia. Your husband's cronies put an end to her."

"What are you talking about? That's not true."

"I'm in the medical community, Marianne. I hear things. The Nazi party is getting rid of 'undesirables'. They're killing people in mental institutions, handicapped people. Even children. People who will not adequately propagate their Aryan race. I know you don't want to believe these things about your husband and maybe he's not doing it personally, but he knows and condones it by being a member of the SS. You need to open your eyes and see what's going on in your husband's world. See what world you're creating for your children. Marianne, I want you and the children to leave him. He returns to Russia in two weeks. Let's get out of this hellish new world we're living in. I can take the family to a veterinary conference in Sweden or Switzerland, and we can stay. I have connections that can take care of us until this is all over."

"No, Father, I don't know what the Nazi's are doing, but I know Eric is not a part of killing anyone other than the Führer's enemies. And what you're saying is treasonous. You'd better watch yourself."

"Are you threatening me, Marianne?"

She softened.

"Of course not, Dad, but you're threatening my family. Nothing is going to break us up. No matter what happens, my family's staying together. Nothing's more important to me. I love my husband and he is a decent, good man. I don't know about everything else, but I do know Eric."

"Ok, Marianne, OK." Martin sighed. "And OK for you too, Gunther." He playfully shook the drooling dog's jowls and leaned to whisper loudly into his pointy ear. "Stay out of the path of the Hitler Youth next time."

Marianne thanked her father and he bent to allow her to kiss his grey stubbled cheek. As her cab pulled away, Marianne watched her father's face appear in the clinic window and raise his hand goodbye. She wished he understood how much she loved Eric and how wrong he was about him. Surely, he must know Eric would never condone the things he was accusing him of. As she turned around in the cab, she had a hard time shaking the nagging feeling in the pit of her stomach, as she tried to convince herself his theories about Brigitte's death were dead wrong.

*****

She was always surprised by how elegantly handsome Eric was. Marianne adjusted the bed sheet self-consciously to cover her belly as he got out of bed. She watched him dress, his muscled shoulders showing no sloop or sign of aging, only the slightest graying at his temples indicating he was no longer the young man she had married fifteen years ago. His black uniform was crisp and cold, the silver eagle staring down at her from his shoulder as he leaned over to pull on his boots, which he refused to leave at the front door despite the path of mud they left trailing from the door to their bedroom. He had arrived late the night before and had not yet seen the children. The seven months he'd been gone seemed like an eternity. Frequent letters home and packages filled with treasures of stockings, linen, chocolate, and sometimes jewels, were only a small consolation. With Eric home, her family was whole again.

The door crashed open. Hans and Erika broke through the doorway, their shoulders jostling to be the first one in. Erika rushed into her father's arms.

"Papi! When did you get home? I missed you so much!"

Hans stayed in the doorway and raised his arm to greet his uniformed father.

"Heil Hitler!" he shouted.

Eric beamed and returned the greeting, equally as enthusiastic.

Seven-year-old Christa followed behind, shyer. Seven months in the eyes of a seven-year-old seemed like literally an eternity. She crawled into her parents' bed and curled up next to her mother.

"What did you bring us?" she peeped.

Eric's laughter echoed through the room as he scooped up the suitcase he left by the dresser last night, when Marianne had dragged him into bed, all material possessions forgotten. The scent of his body still lingering on her, Marianne beamed a contented, satisfied smile as Eric opened his suitcase to the shrieks of their two daughters. Dolls and chocolates for Christa; perfume and a gold silk scarf for Erika. Marianne raised her eyebrows in discontent. She would have preferred dolls for the thirteen-year-old as well, but Eric knew how to win his eldest daughter's affection.

Hans' gift raised her eyebrows further. The ebony and silver metal glistened as Hans turned the pistol over in his hands, his adoration of his father bursting through him. Eric radiated at his son's excitement, so obviously full of pride in the boy that Marianne held her tongue. When Hans left with his new Luger, the two girls following behind in giddy chatter, Marianne finally scolded her husband.

"He's too young for that gun. And Eric, he's violent enough already. You should see how he parades around the neighborhood and comes home nearly every night bloody and bruised from fighting."

"Hans is learning how to be a soldier. That's what good German boys should be doing."

"I don't want him to be a soldier."

Eric's eyes narrowed, glaring a look of contempt that nearly buckled her knees.

"Well, that's what he is going to be. A soldier for our Führer. If you raise him to be anything less than that, I'll find someone else to raise him while I'm gone."

She was shocked silent. He had never seen him look at her like that before. Fear flashed through her as she spoke quickly to soothe him.

"I'm just scared for him. I still see him as a boy."

"Boys not much older than him are fighting at the front." Eric sighed at her stricken expression. He sat back down on the bed next to her. "Enough talk of that. Don't you want to know what gifts I brought for you?"

Marianne glowed as his face transposed back to the boy she married. He removed a layer of navy cloth from the bottom of the suitcase to display a mass of rich ginger fur. He reached in and revealed a full-length mink coat. She gasped,

"Just like Hilde Müller!"

Eric laughed as she quickly disposed of her nightgown and poured herself into the plush sleeves of the fur.

"Exactly like Frau Müller," he concurred with a grin. "In fact, speaking of the Müllers, I have something to tell you. I have been promoted to Sturmbannführer. Standartenführer Müller showed me the orders on the train last night. And, you'll be happy to know, I've been assigned for six months to the SS training academy right here in Munich."

"Munich! You're going to be home!"

She leaned back on the bed, naked underneath the opulent fur. She peered back into the suitcase and discovered a silver jewelry box nestled beneath the navy cloth. She met his eyes and he smiled and nodded. As she slid the diamond bracelets up her arm and gazed in awe at the amethyst ring, sapphire necklace, and the collection of loose rubies and pearls gleaming from the purple velvet-lined box, Marianne murmured,

"Where did all of this come from? How can we afford all of this?"

"Shhh... Don't worry about that."

He stopped her next question with a kiss as she pulled him, uniform be damned, back into bed.

*******

Eric's six months home passed much the same as the months he had been deployed. Marianne saw him irregularly. He was gone for days, often weeks, at a time. Sometimes Marianne would arrive at his temporary assignment, the prison camp in Dachau, to surprise him with lunch and he rushed her off, seemingly agitated by her intrusion. The nights he was home, he ate a hurried dinner then locked himself in his office, begging off any time with the children to spend with his briefcase and a multitudinous pile of papers ominously labeled 'Streng Vertraulich', Strictly Confidential.

At least twice a month, Eric whisked Marianne into Munich's elite social scene: dinner at white linen restaurants with endless pours of Riesling, Die Zaubergeige at the National Theater, or the Ninth Symphony at The Munich Philharmonic. Occasionally, depending on the company, the shows were followed by raucous laughter at the Hofbrauhaus or ParkCafe. Marianne was proud of her sophisticated, charming husband.

She secretly enjoyed watching other officers' wives steal lingering glimpses of Eric above their wine glasses, knowing it was Marianne who would go home with him at the end of the night.

Marianne made flighty, mundane small talk with the other lower officer's wives, but became anxious when accompanied by Eric's superiors' wives. Eric watched her with eagle eyes those nights, afraid, like she, that Marianne would say the wrong thing. Marianne cautiously limited the conversations to her children, their children, and who had last seen or heard the Führer. Marianne gauged her success by Eric's response when they arrived home: he either swept her to him and carried her to bed, or spoke little and turned his back, ignoring her pleas to speak to her. The next day he berated her for neglecting to mention Han's newest marksmanship medal or forgetting Frau Lehmann's second daughter was pregnant with her fourth child. But he would eventually come around, succumbing to her tears.

"I'm just trying to teach you, Marianne. If we want to be something in this life, you have to learn how to rise to the top. The right words and the right people will take us places."

The rare evenings and weekends when Eric was home were spent primarily with Hans, training the boy to be an officer. Marianne watched her only son and worried. Now fifteen and nearly six feet tall, his Hitler Youth uniform was lined with medals and badges. Hans had all of Eric's ambition, but none of his charm or sensitivity. Hans was worshiped by a pack of neighborhood hoodlums who terrorized weaker boys. Marianne's lectures were widely disregarded by both Hans and Eric until the day that Hans raised his voice to her. Eric's backhand across Han's lip brought his tone into check for a few weeks. Hans spoke to Marianne more courteously after that, but his eyes conveyed his contempt.

Erika was gone to BdM meetings five nights a week. Once she turned fourteen, Erika was quick to join the Nazi girl's organization, Bund Deutcher Madel, and Marianne saw her only as she rushed through dinner to get to the next assembly, flag ceremony, or sporting event.

One night during an air raid, Marianne realized it was the first time in nearly a month that her entire family had been in the same room. With increasing frequency, air raid sirens sounded in the middle of the night and the family got up from their beds and raced to the bomb shelter Eric commissioned to be built in their basement. Marianne held a crying, frightened Christa in her arms, Erika clung to Eric, and Hans stood in the corner, agitated to have been awakened, cursing the British and swearing revenge. When Eric was away, Marianne was even more frightened by the air raids, worrying for his safety, praying he was in a shelter, unsure if she could manage without him.

Marianne filled her days with mindless tasks: assembling baskets for the next Frauenschaft meeting, stripping bandages to be shipped to the front, knitting winter socks for the soldiers. She longed for 3 pm when her sweet Christa returned home each day from school. They read books together, sang along to folk songs on the radio, and giggled while Marianne demonstrated the steps of the landler or the polka. Some days it felt like Christa was all she had. In the evenings Martha took her from Marianne's arms and reminded her Christa needed more structure and discipline. Marianne would lie awake, alone, often with Eric snoring by her side, waiting for something she couldn't name.

*****

The POWs showed up on a Thursday. Marianne drew open the kitchen curtains to let in the morning light and shrieked at the sight of a striped-shirted stomach filling the window frame. Martha came running.

"Frau Hofmann! Did your husband not tell you the workers were beginning today?"

Marianne gathered herself. She was not about to admit to her overbearing housekeeper that she didn't know what the woman was talking about.

"Of course, he did. I simply must have forgotten. Now, remind me what all they're doing."

Martha looked smug.

"They are reroofing, painting, and putting in a larger garden. Sturmbannführer Hofmann also requested they replace the sewer system."

Marianne watched the men from her parlor window. Eight men in black striped uniforms were guarded by two low ranking Nazi soldiers. The prisoners were young. The oldest was no older than she and the youngest couldn't be much older than Hans. Their beards made them appear much older, but as she peered at them through the parlor curtains, she recognized the youth in their eyes. That night Eric laughed when she asked how they could afford all this labor.

"Oh Marianne, don't be dense. We aren't PAYING them. They're slave labor. Another perk of being an SS officer, my dear."

He winked at her, but she didn't smile back.

Marianne spent the next eight weeks peeking through the curtains of the parlor to watch the men. Their eyes frequently caught her as she peered through the lace curtains and she quickly spun away, ashamed of her gawking. They were in her yard each morning when she woke and were herded away shortly before she put Christa to bed.

As the weeks passed, she felt she had gotten to know them. The slight boy with the clean, beardless face, the oldest man with the red beard and striking blue eyes, the tall scarecrow with wild flaxen hair. She and Christa gave them names, as the little girl sat in her lap and made-up stories about what their lives must have been like in Russia. The paunchy man with the jowls was certainly a goat herder in Siberia. The bald man: a barber; the pale faced boy: a movie projectionist. Their imagined lives meshed with Marianne's real one.

They were all thin. As each day passed, she believed she could actually see them getting more gaunt. She watched as the German guards ate their sausages and brotchen, giving little notice to their charges other than the occasional glance or yell to hurry up. Every day at noon and 6, the eight men took their short break with a small piece of bread and a cup of coffee. Some days, they only had the coffee. As the days passed, the guards watched less and talked more. At the beginning, Marianne was concerned about the guards' laxness. What if one of the prisoners escaped? What if one came into the house? But the prisoners simply worked, and Marianne eventually felt no threat from the tired, emaciated men.

Hans and his boorish friends often arrived home in their brown Hitler Youth garb, shouted at the prisoners, and threatened to shoot them. Marianne watched in horror as they drew their guns and pretended to shoot. The prisoner's eyes never left the ground as the teenagers spewed profanities. The day they threw rocks as the guards laughed, Marianne stormed out of the house. Hans and his friends dispersed, but Hans gave her a shaded, disappointed look, as if she had shamed him with her behavior.

*****

"The pot of goulash is on the stove for dinner."

Marianne followed Martha into the kitchen, being directed as if she were a child.

"It can sit and cook for the next several hours until all the family is home and ready to eat."

"I know how to serve dinner to my own family, Martha. I did it for years before you came along." Martha looked at her dubiously.

"All the same, the goulash is on, and I'll be back on Tuesday."

Martha was going to Würzburg for the weekend to visit her mother. She acted as if she were leaving a helpless child to tend to the children instead of their own mother. Marianne was glad the meddling woman was going. She hadn't had the house to herself since Eric had hired Martha during her difficult pregnancy with Christa, nearly eight years ago. Martha left long lists of household routines to follow and meals she had pre-prepared, and Marianne nodded along, relieved when the car finally arrived to take Martha to the train station.

With Christa in school, Marianne found herself alone in her house for the first time since her children were born. Fifteen years had passed since she had been truly alone. No one was running through the halls yelling, no nanny or housekeeper was scolding the children or her; instead, it was just Marianne, alone with her thoughts. Quiet moments like this like this reminded her of painting. As a teenager she had spent hours in a sunlit back room her father had converted from a closet, creating life and beauty from a blank canvas.

After Hans was born, her time to paint and sketch dropped dramatically. It ended completely when Erika was born eleven months later and Eric was promoted. From then on, her life was consumed by childcare, then later by social functions, Frauenschaft meetings, charity events, and the role of an officer's wife. Now, this brief moment of solitude brought the longing for her old self, the artist, the independent free spirit, back in waves. She hadn't been that Marianne in a long time.

Alone, she didn't know what to do with herself. Martha had already made the beds and supper was on the stove. Marianne ripped some sheets into bandages to add to the stash she would take to Frau Hilber's house next week. When Christa came flying into the empty house, it was a welcome relief. Of her three children, Christa gave her the most joy. Christa had none of Han's venom or Erika's nonchalance. Even when they were little children, Marianne had struggled to connect with Hans, who refused to let her get close, or Erika who was more interested in Eric, Martha or her neighborhood friends than she was in her mother. But Christa wanted nothing but to be with Marianne. Marianne loved her intensely.

The little girl stood on a chair, her blond braids beginning to stray from the tight loops Martha had bound around her head and stirred the pot of goulash.

"Martha never lets me help," she complained.

Marianne smiled, enjoying her youngest child's favor. Hans had left for a Hitler Youth camping trip and Erika was attending a BdM Home Evening (tonight's topic: 'A People and It's Inheritance of Blood: Racial Policies in the Third Reich'). Once again, Eric wouldn't be home for dinner, having called an hour earlier to tell her he had an unexpected meeting. She was surprised the call hadn't annoyed her. She was content to spend this time alone with her Christa.

As Christa stirred the goulash, Marianne glanced out the window at the prisoners. It was nearing 6:00, their usual mealtime. The two guards had already settled in, sitting in the front of their truck, eating and playing cards. The guards rarely even looked up at the POWs. Eric would be furious if he saw how little attention they paid to these supposedly dangerous men. They were so thin, so very thin. The oldest man, whose red beard had grown sparse and scraggly, caught her staring at him. For the first time, she didn't look away. His eyes stayed with hers for a moment, eyes hollow and gaunt. She had had enough.

"Come down, Christa. I'm taking you to a café for dinner."

"Just us?" Christa smiled excitedly as she jumped off the stool. "But what about all this stew?"

"I have other plans for the goulash. Now go change into your blue skirt and put on your shoes."

After the child skipped giddily upstairs, Marianne removed four bowls from the cabinet and balanced them inside the giant, lidded pot. With two potholders, she grabbed the pot, and pushed open the door with her knees. Her eyes focused on the guards in the truck, who took no notice of her, and she walked nonchalantly toward the colossal hydrangea bushes that lined the house, where the POWs often gathered to eat their late afternoon bread. Stopping at the center bush, she set the pot underneath it, and began to pick the flowers. She smiled and waved to the guards who nodded their heads in acknowledgement, but barely looked up from their card game. She left the bushes with an armful of hydrangeas.

As she walked away, she stared intently at the sparsely bearded man. His eyes left her face for a brief moment and went to the black pot sitting beneath the bush. When he met her eyes again, she gave a slight nod, then looked away. Christa was waiting in the doorway. Marianne dumped the flowers onto the counter.

"Come, Christa. We're going to dinner."

# Rachel
## Warsaw, Poland
## October 1940 – September 1941

Adam's screams in the dank, unfamiliar hallway were drowned by the clatter of a handcart toppling down the stairs toward them.

"Watch out below!" an unknown voice called.

Rachel leapt out of the way, shielding Adam's body against the wall as the hand cart rattled past them, emptying its contents into the stairwell. A woman's berating voice trailed a gangly teenage boy as he chased the cart down the stairs. He smiled at Rachel apologetically as he blew past her in pursuit of the cart that crashed against the stained wall at the bottom of the cracking stairs. Rachel continued her ascent, two more flights up, passing the harangued woman collecting her spewed belongings. Apartment 4B. She stared at the number on the door, the top circle of the B peeling off, leaving a sad, lower-case version of itself. She gave the door a light knock and pushed it open.

"Rachel."

Her mother rose from the table and a smile creased her face, but not before Rachel saw her wipe her eyes. Hella took the baby from Rachel's arms and kissed his pink forehead.

"He's not warm enough," she scolded as she tightened the infant's blanket. "Where's Josef?"

"Unloading the cart with Aron. They should be up shortly."

Rachel surveyed the room. The main room was cramped but accommodated a kitchen with a dilapidated stove and a sink in the corner. A green paint-chipped wooden table with four mismatched chairs hunkered in the center of the room and three mattresses lined the walls. The door to the single bedroom was open. A cracked window in the back wall provided a view of the dirty brick of an adjacent building. A family photograph hung on the wall over the mattresses which had been covered with her grandmother's quilts: desperate attempts to make this hovel homey. The smell of boiled potatoes wafted in from the apartment next door. Hella read her daughter's face.

"We were lucky to get it, Rachel. If we hadn't made the trade with that Catholic family, we could well be homeless. I hear they're setting up refugee shelters for people who have nowhere to go. Rumor has it, we may even have to take in another family."

"Another family? We already have nine people in a one-bedroom apartment."

"Yes, well, four people per room is mandated, but there's talk. There's always talk," Hella sighed. "I'll take care of Adam. Go help your brother and husband. You can put that bag in the back room."

Rachel walked through the apartment, not feeling the luck her mother spoke of. The home she had grown up in, their sunny apartment on Szewska Street, had been traded to an unknown Polish family for this dingy, peeling apartment that was half its size. When the edict passed that all of Warsaw's Jews had to move to the established ghetto, her parents acted quickly, her brother using his university connections to secure them this trade. Rachel and Josef waited until the last possible moment, hoping things would change, hoping to stay in their cozy apartment with the view of the park, hoping their baby would be born outside the barbed wire. At least they had gotten that. Three weeks after her long labor, Rachel still felt sore but managed to help Josef pack the few belongings they could fit into a borrowed wagon.

Two mattresses were pushed against the wall of the bedroom that Rachel, Josef and Adam would share with Rachel's brother Aron. Mother and Father would sleep in the outer room with her mother's sister Dora and Dora's two daughters, Mira and Lilliana, who made up the nine crammed into the tight apartment. If Uncle Ziv came home from the front, that would be ten. Last night, Josef quipped they shouldn't hold their breath waiting for the return of number ten. Rachel kicked him under the table, and he dropped the subject. But she too had seen few men return from the front.

The stairwell filled with new bodies, as more families moved in. She nodded at their tired, fearful faces. Outside, Aron and Josef piled their belongings near the entryway; Aron was anxious to return the wagon to its rightful owner. She didn't know where the wagon had come from and hadn't asked. Aron was always pulling rabbits out of his hat. The crisp end of October air bit her cheeks and she pulled her burgundy coat closely to her and stepped back outside. The streets were packed with overflowing handcarts, loaded wagons, and discontented transients with a lifetime of weight on their backs. Today, the last day for Warsaw residents to enter the ghetto, was the end of wishful thinking.

Rachel evaluated the small accumulation of belongings, now encompassing everything she owned. Josef put down his guitar case, the last item from the cart, and kissed her lightly on the forehead. She forced a smile. His brown eyes had aged a hundred years since she met him, a free-spirited aspiring musician, teaching at the local college to pay the rent. Josef wooed her with love songs outside her bedroom window after afternoons spent strolling through Lazienki Park and reciting poetry by the Chopin Monument. Rachel's father hadn't approved until he got to know the temperate, wry-witted man who adored his daughter. Saul gave his consent to their marriage after ensuring from his future son-in-law that his daughter would be cared for.

After they married, Josef taught full time until he was fired when all Jewish employees were banned from the university. Teaching Jewish students piano and guitar in their home had supplemented Rachel's income as a social worker with the Judenrat, Warsaw's Jewish Council, a job she had arranged to continue in the ghetto.

As of today, she was the only family member still with a job; a bitter pill to swallow when all she really wanted was to be home with her baby. Tomorrow she was to report to ZTOS, the newly named Jewish Society of Public Welfare, for her new assignment. She knew she should be grateful, feel lucky, but found it hard to muster up gratitude. But she did manage to muster a smile for her husband and carried the last load up the crumbling stairs.

*****

"How are we expected to survive on this?" Hella threw the ration cards onto the table.

"Clearly, we're not," Aron said, spooning the last of his bowl of soup into his mouth.

Rachel sat close to the stove, Adam at her breast. She worried constantly about her breasts drying up and not having enough to feed her son. Hella brought Adam to her twice a day at the ZTOS offices where she was able to sneak out for a few minutes to feed her son. Rachel's job consisted of sorting through the multitudes of requests for additional rations, clothing, and work certificates for the tens of thousands of unemployed workers in the ghetto. ZTOS was in the process of opening soup kitchens throughout the ghetto to supplement the paltry ration cards. Many Jews in Warsaw couldn't even afford to purchase the tiny rations they were allotted. The weak bowl of soup and piece of black bread from the soup kitchens was the only meal for many of them. Rachel's salary at ZTOS consisted only of the extra bowl of soup and two loaves of black bread she was able to bring home each night. In the two weeks since they had moved into the ghetto, they had all lost weight.

The small number of zlotys they had brought with them was nearly gone. Josef had used them to buy milk and cheese for Rachel from a street vendor. Josef ate little, giving Rachel his share of bread. She felt guilty taking it but knew she needed to feed Adam. Rachel couldn't meet the eyes of Josef or her hungry cousins, Mira and Lilliana, as she ate the extra portions.

"We need more food," Aron said, looking directly at his father. "I know you have money hidden. We need to use it."

"We have food for now. We should save our money in case times get worse."

"We won't be alive to use the money if we continue to eat like this. Father, if you give me the money, I can use it to make more money."

"You don't even have a job. How can my money make you money?" Saul's voice grew louder.

Josef cleared his throat, interrupting the conversation. Rachel looked at him questioningly. She watched her husband give Aron an admonishing look, clearly intending to shut him up.

"I have news," Josef announced, "I've found work."

"You found a job? How? What kind of job?" Rachel asked excitedly, forgetting the suspicious interruption.

"I ran into Chaim Lowen while applying for factory jobs this afternoon. He was in my education classes at the university. He's starting a school in his apartment on Sienna Street. The pupils pay thirty zlotys a month to attend. He'll give me ten zlotys per pupil every month to provide piano, guitar, and voice instruction."

"But Josef, those schools are illegal. You could be arrested. Or worse."

"What would you have me do, Rachel? Allow us to starve? Beg on the streets? Wealthy families will pay me to teach their children. I have no intention of turning that down."

"Josef and I went to the house on Sienna Street. It has a courtyard that backs against where the ghetto wall's being built."

Josef gave Aron another look of warning, but Aron ignored him this time and continued.

"With money and supplies, I could trade with Poles on the other side of the wall. Chaim said there are openings in the wall. I look Aryan enough that if I get through, I can spend some time on the other side getting us supplies and food."

"Absolutely not!" Hella and Rachel spoke almost in unison.

"Do you realize you could be shot? Are you crazy?"

"No, Aron," Saul's jaw tightened. "We can use my money to buy food here in the ghetto, but you can't take such risks. I will not allow it."

"How long will the money last, Father? A few months? Maybe a year? And then what? No money, no food. Rachel's job pays for an extra bowl of soup. Do you think nine of us can live off Josef's fifty zlotys month? Look at your grandson, look at your nieces. We can spend your money until it's gone, or we can use it to provide long term for this family."

"You can have my money," Dora's voice rang from the back of the room where she sat on a mattress brushing her youngest daughter's black curls. "I'll give you every cent I have, Aron. I've sewn the money Ziv left me into my skirts. You can have it, but you must promise to take care of my girls."

Aron met his aunt's eyes and nodded his promise. He turned his gaze to his father.

"You must be careful, Aron. It's not worth your life."

"Of course it is, Father. There's nothing else I'd rather give my life for."

Saul's eyes filled with tears as he clutched his only son's hand. Rachel pulled her own son close, very much afraid.

*****

In late spring, Rachel asked her mother to stop bringing Adam to her office to nurse. In the eight months since they had moved into the ghetto, conditions and the health of its citizens were deteriorating rapidly. Every contact Adam had with a person other than a family member caused Rachel panic. Several days a week, Rachel left the piles of requests and requisitions in the office to assist in the soup kitchens. She walked past lines of filthy, lice ridden, helpless people, most of them shaking with cough and dripping with fever. Her own thin frame in her worn coat looked healthy compared to the destitution of others.

The refugee centers ZTOS established held thousands of homeless men, women, and children. Thousands more were being shipped into the ghetto weekly from cities and villages across Poland. The housing shortage was dire. More and more people were living on the streets, begging for food, pleading for help. She looked at the emaciated babies in the arms of their mothers and felt waves of guilt at the thought of her own child, whose cheeks were still round and whose arms, while not plump, still had the energy to wave giddily at his uncle bringing home milk, vegetables, and an occasional piece of unidentifiable meat.

Rachel persuaded Simon, her ZTOS supervisor, to give her father a job. Saul now helped organize the house committees in each apartment block. Every apartment building in their sector was assigned a chairperson who reported to Saul. Each house committee chairperson accounted for the residents of their apartment building and assessed what each person was able give to charity. A soup pot was passed around each week for contributions to the hungry and poor. Giving was technically not compulsory, but there were ways to make the stingy more generous. Aunt Dora, their building's house committee chairwoman, was notorious for posting signs at the entrance of their building listing the names of everyone who did not give that week. Rachel couldn't help but laugh at the sudden increase in generosity the next week by those unfortunate enough to be the target of Aunt Dora's wrath.

Her father's job paid nothing but enabled him to obtain a work permit. The work permit prevented him from being assigned to a forced labor brigade. Her brother used his infamous and inexplicable connections to enroll in a drafting course offered by the Judenrat's ORT organization, one of the few vocational programs allowed by the Germans. Students who enrolled in ORT courses were also exempt from forced labor. Hundreds applied for a few slots, and Aron, of course, managed to get accepted. Rachel had no doubt bribes exchanged hands for nearly all those enrolled. The ORT also offered sewing classes for girls, which were easier to get into as girls were not at risk of being drafted into forced labor, and fourteen-year-old Mira enrolled. Rachel hoped Mira could get a job as a seamstress in one of the German factories when she completed the program and secure a work permit for herself.

Rachel worried most about Josef. He was content to go off to his teaching job every day. The zlotys Josef brought home supplied Aron with resources to trade on the black market and enabled the family to supplement Aron's goods with enough to keep them all fed and clothed. But Rachel fretted Josef didn't seem concerned about obtaining a work permit. Josef left the house each morning confident he could avoid the soldiers spot-checking identification cards and loading trucks full of young men without proof of gainful employment. Every night she watched the clock nervously. If he was five minutes late, the whole house became worked into a frenzy with her worry. But every night he strolled blithely through the door and teased her for being an old worrying babushka.

Worry filled Rachel's days and nights. Worry about food, Adam's progress, being warm enough. Worry about work permits and Josef being picked up for forced labor. Worry about Aron and his smuggling. Increasingly, signs were posted around the ghetto warning of the consequences of smuggling.

That consequence was death. Aron waved her off when she brought it up.

"If I wasn't doing it, then we'd all be dead anyway, so what difference does it make?"

When Rachel looked at the disintegrating souls in the soup kitchen lines, she knew her brother was right. She tried to keep her mouth shut but couldn't stop the constant ache of anxiety in the pit of her stomach.

Rachel's favorite time of day was late afternoon when she returned from her job with a loaf of thick black bread and scooped Adam into her arms. She just breathed him in. His spiky chestnut hair made him look like a porcupine as he crawled across the chipped plank floor to greet her.

*****

Tufts of grass peeked through the cracks of cement in the courtyard behind their building. Rachel sat on a blanket spread upon the concrete, imagining a picnic in the warm sun. She watched Adam and Lilliana play. At twelve, Lilliana was somewhere between a young woman and a child, dancing and spinning under a lone brick-encircled tree. She twirled and spun with Adam until she was out of breath, then collapsed with Rachel on the blanket and asked her to braid her hair. Rachel stroked the child's beautiful ebony curls. Her own hair, the color of fallen leaves, had long been neglected. Rachel tried to remember the last time she looked in a mirror. The girlish vanities, so important to her just a year ago, were inconsequential now.

"My mother says Papa's coming home soon."

Rachel continued braiding slowly, coming to terms with Lilliana's words.

"Oh, I see," Rachel said cautiously.

Lilliana tossed a ball toward Adam who scurried after it, his pants' knees a dusty grey from the dirt. Lilliana took a long breath and continued speaking.

"We haven't seen him in three years. I can't see his face anymore. Momma has his picture on the wall, but that's not what he really looks like. I can't remember how he really looks, but it is not like that. I don't think he's coming home. I think Momma's wrong."

Rachel stopped braiding Lilliana's hair.

"You can't give up hope. He might still come home."

"No, I don't think he will. I think my mother tells us he will so we don't feel bad and Mira and I tell her we believe her so she doesn't feel bad. But we all know the truth. But no one will just say it. There's a whole lot of pretending going on in this place, but no one's really fooled, I think. It's just easier for everyone to pretend not to know."

Rachel pulled her cousin close to her and held her.

They watched as Adam poked at an ant pile with a stick. In this courtyard, today in the sun, it was easier to just pretend.

*****

The papers on her desk flew to the floor as the entire building shook. Screams pierced through the hallways.

"They're bombing! Everyone to the cellar!"

Simon barreled through the room leading the panicked chain of bodies into the hallway and down the stairs. Rachel pushed her way through the crowd but headed toward the door. Adam. She had to get to Adam. Fear pulsed through her as she raced through the streets, dodging panicked people looking for cover. She could see the smoke rising on the other side of the walls as the rockets flashed red and yellow towards the earth. Relief flooded her as she arrived, breathless, to find her apartment building still standing. She fled to the cellar and pushed through dozens of praying neighbors to find Adam safe in a smiling Josef's arms.

"It's the Russians, Rachel. Don't you see? The end is near. Soon this will all be over."

She kissed her husband and held Adam as he cried. Yes, soon this would all be over. Today, there was hope.

*****

Typhus waved in like a massive fog thickening the heat of the summer. Rachel walked down Grzybowska Street to the public kitchen to deliver the daily requisitions list. A child, maybe six years old, maybe ten, one could no longer tell, lay on the side of the road, his belly protruding from scurvy. His red-faced mother rocked back and forth next to his swollen body, an empty hat next to them.

"A coin, a coin please for my child," the woman whimpered.

Masses of people, just as skinny, just as swollen, stepped over them to continue down the street. Rachel couldn't take notice as the scene repeated itself a dozen times over, with new mothers and new children replacing the ones passed by.

The soup kitchen overflowed with sweating hordes of people, one blending into another, individuals unidentifiable as they moved as a mass toward the thin, watery soup with the hope of a floating potato fragment.

"A typhus breeding ground," Rachel turned around at the sound of Vera's voice. "This place is a breathing graveyard."

Vera worked as a nurse in the hospital at Gesia Street and was also her building's community chairwoman. Rachel had become friendly with her, as Vera regularly delivered her building's food donations to the soup kitchen and was often first in line at Rachel's office to request additional supplies for her apartment building. Her crisp no-nonsense manner could give Aunt Dora a run for her money.

"How bad has it gotten?"

"Hundreds dying every day. Have you walked past the hospitals lately?"

Rachel shook her head. She had travelled only the triangle between home, the ZTOS office, and the soup kitchen these past few days, afraid to venture much further based on the rumors of spreading disease.

"Jammed to capacity. Mothers are leaving their children on the doorsteps hoping we will have no choice but to take them in. But whether they die at the hospitals or die in the street, it really makes no difference. No medicine, no vaccines, there's no chance for them. And this is only the beginning of it. Mark my words, typhus is going to make way for TB, and that will be the end for most of these poor souls."

"Aren't you afraid working at the hospital? How can you risk being around so much disease?"

Vera looked at her sideways.

"Perhaps you should ask your brother."

"What do you mean? How do you know my brother?"

"Everyone who needs to know Aron, knows Aron." She took the requisition list from Rachel's hand.

"Why don't you head on out of here? I'll deliver this for you," Vera said, and smiled coyly as she delivered the papers and small bucket she was carrying to the cook, leaving Rachel wondering.

*****

Aron handed Rachel a small package with a satisfied look on his face. In the weeks since Aron's ORT course ended, Aron spent his days dodging patrols and Hella complained he was never home. Today, Rachel had been surprised to find him waiting for her in the courtyard.

"What's this?"

"Open it."

The courtyard was full of families from the building, gossiping about the latest rumor, hanging their clothes to dry in the beating sun, or simply escaping the oppressive heat of the apartments. Before Rachel had the chance to confront her brother about Vera's words, he took her arm and asked her to walk with him. Lilliana rolled a ball to Adam across the courtyard. Rachel unwrapped the brown package.

"Oh my God. How did you get these? How much did this cost?"

Inside the rumpled brown paper, lay two vials of typhus vaccine.

"That's all I could get. There's a doctor in Lvov the Nazis hired to make the vaccines, but he's arranging for some of it to be smuggled to the ghettos. Each of us was allotted two vials for our efforts but any more we have to buy at market rate. A thousand zlotys a vial. Hospital workers only have to pay five hundred. We donated several in our families' names to the doctors. Those donations will permit our families front of the line medical care if we ever need it."

"Do you realize how much danger this puts you in? If you're caught, you'll be shot."

"Understand that I don't care. I fully expect to be shot any day now, so I need to do as much as I can while I'm still here."

"If you get a job and a work permit, then you'll be safe."

"Don't be naïve. And how about instead of nagging me, you thank me." He turned his back to her, his shoulders tense. She placed her hand on the back of his arm.

"Thank you, Aron. This vaccine could save Adam's life. I'm just so afraid for yours."

Aron turned back to her.

"You know, Rachel, we could use you. Your Aryan looks could get you far on the outside. I could get a couple of documents for you and together we could get twice as many supplies through. We could make a fortune and help a lot of people."

"Never, Aron. I could never do that. I'm not brave like you."

"It's not about bravery. It's about survival and hope."

"This from the man who expects to die every day."

He snorted and took the vials from her to rewrap them. "The first vial is, of course, for Adam. I was thinking the second vial should go to you. You're the one at the soup kitchen being exposed to the walking dead."

"I won't take it."

He opened his mouth to speak, and she shut him down. "Don't ask again."

"Then one of the girls?"

She swallowed and watched Lilliana chase the crawling Adam behind the scraggly tree. Lilliana's giggles filled the courtyard.

"Lilliana's younger and smaller."

"Yes," Aron pondered, "But Lilliana rarely leaves the house or the courtyard. We can keep her more contained. Even when Josef takes her to his school, he's able to monitor her exposure. Mira's in ORT classes. She's more at risk."

Rachel watched Lilliana with her wild black braids flying, and Rachel's stomach lurched. Shame poured through her as she realized Adam not getting the vaccine wasn't even an option she would consider. Was saving her own child condemning another?

"What kind of a choice is this? I can't make this decision. You decide. Don't tell me who you decide, just make the decision."

His eyes bore into her.

"Someday, Rachel, you're going to have to stand up. You can't choose to be helpless and survive here."

She looked away. Aron glared at her angrily and snapped,

"But, today, as usual, allow me to carry the burden."

He shoved the package back into his pocket and left her to watch the children through her tears.

*****

Rachel dodged the black-capped undertakers loading bodies onto their carts. They pushed their loads from doorway to doorway, adding corpses to their piles until the carts overflowed with the daily dead. The stench of rotting flesh festered in the streets. Walking corpses shuffled along the alleyways, children shook cups, pleading for coins or food. Luckier residents scurried to their jobs or rushed frantically to get in line at whatever vendor was rumored to have an elusive food item, medicine, or rare, coveted treasure. The line at the baker's had formed around the corner, but Rachel saw Vera near the beginning of the line and rushed to her.

"Will you buy two loaves for me?"

She handed Vera her zlotys. Tomorrow was Rosh Hashanah and the lines formed to get challah for the celebration. The bakery had made hundreds of batches of the leavened bread. Rachel speculated much of the bread consisted of sawdust but tried to push that thought out of her mind and focus on the holiday. A new year was supposed to be a fresh start. She hadn't had time to even think about her resolutions and what she hoped to change in herself.

Rachel felt a flash of concern for the people standing in the long line. The Nazis had issued a proclamation prohibiting groups of people to gather for prayer. Any violators would be shot. Execution was the threat for every violation. Proclamations came down weekly for what you could or couldn't do, what minor infraction warranted arrest or, more frequently, death. There were so many proclamations, they all blended together to mean nothing.

She sidled next to Vera in line, ignoring the dirty look from the woman behind her. She wasn't cutting, she rationalized, she was just adding to Vera's order.

"I'm glad to see everyone's still planning to celebrate."

"I just hope we still have something to celebrate after tomorrow."

Rachel nodded in agreement. The Nazis always seemed to choose Jewish holidays to enact something particularly horrible. The year before on Yom Kippur they had announced the mandate establishing the ghetto. Each Jewish holiday since had been met with an increase in abuse from the Nazi guards. The undertakers' cartloads doubled the morning after a holiday. It was the Nazi's way of punishing the Jewish population for the crime of being Jewish.

"I saw Aron this afternoon. He seemed agitated but wouldn't tell me anything. He'd been looking for Josef all morning but couldn't find him," Vera whispered.

Vera and Aron had become a couple shortly after he delivered the typhus vaccine to her. Rachel was pleased to see Aron with the petite, practical nurse. She had hoped Vera would tame Aron's risk-taking, but instead it had only escalated since summer. When the supply of typhus vaccine dried up, he moved on to smuggling medications from the university where he was formerly a pharmacy student. More than once, he disappeared for days at a time, leaving them all convinced he was dead. But then he would resurface, appeasing his angry mother and sister with gifts of shoes, vegetables, and even soap.

"Josef took his students to the orphanage for a performance today. I was hoping to swing by, but Simon was called away and I had to stay at the office. Why did Aron need Josef?"

"I don't know. But something's up."

The impatient storekeeper waved his hand to indicate it was Vera's turn. After paying for her challah and leaving Vera, Rachel rushed home worried, anxious to find Aron.

"Adam Czerniakow has been ordered to deliver 5000 young Jewish men to be sent to forced labor camps," Aron exhaled, nearly out of breath.

Adam Czerniakow was the president of the Judenrat. Czerniakow was widely respected and held enormous power in the ghetto. Rachel knew from the records she processed with ZTOS that Czerniakow and his council were responsible for managing most of the supplies, food, medication, and housing that existed in the ghetto. But he possessed only the power the Nazis permitted him to have.

Aron continued,

"But we won't allow it. The community is going to refuse to send anyone. No one will volunteer."

Hella's worried face turned to her son and son-in-law, Josef, neither holding a work permit, and therefore, both in imminent danger.

"What will the Nazi's say to that?"

"We'll see, Mother. We'll wait and see."

"Both of you stay home for the next several days. You must stay off the streets. They'll round up anyone without work permits."

"I'm leaving the ghetto as soon as curfew ends in the morning. I made plans for a shipment tomorrow and I've found a place to stay for a couple of days on the other side." Aron said.

Hella slammed a plate onto the table and glared at her son. Rachel grasped Josef's hand. Unlike Aron, Josef could not easily pass for an Aryan. His dark hair and olive skin would raise immediate suspicion on the outside. He would need to stay in the ghetto.

Josef spoke quietly.

"Aron and I have discussed this. If the Nazi's are looking for us, they're just as likely to go door to door and find us here. I'm going to the school in the morning and will stay there for a couple of days. If the Nazis come looking for me, I have a place to hide. Our school is set up with just this in mind."

Aron discreetly offered to sleep in the main room that night. With Adam curled up with Saul and Hella, Josef and Rachel retreated alone to the bedroom.

"It's going to be ok, Rachel. I'll come back safely." Rachel held onto him and cried. He kissed her softly.

They made love somberly. Wrapping her arms around him, she felt his skin pulled tight against his bones. When they first met, she used to tease him about his belly, the softness of a musician, not a laborer. She knew he could never survive a labor camp.

"Promise me you'll hide. If they catch you, you must run. Adam needs you. I need you."

He quieted her with a kiss and held her until the morning light signaled the end of the curfew. Only after he left, a bundle of food and clothes over his shoulder, did she close her eyes to sleep for a few fitful hours.

The Nazis entered the ghetto in full force that afternoon. Grey-green uniforms armed with handguns, machine guns, and growling shepherds patrolled the streets. Alongside the Nazis, hundreds of Jewish policemen, paid to do the devil's dirty work, verified work permits and arrested any men without the correct papers.

Hella refused to let Saul leave the house, even though he was not who they were looking for. Thousands of young men were taken from the streets. Gunshots rang from the alleyways and streets. On her way home from work, Rachel walked past the labor office and stepped inside the doorway of a tailor shop to watch. Thousands of men were lined up in military formation. The Jewish police force surrounded them, ensuring no one would escape. While a few of the young men wept, most stood quietly, their heads bowed to the ground, as if shamed by their arrest.

Rachel scanned the lines, relief piercing her when she didn't see Josef or Aron. She recognized Pawel, the lively boy from upstairs with the rogue handcart that first day they moved in. She could imagine his mother's despair. Rachel forced herself to turn away and ran home as the curfew neared.

When not enough men were taken the first day to satisfy the quota, the manhunt continued. The police force went door to door, taking every young man they found. On the second day, Jewish police banged on her door. Rachel stared them down as they searched the small apartment. Jews hunting for Jews. It was despicable. She would have preferred them to be Nazis.

"Where are your sons?" they asked her mother. "Two men ages 21 and 26 are registered as living here."

Hella stuck out her chin defiantly.

"I haven't seen either of them in days. If you can't find them, how should I be able to?"

They left for the next apartment, to take someone else's sons. After four days, the manhunt ceased, the gunfire in the streets silenced. The 5000-man quota was met.

By the next afternoon, Josef still had not returned. Rachel raced to Chaim Lowen's apartment. As he opened the door, Chaim's eyes widened at the sight of her.

"Where's Josef? Is he ok?" he asked.

"What do you mean asking me where he is? He's here, with you. He's been here for four days..." Her voice trailed off, fear gripping her, wanting him to be teasing her, to know exactly where Josef was.

"Oh Rachel..." Chaim whispered.

He opened the door and led her to a battered red sofa. She collapsed onto it, her legs weak with fear.

"Josef was here on Rosh Hashanah. The next day when we heard there would be searches, one of our students, a seventeen-year-old boy, was trapped here. His mother sent him to school, not understanding the dangers. Our hiding spot is only big enough for two. Josef insisted Stanislaw take his spot. I tried to convince him to stay, so he'd at least be off the streets. But he insisted on going home to you and Adam. He said if he were going to be taken, he wanted at least to be taken from home where he could see you one last time. When he didn't show up to work today, I worried. But I hadn't heard..."

"He never came home," Rachel whispered.

"Maybe he found another hiding place. Maybe he ran into someone he knew, and they found somewhere for him to go."

"Yes, maybe."

Rachel gathered the strength to walk home, her eyes searching the streets, scanning the bodies on the doorsteps for signs of Josef. She climbed the three flights of stairs to the apartment, her legs growing heavy with dread, afraid to open the door, afraid he might not be sitting there. She pushed the door open and met Aron's eyes. Aron had returned. He sat at the table, Hella next to him, her face welted from tears. Saul stood when she entered the room, and Rachel knew.

"Tell me," she said flatly, the door slamming behind her. Adam, in Dora's arms on the mattress against the wall, cried out for her.

"Just tell me," she repeated.

"Josef was rounded up three days ago. He was lined up with a group of about 200 other men. They were loading them onto trucks. The Nazi guarding his group turned his back to smoke a cigarette and Josef ran. He made it around the corner but ran into another lineup. They shot him on the spot. Shmuel Horowitz, the armband vendor, was on the corner and saw it all. Josef didn't suffer, Rachel. It was quick."

"He tried, Rachel. He tried to get home to you." Saul took her in his arms.

"I told him to run, Papa. I told him to escape. He did what I asked. I killed him."

No reassurances could comfort her. She should never have told him to run. If he had gotten on the trucks, he would at least have had a chance. Dora and her mother wept, the girls whispered quietly in fear, and Aron filled the room with his rage. He paced the apartment, swearing his revenge. All Rachel could see was her child. Adam was without a father. He would never know his sweet tempered, musical father who loved him so deeply.  Adam wrapped his little hands around strands of her hair as they lay in bed that night.  She whispered in his ear as he slept,

"I promise to always keep you safe. They will not take you too."

# Claire
## 1943

*"What the hell are they doing here?"*

*Claire stepped up into the back of the truck, her socks swimming in the bottom of her boots, a thick layer of sand coating the knees of her drenched trousers.*

*"Get them out of here! This is no place for women. Girls, get out as fast as you can."*

*A band of soldiers gathered alongside them as Claire and the two dozen other nurses of the 17th Evacuation Hospital loaded into the truck bed. A thundering echo reverberated from the mountains and a barrage of fire descended upon the beach. Foul grey smoke converged with the stench of burning rubber blazing in the rubble of a collapsing building. The soldiers surrounding the truck scattered into the marshlands. The last three nurses were hauled onto the truck as it clattered forward. An airplane roared overhead, and the nurses cringed, waiting for its fire. Claire scanned the terrain for escape routes from the back of the truck. The flat, marshy land beyond the beachhead offered no trees, trenches dug by the American soldiers offered little cover. There was nowhere to hide from the onslaught of shells. If they were targeted, it was over.*

*The truck rattled through pits and bumps, bruising the terrified women. Ahead, Claire saw a conglomeration of tents in a vast field. Dozens of tents huddled out in the open, directly in the eye of the German snipers cradled in the heart of the mountains, exposed to the wrath of the shelling. Her heart sank as she realized this was her new home.*

*****

Claire's sagging stockings withered on her legs in the sticky Minnesota summer heat. She swatted a mosquito as she slid a letter to her father in the mailbox and lumbered through the door of St. Ignatius Hospital. She was late. Nurse Crawford would write her up again. For a brief moment, Claire hoped Nurse Crawford would fire her, but quickly retracted the thought. She couldn't disappoint her father.

Her father had insisted Claire attend nursing school, and she had, delaying the inevitable shattering of his fantasy that someday father and daughter would work side by side as doctor and nurse. Her plans to find a job doing anything other than nursing changed when her father deployed, and his letters frequently expressed his pride in her. After everything he had been through, if her being a nurse made him happy, then for now, that's what she would be.

When his wife of 25 years succumbed to a slow, devastating cancer he could not cure, Dr. Robert Weber began to dissolve within himself. He went through the motions of treating patients at his small-town Minnesota clinic but numbed himself to the world. Even Claire's threatening to quit nursing school had not brought him back.

December 7, 1941, changed everything. Robert called Claire home and they sat frozen to the broadcast of the attack on Pearl Harbor. Two days later Dr. Weber drove Claire back to school and without telling her, applied for a direct commission into the US Army Medical Department. He left for Europe three months later, promising Claire he would return to her whole. She kept her promise to him, finished nursing school, and took the job at St. Ignatius. He didn't need to hear about her discontent.

Claire darted into the nurse's break room and threw her coat into her locker. Smoothed the front of her crisp, white apron, she peered into the mirror and adjusted her cap, just slightly at a tilt, enough to show off the curls she had worked so hard to perfect this morning.

"Miss Crawford won't approve that."

Barbara Ann's round face appeared in the mirror behind her. Claire sighed and straightened the cap, flattening the blonde curls.

"Miss Crawford has never understood the frustrations of frizzy hair."

"As if you have ever had frizzy hair," Barbara Ann sniffed and touched her own brown tufts wafting out from under her cap.

"What are you talking about, Barbara Ann? You have the most glorious hair I have ever seen. I spend hours each night in curlers, but you wake up with hair like Rita Hayworth."

"If only I looked like Rita Hayworth."

Claire snuck a glance at Barbara Ann, short and doughy in her nurse's uniform, her eyes and nose too small for her full face. The only feature Barbara Ann shared with her brother was that cascade of russet hair. Claire smiled as she thought of Bill and how she had run her hands through that hair as he kissed her at the train station.

Bill had sauntered into the university lecture hall eleven months ago to drive his sister home. Barbara Ann had introduced them. Less than an hour later, he called Claire at her nursing school housing and invited her to dinner. She waited until the next day, after asking Barbara Ann's permission, to say yes. Bill arrived in the lobby with a bouquet of lilies and a charm that made her swoon. The girls in her dormitory peppered Claire with giggly questions about the police officer with the broad shoulders and movie star smile.

Bill became a fixture in the lobby of Claire's dormitory. He charmed her with red and yellow roses, walnut fudge from Pietz's Candy Shop, and trinkets from downtown Minneapolis's department stores. She radiated in his lavish attention. Alone since her mother's death and her father's enlistment, Bill filled that cold, empty space in her life. He was the man she meant to marry.

The day Bill was drafted into the army, he proposed. He departed for training four weeks later, insisting they marry before he left. But Claire put her foot down at the thought of a war wedding, rushing off to the minister with a Sunday dress, a corsage, and a couple of witnesses. And, as much as she loved Bill, she couldn't possibly get married without her father.

Before Bill left, Claire and Barbara Ann rented an apartment together at his suggestion. Bill said he liked to keep his girls together to keep an eye on each other. Claire was flattered by his thoughtfulness.

"Are you going to the USO tonight?" Barbara Ann asked as she pulled up her white stockings.

"No, I'm having dinner with Tom Parker. He had to cancel our usual Sunday night dinner because he has to pull a night shift tomorrow."

"Will his wife be there this time? Bill doesn't like it when you're with him alone."

Claire looked at Barbara Ann cautiously, wondering how she knew that. Claire and Bill exchanged letters weekly, but sometimes it seemed Barbara Ann received more letters from Bill than she did. Had he mentioned concerns about Tom to his sister?

"Bill has nothing to be concerned about where Tom Parker is concerned. Tom's like an older brother to me. We practically grew up together."

Sebastian Parker and Robert Weber had been inseparable in childhood. Sebastian married straight out of high school and took over his family's farm while Robert left the small town of Green Meadow for medical school. Robert was drafted in the first war, and while he was in France, Sebastian died in the flu epidemic. Robert never forgave himself for not being there. After returning to Minnesota to finish medical school, Robert and his new wife, Alice, moved back to Green Meadow, where he established his practice and took Sebastian's wife and three children, including young Tom, under his wing.

When Tom Parker was 13, he began working for Dr. Weber running errands, delivering prescriptions, and transporting patients to and from the small-town clinic. Claire was constantly under his feet, an infant when he came to work for them, and a little girl when Tom himself, under the guidance of Robert Weber, left for medical school at the US Army's Medical Department Professional Service School in Washington, DC.

Tom requested a transfer to Ft. Snelling in St. Paul, at the insistence of his wife, Ginny, a statuesque redhead Tom had met during a brief teaching stint at Fort Des Moines, who had insisted on moving back to the Midwest after six years in DC. When Robert Weber left for the war, he asked Tom to take care of Claire. Dinner with Tom had been a weekly staple for the past eighteen months.

"As for his wife, I don't know if Ginny will be with us or not. She's spending a lot of time in Des Moines lately."

Barbara Ann hmmphed.

"It's just not appropriate for an engaged woman to be alone with another man for that long of a time."

Claire started to protest but was interrupted.

"Ladies, your shift started two minutes ago," Nurse Crawford's head shot out of the door as fast as it came in.

Claire buckled her white shoes, and the girls left the shelter of the nurse's lounge. Barbara Ann went to the post-op surgical unit while Claire headed downstairs to orthopedics. Claire didn't know how Barbara Ann did it—the surgical unit was intense. Claire chose orthopedics after nursing school. It was what she considered the least of the evils. Giving medicine to patients in casts, raising and lowering casted arms and legs, and wheeling broken limbed patients in wheelchairs to x-ray were all things she could handle. She never admitted to anyone how much she hated nursing school: the blood, the urine and feces, changing dressings of open wounds. When Bill returned home, they would marry, have three babies, two boys and a girl, and she would stay home and put nursing behind her. Her father's disappointment could be dealt with after the war. Perhaps grandchildren would take her father's mind off her departure from her medical career. For now, Claire pasted on a smile as she walked through the double doors to the orthopedic wing.

*****

September 3, 1943

Dear Claire,

My unit moved from Morocco to Algeria this week. It seems we're never staying in the same place long enough to get settled in. That's ok, I guess. I won't really be settled in until I am home with you. Thanks for that picture of you in your bathing suit. Monty Krieger thinks you look just like Bette Grable. After he said that, I put the picture inside my footlocker so no one could see it but me.  The women here are covered from head to toe and all you can see of them are their eyes and their feet. Sometimes I wish I could send you one of those getups and have you wear it all the time. You're just so beautiful, Claire, and I'm so far away.

You said in your last letter that you're thinking about working in a clinic rather than in the hospital, hoping it would be less messy. I had to go to the hospital unit last week because I cut my foot on some broken glass that neither Monty nor I could get out (walking barefoot on the beach—next time I'll wear my boots). Talk about messy—the gals working in the army hospitals here have to deal with all kinds of "messy" stuff, as you so sweetly put it. I know you wouldn't want to be in their shoes!

Hopefully this war will be over soon, and I will come home and marry you and all you'll have to worry about are me and our babies.

Take good care of yourself and stay true.

Bill

"Where's Ginny?"

Claire jumped into the passenger seat of Tom's Ford coupe. He shut her car door, walked around the front of the car, and slid into the driver's seat.

"She's in Des Moines."

"Again? It seems like the last five or six times we've had dinner she's been in Des Moines."

"Is that right?" he asked absently.

"I only asked because Barbara Ann thinks it's not appropriate for us to be alone. I told her you're like a brother to me, so it's entirely appropriate."

Tom nodded his head as he looked for the light to change.

"Barbara Ann should keep her opinions to herself," he said.

"She's just looking out for me while Bill is away."

Tom didn't respond. Claire felt his disapproval. Tom had been silent last winter when Bill joined them at dinner one Sunday night. Bill filled the restaurant with his booming voice and more than once Claire saw Ginny cringe. After dinner, Claire suggested to Bill that perhaps they may have wanted a quieter dinner. Bill said Ginny was an old stick in the mud and they both needed livening up.

The following week at dinner, Tom asked if Claire was sure Bill was the one. Ginny told Tom to leave it alone and said she thought Bill was 'simply lovely'. Tom grunted. Claire stewed in anger the rest of the evening. After that, Claire and Tom kept their discussions about Bill to a minimum. Claire didn't dare mention any of it to Bill.

Claire sighed at Tom's silence and lightened the conversation.

"Speaking of Barbara Ann, she's been going on and on about Albert, this wonderful man she met at the USO. From the way she talked, I thought he was the next Clark Gable. Well, I met him last week and he's just awful. He looks like the son of Frankenstein. He leered at me the entire time, even with Barbara Ann standing right next to him. And then Barbara Ann got mad at me, as if I did something wrong. I was certainly glad I needed to be home early. I couldn't stand much more of that."

"Claire, girls like Barbara Ann can't compete with girls like you. She's going to read your friendliness as flirtation. You need to scale it back when her boyfriends are around."

Claire blushed. She didn't know whether to feel complimented or scolded. She answered with sarcasm.

"Thanks for the advice, Pops."

"I'm hardly your father, Claire. But I'll back off the advice. It seems you get enough suggestions in your life already."

Tom looked at her innocently, but she knew he meant Bill. She stuck her tongue out at him playfully, choosing not to brood. She understood Bill. It didn't matter if he didn't.

"So, how's the job going?" he asked, his eyes still on the road.

Claire moaned, "It's tolerable. But Nurse Crawford is an absolute drill sergeant."

"You really should join the ANC. They could use you."

Claire rolled her eyes.

"Really Tom, someone would think you had a quota to fill."

She saw him trying to hold back a laugh. Tom had been teasing her about joining the Army Nurse Corps since graduation. At nearly every meal he extolled the virtues of the ANC, quoting the posters plastered everywhere in the nursing school and in Life Magazine and Ladies Home Journal: 'Save Their Lives and Yours', 'The Touch of a Woman's Hand', 'World War II: It's YOUR War Too'. It had become a running joke.

"You know my father would kill you if you let me join up. And can you really see me in the ANC? Honestly, I can't wait for Bill to get home so I can just be done with it all."

"I think you'll find that there's a lot more to life than an early marriage and babies. After the war, you should travel, see the world, do something for society."

"I'm 23. This is hardly an early marriage. Nearly all my friends are already married and have babies. And I do lots for society already. I volunteer at the USO every weekend, I distribute pamphlets about war bonds, and I even planted a victory garden in my apartment courtyard. I can still travel and be married. Bill and I will travel a lot."

"Bill Vincent hardly strikes me as the type of man to encourage world travel."

Claire bristled. "What do you know about my fiancé? You've met him twice and have no right to form any opinions about what he does or doesn't want to do."

"OK, ok, I'm sorry. Let's not fight. Last time we argued about Bill's favorite baseball team, and you didn't speak to me for an hour. The last thing I need in my life is more silence."

He reached out and put his hand on top of hers, a brotherly pat. She felt a twinge in her stomach and pulled it away but smirked at him when he looked away from the road to her.

"Ok, you're forgiven. But just this once," she said.

He smiled and she noticed how one side of his mouth was just slightly higher than the other. You wouldn't notice unless you really looked. A wrinkle formed on his right cheek, almost creating a dimple. Not like Bill's deep dimples. She remembered in high school Shirley Ingalls thought Tom Parker was "dreamy" when Tom had visited one Christmas with his elegant new wife. Claire had never looked at him that way before. Age had moved him from dreamy to distinguished. He turned and caught her staring and she looked away, reddening.

"Have you heard about Madge Barker and Edward Olafson's wedding? Her Aunt Iva's casserole caught the church basement on fire, and they had to have the reception in the barn!"

Tom laughed and the talk turned safely to Green Meadow gossip and the antics of their shared hometown.


September 8, 1943

My darling daughter,

I can't write much today as we're striking the tents to move on. The boys' missions have been successful but that doesn't limit their casualties. Our hospital tents are always full. A funny coincidence has happened. A Minneapolis Tribune reporter has been assigned to our field hospital for a month. He's writing articles about the move into Sicily and Italy as well as how the evacuation hospitals deal with the casualties. He knows I'm from Minnesota and keeps following me like a Labrador, hoping for a jazzy story with a hometown angle. I hide in John Keller's tent, as the last thing I want is my name splashed in the newspaper like I'm some sort of hero. These boys are the heroes.

I'm sure you remember Colonel Keller. He and his wife Mildred spent a weekend with your mother and me several years back. We went to medical school together before he moved out East. I have no doubts when he heard I was joining, he arranged for me to be assigned to this unit. I'm grateful to have his friendship here.

I think about you every day and I love you desperately. I cherish every letter you send. I believe I should be here, helping however I can, but the hardest part of being here is not being able to see you. The only thing I ever regretted about joining the Army was leaving you. I love you, Angel.

Dad


*****

Claire followed Barbara Ann into the hallway, dreading another day at work.

"I need to sign my time sheet," Barbara Ann said as she passed the double doors to the reception desk. Claire followed, in no hurry to get to the orthopedic ward. As they turned the corner, the familiar shape of a man's uniformed back and slightly greying hair hovered over the reception desk.

"Tom?"

Tom turned around and flashed a broad smile.

"Claire! I was just asking for you. I knew you worked on this floor." He nodded to the receptionist who disregarded them and went back to her filing. "You left your scarf in my car last week."

He pulled the bright yellow scarf, now folded into a small square, out of his pocket and handed it to her.

"You came across town just to return my scarf?" Claire was flattered. Barbara Ann's eyebrows nearly hit the roof.

"Actually, no," Tom cleared his throat, embarrassed. "I'm picking up a friend for lunch. I thought since I was coming here anyway, I'd drop your scarf."

Claire blushed at her presumption.

"Oh, of course."

Tom's eyes left her and Claire turned her head, following his gaze to a lithe brunette who had just turned the corner.

"Tom! I hope I didn't keep you waiting." The woman eyed Claire and Barbara Ann and smiled.

Claire recognized Ava Sorenson instantly. Ava's husband was killed at Pearl Harbor two years ago. She was the head nurse in general surgery and from what Claire heard from Audrey Leland who worked in pre-op, Ava's department had the highest turnover of nurses in the hospital because she guilted her girls into joining the Army Nurse Corps. The only reason Ava herself hadn't joined was she had a three-year-old daughter at home.

Tom's eyes lingered on Ava before he caught himself. Claire didn't blame him. Ava Sorenson was one of the most breathtaking women Claire had ever seen. And not in the way Claire knew herself to be attractive. Claire was pin-up cute; Ava Sorenson was a beauty. Claire watched Tom force his eyes from Ava as he remembered Claire and Barbara Ann.

"This is Claire Weber and Barbara Ann Vincent. Claire grew up in my hometown. In fact, her father is Dr. Robert Weber, who was my mentor."

"Very nice to meet you," Ava said. She eyed the ring on Claire's finger. "Is your fiancé in uniform?"

"Yes, he's currently in North Africa."

"Have you considered joining him? The ANC is desperate for good nurses."

Claire opened her mouth to reply, but Tom cut in.

"Don't bother, Ava. The ANC isn't for Claire."

"Hmmm," Ava lost interest in Claire and turned to Barbara Ann. "What about you?"

Barbara Ann squeaked, and Tom saved her.

"Ava, I've made us a reservation at The Lexington. We should get going."

Ava turned her entire attention to Tom, forgetting her two potential recruits and took the elbow he offered.

"Have a good afternoon, girls. Claire, I'll call you about a time to pick you up next Sunday."

Claire and Barbara Ann watched them leave.

"I thought he was married," Barbara Ann sputtered.

"He is. Maybe she's a friend of his wife's."

Barbara Ann harrumphed. "Yes, and I'm the queen of Sheba."

Claire glared at her as Barbara Ann turned her back to her to sign her timecard. Ava Sorenson and Tom Parker? Could it be true? Claire worked the rest of her shift trying to push the thought to the back of her mind. If Ginny had left Tom, he could date whomever he chose. Maybe she would write Bill about it. Then again, Bill might be even more upset if he knew Tom was now single. No, she would keep it to herself.

*****

"You should wear my blue velvet hat tonight. It would be smashing with that skirt."

Claire handed Barbara Ann the black eye pencil and turned around.

Every Saturday night, Claire and Barbara Ann volunteered at the USO. They served coffee and donuts and danced with the homesick enlistees training at Ft. Snelling, most awaiting transit overseas. Since the US joined the war four months earlier, thousands of young Minnesotan men were sent to Ft. Snelling for physicals and preliminary training. Local girls flocked to volunteer at the USO clubs that popped up around the city to give the boys a 'home away from home' and provide them with some fun before shipping overseas.

Barbara Ann made the finishing touches on Claire's pencil drawn seams down the back of her legs, a trick they used to give the illusion of stocking which were impossible to get since the war. A rap sounded at the door.

"Stay put, you don't want them to smear."

Barbara Ann opened the door, and both girls froze. A western Union Telegram boy stood nervously in the doorway. Barbara Ann gripped the door, her knuckles whitened. Claire's stomach lurched. Barbara Ann paled.

"I have a telegram for Claire Weber," the pasty boy said apologetically. For a brief second, Barbara Ann was visibly relieved. She quickly flashed to sympathy. Claire staggered to the door and took the telegram. The room spun as the door shut quietly behind the delivery boy.

WESTERN UNION MISS CLAIRE WEBER
212 ELDER AVENUE MINNEAPOLIS MINNESOTA
THE SECRETARY OF WAR DESIRES ME TO EXPRESS HIS DEEP REGET THAT YOUR FATHER MAJOR ROBERT J WEBER HAS BEEN REPORTED MISSING IN ACTION SINCE FIFTEEN SEPTEMBER IN ITALY IF FURTHER DETAILS OR INFORMATION ARE RECEIVED YOU WILL BE PROMPTLY NOTIFIED=
UL10  THE ADJUNCT GENERAL


Claire crouched against the closed door, hardly breathing. The wood trim of the door gouged her in the back. Barbara Ann slid the telegram from Claire's trembling hands.

"He's missing. This doesn't mean he's dead. They could still find him," Barbara Ann's voice wavered.

"I n e e d  t o  find out for sure."

*****

Claire's leg shook, jittery, in the rickety chair against the wall of the Tribune office. The clacking of typewriters echoed throughout the smoky room. No one noticed her as they sped by with ink spattered shirts to whizzing telegraph machines and the buzz of impatient phones.

It had been over four hours since she had arrived and demanded to see the editor. Night had fallen, but the room filled with even more employees after 6:00 had come and gone. Three hours ago, the editor told her he'd call as soon as he heard anything. She firmly told him she would wait. So, Claire sat, stretching her legs occasionally as she crossed the room to a stale coffee pot. At the end of hour four, a high heeled woman approached the editor's office with a folder, giving Claire a discreet glance before she disappeared into the office. When the woman reappeared, Claire tried to catch her eye, but the heels escaped in the opposite direction. Ten minutes later, the door opened, and the editor waved Claire in. He was nearly bald, with only a cluster of black hair circling his shiny scalp.

"Miss Weber," his hoarse voice held a twinge of sympathy. "Our 5th Army correspondent responded. I'm sorry. I wish there was more I could do."

He handed her the folder. She opened it to a thin sheet of paper, its black ink smearing the edges. As she read the words, the page blurred in front of her. Quivering, she rose and whispered her thanks to the editor. She couldn't feel her legs as she descended the stairs into the lobby and out the thick glass doors. She leaned against the brick building for support and opened the folder, the correspondent's words seeming more surreal in the flickering streetlight.

MAJOR ROBERT WEBER NOT MISSING IN ACTION. HE DESERTED.

*****

"I need to see Dr. Tom Parker."

The green garbed woman behind the reception desk eyed Claire's uniform and picked up the phone. Claire had worn her nursing uniform intentionally that morning, knowing it would open doors. The soldiers at the gate had easily believed her story about picking up medical supplies and allowed her and her waiting cab onto Ft. Snelling. Ft. Snelling Hospital was a flurry of olive green and white. Its corridors were filled with fresh-faced farm boys in crisp new uniforms waiting to complete their final physicals before shipping out to become war heroes.

Ten minutes passed before Tom appeared at the reception desk.

"Claire? What are you doing here?"

"I need to talk to you privately."

He looked alarmed but led her through the hallway and up a flight of stairs to a compact, windowless office. Medical books lined a waist-high bookshelf. A wedding picture of Tom and Ginny sat on the corner of the bookshelf. Tom motioned for Claire to sit in one of the two chairs facing a cherry desk. Instead of circling his desk to the large leather chair behind it, Tom sat in the chair next to her. She could hear his breath as he pulled the chair close. She handed him the MIA telegram and the Tribune reporter's nine-word apocalypse.

"I've contacted every military agency I know, and they all tell me the information is confidential. When they find him, they'll let me know. They said there's nothing I can do. You know he didn't desert. My father would never desert his unit. They're wrong. I need to find out the truth, Tom. I need your help. This morning, I met with Ava Sorenson and signed the papers to join the Army Nurse Corps. I need you to pull whatever strings you have to expedite it."

Tom was quiet for a long time. Her eyes nervously studied the worn grey carpet, but she could feel his gaze on her. He finally spoke,

"Claire, if you join the ANC, there's no guarantee you'll be anywhere near Italy. Nurses don't even know where they're going until they get there."

"I know you have connections, Tom. You worked on that board in D.C.," she whispered. "You can get me assigned to a Europe-bound unit."

Tom did not speak. Silent seconds seemed like hours. The silence in the room was unsettling. Finally, he spoke,

"What's your plan when you get there? Are you going to comb the beaches of Italy hoping he'll turn up? Desert your own unit to go searching for your father? You aren't Dick Tracy. There aren't clues waiting to be found on the battle grounds of Italy. Claire, I know you're scared. We both know your father didn't desert his unit. This is a misunderstanding and will work itself out. There's nothing you can do there that you can't accomplish here. I'll help you write more letters and together we'll try to find out what happened."

"Can you do this favor for me or not?" Claire frightened herself with her own tone of voice. She softened. "Please Tom, please do this for me."

"It doesn't seem I have much of a choice. I can't do nothing then watch you get shipped off to the Pacific." He reached out and took her hand in his. "Are you sure about this, Claire?"

"Yes, I'm sure."

She met his eyes and prayed she convinced him more than she convinced herself.

He squeezed her hand. "Ok, Claire, ok."

# Min-He
## West of Shanghai, China
## August 1943

Min-He finished washing her face and slipped into the canary yellow silk dress the kempei pointed to when he delivered her to the third-floor room. She had been surprised when Soon-Yee was dropped off first in the room next to hers. She assumed they would all be rooming together. She was relieved to hear Eun-Su go into the room on the other side. At least they were right next door.

The suite was the most elegant room Min-He had ever been in. A rich yellow-brown elm wardrobe with matching bedside tables adorned the room. Mahogany curtains hung from tall windows. There was a small, private toilet room with a bidet and a bathroom with a pedestal sink and a big, clawed soaking tub just like the pictures in the Hollywood magazines that some of the girls brought to school. She smiled, imagining Soon-Yee's joy when she saw it.

Min-He wondered if she would have time to bathe but was uncertain what she was supposed to be doing. They hadn't eaten since that morning on the ship and the kempei left no directions other than telling her to change into the yellow dress. She opened the long curtains and looked out onto the busy street below. As evening fell, the clamor from the street rose up to the third floor like an urban symphony. Cars and military trucks dodged rickshaws and bicycles. A Japanese soldier leaned against a brown, stone building smoking a cigarette. A woman with a baby strapped to her back gestured wildly at a grocer holding a red cabbage.

"Shanghai is a cesspool."

Min-He gasped and turned to see a man standing in her doorway. He wore the same uniform as the kempei but without the white armband. A yellow and red striped patch with two stars flanked the collar of his jacket. She knew enough to know that meant he was an officer. She didn't know what to say so she bowed slightly and stared at the floor. She heard the door shut and lock.

"What's your name?"

"Miyuki Ota", she replied, knowing it would be a long time before she would call herself Min-He Oh again. At the sound of her Japanese name, her eyes filled with tears, missing her mother, who never let that name be spoken in their home.

"Where are you from Miyuki Ota?"

"Sokcho, Korea," she took a step back as he slowly moved towards her. She kept talking. "Mr. Park hired me as a nurse, and we just arrived this afternoon. My friend Soon-Yee..."

The officer interrupted.

"Did you have a boyfriend in Sokcho?" He now stood inches in front of her. The smell of tobacco and gin wafted from his breath. His black mustache absorbed a pool of sweat on his upper lip. He was short, only a few inches taller than she, but thick, his shoulders nearly twice the size of hers. He was as wide as Mr. Park, but this man was pure strength. With the window behind her, she had no room to step back any further and was trapped between his body and the glass panels.

"I...no."

She didn't know how to respond. He moved in closer. "That's very good news."

With one arm, he grabbed her waist and pulled her to him. His mustache pressed against her lips and his tongue forced into her mouth. She yanked her head back and screamed,

"No! Get off me!"

With both hands, she pushed him. To her surprise and relief, he let go of her and took a step backward. They stared at each other and then he smiled.

"I'm afraid you don't understand," he said.

Before Min-He could process his words, the man's fist flew into her cheek. The unexpected blow shocked her for a moment before the blinding pain pierced into her head. She fell to her knees. The man grabbed her by both arms, picked her up and threw her onto the mattress. Her body curled into the fetal position, her arms covering her head, terrified of another blow. She couldn't think; her head pounded. He was on top of her, forcing open her legs with her knees. She screamed, knowing

Soon-Yee and Eun-Su would hear, would come running to her rescue. His fist slammed into her jaw, blood filling her mouth. The yellow silk bunched around her waist, the buckle from the officer's belt dug into her thigh. With one hand he ripped her underwear, the seams digging into the flesh of her hips as he tore them away from her body.

'No, no, please no', she pleaded in her head, her swollen, bleeding lips unable to form anything but moans. She felt his rough hands reaching down, spreading her open. After several bruising thrusts, pain shot through her body as he entered her, grunting, his sweat burning her as it dripped onto her face. Her eyes squeezed shut as she turned her head to let her tears fall onto the mattress. His left hand grabbed a fist full of her hair and pulled her head to face him.

"You look at me, whore. Open your eyes and look at me."

Rage shot through her body, blocking the pain. She squeezed her eyes tighter.

"You will look at me," he growled through clenched teeth.

Min-he reeled as the base of his palm pounded into her cheekbone, once, twice, matching the pattern of his thrusting. Her fight was gone. She opened her eyes. She stared into his forehead as he climaxed, wishing him death, painful death, hoping he would be castrated by the Russians, imagining him dying on a battlefield. He lay on top of her, his full weight on her chest blocking her breath. Then he pulled off, stood, and buckled his pants.

"I have to admit I was surprised you were a virgin," he said to her as casually as if they had just taken an afternoon stroll. "The Korean said all of you were, but you never know. It's so rare to get your money's worth nowadays."

Min-He's head couldn't wrap itself around what he was saying. Money's worth? She didn't know what that meant.

"So long, Miyuki Ota. We'll see each other again soon, I'm most certain. And don't worry. It'll all come naturally after a while."

The room still echoed with his laughter as the door slammed shut behind him.

Min-He rolled over and forced herself to sit up. She had to clean up. She had to get him off her. Doubled over, she limped to the toilet room. The water from the bidet flushed away the man's filth from her body. She made her way slowly to the bathroom, pulled off the bloody yellow dress and turned on the faucet of the clawed tub. She just needed to wash then she would go next door and Soon-Yee would help her. Soon-Yee would hold her and comfort her while she reported this to the police. The kempei who brought them here was probably still downstairs. Soon-Yee would know what to say and would help keep this secret from her family. She just needed to wash first.

The water filled with blood as she splashed water onto her face, her legs, her breasts. Only then did she weep. She sat naked on the floor by the tub as grief and shame filled her body. What would her father say? Who would marry her? What if her family found out? A scream pulled her out of her own head, and she froze. Had she screamed? No. Another scream shattered from Soon-Yee's room on the other side of the wall. Min-He got to her feet and grabbed the bloody dress from the floor. As she stepped back into the main room, a flood of relief and shame hit her as she saw the kempei from the docks standing by the dresser. She covered her nakedness with the dress in her hands.

"Please help me. I was coming to find you. A man came was just here and, and..." she stuttered, "He, he raped me," she whispered, embarrassed by the words. But she raced to continue, "I think he's gone next door and is hurting my friend. Please go help her. Please stop him."

The kempei didn't move.

"I've always thought it would be easier if they'd just tell you the truth before you actually arrive here. But the damn Koreans just want to make things easier on themselves, so they leave it to us. It's not surprising really."

"What truth?" she whispered, her knees weak. She grabbed onto the table to support herself.

"You weren't brought here to be a nurse. You were brought here to provide a different sort of comfort to the Japanese army."

"Eun-Su," she whispered, the girl's words on the ship echoing in her mind.

He approached her and smiled gently. He touched her bleeding, swollen face and traced her cheek with his thumb.

"Later I'll bring you some bandages and some clean clothes."

Min-He couldn't breathe, couldn't process what he had just said. This couldn't be true. She let herself be led to the mattress and sat down. He sat beside her and placed his hand on her knee. She realized for the first time since he had begun speaking that she was naked, the dress having dropped to the floor when she grabbed the table. The kempei began unbuckling his belt.

"No. You can't really think..." Oh my god.

"It'll be easier if you just relax. The lieutenant colonel was rough with you. I don't need to be."

He smiled at her, but she read the threat in his eyes. He leaned her back and she let him crawl upon her. She was numb. Still raw from the lieutenant colonel, she cried out in agony when he pushed himself into her. She felt like someone was scraping out her insides. He didn't speak to her and when he finished, he disappeared into the toilet room. She heard the bidet running and he reentered the room a minute later. She didn't look at him. He spoke from the doorway.

"It will take some time to get used to, but you need to remember your job here is even more important than being a nurse. These men need you. You're one of the emperor's children and this is the path chosen for you. You're a soldier whose job it is to help our men be able to fight for our Emperor." The door slammed shut behind him.

Four more men came to her that night. After the second, she didn't even bother to get up from the mattress. She didn't speak, didn't acknowledge, she just laid there. Throughout the night, screams came regularly from Eun-Su's room on her left. After the first scream in the bathroom from Soon-Yee, her room was silent. Min-He prayed Soon-Yee was spared this hell. But she knew the truth. When the final man left, she waited for a long time to hear the sinister turning of the doorknob but when none came for a long time, she took herself to the tub, sat in the cold water, and cried.

When Min-He woke the next morning, she wished she had not. The realization of where she was, and who she now was, hit her in agonizing waves. Her face throbbed and her lower body was on fire. Her legs trembled so uncontrollably she resorted to crawling on her hands and knees. She yelped in pain from the burning as she squatted on the toilet. She pressed her head against the wall in the bathroom, listening to hear if Soon-Yee was moving around next door. She gave the wall a few taps and waited; there was no response.

She crawled back to the bloodstained mattress and watched the light from the window make patterns on the wall. Out there, people were going on with their normal lives, going to work, buying groceries, chasing their children. Her life was over. There were no more tears left in her to cry.

The door opened and she froze. She couldn't do it again. It would kill her. She forced herself to open her eyes to face the horror. A Chinese woman, pushing a cart carrying two large baskets and a tray of food, entered the room. Min-He watched as the woman gathered the yellow dress from its heap on the floor. She disappeared for a few minutes into the bathroom with a scrub brush and a jar of soap. Min-He's eyes refocused on the old woman who now stood at her bedside. The woman said something in Chinese. Min-He rolled over, filled with shame. What this woman must think of her.

"I must change the sheet," the woman said in stunted Japanese. "You must eat. Come."

The woman knelt and gently coaxed Min-He to a seated position, wrapped a clean sheet from the cart around her, and helped her over to the table. Min-He hadn't realized how hungry she was until she sat in front of the plate of rice and cabbage. She hadn't eaten in nearly 24 hours. As she ate, she watched the woman change the blood and semen-soaked sheet. The woman didn't flinch or judge. Instead, after placing a clean cover on the mattress, the old woman put her hand on Min-He's bare shoulder and whispered in Chinese what Min-He thought was a prayer. Maybe that was just what she hoped.

After Min-He finished eating, the old woman cleared her tray and returned with a small, white embroidered bag. She took Min-He's face in her hand and gently applied a thick gooey salve to her wounds. When she finished, she handed Min-He the bottle and pointed to her genitals. The woman stroked Min-He's hair with her wrinkled hands, and for a brief moment placed the side of her face against the top of Min-He's head. She walked out the door without another word. Min-He watched the door close and realized she was wrong. There were plenty of tears left.

One of the baskets the old woman left contained two silk dresses, a new skirt and blouse, and three pairs of underwear. Her original clothes had been removed from the room. It occurred to her that perhaps this should anger her, as her clothes had been the only things left that truly belonged to her. But instead, she was grateful. She didn't want any reminder of who she was yesterday, who she could never be again. She applied the salve the woman had given her.

Limping to the bathroom, she tapped on the wall to Soon-Yee's room, hoping for some indication she was there, that she was ok, but there was no response. She returned to her bed, curled up her legs and closed her eyes, blocking out the pain.

Voices in the hall brought her back to the world. Yelling came from Soon-Yee's room, men's voices. She couldn't make out the words, but she could hear the anger. Footsteps pounded in the hallway. Gently, she made her way to the door and pressed her ear against it. She still couldn't make out the words. She turned the doorknob and peered into the hallway.

Soon-Yee's door was propped open and standing right outside Soon-Yee's doorway was the kempei. He was wearing civilian clothes, navy blue pants, and a white collared shirt. He could easily be one of Hyo's classmates. He took a step backward as two men came out of Soon-Yee's room carrying a large bundle. She stared at the scene, trying to process what the men were carrying. Soon-Yee didn't have any luggage. It couldn't be her laundry. And then Min-He knew.

Min-He heard herself scream as she threw open the door and flung herself at the men carrying Soon-Yee. Blood gushed down her legs, but she felt no pain as she clawed at the men to get to Soon-Yee. The men stumbled and dropped the bundle. Min-He fell to the floor and pulled the sheet away from Soon-Yee's head. Her body racked with sobs. Soon-Yee's face was blue, her lips swollen, and a red ring circled her neck. Min-He turned to the kempei and began to pound on his legs.

"No No! How could you do this? Why? You did this to her!"

"She did it to herself," the kempei grabbed her by the arms and dragged her, still screaming, back into her room. He threw her on the bed.

"You have today to recover. This afternoon you may rest but tomorrow you'll resume your duties. In two days, you'll be taken to your permanent placement. Your friend was weak and is a disgrace. Unless you want to end up the same way, find a way to accept your fate."

*****

Min-He slouched in the back of the truck as it rattled along dirt roads on the outskirts of Shanghai. Every time the truck bounced or skipped over a rock, Min-He winced, bruised and sore from the seemingly endless line of Japanese officers.

The first night after Soon-Yee's death was silent, as the kempei had promised. The old Chinese woman came to her room, patted her on the back as she lay on her mattress, wavering between cold numbness and body-wracking sobs. She heard Eun-Su's tapping on her wall, attempts to contact her, but Min-He ignored it, unable to move, unable to care.

The next morning, the officers began to trickle into her room, blending together as if they were one brown uniform, ramming into her, ripping her apart. She lost count after twelve, thirteen, fourteen, they still came when she was vomiting, they still came when she bled, they still came when she was unconscious, unable to endure any more.

She regretted awakening this morning, wishing she had just drifted into nothingness, envying Soon-Yee. The morning was quiet until the kempei arrived, ordered her to bathe, and loaded her and her only belongings, the clothes left by the old Chinese woman, into the rattling military wagon.

Hours had passed but Min-He knew they couldn't be far from Shanghai, as the roads were slow and every few miles the driver stopped at checkpoints. Min-He hoped the ride would last forever; she didn't want to go wherever they were going. The kempei and the driver spoke to each other, but not to her, which suited Min-He just fine.

She knew her time of peace had ended when the kempei looked back at her as the truck turned off the main road and he stopped to speak with two sentries at the entry of a Japanese military base. Wooden buildings with iron roofs painted a camouflaging blend of brown, green, and blue were surrounded by hundreds of identically uniformed men. One of the sentries pointed the driver of Min-He's truck to the right, and they rattled on another two hundred feet through an open gate in a tall wooden fence.

The truck came to a stop in front of a white lime-coated house. Min-He felt a flash of pity for the Chinese family who lived here before the Japanese invaded. Like they had done with her, the Japanese took what they wanted. As they pulled up, Min-He saw a long wooden hut with ten individual doors behind the main house. On each door a white sheet of paper was posted. All the doors were closed except for two on the far right. Several Japanese soldiers stood in front of the hut, laughing, smoking, and pushing each other.

A lean man rushed through the walled forecourt of the house to greet them. His mouth turned down when he looked at Min-He, but his eyes were soft. The man saluted the kempei. He didn't salute back but merely nodded his head. Plodding behind the man was a Japanese woman, taller than he, in a garish red kimono. Her round stomach protruded beneath the silk and her arms were like the dough Min-He used to make her mother's dumplings. Min-He thought she looked vulgar. The corpulent woman didn't greet the kempei but stared at Min-He for a moment and said,

"I thought we were supposed to be getting two."

The kempei cleared his throat.

"The other one didn't make it. The vendor didn't bring enough girls and the others were slated to go elsewhere."

"Well, we'll have to make do with just the one, although the colonel won't be happy. My girls are busy enough as it is. Is she clean?"

"Only officers these past few days. She was a virgin before that, so she's clean enough."

"The boys will like a fresh face. Let's get her inside."

The woman turned to Min-He and spoke slowly and loudly at her.

"Do you speak Japanese?"

Min-He looked the garish woman in the eye. Did they think she was an idiot?

"Of course," she said. She kept her voice low, afraid to show any emotion.

"Good. The last one didn't, and no one knew what the hell she was talking about. Get your things and let's go."

Min-He grabbed the yellow bag the old Chinese woman had packed her new clothing in and followed the vulgar woman into the house. Near the entranceway, a long, waist high desk spanned half the room. On the wall to the left of the desk were eight wooden planks hanging from hooks. Each plank was inscribed in Japanese with the name of a different flower. The woman ushered her around the desk, to a large sitting room, with several padded chairs surrounding a center table. Sliding paper-lined doors hid several rooms on each side of the sitting room. The woman led her to an orange padded chair.

"Sit," the woman ordered and sat across from Min-He in a striped orange and white chair with thick armrests.

The soft eyed man followed them and sat next to the woman, whom Min-He assumed to be his wife.

"You know why you're here," the woman said directly. Min-He said nothing. The woman continued.

"You've been commissioned to work for the Japanese army. We are your supervisors. You may call me 'Mother' and this is 'Father'. If you're obedient and loyal, you'll be comfortable here. If not..." she paused. "If not, then you'll be very uncomfortable. Do you understand?"

Min-He nodded, wondering what other choice she had. 'Mother' continued.

"We have eight other girls here. We're supposed to have ten but now you make nine. You'll be known while you're here as Mio. Each of our girls is given a name which represents a flower. You are to be a bloom in the lives of our Japanese soldiers."

Min-He knew she would have laughed at this in her former life. It didn't seem funny now. Mio — cherry blossom. She thought of the cherry blossoms lining her street back home and the rich fragrance of the blooms as she walked to school. Her throat tightened as she willed herself not to cry.

'There are five hundred permanent soldiers based here and we have mobile troops passing through monthly. You receive a half day off every week for a medical examination and rest and you will have two days off monthly for menstruation. You will begin each day at 10 a.m. and will entertain soldiers until midnight. If an officer chooses, he may spend the night and will leave by 5 a.m."

Mother paused and Min-He watched as she studied her, looking for a reaction. Min-He gave her none.

"In exchange for your service, you'll be provided with two meals a day, clothing, necessities as we see fit, and a weekly medical examination. Meals are in the dining room daily at 9:00 every morning and 8:00 every evening. All these expenses will be deducted from your salary and any extra will be held in safe keeping by Father and me."

A bell rang at the front door and two soldiers walked in. Father jumped from his chair and scurried to the front desk to greet them.

"Wait here," Mother said, getting up from her chair. "You'll need a medical exam before we can allow you to stay."

Mother left the building, nodding to the two soldiers as she walked out. Min-He watched as Father took money from the soldiers. The soldiers each removed a wooden plank from the wall and handed it to Father. Father transferred the names from the planks onto a blue ticket, handed the tickets to the men, and directed them around the house to the long wooden hut.

He looked over at Min-He, gave her a quick smile and a nod. He gestured for Min-He to join him behind the desk. Cautiously, she took the cigarette he offered her. Neither of them spoke. Father busied himself with sorted stacks of paper on the desk. Min-He studied a large sign posted on the wall on the inside the main door.

*¥2 Privates    10:00AM – 3:30PM   30 minutes*
*¥3 NCOs      4:00PM – 8:00PM    40 minutes*
*¥5 Officers   9:00PM – 12:00AM  60 minutes*
*¥15 Overnight   Officers Only*
*Mondays: NCOs and Officers Only*

Another soldier walked through the door, this one younger than Min-He. He looked up at the planks and smiled.

"Must not be a busy day... no lines outside," he said to Father.

"Fujiko and Hinata are available now," Father replied.

The young soldier hesitated then shrugged. He looked at Min-He and raised his eyebrows.

"New girl? Is she available?"

"No. She's not ready yet. Maybe in a few days."

Min-He sighed with relief. A few days would give her time to get out of this place. The boy looked disappointed.

"Everyone else but Fujiko and Hinata is a wait? All right. Give me Fujiko."

Father took the boy's money then handed him a blue ticket with Fujiko spelled out in bold letters. The boy walked out the front door and around the corner.

Min-He decided to ask.

"What's wrong with Fujiko and Hinata?"

"Nothing's wrong with them. They're Japanese. The younger boys like you Korean girls. Fujiko and Hinata make it clear they prefer the officers."

"The other girls are Korean?"

"Yes, we have six Korean girls and two Japanese. With you, we have seven Korean girls now."

"How long do I have to stay here?" She blurted out, willing to take the risk. Father stared at her for a moment then looked back down at his books.

"Until your debt is repaid. Mother has records of the advance paid to your family and will keep track of your living expenses."

"How long will that take?"

Father stopped writing and paused for a long time. He whispered,

"No girl has left here yet."

Min-He perched herself on the end of a bench behind the desk. Several soldiers went in and out as she stared at the white walls. Father said she wouldn't have to work for a few days. There had to be a way out of this place. She could sneak out at night and walk back to Shanghai, blend in with the crowd at the harbor then get on a boat home. She took a deep breath thinking of the options. If she had to, she could sell herself a couple of times to get the money for ship fare. She almost laughed out loud. She thought of her old self, three days ago, considering selling herself so casually. Three days of rape had destroyed that Min-He. Now she just had to figure out who the new Min-He was and if that new Min-He could survive.

Several batches of soldiers later, Mother walked in the door followed by a tall, uniformed man with wire-rimmed spectacles.

"Come."

Min-He followed her through a sliding paper door into a room adjacent to the reception area. A steel medical table with a paper-thin mattress encompassed most of the room. Shelves with clear bottles filled with murky liquids lined two walls. A rusting metal sink hung precariously from the far wall.

"This is Major Kono. He'll be performing your weekly exams. Dr. Kono, this is our newest girl, Mio. They said she was clean. I hope that's true."

She slid open the paper-lined door and walked out. Min-He peered up the scholarly doctor, relieved to be with someone who would finally be gentle with her. Maybe he could give her something to ease the throbbing pain.

Major Kono cleared his throat. "Undress and lie on the table."

Her heart began to pound. How many men over the past three days had seen her naked, yet she couldn't bring herself to undress in front of this man.

"Get undressed. I don't have all day."

She unwillingly slipped off the black and pink dress the old Chinese woman had given her at the hotel and kept her head down.

"Underwear off!"

Tears ran down her face, as she slid off her underwear, humiliated. Blood and pus streaked the lining of her panties. Naked, she hid them under her dress on the floor next to the wall. She got onto the table and the doctor pushed her down and propped her legs into two stirrups.

At the first jab of a cold sharp instrument, Min-He cried out in pain. He pressed his rough hands on her abdomen, ignoring her cries.

"Swollen and a little roughed up, but no signs of disease," he said, more to himself than her.

With her head turned to the side, Min-He could see out of the corner of her eye. The doctor, still standing, was between her legs. Her eyes widened as she saw his hands go to his own pants and pull out his erect penis.

"No, please no," she cried.

He grabbed her arm as he leaned over her, digging his nails into her flesh.

"You shut up or I'll add fresh bruises to that banged up face of yours."

Min-He gasped as he slid into her. She clenched her eyes shut until it was over, grateful it was quick. The doctor buckled his belt then went to the shelves and pulled off a small brown jar. He opened the lid and applied a salve to her vagina. Placing the jar on the table by the door, he said,

"Apply this three times a day for five days. Cold compresses with a wet rag will reduce your swelling. Because you were a good girl, I am ordering a day of rest for you. You'll find a box of condoms in your room. If you want to continue to be free of disease, you must be sure they are used every time. Douche with the red liquid in your room after every customer and bathe daily. Stay clean. I'll see you next week." The door slid open then slammed shut.

She curled herself into a ball, hugging her knees until Mother let herself into the exam room several minutes later.

"Doctor Kono only indulges himself with the cleanest girls. Take it as a compliment. He must have taken a liking to you since he's giving you a day off." She sighed audibly, "Now not only am I down a girl, I'll be losing money on you for 24 hours. Get up and get yourself dressed."

With the brown jar gripped tightly in her hands, Min-He followed Mother out the front door and around the side of the stone house. Every step felt like broken glass between her legs. They passed a tin-roofed building with two entrances. Water puddles formed by the first entrance and the smell of stagnant water and mud wafted beside the doorway.

"That room is your bathhouse. We expect our girls to bathe regularly. You'll have personal time every morning from 5 when the officers leave to 10 a.m. when the privates can begin their visits. Use that time to bathe, do laundry, and clean your room. I expect your room to be tidy and clean at all times. The toilets are here," she nodded to the second door. Five pairs of toilet slippers sat in a row alongside the building.

In front of her now was the long hut with all the doors. She counted ten separate entrances, each with a small square window, all of which were open. Five of the doors had soldiers standing in front of them, some of them pacing, impatient. All the doors but the second and third had a pair of women's shoes and a pair of military issue boots lying in front of them. Min-He and Mother stopped at the second door. A wooden plank identical to the planks hanging in the reception room hung from the door. The plank read MIO. Mother pushed the door open.

Inside the wooden walled room was a stained mattress on a tatami mat lined floor. Her yellow bag sat on the mattress. Two clumsy shelves had been nailed to the wall. A folded sheet and a threadbare towel sat on the bottom shelf next to an orange box with bold Japanese lettering. A wood burning stove in the corner of the room was flanked by two buckets and a long putty colored hose. Min-He wrinkled her nose at the emanation of sweat and ammonia. Mother grabbed the orange box from the shelf and held it in front of Min-He's face.

"Every customer is required to wear a condom. No exceptions. If they give you any problems, report it to me. Nothing is more important than our soldiers' health."

Min-He had no idea what Mother was talking about.

"I don't understand."

"These are condoms. Tell me you know what a condom is."

Min-He shook her head. Mother laughed.

"An innocent! Well, you'll find out soon enough. If your customers don't bring their own, give them one of these. They'll know what to do."

Mother replaced the box on the shelf and began to leave. "Dinner's in two hours in the main house dining room. I'll send one of the girls to get you. Tomorrow night after dinner you'll begin work."

As Min-He watched Mother's portly back disappear, she sat on the stained tatami mat and regretted she had not taken

Soon-Yee's path. Instead, tomorrow she would continue her descent into the hell of the living.

# Marianne
## Munich, Germany
## June 1943 – March 1944

At the piercing shriek Marianne leapt from the table and ran to the window. Eric scrunched his eyebrows in irritation. Trying to block out the ruckus, he turned up the volume on the broadcast of the Reich war victories. The announcer was detailing the Nazi glory over the Ukraine when Erika's shriek from the front porch muffled the details.

Through the window, Marianne watched her daughter dart across the yard, chased by her latest boyfriend, a twenty-year-old Wehrmacht soldier she had met at a BdM and Hitler Youth social. Erika's blond braid flew behind her as she ran, giggling and screeching until she was caught. The soldier threw her to the ground and began to kiss her. Marianne blushed and looked to see if the Russian men were watching. They were lined up at the shallow sewer trench, digging, intentionally not looking at the young lovers. Enough. Marianne opened the window.

"Erika! Come get changed for dinner. Your father's home."

Erika rolled her eyes, irritated, but got up, brushed herself off and gave the enthusiastic soldier an exaggerated kiss goodbye. Marianne watched him ogling her oldest daughter as she bounced up the porch steps, her long legs still in her BdM exercise shorts, exposing far too much of the fourteen-year-old's body than Marianne would have liked. Erika entered the kitchen and draped her lean body over her father's shoulders as he turned up the radio further.

"That public display isn't acceptable, Erika," Marianne scolded.

"Mother, it's not public, it's our front yard."

"You need to be careful with that boy. He's much older than you."

"I don't need to be careful, Mother."

"Shhh..." Eric shushed them.

"There's no need to be careful, Mom. If I get pregnant, it will be a baby for the Führer. Greta Frederich just had her second baby and she's only a year older than me. My BdM leader told us having a baby with a pure German boy is the most patriotic thing we can do."

Erika grabbed an apple off the table and brushed by her mother. Marianne snapped the radio off and glared at her husband.

"You can listen to this later, Eric. They replay it constantly. Right now, we need to deal with your daughter."

Eric sighed.

"What's the problem, Marianne?"

"What do you mean what's the problem? Didn't you just hear that conversation with your fourteen-year-old daughter?"

"I heard it. And she's right. If Germany's going to remain strong, we need to increase our population. Rudy's a good Aryan boy and would be a fine sire for Erika's child. She's nearly fifteen. She's old enough. We've only been able to produce three children. The least we can do is to give Germany some of our grandchildren. And it would be nice to have a baby in the house again."

He flicked the radio back on and turned the volume up, ending the conversation. Marianne stared at him, speechless. Just last year Erika had mapped out a plan to someday attend University to study law. And now she wanted only to have a baby. Hans, who had once dreamed of being an architect, now talked only of the war, begging his father to let him enlist. What was happening to her family?

*****

Four days later, the pounding at her door caused Marianne to drop her knitting needle, as she finished her fifth pair of socks that week. Hilde Müller had increased their quota of socks for the soldiers. She wondered if it could still be considered charity work if she was volunteered rather than chose to volunteer. Did you still get credit for being charitable if you did it strictly to impress your husband's boss's wife?

Martha appeared in the doorway of the sitting room followed by two SS men. Marianne rose.

"Heil Hitler," she greeted.

"Heil Hitler."

They spoke in unison. The taller of the two, a second lieutenant with a dark pencil mustache, spoke.

"Frau Hofmann. Your presence is required at the SS security office immediately."

"Is everything ok? Is my husband ok?" Panic rose in her throat.

"This does not involve your husband. We are to escort you to the office now, Frau Hofmann."

Marianne looked at Martha and thought she saw a brief smirk. It disappeared when she saw Marianne glance her way. Marianne stood straighter and lifted her chin.

"Certainly gentlemen. Martha, please bring me my handbag."

A sleek Mercedes, nearly identical to the one that Eric drove, waited in the driveway. As Marianne walked to the car, flanked on each side by an SS officer, she noticed the normally lackadaisical guards standing with their guns pointed at the POWS, more alert than she had seen them in weeks, trying to impress the officers with their diligence. The POWs all stared at the ground, except the red-bearded Russian, who looked from her to the officers. The fear, blatant on his face, terrified her. She refused to meet his eyes, got into the back of the car, and forced a smile.

Marianne had been in the imposing grey SS building dozens of times, attending her husband's promotion ceremonies, bringing him lunch, taking a tour with the Frauenschaft. Never before had she felt the ominous intimidation the building brought with it. Twin stone eagles glared down at her under the massive swastika emblazoned flag as she crossed the threshold. She requested to be taken to her husband's office, but the two iron-faced officers ignored her. They escorted her to the third floor and abandoned her in a white walled waiting room. A matronly secretary hunkered at an extravagantly engraved reception desk beneath a portrait of the Führer.

As she waited, not knowing what she was waiting for, Marianne's stomach began to ache, and she picked at her already scraggly fingernails. She had bitten her nails since she was a little girl. Her mother tried soaking her fingers in vinegar, telling her she'd never get a husband with bitten nails, but the threats hadn't had any effect. Today, they were bitten down so low, blood seeped through to the tips of her fingers.

She watched the minutes on the clock tick by as she waited, listening to the secretary clicking on the typewriter. 18 click click 19 click clack click click...26. The lieutenant from the car finally reappeared and signaled with his hand for her to come with him. She trailed the lieutenant down a long scarlet hallway. Photographs of decorated Nazis, plaques extolling awarded virtues, and framed medals adorned the walls. At the end of the hallway, a behemoth Swastika hovered above an oak doorway, scrutinizing all who entered. The lieutenant paused briefly at an unembellished, more modest door and opened it without knocking.

Behind an enormous cherry desk sat the forbidding Obersturmbannführer Scharf. Marianne knew the man and his horse-faced wife from the social functions she and Eric attended. Eric referred to him in private as a jackass. The lump in her throat thickened.

Seated in a leather chair in front of the Obersturmbannführer's desk, his face as red as the blood beneath her nails, was Eric. Hitler's face glared down at her from a large photograph behind Scharf's desk. The man rose. He was short for an SS officer, no more than 5'10. His thinning brown hair was slicked back with a shiny oil, generating a faint gleam from his scalp. His thin lips twisted into a scowl.

"Frau Hofmann, please come in and sit down."

Eric remained seated. Marianne shuffled uncertainly across the spacious office and perched on the edge of the empty chair next to Eric. She tried to meet Eric's eyes, but he stared straight ahead at Scharf. His face was glacial. The Obersturmbannführer spoke.

"Frau Hofmann, it has come to the attention of the SS that you have been aiding the enemy."

She gasped.

"I'm sorry? What?"

Scharf repeated himself.

"You have been accused of aiding the enemy. It has been reported you have provided illegal nourishment to Soviet prisoners of war."

Marianne gripped the arm of the chair. How could this be happening? She looked at Eric, panicked, but he refused to meet her eyes, instead staring ahead at the photograph of Hitler. Spots flashed in front of her eyes. Why wasn't Eric saying anything?

"This is extremely serious. Treason is punishable by death, Frau Hofmann."

Marianne opened her mouth to speak but only a squeak emerged. She tried to form words but found none that would take shape. Large beads of sweat began gathering at Eric's brow. Marianne's chest tightened and the room became hazy. Scharf's piercing scowl blurred in front of her. Why had she taken such a risk? How could she have been so foolish? A booming voice echoed from the doorway and jolted her back into focus.

"Now Obersturmbannführer Scharf, threatening one of our wives with execution is getting a little ahead of ourselves, isn't it?"

Standartenführer Müller entered the room. All Marianne could think of was his wife's bloody fur coat. Please God, let that stain have come out. She glanced at Eric and saw him breathe for the first time since she entered the office.

"May I sit, Obersturmbannführer Scharf?"

Scharf leapt from his chair, as did Eric. Both men shouted,

"Heil Hitler!"

Marianne didn't think she had the strength to stand. The private accompanying the Standartenführer pulled a chair beside Scharf and Müller plopped himself into it. Scharf looked disgruntled.

"Sorry I'm late, but where were we?"

"Sir, I was explaining to Frau Hofmann and Sturmbannführer Hofmann the severity of the charges against Frau Hofmann."

"Marianne," Müller addressed her firmly, "What's this all about?"

Before she could speak, Eric jumped in.

"Sir, as you may know, Marianne was raised by a veterinarian. She was brought up with the idea that all animals should be fed and cared for. When we were first married, she was always bringing home stray dogs and cats. In fact, some nights I thought our table would go empty, we had so many strays to feed."

He cackled a strained, forced laugh. Marianne looked at him wide-eyed. She had never brought a stray animal into their home. Eric refused to allow it. He lectured about the diseases unknown animals might bring to their children and he heavily researched the breeders of their long line of full bred boxers before permitting the children to choose one from the litter. Eric didn't meet her gaze and continued.

"I think Marianne looked at these Soviets as strays. They were hungry, so Marianne, being the tenderhearted girl she is, fed them. It was by no means intended to aid the enemy, Sir. She was simply being sweet and simple, feeding hungry animals."

Marianne bristled at the word 'simple' but kept her mouth shut. Standartenführer Müller smiled at her.

"My wife speaks highly of you, Frau Hofmann."

Marianne raised her eyebrows in surprise. She had never felt anything but contempt from Hilde Müller.

"And she shared with me the reason for the downfall of her fur coat. Scharf, Frau Hofmann's beloved dog sent my wife into hysterics over the potential damage to a fur coat she values more than she values me, I daresay."

He chuckled at his own joke. Marianne and Eric both forced smiles. Marianne felt like she was going to throw up.

"Given what we know about Frau Hofmann's nurturing background and sympathy towards those who are beneath us, combined with the outstanding service of Sturmbannführer Hofmann to our Führer, I think we can put an end to this matter and expunge the otherwise superior record of the Hofmanns. Don't you think, Scharf?"

"Yes sir, if you think it best, sir," the younger officer grumbled. Marianne could tell he was displeased with this turn of events.

"I do think it best. However, Frau Hofmann, it would be advisable in the future if you put your sympathies toward a charitable nature of another kind, don't you think? Perhaps our German orphanages or knitting socks for our soldiers, hmmm? I don't think we can be so understanding if this happens again. Don't you agree, Hofmann?"

"Yes sir. Thank you, sir." Eric had transitioned to a different shade of red.

They were dismissed with "Heil Hitlers" and Marianne and Eric followed the Standartenführer out of the office. The two lieutenants were still standing outside the door.

"Escort her home," Eric told them, still refusing to look at Marianne.

"Eric…," Marianne began, but she was talking to his back as he walked away.

*****

"Do you have any idea what could have happened if Standartenführer Müller had not intervened? Not only could you have gone to a Konzentrationslager, I could have lost my job and been sent with you."

"I am so sorry, Eric. I had no idea. I was only trying to be humane."

"Humane, Marianne? You were feeding the enemy! Those Soviet POWs are subhuman, don't appreciate or understand your humanity and not only don't deserve your sympathy, they certainly aren't worth jeopardizing our family. Thank God for Standartenführer Müller. That rat Scarf would have sent us both down with a smile. What you did was inexcusable, Marianne. I have been completely humiliated."

"I'm sorry, Eric. But I didn't think those guards saw me. And I was sure even if they had, they wouldn't have said anything, out of fear of you. I just don't understand why they told."

"It wasn't the guards who turned you in. Those lazy cowards wouldn't go to that much effort."

"Then who could have possibly known? There was no one else around."

Eric sighed.

"It was Christa."

Marianne froze. She was sure she hadn't heard him right.

"What? What do you mean it was Christa?"

"Christa told her teacher. And don't look like that – I'd fully expect she would tell her teacher. If someone is committing a crime, we expect good German children to report it, even if the crime is committed by their own parents. Perhaps we need to think of a way to reward her for doing the right thing."

Marianne was numb.

"It was Christa?" she repeated.

"If you were doing what you were supposed to be doing instead of feeding enemy soldiers, your children wouldn't feel obligated to report your crimes. Imagine how she feels."

Marianne's head spun. This didn't make sense. How could her own daughter have turned her in? Christa. Her Christa. Surely there was some mistake. She tried to refocus on Eric.

"What exactly is it I'm supposed to be doing, Eric?"

"Mother t h e children you have. G o t o m o r e Frauenschaft meetings. Perhaps we could be working harder to conceive another child. Have you been to your doctor lately? I'd like to see you wearing that Mother's Cross."

"You know how much I want another child, Eric. Do you think I'm purposely not getting pregnant? How can you say that?"

"As long as we're on this subject, there's something else I need to talk to you about. Now is as good a time as any."

Her hands started to shake at the way he turned away from her, afraid to tell her. She knew something awful was about to come. She didn't know if she could take another blow.

"You've struggled to conceive and carry the children we have. The Führer is asking SS officers to be looking toward the future and repopulating Germany. We need a strong, populous Aryan Germany to continue to thrive."

Marianne's breathing grew shallow. She knew what he was about to say, she had heard the stories, but she had never imagined it would come from Eric.

"Although you may not be able to, I can have more children. Lebensborn homes have been set up around Germany so officers can help our Führer repopulate the Aryan race. Marianne, it's time for me to start visiting these homes and allowing other Aryan women to bear my children." He looked at her in the eye for the first time all day.

"It's not about sex or love. And it's in no way a reflection of how I feel about you. It's a business deal, Marianne. It's my duty to propagate the race and it's your duty to support it as best you can. And who knows? There's an excellent chance one of the girls won't want to raise the child and I can bring him home to you. Then you can have the fourth child you have always wanted. It's a blessing, Marianne, a blessing, and a privilege."

Marianne fled the room, leaving Eric cursing in her wake. She slammed the bathroom door behind her and vomited the bile that had been forming all day. Marianne stumbled to their bed and cried. She heard the door open a crack and looked up, hoping it was Eric, there to tell her he had just been angry and had threatened those terrible things just to punish her; he really didn't mean it. Instead, in the doorway, stood Christa. The child tiptoed to Marianne's bed.

"Mommy," she whispered, "Are you ok?"

Christa climbed onto the bed and began to curl up next to her mother, as she had done most nights of her life. Marianne recoiled.

"Get out."

Marianne glared as her child retracted in surprise and fear. Looking at this girl, who she had loved so much, who had been her calm in the storm of her family and this war, she felt only repulsion at her betrayal. Marianne reached out her hands and pushed Christa out of her bed. The little girl landed on the floor in a heap and began to whimper.

"Get out," Marianne repeated. "Go cuddle with Martha. You belong with her now."

Rage and hate filled Marianne, emotions unlike any she had ever felt before. She didn't know she was capable of feeling this toward a child, towards her child. Towards her Christa.

"Mommy... Please mommy."

Marianne rolled over and turned her back on her.

"Get out and don't come back."

She heard Christa's sobs as she scuttled out of the room. The sobs that racked her own body nearly tore her apart.

The day after her arrest, the Russian prisoners did not show up to work. The yard was left dug up and filled with dirt. Eric hired a crew of carpenters and plumbers to complete the job. Eric reminded her daily what her offense had cost him. Crying alone into her pillow at night, she wondered what it had cost the Russian prisoners. Terrified of the answer, she never asked.

The weeks passed, echoing with her pain. Eric spent longer and longer hours at work, sometimes gone for days at a time without any word, leaving Marianne imagining him in the arms of a twenty-year-old Lebensborn whore, conceiving the child that was supposed to be hers. Eric's departure for western Russia in late September left Marianne relieved. That respite was fleeting, as she realized the diversion of her obsession with her husband was over. She was left with nothing to focus on but her children.

Marianne watched Erika float from boy to boy, a different soldier on their doorstep nearly every fortnight. She watched her daughter's belly and breathed with relief as each month passed with no signs of a child growing within her own child. With Eric gone, Hans disappeared as well, into the depth of the Hitler Youth. Other mothers at Marianne's Fraunschaft meetings bragged about their sons' Hitler Youth accomplishments; Marianne stayed quiet, distancing herself from pride in the son she knew she was losing to the Reich.

And then there was Christa. For days after Marianne banned her from her room, Christa approached her, attempting to climb in her lap at the dinner table, curling up next to her on the couch, desperate to win her mother's affection. But each time, Marianne pushed her away, unwilling, unable to hold the child who had betrayed her. Until, like a lost puppy, Christa eventually sought the sterile arms of her housekeeper, and stopped trying.

As Marianne watched her child shrink away, her heart burned with sadness and regret, but the betrayal she felt in the pit of her stomach overwhelmed her and forgiveness was unconscionable. The gap between them was a sea, Marianne never speaking to her youngest child: not to scold her, not to acknowledge her. Christa disappeared into the walls of the hollow house.

*****

Marianne politely rejected the offer of a ride from Frau Huber's home. The regional Frauenschaft meeting had taken place in Schwabing, an area of Munich whose cafés, pubs, and galleries were more inviting to Marianne on this Tuesday afternoon than returning home to any of her three children or her scrutinizing housekeeper. The artist's district had always attracted her; she had spent countless days in her teens meandering through the galleries, fashioning her own work after the inspiration from the artists she spoke to, sitting in cafés sketching passersby and pouring through art books at the quiet, inviting bookstores. That was all before Eric. Everything changed with Eric, embarking on the path that led her in the direction of an officer's wife, not the Bohemian artist she had once imagined she would become.

The early March sun lazed gently over her as she strolled down Theatinstrasse through the crowds of vendors, mothers with strollers, merchants returning to work from lunch, soldiers in tight, patrolling packs. She passed the tripled arched Feldherrnhalle and gave the Nazi salute. The sounds of 'Sieg Heil' surrounded her, as compelled by all Germans when they passed the historic hall where a monument to their fallen comrades loomed. She stood for a minute after passing the hall and observed. Several people circumvented the hall and walked out of their way to the alley running behind the Feldherrnhalle. She smiled to herself. Her father had been right after all.

Last fall after she and her father had enjoyed a lunch in a nearby cafe, he had told her anyone who didn't want to salute Hitler would take the Drückebergergässchen, or "evader's path" behind the Feldherrnhalle to avoid having to salute. She hadn't believed him — who would take the time to walk several minutes out of their way just not to salute? But she was surprised to see it actually happening. She circled the side of the building and walked down the evader's path. Normal alleyway, normal people. She wondered if everyone knew what she knew, if everyone on this street was anti-Hitler. Or were most just normal Germans, oblivious to the insidious nature of the path they were on?

Strolling aimlessly through the side streets, she paused at a flower cart and purchased six red tulips for the kitchen window—'Fresh from Holland' the vendor told her with a nod. Putting her nose to the bouquet and weaving slightly to avoid a child escaping his harried mother, she almost missed it. She looked up in time and was brought to an abrupt halt. There, in a glass window etched at the top with "Vogel Gallery", was a painting of a dark-haired girl in a field, the mountains rising behind her. Her painting. Her first year of art school she had entered the piece in a novice art competition. After winning second place to the underwhelming son of the art school's dean, she had gifted the painting to her roommate, Anna. She had lost touch with Anna after leaving school to marry Eric. Could this be Anna's gallery? Perhaps she had married a Vogel. Marianne rushed into the shop.

The meager gallery was empty except for a paint-strewn smocked man in his late twenties, looking up at her through round glasses. He slouched on a low stool behind a counter filled with brightly colored paint tubs. A white cat lounged at the end of the counter, its tail tipped with a splash of green paint. The lingering scent of turpentine brought Marianne back to her art school days. The artist lifted the brush from his canvas as Marianne entered and greeted her.

"Grüss Gott," he welcomed.

She paused at the traditional Bavarian greeting, mandatorily replaced in recent years with 'Heil Hitler'.

"Grüss Gott," she responded hesitantly.

"And Heil Hitler of course," he smiled at her.

"Of course," she replied, slightly frazzled by his impertinence. "Tell me, is this the shop of the former Anna Grüber?"

"I'm sorry. I don't know any Anna Grüber. This is my gallery. I'm Andreas Vogel."

Perhaps Anna had run into hard times during the depression and been forced to sell the painting. Marianne found herself imagining her painting saving Anna's family from starvation. She flushed. Silliness.

"Oh, I see. I was wondering because that's my painting in your window. I had given it to a friend years ago and was just surprised to see it there."

"You owned 'Elisabeth's Retreat'? That's one of my favorite pieces. I've had several offers for it, but none large enough to force me to part with it just yet."

"Oh, no, I didn't own the painting. I painted it. It's my work."

"You're the artist?" He eyed her skeptically. "What's your name?"

"Marianne Hofmann. Well, it was Marianne Bauer when I painted it, before I was married," she said wistfully.

"M. Bauer. Yes, that's the artist. I can't believe it."

The young man rose to his feet and circled the table, his hand extended to her.

"I'm Andreas Vogel. It's a great pleasure to meet you, Frau Hofmann."

She took his hand and her eyes dropped to his left arm, absent a hand. His sleeve was sewn together, and the arm hung passively by his side. He noticed her eyes shifting and lifted his left arm to her. She blushed.

"Poland, 1939. While the left arm was a great loss, it enabled me to be here today in this shop rather than on the Russian front. A good trade for me in the long run." He winked at her. Uncomfortable with the subject, she quickly changed it.

"How long have you had the painting? I'm wondering if you might have the address of the seller. I'd very much like to contact her. Her name was Anna Gruber, but perhaps the painting was sold under her married name."

"I'm sorry, Frau Hofmann, the painting was brought to me about a year ago but wasn't brought in by the owner. Well, not by the original owner at least."

He grimaced then lowered his voice, even though no one else was in the gallery.

"A couple of SS officers brought in a small truckload of paintings they confiscated from Jewish families preparing to be resettled. This was amongst them."

"But Anna was not ..." Marianne then trailed off, remembering Anna saying that her grandfather would not be present at Christmas one year as he didn't celebrate the holiday. She had thought nothing of it fifteen years ago. But today, Jewish grandparents would mean certain deportation. Marianne's eyes welled up for the sweet girl with the high-pitched laugh and frizzy, untamable curls.

The bespectacled young man drew a wrinkled handkerchief from his shirt pocket and offered it to her.

"I'm sorry to be the bearer of such news. Perhaps the fate of your friend isn't sealed. Perhaps she left the painting with friends before leaving the country on her own."

He was unconvincing. She pulled back her shoulders and wiped her eyes, embarrassed. She knew she shouldn't be crying front of a stranger, and certainly not over the fate of a Jew.

"Yes, perhaps. Please, may I see the painting?"

Andreas walked to the window and removed the painting, gripping the top with his good hand and resting it on his stumped left arm. He laid it on the counter in front of her, presenting it with a flourish of his right hand. It was beautiful. She had not thought of this painting in years, the shades of light cascading down from the mountains, the emotion in the little girl's eyes. She was amazed she had once produced this. She stared at it for a long time before it occurred to her to be self-conscious. She looked up from the painting to find the shopkeeper watching her. She reddened.

"I'm sorry. It was just so long ago. It seems like a different world."

"It's a magnificent piece. I'd be very interested in acquiring more of your work. Do you have others for sale?"

"No," she sighed sadly. "It's been years since I painted. In fact, this was one of the last pieces I completed. Since having my children, I've simply..." she searched for the words, "...I've simply forgotten that part of myself."

"Well, perhaps it's time to get it back. I'd love to commission a few pieces from you. If years ago you were able to create this, then that talent must still be inside you somewhere."

"Oh, I couldn't. I don't have anywhere in my home to paint. I'm not sure my husband would approve of my turning a study or a bedroom into a studio."

She gave a false laugh, hiding her disappointment as she realized that Eric would never approve of her painting again, much less selling her work. If what she did wasn't contributing directly to raising the children or promoting the war effort, Eric wasn't about to allow his wife to have anything to do with it.

"I'll tell you what," Andreas smiled at her conspiratorially. "I could use some help around here. In exchange for working in the gallery a few hours a week, you can use the space to paint. In all honestly, we don't get more than a couple real customers a day and a few dozen browsers, so you can paint at the counter while you're working. That will allow me to concentrate on my own work without dealing with the customers, and I can run a few errands during the day. After hours, you'd be free to use the studio space as much as you'd like. However, once you finish a piece, I get first dibs to buy it."

He flashed a boyish smile.

All the reasons this was a terrible, unworkable idea filled her head but she found herself outside the gallery door an hour later with a work schedule in her hand and a promise to be there at 10:00 the next morning. As she rode the bus home, she began to generate her excuses. With Eric away, it should be easy. The children were in school all day. Martha would be happier with Marianne not there getting in the way of her dominating the household. She could invent emergency Frauenschaft meetings she must attend, tell her family she was volunteering at the Krankhaus nursing wounded soldiers, say she was helping her father at the clinic while his secretary was on vacation. As the bus deposited near her front gate, she was bursting with excitement. For the first time in years, Marianne felt a glimmer of hope.

# Rachel
## Warsaw, Poland
## November 1941 – June 1942

The angry red rash on Lilliana's chest created a breathless hush in the room. For a split second, the room was completely silent. Hella's cry pierced the thick silence as she snatched Adam into her arms and fled the apartment. Dora rushed to her daughter, feeling desperately for fever. Lilliana began to cry. Five days after the initial rash, a fever would indicate full out typhus. As if in slow motion, Rachel watched the door slam shut behind her mother and then met Aron's eyes across the table. The secret question between them now had an answer. He had chosen Mira.

"Mira!" Dora's voice echoed in the small apartment. "You must leave! Quickly! Gather your things and go to Noemi's house. Her mother will allow you to stay."

"There's no need for that," Rachel said quietly. "Mira's been..."

Aron jumped up from the table and interrupted her. "Noemi's house is an excellent idea. Rachel, I'm sure your mother will find a place suitable for herself and Adam, but Mira can stay at Noemi's."

Aron's eyes bore into her, and Rachel understood immediately. How do you tell a mother you chose one of her children over the other? That they chose to vaccinate Mira and Adam instead of Lilliana? Rachel stirred her thin soup in shame.

"She stays here until she gets the fever," Aron ordered. "I don't want her in a hospital where she could get infected or contract something worse. Perhaps this is just a skin rash."

"Of course," Dora nodded. "I am sure it's just a skin rash. Lilliana, we'll stay here for a few days then it will clear up and everything will be fine. Maybe Aron can get us some cream."

Dora brightened and began straightening the blankets on the mattresses. Lilliana's red puffy cheeks turned to Rachel who nodded at her encouragingly. But that morning when she left for work, Rachel took her extra set of clothes. Lilliana did not have a skin rash.

Five days later, Aron took the burning child to the hospital. He stepped over emaciated bodies, both dead and alive, piled in front of the hospital door. Vera met him there and took Lilliana to the bed she had set aside for her. Rachel met the cleaning crew at the house. Ghetto law stated that any apartments affected by typhus be disinfected. She hung a sign on the front door of their building indicating the recent presence of the disease. The Nazis were terrified of typhus. Aron joked they should have hung the sign months ago and guaranteed themselves peace from Nazi raids. No one laughed. Adam and Mira returned to the apartment after the disinfection. Rachel guiltily watched her mother and Dora fuss over Adam and Mira, checking for signs of infection. Aron and Rachel had vowed they would never reveal why there was no need to be concerned about the other two children.

"Lilliana will be home soon," Dora told Rachel when she first got home.  "I'm so glad Vera is there for her and as soon as she's well, Vera will bring her home. Aron's connections got her the best care the hospital could provide, right Aron?"

Aron nodded, a pained smile on his face. Dora repeated the same lines verbatim when Saul came home. Hearing Dora's need for reassurance a second time, Rachel retreated to the bedroom and prayed.

Aron had forbidden them to go to the hospital for fear of contagion.

"Lilliana has Vera there and our visiting and getting sick isn't going to make her better."

Rachel ignored his words and passed through the hospital door. A long hallway lay in front of her, bodies lining the floor on either side. She walked along the middle flanked by death. Rachel covered her nose to repel the repugnant stench of rotting flesh. Those who could still speak reached out to her, begging for water, for help. She looked straight  ahead.  The November  cold  lashed  through  the corridors. A nurse scurried by and stopped barely long enough to answer Rachel's question, just pointed to a door on the right where she would find Vera.

Rachel entered a large, icy room. The only difference between it and the hallway was the presence of beds. Skeletal bodies, many three to a bed, filled the room. A handful of doctors and nurses stood by the bedsides, reading charts or changing sheets. No one seemed to be administering medicine. Vera's red hair stood out across the room as she leaned over a young boy, laying a dirty cloth over his forehead. Rachel called her name.

"Good God. What are you doing here?" Vera demanded, "Have you been vaccinated?"

Rachel considered lying, but then shook her head.

"I have to see Lilliana. There were only two vaccines. I couldn't choose. I should have chosen Lilliana. This is my fault."

Vera's face softened. Aron had obviously told her. Vera sighed and looked around. "Ok, come with me."

She led her through the large room and back into the hallway. As they walked, Vera offered an occasional reassurance to the dying patients on the floor, promises to bring water, soup, or a blanket. Vera opened a supply closet and handed Rachel a white handkerchief. Rachel covered her mouth and nose with it as she saw some of the nurses do. They turned left into a much smaller room with only ten beds. In the corner, a thin green sheet hung from a makeshift barrier. Vera pulled back the sheet. Lilliana lay in the bed, covered with a thick blanket, her face dark red and sweating.

"This is what smuggling in thousands of zlotys worth of vaccines in the ghetto gets you: a private medical paradise for your family member," Vera sighed. "We give her clean sheets, water, soup broth, and blankets, but no medicine to heal her. Even for the family of the infamous Aron Kaplan, there is no medicine."

Vera's voice was bitter. Rachel wondered how she did this: facing the thousands of dying people, unable to help them, for most not even being able to provide minimal comfort.

Vera poured a bit of water out of a pitcher and placed a wet cloth on Lilliana's forehead.

Rachel knelt down next to the bed.

"Lilliana, can you hear me? It's Rachel. I'm here to visit you."

Lilliana's red face turned towards the sound of her voice but her eyes closed before they met Rachel's.

"She's delirious. Her fever has been extremely high for 48 hours now. I was able to get her something to reduce her fever, but so far, it's had no significant effect. I can't risk another dose. Another patient might get some benefit out of it, whereas Lilliana isn't responding," Vera said apologetically.

Rachel nodded numbly.

"Is she going to die?" Rachel whispered, not able to take her eyes off the nearly unrecognizable face of the child who two weeks ago was racing through the courtyard, her laughter spiraling off the walls.

Vera didn't speak. Rachel turned and looked at her.

"Is she going to die?" she repeated.

Vera looked away briefly, then nodded almost imperceptibly.

"I'm sorry."

Neither of them spoke for a few moments as Rachel watched the little girl, the only movement the water dripping from the cloth on her forehead. Rachel reached out to wipe the droplets from her cheek and Vera touched her shoulder, stopping her.

"You better go. It's not safe for you to be here. You don't need to bring typhus home to the rest of your family."

Rachel rose. "When?"

Vera understood.

"A few hours, maybe a day. She won't last long with that fever."

"Does Aron know?" Vera nodded.

"He checks in on her twice a day."

Rachel thought of his hypocrisy, but she wasn't surprised. As if Aron could stay away. He was just as responsible for this as she.

Words did not need to be spoken when she entered the apartment that evening. Hella and Dora clung to each other weeping. Aron met her eyes and gave a single nod. Beautiful, soulful Lilliana was dead.

*****

Adam began to walk that winter, his thin, spindly legs tottering toward her. Every time he fell, his little face squinched up, determined to try again. She laid out all the blankets and pillows around him to brace his fall.

"How is he supposed to walk on those blankets?" snapped Aron after Adam tripped over a wadded-up corner.

"I don't want him to get hurt."

"It's not like he has far to fall. God, Rachel, he's going to get a scraped knee in his life."

"Not if I can help it."

She looked over at the bedroom door, wishing she had kept her voice down. Since Josef and Lilliana's death, Dora and Mira had moved into the bedroom and Aron, Adam, and she had moved into the main room with their parents. At first Dora refused to allow Mira to return to school, out of fear of getting typhus. Aron and Mira concocted a story about being able to get her a vaccine after Lilliana's death. In her own guilt, Rachel had overlooked Mira's devastation. Mira hadn't known she was the only one of the two vaccinated. Aron had to tell her immediately after Lilliana became sick, before she mentioned the vaccine to her mother. The black circles of guilt had lain under Mira's eyes since.

The deaths of two of their family had prompted Aron to finally get a legitimate job. He couldn't risk not having a work permit and being rounded up and forced to leave the family alone. He was employed as part of the construction crew of the bridge over Chodna Street, connecting the large ghetto and the small ghetto. Food prices were skyrocketing, and even the basics such as bread and potatoes were harder and harder to get. Aron's smuggling was now limited to nights and their income was significantly reduced. He constantly tried to get Rachel to join him outside the ghetto.

"With your looks, you could easily cross over and we could get meat and milk."

But she refused. She couldn't risk leaving Adam. Without her, he wouldn't be protected. Her family loved him. But they wouldn't die to keep him safe. Not like her. Only with her there, did she know he was ok. Nothing else mattered. So she traded away her clothing, her wool coat, her mother's rings, in order to get what the ghetto had to offer to put in their soup and to get coal for their stove. It was more than most had. With these things, they could survive.

Winter brought more death and devastation, the bodies piling up in the doorways, not enough undertakers to transport them all to the cemetery. The sewage pipes froze and human waste blended with the garbage already heaping in the streets, creating an unearthly stench hanging in the cold air. Homeless mothers and children froze together in the streets, staying where they died.

Rachel walked past an infant, trying desperately to suckle the limp breast of a mother already dead. She continued walking, then stopped and returned to the harrowing sight. She cradled the cold, bony infant in her coat and walked her to the orphanage. A weary CENTOS worker took the child, too weak to even whimper, listened to Rachel's story, and nodded. Rachel wondered if the woman thought she was making it up, trying to be rid of her own child. But it didn't matter. The child might now live a few more days. Walking away, she felt neither heroic nor satisfied. One child might live a while longer. Josef didn't. Lilliana didn't. The thousands of others she passed by every day without looking at their faces wouldn't. It was impossible to be a hero in the ghetto, she told herself. It took everything one had just to be human.

*****

Saul burst through the door of the office where Rachel sat, her eyes blurred from the mounds of requests piled in front of her. He nodded apologetically at Simon, who had spilled his ersatz coffee as the door slammed against the wall.

"Papa, what happened?"

Saul scanned the room of office workers, all interested eyes on him, and gestured for Rachel to come into the hall.

"What's going on? What happened?" Unexpected visits were never good news.

"Where's Aron? Have you heard from Aron?" Saul's eyes were wild with fear.

"Not since Sunday night." Her voice lowered to a whisper as she scanned the hallway. "He was going over for supplies. He should be back tonight."

"They have taken over a hundred prisoners arrested for smuggling from Gesia Prison. Ten policemen, even pregnant women. They've shot them."

"Aron's not with them." Rachel whispered, "We would have heard if he had been arrested."

Saul nodded, convincing himself.

"Someone would have told us. Yes. My heart can't take this, Rachel. Every week it's something else."

Rachel put her hand on his cheek, which was growing more sallow each day. The six months since Lilliana's death had bought incredible food shortages. The Nazis had lowered their food rations even more and prices on the black market were astronomical. The soup she brought home each night barely supplemented their allotted ration. Only Aron's skimming off the top of his smuggling loot kept them from starvation. All her previous judgment about his activities ended the day he brought home a week's supply of milk, real milk, for Adam.

"He'll be home tonight, Papa. Aron is smart. He'll know when to stop. It's going to be ok. We are all going to be ok."

Saul smiled gently at her loving lies.

Her father was right. Every week it was something else. On a late Friday night in April, fifty members of the resistance were arrested from their homes and shot in the street. At the first word of it, Aron fled the house, despite the curfew, and Hella cried until he returned the next morning. The Nazis had targeted members of the underground press. But the illicit newspapers continued, undeterred. The next week, rumors flew about a massacre in the Lublin ghetto. 3000 people who didn't have work permits had been taken by truck and shot.

"I don't believe that," Aunt Dora insisted. "I won't succumb to such hysteria. They were taken to work camps. The Nazis would not kill their own slave labor force. They need us."

Rachel glared at Aron that night, daring him to contradict Dora. Aron had told her once that to be in denial was to be six feet under, but denial was a comfort to Aunt Dora, Mira, and her parents. Hell, it was a comfort to Rachel. Maybe Aunt Dora was right. Maybe.

*****

"It is absolutely out of the question."

"At least see her, Rachel. Listen to what she has to say."

Rachel glared at her brother. She could hardly wrap her mind around what he was suggesting. Her breathing grew shallow at the thought of it. But what if... No, she couldn't bring herself to consider it. She told him as much.

"Well, that's too bad, because she's in the next room and it would be rude not to see her. I'm bringing her in."

Aron got up from the table and Rachel listened to the muffled voices next door. She was furious. He lured her to Rysiek's house with the promise of a card game with friends. Rysiek, his girlfriend Dita, and Vera sat at the table, but no cards had been brought out.

"This could save his life," Vera said.

"You don't have children. You don't understand," Rachel snapped back.

"But I see. I see children die every day. Hundreds of children every day, Rachel. This could be Adam's only chance." Vera refused to look away from Rachel's icy glare. It was Rachel who broke the stare to turn her head toward the Polish woman who accompanied Aron into the room. She was petite, but clearly well fed. Dark brown braids circled her face, and she wore the crisp white uniform of a Polish social worker.

Aron pulled out a chair for the woman and she sat on the edge of it, her eyes focused into Rachel, ignoring everyone else in the room.

"As your brother may have told you, my name is Irena Sendler. I'm a social worker, as I understand you are as well, Rachel. I work with a group of organized Polish friends outside the ghetto and our mission is to help the Jews."

Rachel nodded. Aron had alluded to this group in the past. She knew they were able to assist in finding hiding places and members of the organization were some of Aron's main smuggling contacts.

The woman continued.

"I understand you have a young child. Aron said his name is Adam and he's nearly two?"

Again, Rachel could only nod. The presence of this woman, what Rachel knew she was going to say next, terrified her.

"Rachel," the social worker said softly, "I can help Adam. I can help him escape the ghetto and can find him a place to hide until the war is over."

"I can't," Rachel said, her voice barely above a whisper. "He is my child, I can't leave him."

"I understand…," Irena was interrupted by Aron pounding his fist against the table.

"God damn it, Rachel. Don't you see what's going on here? Are you blind to the children dying in the streets? Are you completely ignorant to what's going to happen? Do you think we're somehow immune to what happened in Lublin? Do you think that last month the Germans made inventory lists of all the registered workers so they could buy us Hanukkah gifts? It's coming, Rachel. I know much, much more than just what you've seen and heard. If you keep Adam here, you're a selfish cow and you're sentencing him to death."

Tears poured down Rachel's cheeks and she gasped at the boldness of Aron's last statement. His voice softened as he continued.

"Rachel, I know how much you love Adam. It's because you love him so much that you need to do this. This is his only chance. I believe that with everything in my heart, and I know you do too."

Rachel did not wipe her tears but spoke directly to the woman through them.

"If you take him, can you promise me he will survive?"

The woman looked intently into Rachel's eyes.

"No, I can't. But I can promise that if he stays, he will die."

*****

"Please, Aron, let's wait. Just another week. I want to be with him just one more week."

"No. Irena is coming tonight and it's now or never."

105

Rachel buried her face into the squirming child's brown curls. Feeling the wetness on her cheek, he turned to her and placed his small hand on her face.

"Mama cry?"

"Mama's happy to be with her Adam, that's all. Mama's not sad."

Adam wrapped his thin arms around her neck and she breathed him in. He wiggled away and toddled over to Hella, who handed him a slice of potato. Rachel had asked Simon for time away from work and spent every second of the past three days with her son. She changed her mind almost hourly over the past three days and asked Aron numerous times to cancel the plan. Each time Aron refused and reminded her of Irena's words: If he stays, he will die.

"It's time, Rachel. Do you want to give it to him or should I?"

Aron took a small syringe out of his coat pocket, the sedative for Adam. Irena had been explicit in her instructions. Thirty minutes before her arrival, Adam should be sedated. Irena most frequently dealt with older children, who were able to be quiet as instructed. A twenty-month-old was a different story.

"You do it. I can't," she whispered.

Rachel called Adam back to her and pulled out a storybook.

"Look at the lamb, Adam. The lamb says 'baa'."

Aron crouched down by Adam, engrossed in his book and munching the potato.

"I love you, little man." He pulled down the side of Adam's trousers.

"No, Aron, don't do it. Let's not do this."

Rachel pulled Adam closer to her, and Aron, without looking at his sister, inserted the needle into the child.

Adam's eyes widened in shocked betrayal, and he began to scream. Rachel began to cry with him and rocked him back and forth. Hella and Saul surrounded them, hushing and kissing the little boy. His cries grew weaker as the sedative settled in and Rachel cradled and rocked her son, whispering, "I love you, Adam. Mommy will always love you" until his eyelids closed and his breaths grew deep. She rocked him until a quiet knock sounded at the door. Irena Sendler came in carrying a heavy, grey gunny sack. She walked over to the child, cradled in Rachel's lap, knelt down, and put her small hand on his forehead.

"Adam Josef Zylberman. Born October 7, 1940." Irena looked into Rachel's swollen eyes and Rachel nodded. "Downstairs a Polish potato vendor I trust is waiting. We will conceal Adam in the gunny sack and hide him under the potatoes. Jan will go directly to the Dzielna gate and I've arranged a meeting place with him outside the ghetto. From there, I'll take Adam to a family who is waiting for him. He will hide with a Polish family as an orphaned nephew. They are prepared to care for him until the war is over and then he will be returned to you. New identity papers have been made for him."

Rachel clutched Adam, panic rising inside of her.

"I don't think I can do this. I can't. I need to keep him."

Irena looked to Aron. Hella began to cry. Aron took the gunny sack from Irena and approached his sister.

"Rachel, you have about 30 seconds to make a final decision. You can hand me Adam and save his life, or you can hand him over to the Nazis to murder. That's the decision. Do you want him to live or die? Choose."

"You don't know, Aron, you don't know he will die."

Aron looked her squarely in the eye.

"Yes, I do. If you do not hand him to me right now, you are condemning him to death."

Rachel could hardly bear it. She lost Josef and now she was losing Adam. She felt like her heart was being shredded into a thousand pieces. She looked through her tears at Irena.

"Will you give him something? I've written him a letter. Can it go with him?"

Irena shook her head.

"I can't send anything with him that will identify him. But I will bury it with his identity so he will have it after the war."

"How will we find him after the war? How will you remember where he is? What if you're killed?"

"I have buried jars in a secret location with the names and locations of all the children. Only a small number of trustworthy people know the whereabouts of these jars. Like me, they are willing to die rather than reveal the whereabouts. That is the only promise I can make to you."

Irena looked to the window.

"I need to go. The vendor is waiting and if he stays there much longer, we will raise suspicion."

Rachel kissed her child and held him close one more time. Then, without lowering her gaze from Irena's, she handed Aron her only child.

"I trust you with his life. Please take care of my son."

Aron and Saul placed Adam gently in the bag, each whispering his own goodbyes and promises to the sleeping little boy. Hella kissed him one last time then clung to Rachel, both women sobbing.

Aron handed the enveloped child to Irena. "We don't know how to thank you."

"God be with you. I promise to do my best to keep him safe and God willing, he will return to your arms again. "

The social worker placed the bag delicately over her shoulder and with a final, sad smile to Rachel, she and Adam left.

A moment passed in silence.

"No," Rachel stood. "No. I'm going to get him."

Aron grabbed her arm.

"No, you're not. He's gone, Rachel. He is safe now."

"No, he's mine. I want him back. I'm going to get him!"

Aron wrapped his arms around her and held her as she kicked him.

"You get him back for me, Aron, you get him back. I want my baby. I want my boy."

She turned to face him and began punching his chest and arms.

"You get him back! You get him back."

Saul hugged her from behind and broke her away from Aron. She turned to her father and sobbed into his chest.

"My baby. I want my baby."

"You have saved him, Rachel," her father whispered. "You have made the greatest sacrifice a mother could make. You have saved him."

Rachel's anger faded to overwhelming grief, and she melted into her father's arms. Aron backed quietly into the bedroom, where Rachel's sobs were nearly surpassed by his own.

# Claire
## USS Sherman
## September – October 1943


September 24, 1943

Dear Colonel Keller,

Yesterday I received a telegram from the War Department informing me of my father's MIA status. After making inquiries, I discovered the Minneapolis Tribune reporter assigned to your unit believes my father deserted. I am leaving for Europe with the 17th Evacuation Hospital within the week. Please contact me as soon as possible with information about my father's status. I'm desperate to know where he is. As soon as I arrive at my location, I will do everything in my power to make personal contact with you. If arrangements can be made for me to join your unit as part of your nursing staff, I would be grateful.
My father cherished your friendship and I'm sure you must know the truth about what happened to him.

Claire Weber


October 3, 1943

Dear Tom,

I arrived in New York City yesterday afternoon and boarded the ship USS Sherman this morning. As you likely know, I've been assigned to the 17th Evacuation Hospital. There are 48 nurses, 30 doctors, and a slew of other medical personnel. There are nearly 400 people in my unit and the Sherman has three other evacuation hospitals being transported along with us, so there must be a couple of thousand people aboard.

I was told the nurses of the 17th have been together for several months in North Carolina. I fear the other nurses will be suspicious by my arrival and will find me less than competent. A handful of their unit's nurses were deployed elsewhere at the last minute, so perhaps they'll just view me as a replacement, which maybe I am. I hope I can live up to everyone's expectations of me. Thank you for lending me your emergency medicine manual. I think I studied it on the train more thoroughly than I ever studied any textbook in college.

If you could see me right now you wouldn't recognize me. I'm wearing a worsted navy-blue dress uniform (it's awful), and I'm a second lieutenant. I'm the same rank as Bill. Can you believe it? I hope he gets a laugh out of that.

I've been assigned a large cabin to share with nine other nurses in the lower deck of the ship and it has no portholes. I'm worried I'll get seasick. We're just sitting in the harbor now and may be for several more days.

Tom, I can't thank you enough for the strings you pulled to get me here. I know in my heart because of you, things are going to be ok. I would like to write to you and--

"Claire? It is Claire, isn't it?"

Claire looked up from her letter at the two identically uniformed women standing at the end of her cot.

"Yes, hi. Claire Weber from Minnesota."

"I'm Marie Salazar and this is Bonnie Grund. We just wanted to welcome you to the 17th. We're headed up to the mess for dinner. Would you like to join us?"

Claire liked the women instantly, especially Marie, her thick, unruly hair and dark flashing eyes singing out her Italian heritage. Marie talked quickly, with wild gestures, as she described her Mama's gravy in contrast to the thin, pasty, pasta-like substance on their trays. Marie's thick New York accent contrasted Bonnie's lilting southern twang and both women teased Claire about her Minnesota vowels, a comment Claire had never heard before. She never realized Minnesotans had an accent. Bonnie was quiet, Laurel to Marie's Hardy, her blonde hair piled onto her head and green eyes hidden under long lashes.

"How long have you two known each other?" Claire asked.

Marie shoved mysterious orange bits to the left of her tray.

"Let's see, Bonnie and I first met in December when we were both sent to Fort Bragg."

Bonnie nodded. "I had just joined the corps, but Marie had been assigned to Ft. Lewis, Washington before being reassigned to Fort Bragg."

"Is that where you received your training?"

"No, we both went to nursing school previously. Marie in New York and I went to school in Georgia."

"I mean your military training."

"Military training? We haven't received any military training other than who to call what. The men in our unit got an eight-week military course on base. We were sent to work in the hospital. Why? Did you receive military training?"

Claire shook her head, relieved that these two women didn't seem to have much more military experience than she did. Marie continued,

"I was an emergency nurse before joining and Bonnie worked in post op. We both worked in the emergency department in Ft. Bragg."

Claire's relief faded. Even without more military experience, these two, and likely the rest of the women buzzing around the ship's cafeteria, were prepared to work in a combat hospital.

"How about you? What did you do before you joined up?"

Claire tried to be vague.

"I was working at a large hospital in Minneapolis..."

She was saved by the appearance of a broad-shouldered woman with a barrage of decorations on her uniform. The woman stood behind Bonnie. Marie and Bonnie rose, and Claire followed suit.

"Please ladies, sit down, continue your dinner. Lieutenant Weber, I wanted to introduce myself. I'm Major Lois Beck. I'm the head nurse of the 17th Evacuation Hospital. Welcome to our unit. You come very highly recommended."

"I do? Thank you, ma'am."

"We have highly prepared and competent nurses in this unit. I have no doubt you'll fit in well here. Ladies, have a nice evening. We have a nurse's meeting at 0800 sharp. I'll see you then."

"Highly recommended, huh?" Marie looked at Claire, impressed.

Claire blushed and mumbled something intentionally inaudible. She looked up and met Marie's black eyes and was comforted by her open smile.

"So, tell us about Minnesota, Claire. What is this I hear about ice fishing? Is that really true? How's that done? And more importantly, why would anyone want to do that?" Claire smiled at Marie gratefully and, accompanied by Marie's hoots and Bonnie's giggles, told a story about her Uncle Earl's truck plunging eight feet under the ice and his reappearing on the surface with a twenty-eight-inch walleye in his icy mittens.

*****

Marie perched on the edge of Claire's bunk as she finished her third letter to Bill in as many days. She desperately needed to connect with him. She was nervous about Bill's reaction to her joining the ANC. She needed to find the right words to help him understand.

"You must have a lot of people," Marie laughed, "you've done more letter writing since you've been here than I've done my entire military tour."

Claire blushed.

"Not really. I'm writing to my fiancé Bill. There's just Bill and my father."

"That's your whole family?" Marie asked incredulously.

Claire nodded and quickly changed the subject. She wasn't ready to talk about this.

"What about your family?"

"My family?" Marie hooted. "If I wrote letters to all my family, that's all I'd be doing. I have six brothers, four grandparents, eighteen aunts and uncles and so many cousins I can't count them all. Do you want to see their pictures?"

Claire nodded, surprised she really did want to see them. Marie disappeared for thirty seconds then reappeared with a bulging photograph album. She opened the book to pages of a laughing, dark-haired family. She beamed as she pointed out her six little brothers to an incredulous Claire.

"Six little brothers!"

"My parent had only me for ten years. They thought they couldn't have any more. Then the year my mom turned thirty she had six boys in five years, ending with Ralphie and Joey, these scampy twins. The oldest here is Mario. He's fourteen and tried to join up at every enlistment office in Brooklyn, telling them he's eighteen. Good thing he looks twelve!"

Claire laughed with her.

"And that," continued Marie, "is why I only write to my mother. I couldn't keep up with the rest of them. Don't worry though. She keeps everyone informed about everything, whether they're interested or not!"

"They're amazing, Marie. I always envied the large farming families at home. I've wondered what it would be like to have so many people to care about."

Marie looked at her expectantly.

"I'm an only child. My mother died from cancer three years ago. My father's a physician with the 173rd field hospital."

"The 173rd," Marie looked thoughtful. "My cousin Theresa is with the 173rd. In Italy this past month, right? My mother and aunt compete for the 'most patriotic daughter award' so I hear about Theresa every other letter."

Hope flashed through Claire.

"Your cousin is with the 173rd? Marie, if I tell you something will you keep it to yourself? Your cousin might be able to help me. This is awkward, Marie. I am in a...", Claire searched for the word, "...precarious position."

"Sugar, I don't judge nobody. Nothing passes these lips. My Mama gossips enough for the both of us, so I've never felt the need to, and I don't intend to start now."

Claire took a breath and put her trust in Marie.


October 15, 1943


Dear Tom,

I can't express to you my disappointment at being assigned to North Africa. I was sure we'd be heading directly to

Italy, but our unit was rerouted and we're expected to be here for at least a month. We've received no mail at all. I've had no word from the War Department, no word from Colonel Keller, and no word from Bill. My only beacon of hope right now is that my new friend, Marie Salazar, is writing a letter to her cousin who's a nurse in my father's unit. I haven't had a full night's sleep since that terrible day I received the telegram.

I'll try to focus on the positive and not lace my letters with too much self-pity. My unit has settled into camp since arriving in Morocco three weeks ago. Morocco is as unlike Minnesota as root beer is to apple brandy. Many of the buildings here are surprisingly modern, however donkeys fill the streets and women do their laundry in the open on stone laundry basins built around riverbeds. Houses as big as palaces line the hillside and there's a great disparity between the wealthy and the poor. But the people have been friendly, and the children's smiles are infectious.

We're living on the third floor of a former French elementary school in a town outside of Casablanca. One big room is divided by little half walls so we each have our own little cubby hole with a cot and a small table. We call them our "compartments". In all honesty, the work isn't nearly as hard as I expected. Soldiers aren't being sent here from combat and most of our patients are here because of accidents or common illnesses. At first, we were given pills to prevent us from contracting malaria, but the pills made us all so sick we've been permitted to stop taking them. So, we've seen a few cases of malaria but there's no need to worry. I'm being careful and staying clean.

Sometimes in the afternoon the girls and I watch the paratroopers practice their jumps. Each time we watch, we wonder which of the paratroopers we'll see next with a broken leg or arm from a bad landing. My experience in ortho is definitely paying off! I worry, however, I don't have the skills I need if we ever do see combat wounded.

This evening the girls are going to the beach. The sun here is so hot. Last week one of our nurses, Bonnie from Macon, Georgia, burned so badly after just 45 minutes she had to spend the night and all the next day in cold, wet towels. The Mediterranean Sea is like warm crystal, but it's a strange sight to swim while Moroccan men and their camels are walking along the beach. Camels are terrible animals. They hiss and spit and smell worse than a pig farm.

Please write to me if you hear anything at all, even the slightest rumor.

Yours, Claire

Marie's head popped up over the divider between their compartments. Claire placed her letter into the thin envelope, not bothering to seal it. The army censors would read and black out anything they felt threatening, so she tried to keep things as general as possible.

"Give me five minutes," Claire said.

"All right, but if you wait five minutes, you'll be in the back of the crowd for mail call." Marie disappeared with a grin into her own side of the wall.

"Mail call!"

Claire raced down the stairs, almost knocking over a nurse in the stairwell. Claire nearly burst with excitement at the sound of her name called from the canvas bag laden truck. Three letters and a package were tossed her direction: the package from Barbara Ann, one letter from Bill, and another from Tom. Her breath stopped short at the fourth letter, a nearly translucent envelope with the "The United States War Department" insignia stamped across the front. Escaping the bustling crowds, she fled up the stairs of the school building to the relative solitude of her compartment. She ripped open the envelope.

MISS CLAIRE WEBER
17TH EVACUATION HOSPITAL   APO 42
THE SECRETARY OF WAR DESIRES ME TO INFORM YOUR FATHER MAJOR ROBERT J WEBER'S STATUS HAS BEEN CHANGED FROM MISSING IN ACTION TO ABSENT WITHOUT LEAVE SINCE TWENTYFIFTH SEPTEMBER IN ITALY IF FURTHER DETAILS OR INFORMATION ARE RECEIVED YOU WILL BE PROMPTLY NOTIFIED.
UL10  THE ADJUNCT GENERAL

Bitter disappointment flooded her. She crumpled the letter and threw it onto the tile floor. She tore open the letter from Bill.

October 20, 1943

Claire,

I don't understand this at all. I'm very sorry to hear of your father's MIA status, but your actions make no sense. What possible outcome do you hope to achieve by enlisting in the Army Nurse Corps? Please contact your superiors and request a transfer to the states immediately. Put an end this nonsense. I'll do whatever I can here to find out what happened with your father. Please return to Minnesota immediately.

Bill

October 14, 1943

Dear Claire,

I hope this letter finds you safely in North Africa. I was led to believe your unit was headed directly to Italy, but apparently plans change as things seem to do quickly in the Army, and your unit was reassigned to Morocco. Don't be discouraged. Your unit is designed to be mobile and with the US rapidly increasing its troops into Italy, I expect that'll be your next destination.

I imagine you're settling in to Army nursing. The head nurse of your unit, Lois Beck, is a colleague of mine. I requested you be assigned to her unit. I know you can go to her if there's anything you need.

I've been able to find out very little about your father. I've written a dozen letters to the War Department pleading for an investigation. The editor at the Tribune has been closed-lipped, suspicious perhaps I'll leak a scoop on a story. I'll continue to make inquiries and hopefully can make some headway to find our answers.

I miss our weekly dinners. Take care of yourself, Claire.

Tom

"Nurse Weber, I need you in surgery."

Claire turned her head to see Major Lois Beck looming behind her, watching as she wrapped the paratrooper's wrist. He winced as Claire turned around.

"Sorry," Claire whispered to him.

"I can't right now," Claire stuttered to Major Beck, "I'm in the middle of setting his arm."

"One of the medics can take over for you. I need a nurse to assist. A jeep accident has come in and one of the soldiers needs abdominal surgery."

"Isn't there someone else who can go? Someone else who is available?"

"I'm asking you, Nurse Weber. Come on. A medic will be right over to finish your arm, Sergeant." Nurse Beck smiled compassionately at the paratrooper.

"Aww, Ma'am, he won't be nearly as nice to look at as Nurse Weber here."

"He certainly won't be, Sergeant. You'll have to make do."

Claire smiled weakly and followed Major Beck into surgery. Her head swam as she raced to keep up with Major Beck's long strides. They stopped at a pair of sinks to scrub their hands and Major Beck helped her into a white surgical gown, tying it behind her back. A medic wheeled the unconscious patient into the room. Dr. Heinz, a stern-faced physician with slicked-back silver hair, joined them at the sinks. As the doctor prepped, Claire followed the head nurse into the operating room.

"Claire, you're going to assist Dr. Heinz. I'll be standing behind you as your assistant."

Claire nodded shakily, terrified. She hadn't assisted in a surgery since nursing school, and even then, was always surrounded by others whom she eagerly allowed to take the lead.

"Set up the doctor's tray and clean the patient's abdomen," Lois Beck's firm voice spoke to her from behind.

Claire took a deep breath and willed her hands steady. She pulled the wheeled tray next to her and placed each instrument from the case below onto the tray in front of her. Major Beck reached below and laid out the tools Claire missed. Her face burned. As the doctor entered the room, Claire gauzed the young soldier's abdomen with antiseptic. She resisted the urge to look to Major Beck for approval.

Dr. Heinz asked for a scalpel and Claire shakily handed it to him. Her breathing was heavy behind her mask; she was sure they all noticed. Claire's stomach churned and she averted her eyes as the doctor pried the boy open.

"Please place the retractor," Dr. Heinz ordered as he completed the incision and handed her back the scalpel.

Claire eyed the surgical tray. She recognized nothing on that tray to be a retractor. The only retractor she had ever seen was a small hook-like device. She froze. Major Beck reached from behind her and placed her hand on a large circular ring. Claire picked it up.

"That is a ring retractor preferred by Dr. Heinz for his abdominal surgeries."

Major Beck appeared at her side and her low voice guided her in the proper placement of the round metal retractor into the boy's abdomen, holding back the tissue for surgery.

"See how it creates a large area for the surgeon to work without the need for a manual retractor or a partially opened surface?"

Dr. Heinz grumbled,

"I didn't know we were a teaching hospital, Major Beck."

"I understand, Dr. Heinz."

Lois smiled at the doctor behind her mask but retained her position beside Claire. Claire looked at the boy's open abdomen. She had been so preoccupied with perfectly placing the retractor, she hadn't had time to be squeamish. With fascination, she followed Dr. Heinz's graceful hands as he sealed the young soldier's internal bleeding. She handed him each requested instrument, her eyes riveted to the surgery.

"We're all done here. Nurses, stitch him up and deliver him to post-op."

Dr. Heinz left the room, leaving Claire standing at the table. She had stitched dozens of split knees, fingers, and eyebrows in her nursing school days, but closing a surgical incision put this boy's life in her hands. If she did something wrong and caused an infection, he could die.

"Lieutenant Weber?" Lois Beck's voice behind her prompted her out of her petrified state. Tears filled her eyes.

"The operating room is no place for tears, Claire."

"I don't know how to do that," Claire whispered, her face flaming at the confession.

"That's not an excuse. I'll walk you through it."

Major Beck circled the surgical table and talked her through each step until the stitches in the soldier's abdomen were precise. As the medic rolled the patient out of the room, Major Beck followed him out without another word. Alone in the room, Claire let the tears flow. She knew today was likely her last in North Africa and the thought of being sent home was too much to bear.

Claire stood outside the head nurse's door in what was clearly a former school office. Claire remembered entering such an office in 3rd grade when she had been sent to the principal for kicking Alfred Dougan after he kissed her on the playground. This was infinitely worse.

"Come in," a voice called from behind the door and Claire entered to find Lois Beck, still in her surgical whites, writing a letter at a bamboo desk.

"You wanted to see me?" Claire croaked, her throat dry.

"Please come in." She motioned to a wooden armchair and Claire perched uncomfortably on the edge.

"Major Beck, I want to apologize for this afternoon. I don't have a whole lot of experience in surgery. I'm very sorry."

"It's quite obvious you don't have the experience I was led to believe you did. I watch you, Claire. I see how you avoid the more severe patients, managing to be in the right place and the right time to accept patients with broken limbs or more minor medical complaints."

Claire burned with shame.

"That behavior is easy to overlook here in Morocco, but we're a mobile hospital and I expect we'll be sent into a combat zone in the next few months. That behavior is not only unacceptable, but unforgivable and could cost the lives of soldiers."

Major Beck was silent for a moment before continuing. Claire could feel the major's eyes boring into her. A cockroach scurried across the floor past Claire's feet, and she stared at it though her tears, wishing she could trade places with it and crawl into the walls.

"However," Major Beck's voice softened a bit, "I also see how gentle and compassionate you are with the soldiers. You've developed an excellent rapport with most of the nurses and you do have great skill in orthopedics. So, I don't think a discharge is necessary."

A flash of hope surged through Claire. But then Nurse Beck continued.

"After observing you for the past three weeks, I've made plans to send you back to a military hospital stateside."

Claire's heart dropped. It was over. The tears overflowed onto the floor, startling the cockroach and sending him scurrying back to his corner.

"I am so sorry, Major Beck," she whispered and rose from her chair, formulating the words in her mind to tell Marie and Bonnie.

"Sit down, Lieutenant Weber. I'm not quite finished. As I said, I have made plans to send you back to the States. However, a letter I received two days ago prompted me to change those plans."

Claire sat back down, her breathing shaky, hope creeping its way back to her.

"Apparently we share an acquaintance with a Dr. Tom Parker."

Oh, thank God for Tom. Major Beck continued.

"Dr. Parker and I worked together at Walter Reed for nearly a year when he was completing his residency, and I was just out of nursing school. He informed me he requested you be assigned to my unit and asked that I take care of you, as you were somewhat inexperienced, but had, in his words, "incredible potential with the right guidance". He asked, as a favor to him, to keep you under my wing. So, Lieutenant Weber, as a favor to an old friend and a highly respected doctor, I'm going to do as he asks. But, if you choose to remain here, you can consider yourself in nursing boot camp. You will do everything I ask of you, study every night, and make it your number one priority to learn everything you can about combat nursing. Is that clear?"

Relief flooded Claire.

"Yes, thank you. Thank you so much, Major Beck."

Claire nearly ran from the room and collapsed on the cot in her compartment. She picked up Tom's medical book and flipped through the index to abdominal surgeries.

Marie's head popped up.

"We're going to the beach again. Harold has a swell friend he wants you to meet. He's from Iowa, which is practically Minnesota, right?"

"Marie! I'm engaged!"

"Oh, yeah. Bill."

Marie rolled her eyes and Claire laughed and threw a pillow at her as she ducked back behind the wall. All that mattered right now was she was getting a second chance. She was getting to stay.

# Min-He
## West of Shanghai, China
## August 1943

Min-He stood and listened to the sounds of sex coming from the wooden room on her right. Her stomach churned in revulsion. She sat on her mattress, covered her ears, and squeezed shut her eyes until the noises stopped, replaced by soft voices. She opened her eyes and studied the room. A white sign hung on her door. It was a list of rules for the soldiers. All were numbered "1".

1. Entry to this comfort station is permitted only to Army and paramilitary personnel.
1. Visitors must pay at reception and obtain a ticket and a condom.
1. The ticket is valid for only this occasion and if not entering a room can be refunded. There is no refund once it has been handed to a hostess.
1. On obtaining a ticket, the visitor is to enter the room with the name shown. The time allowed is 30 minutes for privates, 40 minutes for NCO's, 60 minutes for officers.
1. Drinking alcohol in the room is prohibited.
1. Visitors must leave immediately after their business is completed.
1. Anyone who fails to observe the regulations or who infringes military discipline will be ejected.
1. Contact without the use of a condom is prohibited.
1. Entry time: 10am-3:30pm for Enlisted Men, 4pm- 8pm for NCO's, 9pm-12am for Officers.

A timid knock sounded at her door. Her hands began to shake. Mother and the doctor had promised her the day off. She rose and opened the door a crack. Standing in front of her was a child, her long hair in a red ribboned braid, wearing a poorly tied cobalt kimono. Her round face was adorned with thick make-up. She wondered if this was Mother and Father's child.

"Yes?"

"Hi, Mio. I'm your neighbor Umeko."

The child pointed to the door where minutes before the noises had come. Min-He's eyes widened. Certainly this girl, this child, couldn't be doing this work. It wasn't possible. Umeko, plum blossom child, the name certainly fit this tiny, pink cheeked waif standing in front of her.

"You... work here?" Min-He asked incredulously.

The girl giggled.

"That's everyone's reaction. I'm older than I look. I'm thirteen. Can I come in? We're lucky; this afternoon is slow. Most of the NCO's are on some training mission for a couple of days."

The girl slipped by Min-He and plopped herself down on the tatami mat. She pulled a bottle of dark liquid out of her kimono.

"Look at what one of the officers gave me last night! Let's get to know each other!"

Umeko took a long drink from the bottle, grimaced, and handed it to Min-He. Min-He took the bottle but nodded at the sign posted on the door.

"It says we can't drink in the room."

Umeko laughed.

"You can read? I wish I could read. I went to school for a few months when I was little, but never finished the year. Well, whatever it says, don't worry about it. If we can't find a little fun, we'd never survive. Go ahead."

Min-He raised the bottle to her lips. The brown liquid burned her throat and tongue. She choked. Umeko giggled again.

"Did you come from another pi house or are you fresh off the virgin boat?" Umeko asked, taking another long swig from the bottle.

"Fresh off the boat, I guess. What's a pi house?"

"This is a pi house. House of pussy, house of cunt, that's what we are to the Japanese. Pi."

Min-He turned a deep red. She remembered the chanting men on the boat. Less than a week ago, it seemed another lifetime. If she had known what that word meant then, what would she have done? Taken the road Soon-Yee travelled? Tried to escape? Or would she be here just the same?

"I was in a hotel in Shanghai. There were officers…"

Umeko nodded knowingly. "The officers always get the ones right off the boat first. They want them before they're diseased and all used up." Umeko spoke as if she were talking about kimchi recipes.

"How do you do this? How do you survive?" Tears filled Min-He's eyes. She felt foolish crying in front of this woman-child.

"It gets easier. The first week is the hardest. After that it doesn't even hurt. I can teach you how to make it easier, how to make it over faster." Umeko paused. "Maybe we can help each other. I can teach you how to survive here."

"You said we can help each other. I don't have anything to offer you," Min-He said.

"The other girls don't really talk to me much. Most of them are nice, they just…" her voice trailed off. "Maybe you can just… talk to me."

A loud knock sounded from next door.

"That's me. I gotta go. I'll come get you for dinner. If I leave the bottle, you won't drink it all, will you?" Min-He shook her head. Umeko smiled and darted out the door to the waiting soldier. Minutes later, Min-He could hear groans coming through the wall. She took a long, drink from the brown, bitter bottle.

*****

The dining room was behind one of the sliding paper doors inside the main house. Two rectangular tables parallel to each other were headed up by a smaller table where Mother and Father sat. When Umeko and Min-He entered, the chatter of the girls silenced. Two older women, in their late twenties, were the only ones at the far table. Min-He knew instantly they were Fujiko and Hinata, the Japanese women that Father had told her about. Both women stared at her unpleasantly. One, in a gold robe that gaped open, hiding nothing, leaned over

125

and  whispered something to the other. They both cackled, not bothering to disguise the object of their hilarity.

"Bitches," murmured Umeko, as she led Min-He to the end of the closest table.

Five women shifted over to make room for them. No one blinked, as if sitting at the other mostly empty table was not even an option. At the other end of her crowded table sat two teenage girls, wearing identical blue blouses and white skirts, obviously twins. Beside them, a sad-eyed woman tended to one of the most beautiful girls Min-He had ever seen, a girl about twenty, with blank eyes staring at the wall, not even registering. Next to Min-He was a girl with hair as short as a Japanese soldier. Neither Mother nor Father acknowledged Min-He as she sat down. A Chinese girl, barely older than Umeko, brought in bowls of cabbage and began serving. The short haired girl spoke to Min-He.

"Welcome to Hotel Whore," she scowled. The girl with the blank eyes began to hoot, a loud, brittle cackle. Spittle dribbled down her chin. The sad-eyed woman took a cloth and wiped it off.

"Quiet, Kiku, you're going to get yourself in trouble," she whispered. Mother looked over and frowned but said nothing.

One of the twins smiled at Min-He.

"You must be Mio. I'm Ren and this is my sister Ran. This is Botan," she nodded at the short haired girl. "This is Kiku and Ayame."

The sad-eyed woman known as Ayame stopped fidgeting with Kiku long enough to nod in Min-He's direction.

"You've clearly met Umeko," Ran continued. "Over there is Hinata and Fujiko. They prefer to um, keep to themselves."

Botan snorted and Ran shot her a look. "You're welcome to sit with us at mealtimes."

"Thank you," Min-He said softly.

"Where are you from?" asked Ren.

"Sokcho," Min-He replied. "I arrived a few days ago."

"You're lucky then," Ren said, "this is a fairly easy assignment. Our first assignment was at a base at the front."

Ran nodded and added,

"We lived in tents and had fifty men a day every day. Here at least we get meals and breaks each morning."

Min-He's eyes grew wide. They talked about it as casually as Umeko had spoken about being raped by the officers. This was some kind of a nightmare and she couldn't seem to wake up. The cabbage stirred in her stomach.

From the other table, one of the Japanese women, Min-He didn't know if it was Fujiko or Hinata, called out to the front table,

"Mother, I thought we were getting two new girls."

Min-He went cold.

The other girl piped up loudly,

"Oh Hinata, don't you remember? Mother told us the other girl hung herself. Those Chosenjin Korean filth are weak. Japanese penises must have been too much for her to handle."

The two women broke out in hysterical laughter.

"I need to go," Min-He whispered and scrambled to her feet, barely making it out the door before vomiting on the side of the white stone. She heard the laughter echoing in the dining room. Umeko was at her side in seconds. She took Min-He's arm into her own tiny hand and led her to the bath house to clean her face.

"Come. Let's go to my room," Umeko said as she handed Min-He a cloth to dry her face. "I have some time before the officers come."

Umeko's little room was identical to Min-He's, except the shelves were lined with trinkets. China dogs, blue and green glass fish, and three yellow-haired China dolls smiled from the shelves, reminding Min-He of a little girl's room from home. Glossy Hollywood magazines littered the floor by her bed. Umeko pulled the stained sheet off her mattress and replaced it with a folded one from her top shelf. She patted the mattress for Min-He to lie down. Min-He rested her eyes as Umeko began to talk.

"Don't let Fujiko and Hinata bother you. They were prostitutes in Japan before the war and volunteered to come here."

Min-He's eyes shot open in disbelief.

"It's true," Umeko continued. "They thought they'd only have to serve officers and are angry they have to serve enlisted men too. They think they're better than the rest of us. Do what you can to stay out of their way."

Umeko began to change into a flowered cotton dress. "Did you know the girl who killed herself?"

"Yes. Her name was Soon-Yee. She was my friend."

Umeko looked genuinely sad. Min-He, not wanting to be alone with her own thoughts, encouraged Umeko to talk.

"Tell me about the other girls."

"Ren and Ran...can you believe Mother named them Ren and Ran? Ridiculous. They've been here the longest. Almost two years, I think. The officers buy them together, they like the twin thing."

Min-He was tempted to ask what she meant, but she wasn't sure she could handle the answer. She tried to imagine herself having this conversation a week ago. Umeko continued her chatter.

"The twins are the only ones here, besides you now, who are even worth trying to talk to. The others, I don't know, they're just...haunted."

Min-He sat up on her elbow to listen. Umeko talked as she liberally applied pink make up to her cheeks.

"Ayame came about nine months ago, shortly after I got here. She spent the first months just lying in bed. She wouldn't come to meals, wouldn't talk to anyone. Mother had to beat her to get her to snap out of it because the men were afraid to come to her. Father told me her husband had sold her to the Japanese military. She has an infant daughter and doesn't know what her husband's done with her. When Kiku arrived a few months ago, Ayame became her mother. She follows her around and takes care of her, making sure she has everything she needs."

"What's wrong with Kiku?" Min-He couldn't shake the image of the beautiful, dazed, drooling Kiku.

"Opium," Umeko said simply. "And morphine. And I don't know what else. Dr. Kono keeps her supplied and Mother puts up with it because all the boys want to be with her. They don't care she's not all there because she's beautiful. She doesn't care what's happening to her as long as she has her drugs."

Min-He thought of the porcelain doll on Umeko's shelf: beautiful to look at, glassy eyes, hollow inside. She felt a bolt of envy: what it must be like to feel nothing.

"And then there's Botan."

Umeko leaned in close to a small mirror and started to apply even more make-up to her already painted face.

"Botan came here two months ago. Pregnant. Mother was angry she'd gotten stuck with a pregnant girl. Dr. Kono gave her the shot, but it didn't work."

"The shot? What shot?"

"If you get pregnant, you get the 606 shot. You also get it if you get venereal disease. It's the cure-all around here."

Min-He had no words.

"But 606 didn't work on Botan. She must've been too pregnant. She went into labor a week later and gave birth in her room. Mother didn't even call Dr. Kono. She and Ayame delivered it."

"What happened? Where's the baby?"

Umeko shrugged.

"No idea. It was alive though. Mother left with the baby, and he never came back. Botan has been nothing but angry since. Just full of hate."

"Umeko, how is it you're not full of hate? You're still a child. How can you do this and still be so normal?"

Umeko was silent for a long time. She looked about to speak when there was a pounding at the door. Min-He rose from the bed and let the hairy Japanese officer who had entered the room take her place. As Min-He walked out the door, Umeko's voice followed her out.

"This is my normal, Mio. For me, there is no other normal."

Back in her own room, Min-He sat on her mattress and gulped the bitter liquor Umeko had left behind. But remembering her promise not to finish the bottle, she closed her eyes, just for a moment, convinced she would never fall asleep.

She woke up what seemed like seconds later to a shrill scream. Hours must have passed as blackness engulfed her room. Another wail came from Umeko's room. Min-He leapt out of bed, forgetting her own pain, and stepped out into the dark night. Without thinking, she banged on Umeko's door.

"Umeko, are you all right? Umeko!"

A brief second of silence was followed by a growl.

"No, no, it's ok," she heard Umeko whisper to the unknown entity inside.

"Go away, go back to bed," she yelled out to Min-He. "Go away."

"But Umeko..."

A furious male voice came from within. "Go away bitch or I'll shut you up myself."

"Mio, go!"

She heard a slap and Umeko's whimper. She backed away from the door and crawled back into her bed. She covered her ears with her hands to block it all out, remembering Soon-Yee's screams, remembering her own. It wasn't until early morning when sleep finally took her.

When she woke to the noon sun shining through her open window, she found a plate of rice and beets inside her door. A jade dog stood in the middle of the pile of rice. On the side of the plate was a bright red piece of hard candy. She hadn't eaten candy like that since before the war. Sweet Umeko.

Min-He wolfed down the cold food, knowing she wouldn't eat again until just before she was expected to "work" tonight. It could very well be the only food she'd be able to stomach all day. Unsure of what to do with herself, but knowing she couldn't sit cooped up dreading nine o'clock, she dressed and stepped out into the blinding light. More young soldiers lingered about, each with a blue ticket, laughing, joking. As she stepped out, a short, balding man in front of Botan's door whistled and clucked at her. She hastened her step to the toilets.

The young Chinese girl who served them dinner the day before was scrubbing the toilet room floor when she went in. Min-He smiled at her, but the girl didn't look up from her work. Finishing up, Min-He headed next door to the bathing room. The large room held four sinks, a shower, and an ofuru, a Japanese soaking tub: a luxury Min-He hadn't expected. Against the far wall were two large laundry basins.

Unfortunately, standing at those basins, were Fujiko and Hinata. Min-He quickly turned to leave, but it was too late.

"Oh look, it's our newest piece of Korean trash. Chosenjin!" Hinata spit. "Mother says you'll start tonight. Not that you deserve to start with the officers."

Min-He started to head out the door, but her curiosity stopped her when she heard,

"You really should choose your friends more wisely. There's a reason no one talks to that little brat who's sinking her claws into you."

Seeing her hesitation, the women pounced.

"Little Miss Umeko has 'befriended' a Japanese colonel. Before she arrived, rumor had it he liked children. Young children."

"I heard," Hinata interrupted Fujiko, "he paid a recruiter to find him a little girl who loved old men. The recruiter went into her town and took her right out of elementary school. He heard she had pleasured all the town's men since she was eight years old."

"You know what they do in that little end room. She begs him to rough her up. He gives her candy and food and those disgusting little dolls."

"She puts on all that make-up so she can look just like those little porcelain dolls for him. You'd be smart to stay away from her. That devil-child will suck you in."

Horrified, Min-He stumbled out the door. The women's laughter followed her out. She began to run, blocking out the dull pain between her legs, confused, not knowing what to think. Umeko's brightly made-up face flashed in her head. She had seen those dolls with her own eyes and the candy—exactly as the women had said.

"Slow down there, girl. There's nowhere to run to."

Min-He turned to see Father on a step ladder, painting a windowsill on the main house. Red paint covered the front of his shirt, sweat dripping from his brow.

"Come here and hold up this paint can for me."

Panting, Min-He walked to him and lifted the paint can. He dipped his brush and resumed the short strokes. Red coating the dirty white sill reminded her of the blood on her sheets in Shanghai. She looked away.

"You can't run from here, you know. There's nowhere to go out there where you won't be shot or brought back here for pretty much the same fate."

"I wasn't running away from here," she replied quietly, "I was just running."

"I heard some familiar laughter from around the corner. Does this have anything to do with the Japanese girls?"

Min-He hesitated but needed to know.

"They were talking about Umeko. How she came here."

Father interrupted sharply. "I don't know what those witches told you, but I can guess. That child was wailing like an infant when she arrived here and cried for three weeks straight. Those sheets she slept on were bloody for weeks after she arrived. I told Mother she was too young. She's just a child. But no one says no to Colonel Ishida. Not Mother and especially not that child."

He had stopped painting and turned to her so sharply he nearly fell off the ladder. Min-He caught his arm to stop the fall. He grabbed her upper arms so hard she gasped. His paint brush clattered to the ground. He spoke quickly in an intense whisper.

"I don't know where you've come from or how bad you've had it, but no one here has it as bad as that child. Colonel Ishida does monstrous things to her and there's nothing any of us can do about it unless we hope to get shot. She smiles through it and is tough as a kamikaze, but that child needs a friend."

He let go of her arms and looked around. No one but the gate guards were in sight, and they were smoking and kicking dirt at each other.

"I can't do anything for her, Mio," he said leaning over to pick up his brush. "I can't help her."

They worked in silence, Min-He holding the paint and Father changing the white to glistening red, until Mother whistled from inside for Father to help her check in a group of soldiers who had poured through the gates.

The sun had begun to set in shades of deep purple and crimson when there was a tap at Min-He's door and Umeko paraded through. Despite the pit of terror building in her stomach thinking about the hours to come, Min-He couldn't help but laugh. Umeko's hair was in pigtails standing straight out from her head. Pieces of wire were peeking out the ends. Her cheeks were painted with bright pink circles and red lipstick covered her nose. Over one shoulder was a satchel and with both hands she was carrying a glass jug with sloshing red liquid. Wedged under her arm was a small container with a white star on the label.

"I knew you couldn't be sad after one look at me!" Umeko burst out. She plopped down beside Min-He on the mattress.

"Thank you, Umeko. That helps a little."

"Mother called me in and told me I could take one less customer before dinner to help you get ready for your first night. It was probably Father's idea."

Umeko placed the jug on the tatami mat floor and removed the starred jar from her armpit and placed it on Min-He's nearly empty shelf next to the green porcelain dog. She unscrewed the lid from the jug and poured the red liquid into the bucket by Min-He's stove.

"This," she said, "is what you use to clean yourself after each man." She held up the hose by the bucket and showed Min-He how to move the red liquid up through the hose and out the other end.

"You just stick this end up yourself and let the red juice flow though. The men will sometimes wash themselves with it as well. Sometimes if you do it as soon as they're done, they'll take it as a hint to leave and you'll get the rest of the thirty minutes to yourself. But just as often they like to watch you do it."

Min-He felt her face grow hot. Umeko laughed at her and continued her lesson. She pulled the starred jar off the shelf.

"This is Secret Star Cream. If you use this on top of the condoms, it'll make it go in easier and hurt a lot less. The men are supposed to bring condoms and cream, but they always forget the cream and sometimes don't bring condoms, so you have some of your own to give them. Never let them do it without their steel helmet." Umeko laughed at her own joke.

Min-He, still bright red, forced out,

"I don't know what a condom is. I opened the box and saw the disk, but I don't know what to do with it."

Umeko giggled as she pulled a condom out of the box, unwrapped it and gave Min-He a demonstration on her hand.

"They're going to ask you to put it on for them. I couldn't do it right at first either, but you'll get it. And if you do it for them, they get excited and don't last as long once they start in on you. Enlisted men are the easiest. It's usually over fast with them. Some of them are actually more interested in talking than anything else." Umeko suddenly got serious. "The NCO's are more arrogant and aren't as nice. But the officers are the worst. They take forever and want to do weird things. Mio, you've got to just do what they ask. If you resist, it's worse."

"The officer I heard you with last night..."

Min-He stopped at Umeko's stricken face. Umeko shook her head, not wanting her to go any further.

"How do we get out of here?" Min-He asked. "Let's run together. We can get to Shanghai and hide."

"Oh, Mio, there's nowhere to run to," Umeko echoed Father's words. "There are guards at the gate day and night. If we made it outside the gate, the military base is right there. If we made it past the military base and tried to run, we'd be either caught by the Japanese or killed by the Chinese for being Japanese collaborators. A few months before you came, there was another girl living in this room. She managed to bribe one of the guards and ran away. She was caught and returned. Mother brought us all into the courtyard to watch her be punished. Mio, she was beaten so badly I couldn't even recognize her face. And then the Colonel had her sent to the front with the next group of mobile soldiers. I can't imagine she survived there for long.

"Let's not talk about that right now. We need to get you ready before dinner so Mother can see you. Come, I'll brush your hair."

Umeko pulled from her satchel a hairbrush and an assortment of cosmetics. She hummed an old Korean folksong as she pinned up Min-He's hair and applied a light coat of make-up to her face. She helped Min-He dress into a navy blue, short-sleeved dress. When she looked in the hand mirror, Min-He was surprised. Despite her own garish appearance, Umeko had made Min-He look subtle and elegant.

"Maybe they'll treat you like a lady," she smiled at Min-He sadly and took her hand to take her to dinner.

Dinner passed too quickly with more than a few sneers in Min-He's direction from the Japanese women. After the partially eaten meal, Umeko dropped Min-He off at her room with a kiss on the check. Min-He reflected on the irony of little Umeko mothering her. She set the condoms by her mattress and applied some of the Secret Star cream Umeko had brought to ease the pain. Despite the fact she knew it was coming, she jumped at the rap on the door. Min-He took a deep breath. If little Umeko could do this day in and day out, so could she.

Min-He rose and opened the door to a thin shouldered man. He was not in uniform but wore a beige shirt with a small stain by the collar. She bowed her head.

"You're Mio?" he asked. He shifted on his feet uncomfortably. Min-He nodded and stepped aside to allow him to come in. He walked into the small room and turned to her, as if expecting her to do something. She shut the door behind her and just looked at him. She had no idea how this worked. The three days at the Shanghai hotel had been a series of rapes. This was... what? Consensual? A business transaction?

The man raised his eyebrows at her. "You're new here."

"Yes," she said, leaning against the door. If she stepped away from the door, she would fall. He noticed her shaking and reached out his hand for her to take.

"Why don't you come and sit down?"

She closed her eyes for a moment, took a deep breath and reached for his hand, letting him walk her to the mattress.

He sat down next to her. He put his hand on her knee and began to kiss her neck.

"Mother told me to take care of you tonight," he murmured.

Min-He was surprised. A kind gesture from Mother was unexpected. The man reached in his pocket and pulled out a condom wrapper. He handed it to her. Her hands shaking, she managed to open the package while he unbuckled his pants. She looked up from the wrapper to find him standing directly in front of her, his penis erect, waiting. Her face crimson, but remembering Umeko's directions, she slipped the condom over his penis.

"Now that wasn't so bad, was it?" He laughed at her.

He pushed her shoulders back onto the bed and slipped between her legs. Her swelling had gone down in the past two days and the Star cream eased the chafing, just as Umeko had said. She could survive this. She had to survive this. As he pumped against her, she turned her head, and silently prayed the minutes away.

The man didn't stay his full allotted hour. After he finished, he threw his condom in the empty bucket and awkwardly patted her on the head before he left. Min-He didn't know what time it was but figured she had twenty minutes or so before the next one. She could hear thumping next door so she knew Umeko was still with a man. She sloshed the red liquid up into her vagina, unable to figure out how to use the hose. She gasped as it stung for a moment. Min-He welcomed the burn, imagining it peeling away the layer of filth left behind. She applied some of the healing cream the doctor had given her and on top of that, the Star Cream. Then she waited.

The next soldier was in full uniform, his saber by his side. He didn't speak to her, but walked right in and unbuckled his pants. His pants dropped to his knees. Min-he started to reach for a condom.

"No!" he ordered.

He pushed her to her knees and grabbed her by the back of the head, pulling her head towards him, her hair in his hands. Min-He didn't understand what was going on. His penis hit the side of her cheek as she quickly turned her head. He grabbed her chin with his hand and yanked it toward him.

"Put it in your mouth!"

Bile rose in the back of her throat. This couldn't be real. Is this what Umeko meant by officers wanting vile things? Instinctively, she clamped her mouth shut. She could not do this.

Suddenly, flashes of light sparked in her eyes. His right fist flew again into the side of her head.

"You do it!"

Her head throbbing, Min-he opened her mouth and gagged as he forced her head back and forth. When he was finished, he pushed Min-He backwards, and stomped out of the room, not even buckling his pants. Min-He crawled to the empty bucket and vomited. Not even bothering to go back to the mattress, she laid on the floor until the third knock of the night hit her door.

The last officer, old enough to be her grandfather, refused to meet her eyes, said little and got down to business quickly. She was grateful when he got up to leave without a word. If the third officer wasn't spending the night, she would get to be alone. She lay on her mattress and listened. When she heard Umeko's third officer shut her door behind him, she got up, knocked on Umeko's door and crawled into her bed beside her. She cried herself to sleep in the child's mothering arms.

# Marianne
## Munich, Germany
## April 1944 – July 1944

"Tell me, meine kleine Marianne, what have you heard from your SS Sturmbannführer?"

Marianne rolled her eyes at Andreas as she unwrapped the last of the four watercolors Andreas purchased at an auction earlier that day. They were lovely: muted colors with light flowing effortlessly off the images of water and the mountains. She was sure they were worth far more than Andreas had paid. He was a master of discovering items that needed to be parted with in desperation. She wondered at the origin of these beauties.

"Your mockery of me doesn't suit you, Andreas. Knock off the "kleine" Marianne business. I'm hardly little."

She patted her rear end, more ample of late with Eric's shipments of chocolate and meats from the East.

"Ah, but your Führer likes his women robust and healthy."

"OUR Führer, Andreas."

"Didn't I say that?" he laughed.

"It must have been a slip of the tongue," she conceded.

These past weeks, Andreas had been more open about his politics than Marianne felt comfortable. Like with her father, she always felt herself looking over her shoulder.

"So, are you avoiding the question?"

She sighed.

"Eric's regiment left for Russia from the Ukraine last week. His battalion follows the Wehrmacht army to clean up and restore order after each battle. He's received several commendations," she said proudly.

She watched Andreas's eyes raise and suddenly felt embarrassed. She wished she hadn't told him that. To hide her blush, she turned to the wall and began repositioning one of the new paintings.

"There, that looks better, doesn't it?"

"What does he clean up?"

"I'm sorry?"

"You said he cleaned up after the Wehrmacht army leaves. What does he clean up?"

She turned and studied Andreas. He stopped wiping off the display table and his grey eyes steadily held hers, waiting for an answer. She realized she didn't have one.

"I don't know. I never actually thought about it. I assume they clean up the mess of the battle, repair destroyed homes, that sort of thing."

"Why would they do that? Isn't that defeating the point?"

"I don't know, Andreas. What difference does it make?" She found herself getting defensive, upset at his accusatory tone, frustrated at her own ignorance about her husband's activities.

Andreas spoke softly, almost cautiously,

"Marianne, what your husband's doing makes all the difference in the world. I've heard rumors about what's going on in the East."

Marianne felt her stomach turn. She'd heard rumors too, of course. Everyone had. No one really knew what was happening there, and this was war after all, so of course there were going to be horrible things happening. That didn't have anything to do with Eric. He wasn't even fighting; he was just following the army. Political clean up. She opened her mouth to tell Andreas just that when the bell on the door clanged. An older couple said their "Heil Hitler's" and browsed through the new merchandise. She would have to remember to tell Andreas later. Political clean up. Eric was like a politician. Yes, she would say that, and he would understand. But Andreas followed the couple out to deliver a piece to their home and she didn't get a chance to tell him.

*****

"So, Abraham and Hiram meet in the African jungle, each with a rifle.

'What are you doing here?' asks Hiram.

139

'I've got an ivory carving business in Cairo, and I shoot my own elephants,' says Abraham. 'And you?'

'I manufacture crocodile leather goods in Perth and shoot my own crocodiles. And what happened to our friend Isaac?'

'He's turned into a real adventurer. He stayed in Berlin.'

Martin hooted with laughter, toppling a paint pot with his elbow. Marianne grabbed a cloth and wiped up her father's spill.

"Oh, Andreas, I don't know where you hear all the good ones," Martin cackled. The wine bottle on the counter was nearly empty, but Marianne lifted its remnants toward Andreas's handsome, jittery friend.

"The last of the wine for you, Franz?"

Franz shook his head and nervously looked away from the door.

"Andreas, you had better be careful," he said, "People are arrested for less than that."

"Oh, Franz, you sound like me when I'm scolding my father," Marianne slurred.

"To selling her first piece!" Andreas cried.

Andreas, Franz, and Martin raised their glasses to Marianne's joyful blush. Shortly after starting to work at the gallery, Marianne invited her father to lunch in Schwabing. After leaving the café, she took him to Vogel's, and introduced him to her private world. He was proud of her but had been practical, even for him.

"What will happen when Eric comes home? He'll be furious you've been hiding this. You'll have to make a choice."

"Well, of course I'll choose my family, Father, you know that."

She knew she would. This was just temporary. But maybe, just maybe, she could continue to have both.

Martin liked Andreas and Franz immensely. Marianne sipped wine and listened to them talk politics. Their friendship had bloomed hesitantly, each trying to gauge and determine the others' politics before sharing their own. Soon Martin became a regular in the gallery, bringing brötchen and rotwurst for Andreas and slices of cod for his Siamese cat, Mitzi. It served to relieve some of Marianne's guilt as well. Now when she told Martha she was visiting her father, it was occasionally true.

Light was fading in the alley outside the door. She had been due home hours ago but had been convinced to stay when Andreas arranged the little surprise party for her first sale. Franz, Andreas's roommate, had arrived nearly an hour ago to take Andreas to dinner, but had been forced to join their spontaneous party and made to wait. Marianne knew Franz didn't like to be around her. Andreas had confided to Marianne that Franz was nervous to learn she was married to member of the SS. Marianne didn't think that justified him being afraid of her, but she forgave him and tried to be especially kind. It made Andreas happy to see them get along. Andreas talked about him incessantly and it was obvious their friendship was important to him.

These last months had been the most liberating of her life. Once she got out the door at least. She fought every day to come up with new lies about her whereabouts. Lies to Martha about why she wasn't home. Lies to the children about why she wasn't at their every sporting, theater, BdM, or Hitler Youth event. Lies to the Frauenschaft women about why she was no longer attending the meetings regularly. Every day, as she told her lies and took the bus to work, she swore she would tell Andreas she could no longer work there. That today would be the day she returned to her normal life. But each day, the moment she stepped foot in the gallery, it all changed. She changed. She became the woman she imagined herself to be: a free spirit, creating beautiful art, laughing at jokes, and drinking wine. Her life in the gallery was her fantasy world. Each day when she left, she returned to her real world. She was not yet ready to give up this fantasy.

*****

"Where are you going?"

Christa watched Marianne pick up her handbag. Erika and Hans sat at the breakfast table with her, the first time she remembered seeing all three of her children together for a meal in months. She felt a pang of guilt. What kind of mother doesn't take advantage of this rare time with her children? Hans was focused on his potato pancakes, his appetite as large as it had ever been. She barely recognized him. He filled out the chair, his broad shoulders bringing flashes of Eric. She tried to remember the last time she had a conversation with Hans other than handing him money for lunch or demanding he bathe before sitting on her furniture after a football match.

Erika was picking at her food as she was leafing through the July issue of "Frauen Warte": the magazine for good German mothers. 'God forbid', thought Marianne. But Erika still looked as thin as ever in her BdM uniform, her blonde hair tight in a thick braid, looking more of a child than the young woman she was turning into. The effects of the midnight air raid last night left circles under her eyes, which Erika was attempting to cover up with makeup. Marianne would need to speak with her about that. Eric had thrown out Marianne's powders and rouges months before he left, reminding her that good German women do not wear makeup.

Marianne looked icily at her youngest child. "I have errands to run."

In truth, Andreas and Franz had gone to Nuremburg to visit a friend and scout out an insider's tip on some artwork and had asked Marianne to stop in the gallery to feed Mitzi.

"Can I come with you?

"No."

Martha slammed down the spoon by her pot and glared at Marianne.

"Frau Hofmann. You promised me this weekend off work to visit my mother. I cannot take Christa with me. My mother's nerves do not handle children."

Marianne sighed. "Erika..."

"No! I have a date and then I'm going swimming with my friends. I'm not taking her."

Hans didn't make eye contact and Marianne didn't bother to ask. She sighed loudly. Asking a neighbor would bring too many questions. She would have to take Christa with her.

She begrudgingly grasped Christa's hand to lead her quickly through the busy marketplace. Christa's hand felt larger than she remembered. Christa recoiled slightly but allowed her mother to lead her along the wet street. The sky began to spit a light rain, flattening Marianne's blonde hair against her scalp. She picked up her pace as she spoke to the child.

"Now, I'm doing a favor for your grandfather. He asked me to feed his client's cat."

She would need to find time to get to her father before Christa could ask him about it. The last thing she needed was for Christa to sense any doubt in her story and tell on her again. If Martha found out, she would never let Marianne leave the house without threat of telling Eric when he returned.

"The cat is in an art gallery just up this street…"

As they approached the gallery, Marianne stopped short. The door was propped open, allowing the rain to seep through the crack in the doorway. Two SS officers filled the small gallery. One was digging through the drawer on the counter and the other was busy piling several pieces of art onto the table. 'Elisabeth's Retreat' stuck out from the bottom of the pile.

Paint was splattered across the floor. Jars, brushes, papers, and ink pots were strewn throughout the shop. Marianne's art table had been knocked on its side and all the drawers of the back cabinet were flung open, their contents heaped onto the floor. The walls were bare where the paintings that now lay stacked on the table, had once hung.

Anger conquered fear. Marianne, still gripping Christa's hand, marched into the gallery.

"WHAT is going on here?"

"Who the fuck are you?" one of the officers growled.

"I'm Frau Hofmann, wife of SS-Sturmbannführer Eric Hofmann. I'm also a frequent customer of this gallery and demand to know what's going on! I have commissioned art through this gallery and my husband would not be pleased to discover it destroyed or pilfered!"

Marianne's hands started to shake, but she put one hand on her hip and squeezed Christa's hand tighter to hide the shaking. Using Eric's name could be dangerous. The men looked at each other trying to assess the gravity of this Sturmbannführer's wife's outrage. The elder of the two spoke.

"We are acting under direct orders of the SS. The man who runs this shop is engaged in illegal activity and we're here to arrest him and compile evidence."

"What illegal activity? I've done business with Herr Vogel for months and have not seen any evidence of illegal activity. In fact, he served the Führer and was wounded in Poland. Of what is Herr Vogel accused?"

The younger officer looked at Christa.

"This may not be appropriate for young German ears, Frau Hofmann."

Marianne glared at him, waiting. She would figure out how to deal with Christa later. Fear for Andreas engulfed her.

The other man spoke, not concerned about innocent ears.

"Andreas Vogel is engaging in homosexual activity, a crime against the Führer. He's wanted for arrest and questioning. If you know of his whereabouts, it would be in your best interest to reveal them."

"Of course I don't know his whereabouts. I came to the shop today to pick up a painting I ordered, that's all." She started to back away, still holding Christa's hand. The officer sneered at her, clearly sensing her fear.

"Aren't you forgetting something, Frau Hofmann?" Marianne paused, terror rising in her throat.

"Your painting. Don't you want the painting you'd come for? Describe it for us and we'll help you locate it."

She let go of Christa's hand and marched bravely forward. She cleared three paintings from the stack until she reached 'Elisabeth's Retreat'. She clasped the painting to her chest and headed towards the door.

"Come Christa, let's go."

"But Mutti, what about the cat?"

Both men stared at her with interest. She spoke quickly. "I told her Herr Vogel had a cat she could pet. The cat was here on my last visit. Come Christa, now's not the time to worry about a cat. These men have work to do."

She pulled Christa around the corner and leaned against the brick wall, her heart pounding in her chest. Rain pelted down upon them. Christa watched her mother wide-eyed but knew better than to speak. Marianne opened her purse, took out a sheet of paper, and memorized the address scrawled in Andreas's handwriting. Turning her back to Christa, she shoved the scrap of paper in her mouth and swallowed.

The clinic was not crowded for a Saturday afternoon. Marianne counted only two waiting patients after she flew through the door, the bell's ring drawing the attention of the waiting patients. A schnauzer in the lap of his owner yipped at the intrusion. A hulking shepherd snarled at her, and Marianne felt her stomach drop, not at the threat of the dog, but at the sight of the owner. Obersturmbannführer Scharf. She hadn't seen him since the day he had her arrested. The words Eric used to describe him would normally bring a smirk to her face but today they only sat like lead in the pit of her stomach. She lowered her head, hoping her flat, drenched hair would conceal her face. Please God, don't let him recognize her.

"Frau Hofmann," he announced.

Shit. She turned to face him and presented him with her fakest smile. His thin lips took a shape somewhere between a grimace and a leer.

"Obersturmbannführer Scharf. What a pleasure," she said.

The massive dog, growling a low, deep growl, eyed her. She didn't approach him. Scharf followed her eyes.

"Sit!" he commanded. The dog's haunches hit the floor but Marianne could see the tension in his body, cautious, suspicious. She knew how he felt.

"You have no pet," Scharf said flatly.

"What? I have a pet. We have a boxer." She felt Christa huddle behind her, sensing her fear.

"Oh. I see. I don't have a pet here today you mean. This is my father's clinic. Christa and I are here to visit him." She pulled the child out from behind her. The shepherd's growl grew louder. Marianne bristled defensively.

"Perhaps your dog should be muzzled in a public place," she said, "Growling at small children is hardly acceptable manners for a pet."

"Luther is neither a pet nor is he expected to have good manners, Frau Hofmann. He is a trained military dog."

"Well," she challenged, "let's hope that means he's less likely to attack innocents than his master."

Scharf laughed, but his steely eyes narrowed. She regretted her affront. Why couldn't she be less conspicuous?

The last thing she needed was the ire of this man right now. She smiled sweetly.

"I'm teasing, of course."

"Of course." He smirked back, unconvinced. "So, your father is Tiermediziner Braun? I remember your husband mentioning your father being a veterinarian the day you 'visited' our offices, but I didn't realize it was Doktor Braun. I'm surprised."

"Why is that?"

Like Luther, her hackles raised. She knew he was lying. When she married Eric, she had to document her heritage back three generations to prove her Aryanism. Scharf would have known everything about her before her arrest, especially when taking such a risk as arresting the wife of a fellow SS officer.

Scharf looked at the pale, elderly man with the schnauzer who pretended to be taking no interest in their conversation. He glanced over at the receptionist, who quickly resumed typing when she caught his eye. He leaned into Marianne and whispered in her ear.

"Rumors of certain political leanings by Tiermediziner Braun have been heard here and there. But nothing to be concerned about, especially since his son-in-law is so very well connected."

Marianne glared at him, but kept her voice low, aware of the danger.

"Whatever rumors you may have heard are absolutely false. My father is a decorated war veteran and a loyal and dedicated German. I take offense you suggest otherwise."

Scarf looked at her for a moment then laughed.

"Like you, Frau Hofmann, I'm only teasing," he said too loudly. The old man with the schnauzer smiled broadly as if in on the joke. Scharf continued. "A fine veterinarian is difficult to find nowadays. So many of them have been sent to the front."

Marianne keenly felt the not-so-veiled threat. An alarmed Karin leaned over her desk.

"Obersturmbannführer Scharf, the Tiermediziner will see Luther now."

The secretary stepped between Scharf and Marianne, bringing a quick end to the confrontation.

"I believe I will leave him and my aide will pick him up on Monday." He handed the leash to Karin. "Give your father my regards, Frau Hofmann."

He squinted and marched out the door, the bell clanging behind him.

"Karin, I need to see my father right away. Will you watch Christa please?"

"Of course. Take Luther back to him." She handed Marianne the leash. The dog's growl still resided deep in his throat. Marianne looked at Karin incredulously. Karin rolled her eyes at the dramatics and walked back to her typewriter. "And remind him Herr Dort is still here with Fritzi."

The old man nodded and smiled at the pretty receptionist.

When Marianne walked through the door of the examination room, Martin turned, clearly expecting Karin to be accompanying Scharf and Luther.

"Marianne! What are you doing here?"

She handed over the leash of the disgruntled shepherd.

"Vati, we have problems. Obersturmbannführer Scharf said there are rumors about you and implied he could have you sent to the front."

"No one's sending me anywhere, Marianne. Your husband's connections with the SS have made me indispensable in tending the Munich contingent's dogs. Scharf is just an overblown egomaniac like the rest of them. Last time he was here with Luther, he told me at least three times how he had you arrested."

"I knew he was lying," she grumbled.

Martin led Luther, much more amiable without Scharf, to a metal crate in the back corner of the examination room. Marianne continued.

"But those aren't the problems I'm here about." She told him about her visit to the gallery.

"They said Andreas is a homosexual. How can that be? Do you think it's true?"

"I had my suspicions. I think Franz is much more than a roommate."

Marianne cringed at her own ignorance- the thought had never crossed her mind. Her terror surged. Being targeted with the suspicion of homosexuality was dangerous enough, but if the Nazis found evidence of their relationship, both Andreas and Franz were in tremendous peril.

"What are we going to do, Vati? When Andreas returns, they'll arrest him. They'll send him to a KonzentrazionLager."

"We need to make sure he doesn't return. Do you know where he is?"

"Yes. He gave me the address where he's staying in Nuremburg in case anything happened with Mitzi."

Martin walked to the door and confirmed it was shut securely. He lowered his voice to a near whisper.

"You need to go to Nuremburg and warn him. He needs to get out of Munich, preferably out of Germany. Marianne, I'm going to give you the name of a man in Würzburg he needs to see."

Martin pulled a pad of paper from his breast pocket, scribbled an address, and handed it to Marianne.

"Listen carefully. He needs to go to Herr Bergen at this address and tell him "Herr Tier" sent him for the dog food. If Franz is implicated, he needs to get to Herr Bergen as well, but separately, so as not to draw attention. Do you understand?"

"Yes, of course."

"He must destroy this address after he memorizes it. You must get this to Andreas and Franz right away. Go quickly and don't arouse suspicion." Intensity burned on her father's face. "You need a reason to be going to Würzburg."

"I have Christa with me, Vati. Can you take her today?"

"No. It's perfect. Take her with you. Taking your daughter on a weekend day outing is a perfect excuse if you're questioned. A mother with a child is unlikely to raise suspicion."

"But I don't know if she can be trusted. You know what she did."

"You must trust her, Marianne. You don't have any choice. It's time for her to be your daughter again."

Marianne headed straight to the train station at a near run. Christa limped close behind, confused and starting to whimper. Marianne stopped and studied her daughter. Her wispy dark blonde hair had blown into a tangled, wet mess, her face red and splotchy from the rain. Christa's shiny red boots were brown with the muddy slush from the streets. A pang of guilt shot through Marianne. Three blocks back Christa had fallen, and Marianne had slowed only briefly to give her time to get back up. The child's knees below her cotton dress were bloody and torn.

She reached for her daughter's hand and pulled her into the doorway of a closed shop. She drew a handkerchief from her handbag and wiped the blood from the girls' calves. Marianne knelt and looked directly into Christa's blue eyes.

"Christa, I need you to listen to me and listen closely. You and I are taking a little trip. You must never tell anyone what happens today. Do you understand? Someone is in danger and if you tell anyone, Martha, your teachers, Erika or Hans, or even Daddy what happened today, then Mommy and Grandpa will be in danger too. Do you remember how mad I was when you told your teacher about giving the Russian prisoners that pot of goulash? Do you remember how much trouble I got in?"

The little girl nodded, thick tears rolling down her cheeks. A trickle of mucus blended with the tears beneath her nose. Marianne gently wiped her daughter's face with the handkerchief and looked intently at her youngest child.

"Well, this would be much, much worse than that if you ever told. I need you to promise me, Christa, whatever happens today, you must never tell a soul. Can you promise me?"

Christa looked her mother in the eye, stood up straighter and nodded.

"I promise, Mommy, I promise. You can trust me. I'm so sorry about before. I didn't mean to get you in trouble. I'll never do that again. Please Mommy, you can trust me."

Marianne reached out and gathered the child to her chest, her own tears falling into Christa's tangled blonde hair. "I know I can, I know I can." She kissed her baby's wet cheek for the first time in months. A sense of calm flooded her body. She wiped Christa's tears.

"Let's go on a little trip".

Marianne hadn't been to Nuremburg in nearly three years. The train was jammed beyond capacity: uniformed German boys as young as Hans, eager to get their turn to fight for the Vaterland; empty eyed soldiers returning from battle, many with lost limbs and their scarred souls bared; unmarried working women with small parcels, off to visit a parent on a Saturday; or, like her, mothers with children, on holiday or an errand. She tried to blend in with the normalcy, but trembled, terrified someone would read the mission behind her eyes.

As the train arrived in the city, Marianne was awed by the destruction of the allied bombing. The reason for the overcapacity of the train became clear. Rail lines had been obliterated. Rubble lined the city streets. Vast jumbles of concrete, steel, and rubble encroached where buildings once stood. A pack of boys, grey with a layer of sludge, leapt into a pile of bricks from the roof of what was once a school. Nuremburg's elegant, ancient architecture lay in ruins. Marianne's eyes filled with tears. What a horrible waste. The train crept into the station.

Marianne repeated the address in her head over and over. She was afraid to ask someone how to get there. What if they were able to identify her later and knew why she had come? That's unimportant, she told herself. She didn't have a choice. She needed to get to Andreas. She stopped an elderly kerchief-wrapped grandmother carrying a loaf of bread. The building was just a few blocks away.

Marianne and Christa stood across the street from the apartment building. Marianne knelt.

"Christa, go knock on the apartment door. I'm going to follow you into the building but will stand at the end of the hall. Tell whoever answers the door that you're collecting donations for the war orphans. Try to get the person answering to talk to you so I can hear his voice. Try to see who else is inside—I need you to be able to describe them to me. If a man in a uniform like Daddy's answers, I need you to put your hand on your hip. If that happens, I'll meet you outside. Don't under any circumstance tell anyone your name. If asked, tell them you are Greta Schmidt and then get out of there."

Christa nodded at her. Her daughter's confidence amazed her. Guilt waved through Marianne as she followed Christa up the stairs of the apartment building. She was putting her child in danger. She was putting her whole family in danger, including her husband. If she was caught here, trying to hide a fugitive the Nazi's were looking for... she couldn't even finish the thought.

She watched Christa plaster on a smile and bang on the door of apartment four. No answer. Christa looked over at Marianne and she signaled for her to knock again. Christa banged louder. The door creaked open. Christa looked up. Marianne wished she could see what Christa saw.

"Hello sir, I am Greta Schmidt and I'm collecting for the war orphans. Would you care to make a donation?"

Surprisingly cheery. She should sign her up at the Munich theater school. Marianne breathed a quick sigh of relief. No hand on her hip. But what if Christa had just forgotten? She could hear the murmuring voice of a man but was too far away to make it out.

"I'm very sorry sir. I don't hear very well. The building next to my school was bombed and I lost hearing in one of my ears. Could you speak up?"

Marianne looked at Christa in awe. Who knew she was such a wonderful liar? It was a strange sense of pride.

"I said I'm sorry. I don't have anything to give you right now. Please go."

The door slammed shut. It was him. Marianne rushed to the door and flung it open. Andreas's eyes transformed from fear and panic to confusion.

"Marianne! Why are you here?"

She opened her mouth to speak then stopped, taking in her surroundings. The apartment was ransacked. It was the art gallery all over again. Andreas's face was ashen and tearstained. She ran to him and took him in her arms. He crouched to the floor. Behind her, the little girl stepped in and shut the door.

"They took them, Marianne, they took them. Franz and I argued this morning. A stupid, senseless argument. He wanted to extend our stay, but I wanted to collect our new inventory and get it back to the gallery. It was so ridiculous." Andreas gulped air as Marianne soothingly caressed his back.

"I was angry, and I went to some galleries alone to cool off and Franz stayed here with our friend, Albert. I came back and they were being led out of the apartment. The SS had them under arrest. Franz was bleeding. His face... his eye was so swollen. He saw me standing at the corner, I know he did, but he refused to look at me. He didn't want them to know I was there. I just stood there, staring. I didn't say a word. I'm such a coward. I let them take him and I didn't even say a word."

"Andreas, there was nothing you could have said or done. They would have taken you too. Nothing would have stopped them from taking Franz and Albert. Franz knew and that's why he wouldn't look at you. He was protecting you."

Andreas paced the room, shaking.

"Andreas, why are you still here? They'll come back here to look for you."

"I know. That's why I'm still here. I've been waiting for them to come. I want them to take me. I don't deserve to be free when Franz is arrested. I have nowhere to go, Marianne. They know who I am and will find me anyway. They may as well take me now."

"We need to leave. Get your things and any money you have with you. Christa and I will help you."

Andreas noticed the child in the room for the first time.

"This is your child? She's in danger here."

"The longer we stay, the more danger she'll be in. Let's go."

At the train station, Marianne purchased two return tickets for herself and Christa to Munich and a ticket for Andreas to Würzburg. After forcing him to repeat the address and directions to her twice, she embraced him as his train began boarding.

"Please be careful. If my father is sending you to this man, then he can be trusted and will take care of you. But you must do what you can to save yourself."

"Promise me you'll find out about Franz and help him. Your husband has connections. You must help him."

The idea was ridiculous. How could she possibly help? Even if Eric was home, he would never agree to help. How could she risk herself and her family to ask anyone else?

"Of course I will," she lied. "I'll find out where he is and I'm sure all it will take is a bribe. I'll do everything I can."

Andreas reached out and touched Christa's cheek. "You are a brave little girl, Marianne's daughter. You are lucky to have such a remarkable woman for a mother."

He boarded the train and Marianne took Christa's hand and they walked to their platform. As the darkness fell, Christa leaned sleepily against her mother.

"I'm proud of you, Christa. You don't understand all of this now, but you did a brave, good thing today."

"Mutti, if Daddy's soldiers had been there, they would have killed that man, wouldn't they?"

"I don't know, Christa. I don't know." She pulled her daughter closer and kissed her head. Christa fell asleep in her arms as Marianne watched the Bavarian countryside speed by as it faded into blackness.

# Rachel
## Warsaw, Poland
## June – September 1942

June floated as a blur for Rachel. She went to work every day, walking blindly past the starvation and devastation. She stayed at the office as long as Simon would allow her there. Going home to the apartment without Adam was a lonely ring of hell. The longer hours at work were not spent idly. Urgent requests for more food and medicine increased daily. The undertakers in their black hats, pushing their handcarts with piles of bodies, were ever-present. As the summer heat bore down upon them, the rumors began to fly: they had only forty more days to live, the Germans were going to kill everyone in the ghetto within a month. The rumors varied by the day but were always void of hope.

Walking down the streets, people were infused with panic and anxiety. The newest rumor was the topic of every conversation. No one spoke any more of daily problems or small talk. Every conversation consisted of what someone had heard about the fate of the ghetto and how that could or couldn't be possible. Could it be true? Certainly THAT couldn't be true but this person's cousin in Lodz has seen this or heard that, and the Jewish policemen that knew a friend of a friend said that something was happening in this many days. On and on it went. Rachel just nodded, barely listening, not wanting to hear. Being at home made it so much worse. Each night Dora couldn't wait to tell them the latest horrific rumor. Aron said little and Hella fussed and reassured. Rachel just wanted to put her hands over her ears and scream it all away.

On a mid-July Friday morning, Rachel left the apartment for work. Walking down Zelazna Street, she noticed a queue of people lined up with suitcases. Small children clutched their parents' hands. Some wore winter coats despite the stifling July heat. A pack of middle aged, bearded men stood in front of a tailor shop gesturing animatedly toward the lines. Rachel approached them.

"What's going on?"

"Haven't you heard? The foreigners are leaving the ghetto. Anyone with a foreign passport is being taken out. Americans, British, South Americans, they are removing them all from the ghetto."

"Why? What does that mean?" Rachel watched the lines of people, confused.

"Nothing good," another of the men spoke. "If they're removing the foreigners to safety, what are they going to do with the rest of us? Finish us off."

Rachel walked away, a pit forming in her stomach. The man was right. Why would they remove the foreign nationals? What did they need to protect them from?

Six days later, Lithuanian and Ukranian policemen led by Elite guards of Nazi soldiers, surrounded the ghetto. A proclamation announced that nearly all ghetto inhabitants were to be transported East. Forty pounds of luggage were allowed per person and each person was to be given three days of provisions. 3000 people a day were required to report to the Unschlagplatz to board freight cars and be deported to the East. The next day, Adam Czerniakow, leader of the Judenrat, shot himself. Aron brought them the news.

"They say he was ordered to choose 3000 people a day to be deported. He wouldn't do it. He saw the writing on the wall. He knew what these deportations mean."

"Nonsense," Dora interjected. "He was weak-willed. You don't know what caused him to kill himself. People kill themselves in this hellhole every day."

Saul broke in.

"They say those with labor office work cards and their families are safe from deportation. Is that true?"

"It is," Rachel said. "Anyone with a work permit, as well as policemen, hospital workers and community agency workers like you and I, are safe. Their immediate families are exempt too. We've had a huge rush of people in the past twenty-four hours lined up at our offices begging for work cards. There are none to give. Simon was ordered not to issue any."

"What about Dora and Mira? Can you get them work permits?"

"I've already asked Simon. He's going to try to see what can be done."

"Don't bother," Dora said. "Mira and I decided to volunteer for deportation. We're going tomorrow."

Aron stood up from the table, astonished, and had trouble forming words.

"What? Why? Why would you do that? You are not going voluntarily!"

"What do you want, Aron? For Mira to be found in the street without a labor card and shot? That's what could happen."

"Do you have any idea what you are doing? I've heard about survivors who escaped from those camps and returned to the ghetto. They are death camps! You need to do whatever it takes to stay off those transports!"

"Nonsense. If they were death camps, how would anyone survive to escape? It makes no sense. We're going to be sent East and given jobs. The Germans can't kill everyone. They need us for labor."

"You're not going."

"Aron Kaplan, you may think you're in charge of what happens with your parents, your sister, and your sister's child." Rachel drew in a sharp breath at this accusation. Dora continued. "But you are NOT in charge of me or my daughter. We are leaving tomorrow and there is nothing else to be said on that matter. Hella," she spoke more gently to her sister, "I appreciate you taking in my girls and me but it's time for Mira and me to go off on our own and take care of ourselves. They say those who go voluntarily will get the best jobs and housing. I intend to take advantage of that. I'll write to you when we arrive, and you'll see this was the right choice."

*****

Hella packed two extra sweaters in the small suitcases and when she tried to add a package of cheese, Dora stopped her.

156

"You'll need this more than we do. We get extra rations for volunteering."

Aron left early that morning, refusing to see them off. Mira cried when she woke to find Aron gone. Rachel hugged her aunt and cousin as they shuffled out the door and down the stairs with their bags. Hella and Saul went with them to walk part way to the Umschlagplatz.

Rachel looked around at the empty apartment, shocked at finding herself alone. She realized it had been nearly two years since she had been completely alone. With the constant throng of people in the ghetto, solitude was a nearly nonexistent experience. She hauled Dora and Mira's mattress on its side and leaned it against the wall. She would ask Aron to donate it to the orphanage when he returned. There was no need for it now. First Josef, then Lilliana. Adam sent away. And now the unknown fate of Dora and Mira. She thought of them on the trains at the Umschlagplatz, convincing themselves they were enroute to a labor camp. Rachel prayed they were right.

*****

The Nazis soon increased their quota to 10,000 Jews a day required to report to the Umschlagplatz for deportation. Jewish policemen were given their own quotas. If each policeman did not provide five Jews for deportation every day, they would not receive their ration cards. Some ghetto inhabitants turned each other in for food and for favor. Every man for himself: live another day, stay off the trains just one more day. Aron's absences from home grew longer, and when he was home, he spewed anger.

"Fucking Nazis are using Jews to send their own people to our deaths. Rat bastard collaborators keep their own families off the trains and don't lose a second of sleep about turning in someone else's."

Saul spoke harshly. "You can't judge what another man will do to save his family. In this situation, we cannot judge. Let God do the judging."

"Oh, I can judge. You better believe I can judge. And I'll do what I can to make sure those rats get to face God's judgment sooner rather than later."

"You must not let your anger make you become what they are, Aron. You need to pray for peace, son."

"What would you have me do, Father? Sit around and wait for the Nazis to force me onto a train? Allow someone to turn against his own people in exchange for some extra food? And don't you dare talk to me about being angry. Where's your anger? All you do is sit and pray for it all to be over. Prayer is going to get you nowhere, Father. Has God answered any of your prayers? Where was your God when Josef and Lilliana needed him? Where is God for all these starving children on the streets? Your God has done nothing for us. If He won't act, then don't you dare tell me I cannot."

Aron slammed the chair against the table and stormed into the bedroom. Rachel followed him in, leaving Hella to comfort Saul.

"You can't take this out on Father. He does what he needs to do to get by."

"And I do what I need to. Dad prays. I act. And what about you, Rachel? What do you do?"

"Not this again. I came back here to talk to you, not be attacked. I work, I bring in extra food. That's what I do. "

"It's not enough. You're young. You have connections in the ZTOS office. You must do more."

"I can't, Aron. I'm afraid. I need to survive to return to Adam. I can't take that risk."

"You know why we haven't heard from Dora these past three weeks?" Rachel looked at her brother and his blue eyes pierced her. Every ounce of denial left her body.

"I know," she said simply. The acknowledged truth hung in the air.

"You are more ready than you admit."

"You owe Father an apology."

Aron sighed.

"I can do that. What's one more lie?"

The streets slowly emptied of beggars and homeless children. The orphanages were desolate, the children and their caretakers devoured by the trains. By late summer, the myth of deportation was shattered. Gas chambers and mass graves were no longer rumors, but an acknowledged reality. Everyone knew the trains were a death sentence. Anyone without a work permit could only hide and pray to get through each day without being caught or turned in. Work permits were sold and traded and entitled their holders to one more day.

Rachel rubbed her eyes and flipped through the stack of papers in front of her. Simon slumped at the head of the conference table, surrounded by six of Rachel's ZTOS coworkers. The application before them was completed, an entreaty to the Judenrat to request 10,000 more work permits. They had to decide how to convince the Germans they needed more workers. With fewer ghetto inhabitants in need of their soup kitchens, the team had reallocated the ZTOS kitchen staff to keep everyone working. Rachel glanced at her watch, wondering what she could get for a midday meal, when the door slammed open. Four Ukrainians in Nazi uniforms poured through the door.

"Get up! Get up!"

They pointed their guns at the eight frightened men and women. Rachel reached into her blazer pocket and pulled out her papers.

"We have work permits. We are employed with ZTOS and exempt from deportation." She was surprised by the tone of authority in her own voice. The other workers followed her lead and pulled out their papers.

"Those papers are no longer good."

One of the women began to cry.

"Schnell, schnell!" the guard yelled.

Rachel followed two guards out the door, the other two guards close behind. One of them jammed the edge of his rifle into her back as they climbed down the stairs. The hallways were completely empty, the other employees having disappeared at the first sight of the guards. They joined a group of fifty other building employees who had been rounded up and began to march in a direction Rachel instantly recognized: North to the Umschlagplatz. Around her, people were dazed, some crying, some quietly stoic. This couldn't be happening.

She had papers. She was protected. A lump formed in her throat. She thought of her parents' agony at hearing of her fate, and of Adam. He would never know her, never know who his mother was. She had failed him.

As they rounded the corner, the hospital was in sight. She pushed her way to the edge of the marching line. If only she could see someone she recognized, they could let her parents know what had happened. She wouldn't just disappear. She sped up, pushing through to the front of the line. Two men stood smoking outside the hospital, one wearing the blue coat of a hospital employee.

"Vera!" she screamed to them, "Get Vera! Tell her you saw Rachel here!"

The man in the blue coat's expression grew alarmed, and he disappeared through the double doors.

Rachel slowed down and let the fifty others pass, staying in view of the hospital as long as she could. The Ukrainian guard yelled something she didn't understand, and she kept walking. When the guard looked away, Rachel turned quickly, and said a silent prayer of thanks when she saw a flash of red hair appear at the hospital door. She hoped the man in blue had gotten the message right. Her mother, at least, could hold out the delusional hope that Rachel would join Dora and Mira at a labor camp. She smirked at the thought and checked herself, as the man next to her looked at her smile in horror.

The line arrived at the Umschlagplatz. The grey brick wall loomed over them as they crossed through the gate and were herded into the old Stawki Street hospital. Hundreds of people lined the corridors. The stairwells were filled with bodies; Rachel couldn't determine whether they were alive or dead. The guards shoved the group through the hallways into a large room, where they were left. Hundreds more filled the room, leaving almost no space to walk. Crowded masses of people huddled together, many in their own waste, as no toilet facilities were in sight and the doors were heavily guarded, preventing anyone from leaving. Cries and wails blended with desperate calls for loved ones that echoed off the walls. The walls vibrated with the fear of the bereft souls, who knew all too well the future lying before them. Together, they waited for the trains that would deliver their fate.

Rachel spotted Simon on the edge of the large room and shifted her way over to him, trying not to step on anyone. Several ZTOS employees were gathered in a huddle by the wall where they had entered, whispering frantically.

"How could this have happened? This is a mistake. We're supposed to be safe."

"Maybe they'll realize their mistake and come get us."

"Sure, they may realize it, but it will be too late then."

"We don't know if what they say about the gas chambers is true. How could it be true if people are still alive to talk about it?"

"Maybe it's only for the sick and old. We're young and healthy. We can work."

"Yes, we can work. They'll use us to work."

Rachel heard echoes of Aunt Dora in their desperate voices.

More people were crowded in by the minute, some with luggage, others clearly, like them, having been taken unaware. Weeping, cries, and prayers filled the room. Uniformed guards walked through the crowd, delivering random kicks and punches. People held up money and jewels the guards would take, but instead of releasing them, the guards continued on with a laugh. The heat was stifling, making it difficult to breathe. People shed their clothes, trying to find relief. Pleas for water soon replaced the sounds of prayer.

Rachel observed the people around her, heard their cries and felt their desperation. Instead of feeling afraid for her life and joining in the weeping, anger rose in her like a caged beast. These monsters would not see her cry. She would not plead for her life and cry for their pity. She knew where those trains would take them. Looking into the cold, hard eyes of guards, she knew without a shadow of a doubt there were no labor camps waiting for them, no family camps where they would work together for the war effort. All these people would board those trains and be delivered to the lair of the beast.

Fury raged through her. She would not go down without a fight. She watched the guards, with their confident smirks, walk through the crowd. If she were going down, she wasn't going to leave them unharmed. She imagined herself boarding the train, turning to the nearest guard, and clawing his eyes out. The guards' guns sat smugly on their hips. She could grab one and get a shot in before she was shot herself. Her mind raced with possibilities.

A young Ukrainian guard with acne-ridden skin began making his way across the room. He stopped every several feet and spoke to the terrified captives, who shook their heads each time. He methodically moved towards her group. He wore a Billy club at his waist. If he got close enough, she would grab it and beat him in the face with it, then try to get his gun from his hands. Maybe she could get the shot in before the other guards got to her. He moved closer. The gun hung loosely in his hands. He seemed more concerned with asking his questions than securing his gun. She changed plans. When he got close enough, she would grab the gun directly from his hands and shoot him in the chest.

Her heart began to race. He was getting closer. He walked towards them, the gun in his right hand hanging at his side. She repositioned herself on the left of Simon so she would be directly next to the gun when he walked by. Ten feet away. He stepped over a crying woman, his foot landing on her hand. He didn't look back at her squeal of pain. Bastard. He has it coming. Five feet, almost within reach. Three feet, just one more step. The gun now squarely in front of her face, she got into a crouched position, ready to leap. She reached out her arm, eyes now clear with the goal in sight. He opened his mouth.

"I am looking for Rachel Zylberman. Does anyone know Rachel Zylberman?"

She froze. Her hand dropped. Her group stared at her, wide-eyed. No one spoke.

She stood up, strangely disappointed. Her rebellion thwarted by the surprise of hearing her own name.

"I'm Rachel Zylberman."

"Come with me."

She followed him through the maze of people and out the door of the old hospital. They passed through the inner gates, winding through the pathways of the Umschlagplatz. Other guards grunted as they passed but asked no questions. She followed the guard through the gates of the Umschlagplatz and down Zamenhofa Street. He led her into an alleyway and, without a word, turned and left her standing there. She watched his back as he walked towards the Umschlagplatz, then she turned and fled. She ran as fast as she could until she reached her apartment building. She flew up the stairs, flung open the door, and fell into the arms of Aron and Vera. Hella began screaming.

"Oh thank God, thank God. It worked. Thank God." Vera began crying.

"How? Why?" Was all Rachel could choke out.

"You did this, Rachel," Aron said. "Your yelling to the hospital worker was how we knew. Vera saw you and came right to me. I had a favor owed me by a Jewish policeman. That's the only leverage I had. Thank God it was enough. The Jewish Council is hysterical. If the Nazis can violate their promise that ZTOS workers are safe, then none of us are safe. The Nazis say it was an error and agree you should have all been exempt. But they won't release the group. They say the count will be off without them and it's too late. It makes no sense. But thank God you're out of there."

Rachel's heart lurched at the thought of Simon and her coworkers. Her eyes hardened as she looked at her brother. She spoke softly, for only his ears.

"Aron, I am ready."

He met her eyes and nodded.

*****

The man eyed her suspiciously.

"Are you sure?" he asked Aron.

"For God's sake, she's my sister."

"Yeah, well, she was your sister for the past twenty months, but where's she been?"

"She's here now, Marek. That's all you need to worry about. And she's with us."

Marek's green cat eyes pierced Rachel.

"Back off her, Marek." A striking girl, barely out of her teens, smiled from the smoke-filled table. "If Aron trusts her, that's enough for us."

The girl pulled a cigarette out of a case and offered it across the table. Rachel took it from her and nodded gratefully.

"I'm Stefania. That is Artur, Pinkus and Zivia." She gestured with her cigarette toward the three others at the round wooden table in the corner of the café. "And that, as you now know, is Marek."

163

The café stood like a relic of a pre-war era that Rachel barely remembered existed. Waiters in white shirts brought black bread and ersatz coffee. Two violists played Polish folk songs from a corner. Rachel walked by the cafe regularly but had never gone in. The café had the reputation of catering to smugglers, collaborators, and the Jewish elite. Belonging to none of those categories, Rachel had kept her distance. But today, she belonged to one of several small groups gathered at the café tables, each with their own agenda, sipping weak coffee and eating hard bread.

Zivia was a tiny woman about thirty years old, with thick eyebrows that gave her otherwise delicate face a masculine feel. Artur, his hand on Zivia's knee, towered over her even while sitting. His broad shoulders were twice the width of hers and a thick black nest of hair sat on his head as if planted there. Pinkus was fair, blonde, and lean, with a honey-colored mustache. She could tell instantly that like Aron, he had no problems passing to the other side. With a long neck and tilted chin, Stefania reminded Rachel of the ballerinas she had seen perform in the theater before the war. Her hair was tight in a bun with wisps curling out wildly and playfully.

"Is it safe here?" Rachel imagined Gestapo ears at every table surrounding them.

"We come here to meet and relax, not to work," Marek snapped. She blushed at his sharp tone but refused to look away as his eyes challenged her. Aron signaled the waiter for another cup of black water.

"We meet here every Thursday afternoon," Aron said. "I wanted you to get a chance to meet everyone before...well, before we meet again."

"You have a problem with me," Rachel said, still not breaking Marek's stare.

Aron cleared his throat. "Rachel, leave it."

Marek took a long drag from his cigarette. "I do," he said.

Stefania shook her head briefly at Aron, silencing his further protests. Marek continued.

"Your brother is one of our most valuable assets. Every person at this table would give their lives for him. He would give his life for us. Every day I watch him sacrifice for you and your family. He leaves these walls at risk of arrest and execution to feed his family. He saved your child's life. He used a valuable favor that one day could have saved his own life to instead save yours. And where have you been? What have you done? You're young and healthy. But you hide at your job and go home to your apartment every night. You let the rest of us fight for you. I think you're a coward."

Aron's breath drew in audibly. Pinkus blinked nervously and Artur's hand visibly tightened on Zivia's knee. Marek took another drag from his cigarette and blew it callously toward Rachel. She straightened in her seat, not breaking his gaze.

"You're right," she stated simply.

She didn't see the exchanged surprised looks at her response, as she was focused only on the green cat eyes.

"I am a coward. I've been afraid for the past two years. I was afraid of losing my husband, afraid of losing my child. I walked the streets every day with my head to the ground, afraid of drawing attention to myself. I was afraid of losing my parents and my brother. I was afraid they would take me. And then they did take me. They took me and it was then I discovered the one thing I'm not afraid of is death. So yes, I was a coward and I'm still afraid. Only now, I'm most afraid I will leave this earth and the devil will still be standing. I am ready to fight."

Marek put out his cigarette in his last drop of coffee and turned to Aron.

"Oh yes, she is your sister." And Rachel saw, for the first time, the cat eyes smile.

*****

Marek rifled through the small stack of documents Rachel handed him as she peeled the last sticky sheet of paper from her stomach where it was concealed beneath her shirt.

"This is all you have?" he growled.

"It's all I could get without raising suspicion. A Nazi inspector has been auditing our records. I burned as many death certificates as I could without making it obvious. Everyone who once belonged to these work cards is now officially alive."

Marek grunted and dismissed her with a wave of his hand. Stefania was sprawled on the floor on the opposite side

165

of the room stacking guns beneath a floorboard. Rachel walked over to her, bristling.

"Don't take it personally," Stefania whispered as Rachel handed her a handgun from the stack. "He's just focused on his work."

"Perhaps he should be more focused on thanking us for risking our lives, rather than criticizing us for not getting ourselves shot." Rachel glared over at Marek but kept her voice at a whisper.

"Marek doesn't see this job as deserving of thanks. He sees it as a duty."

Rachel watched Marek's back as he carefully peeled photographs from the work permits and applied new ones. His dark hair was unkempt, his shirt stained, more attention obviously given to his mission than his own self-interest. Rachel blushed, ashamed by her expectation of appreciation. She helped Stefania push down the floorboards and rose to wash her hands.

"Where are you going?" Marek called out but hadn't turned around.

"Just to wash my hands."

"Not yet. I need to talk to you both."

Rachel and Stefania joined him at the table. "I have a special job for the two of you."

*****

The two Jewish policemen stood by the bar at the café, ogling them with the subtly of a rhinoceros. Stefania tilted her head back and jutted her chest forward. The tall one elbowed his friend and both of their attentions homed in on the rickety table by the window where Rachel and Stefania sat. Rachel resisted the urge to pull her skirt lower over her knees, and instead followed Stefania's example and crossed her legs, her skirt rising higher across her thigh.

"Here kitty, kitty," Stefania whispered then she broke into a high-pitched giggle, tossing her hair over her shoulder. Her white teeth flashed at the two men. The bait was cast.

"Hello beautiful ladies." The tall one with a choppy mustache leered at them. The shorter one, not much older than twenty, hiccupped and mimicked his cohort's leer, but instead formed a gross gargolyle-esce sneer.

Rachel put her hands in her lap and clutched them together to hide their shaking. Before she knew it, the two policemen were seated at their table, the leerer at her right, his eyes focused on the top buttons of her blouse which, until an hour ago, had been buttoned nearly to her neck. She gave her newly revealed chest a glance and blushed at the sight of her own breasts, exposed nearly to the nipple. He took the blush as a sign of interest.

"Shy, are we?" His sour breath hovered near her ear.

"She's not shy." Stefania gave Rachel a warning look, hidden by a flash of smile. "She just likes you. My sister always gets quiet when she is interested in a man."

"I like the shy ones," he said.

Rachel heeded Stefania's warning and smiled brightly at him.

"Would you like to dance?"

"Nah, I don't dance."

She was disappointed. At least if he danced, she wouldn't have to talk to him.

She let him put his hand on her knee and Stefania took over the conversation, swirling the two men into dizziness with her giggles and smiles.

"Isn't it getting awfully close to curfew for you two?"

Rachel pretended to be shocked at the time.

"Well," she cooed, proud of her first major contribution "maybe you could escort us home?"

"Oh yes, that would be wonderful," Stefania encouraged. "Our parents and brothers left for the East last month, and we have no one to take care of us anymore."

The policeman clearly could hardly believe his luck and winked at the short one.

"Ladies, we would be honored to escort you home."

He squeezed her rear end as she stood to leave and instead of slapping him, Rachel playfully swatted his arm and giggled. As they paraded through the streets, she made sure to stay behind Stefania, afraid she would get lost in the tangle of alleys Stefania was purposefully leading them through. She breathed a sigh of relief when the dreary apartment building appeared in front of them.

The policemen followed Stefania to the door of the basement apartment. About five feet from the door, Rachel dropped her large purse. A resounding thump echoed in the dark hallway. Rachel cringed. It was supposed to shatter. She gulped, but cried,

"Stefania! I think I broke the vase!"

Stefania began screaming at her.

"What do you mean you broke the vase? How can we sell a broken vase? You're such an idiot! Do you know how much that vase was worth?"

Rachel buried her head in the rancid blue shoulder of her policemen and began to wail.

"It's okay, honey," he pronounced. "Why don't my friend and I come in and we can find a way to fix it?"

His friend nodded vigorously.

"Of course, you can come in," Stefania said, throwing a look Rachel's direction. Stefania dug around in her purse and the men shifted anxiously. Finally finding the key, she opened the door, slamming it loudly against the wall.

"Sorry," she giggled, "I always forget how heavy it is. Come on in. The switch in this stupid apartment is on the other side of the room."

Rachel followed the two men into the dark room and shut the door behind them. In the darkness, she eased herself over to the right, knowing Stefania was headed straight ahead. Clear of the men, she took long, bold steps to the far wall.

"What the hell?" The tall man's voice shouted in the dark.

"Hey! Stop! What is this?" yelled the other.

Two loud thumps signaled Stefania to flip the switch and the lights flew on. Aron and Marek each straddled one of the policemen. Zivia, Pinkus, and Artur surrounded them, guns pointing at their heads.

"Nice work girls," Aron grunted, lifting the skinny man to his feet.

"Couldn't you have gotten them inside a little further?" Marek grumbled, rubbing his arms, bruised by the door.

"You fucking sluts!" the skinny man spewed, spitting across the room at Rachel.

"Shut the fuck up," Marek slapped him across the face.

"Who are you? What is this?" the short man squealed like a trapped rabbit.

Ignoring the questions, Marek and Aron pushed them forward. Rachel and Stefania followed them into the back room, where they tied the policemen to chairs. Marek stood in front of them.

"Mendl Tober and David Lask. You are accused of collaborating with the enemy. We have documented evidence that you exceeded your daily deportation quota excessively and willingly in exchange for Nazi favor. We have evidence you told the Gestapo of the smuggling operation on Leszno Street. That information led to the shooting of eleven Jews. What do you have to say in response to these accusations?"

"Lies, they're all lies!"

Short boy began to blubber. Rachel backed her way slowly against the wall. Marek's eyes followed her. She shook her head and slipped through the door, back into the main room. Stefania followed shortly after.

"I just couldn't watch it, Stefania."

"You've no need to apologize, Rachel. You were great tonight. They didn't see it coming. And when you dropped your purse and we didn't hear the vase break, I thought I was going to pee my pants! I had to yell at you extra loud to be sure they heard us coming."

Rachel laughed then stopped short when the crying of the policeman echoed through the walls.

"They better get this done. He's going to draw the attention of the neighbors."

As if on cue, the room next door silenced.

"Does this make us murderers?" Rachel asked.

"No, they're the murderers. We're simply the judge and jury." She put her hand on Rachel's back. "There are a lot more things you should be losing sleep over than this, Rachel."

Rustling and banging reverberated from the next room. "They'll take the uniforms and papers then smuggle the bodies out the back way to the sewers. If they don't make it back by curfew, they'll stay in the sewers overnight."

Aron came out of the back room, holding open the door for Pinkus and Marek, each with a large bag slung over their shoulders.

"Izak, the undertaker, is meeting us at the corner. Zivia's poor brothers just died from tuberculosis. Probably still contagious, you know?" Aron winked. Stefania laughed and opened the door for the men and their baggage. Alone with Stefania, Rachel risked asking,

"What's Marek's story? Are you..., are you with him?"

"Am I with him? Well, yes."

Delayed  understanding crossed her face.

"Oh! You mean with him like that. No, I'm not with him like that. I'm married to Marek's brother. Or I was married to Marek's brother. I guess I don't know officially whether I'm a widow or not. My husband was one of seven thousand men taken away on Yom Kippur in Lodz. No one ever heard from any of them again, so I can only assume my widowhood.

"A month after my husband was taken, Marek was arrested for smuggling. Marek had numerous run-ins with a policeman named Aurbach. Aurbach was notoriously cruel, and it was rumored he sold ghetto secrets to the Nazis. He was dangerous but very powerful. Marek paid him off dozens of times to look the other way after he discovered Marek's smuggling and resistance activities. But Aurbach kept asking for more money.

"When Marek refused to pay more, Aurbach had him arrested. The smuggling ring punished Aurbach by reporting him to the Jewish Council, who stripped him of his position and took away his work permit. The organization Marek worked for in Lodz paid a large sum of money to release him from prison. When Marek returned to his apartment, Aurbach was waiting for him. The bastard was sitting at Marek's kitchen table surrounded by the dead bodies of Marek's wife and three children."

Rachel gasped, her heart sinking into her stomach.

"He planned to kill Marek too, after rubbing his family's deaths in his face. But he underestimated Marek. Instead of falling to the floor in grief, Marek flew into a rage, took a bullet to the shoulder, and strangled the man to death with his bare hands. He came to my apartment six blocks away, covered in blood, and nearly bleeding to death. We pulled out the bullet, stitched him up, and were out through the sewers within an hour. We had no papers and nowhere to go, so we came here. Funny, someone escaping INTO a ghetto, huh?"

Neither of them laughed.

"So maybe that explains a little more about Marek. Unlike most people whose goal it is to survive this nightmare, Marek's goal is to take them and their cronies with him to hell."

Later that night, Rachel pulled the thin sheet to her chin as she lay on the floor, listening to Stefania's breathing become deep. Marek's story echoed in her head. The cat eyes she loathed these past weeks now haunted her with their secrets.

# Claire
## Morocco, North Africa
## October 1943 – January 1944

October 21, 1943

Dear Bill,

I know this is hard for you to understand, but I can't return to the states until I find my father. I love you and I need your support. Please don't be angry.

Claire

Marie barreled through the hospital towards her as Claire wheeled a broken-legged airman down the peeling hallway to X-ray.

"I'll take him. You read this!"

She slapped a beige envelope into Claire's hands.

"A blonde and a brunette. It's my lucky day," the lame lieutenant beamed.

"Enough of your sass, Soldier," Marie laughed and winked as she wheeled him away, leaving Claire to flee into the supply room to tear open the envelope.

October 25, 1943

Dear Marie,

This past month has been a major struggle for the 173rd Field Hospital and we're no longer in Italy. We've been reassigned to Oman and there's a rumor our evac hospital will be disbanded and divided amongst other hospitals. We're in a true state of confusion. I can only imagine what Major Weber's daughter is going through right now. I don't know the truth about what happened to Major Weber, but I can share what I do know and the rumors we're hearing, and hopefully that information can help her in her journey to find answers.

172

On the morning of September 14, we were given orders to strike the camp and were told we'd be moving North with the 15th Army Group at 0800 the following morning. Sometime between 2100 and 2200 hours, Major Weber was seen by at least three corpsmen walking with a duffel bag into the wooded mountain area behind the hospital. All three men confirm he looked behind him suspiciously and seemed to be attempting to conceal himself. As Major Weber is a highly respected doctor, the corpsmen didn't report it and took no action.

The following morning at 0730 Colonel Keller initiated a search of the hospital for Major Weber and delayed the unit's departure until 0900. Five kilometers from Naples, our unit was ambushed by a German regiment and the jeep carrying Colonel Keller, a translator, a doctor, and our head nurse Shirley Byers, was fired upon and all were killed. You may remember Shirley Byers, our nursing school instructor in Brooklyn. I will miss her terribly. A week after arriving in Naples we were replaced by the 111th as we had lost the doctors and our head nurse. We've been in Oman since. These are awful times.

As for Major Weber, there are several rumors flying. One says he was going to the town to San Giordino to see a woman he had arranged to meet there. The three corpsmen confirm he was seen headed up the mountain in the direction of that village, but it's over ten kilometers away from Salerno. No one in our unit believes he deserted. The army investigators who questioned us made that determination based on the corpsmen's description of his departure and the fact he's not been found or reported as a POW. Major Weber was a professional, dedicated physician and to see his name dragged through the mud like this breaks my heart.

I admire Major Weber's daughter for pursuing this on her own. From the tone of the investigators, it seems as if the Army has closed the book. Apparently, an honorable man deserting into the mountains is a common occurrence to them. However, to this unit it is not, and we refuse to believe it.

I wish I could be of more help. This is all I know. I will write again soon on a more personal level, and we can catch up. Stay safe. I love you, dear cousin.

Theresa

November 3, 1943

Dear Tom,

You may notice the postmark of this letter is from New York City. One of our nurses is being sent home tomorrow morning after recovering from malaria and she's going to mail this as soon as she arrives. Now I can write uncensored, and you'll likely receive it sooner than if I were to mail it from Morocco.

I've enclosed a copy of a letter from Marie's friend in the 173rd. I'm very confused by the story. My father would never sneak out of his unit in the middle of the night. There must be a misunderstanding. Hearing of the death of John Keller is devastating. He was a dear friend of my father. All information he may have had has gone with him. I feel like we've taken two steps backward. But I tell myself we can't lose hope and can only plow ahead.

You'd be so proud of me if you could see me here. This month I've assisted in six operations from a hernia repair to a lower arm amputation of a soldier in a grenade training accident. For the first time in my life, I feel like I'm up to par with other nurses. Well, getting there at least. I have you to thank. Nurse Beck told me about your letter to her. Without you, I would've been sent home weeks ago. Nurse Beck has been by my side, teaching me so many things I should have learned in nursing school but never thought were important. The other nurses and some of the corpsmen are letting me practice my IVs on them at night. Marie said if I poke her one more time, she'll have to become a nun, she's so holy. But now some of the soldiers who are hospitalized are requesting me to give them their IVs, because mine don't hurt as badly. These boys are so sweet and many of them are so lonely. The nurses try to keep their spirits up and the single girls flirt a lot. There are plenty of dates for every lonely girl. Not for me, of course.

However, I do have some hopeful news! We're being shipped out next week. They won't tell us where we are going. However, yesterday we received two little brown books: "The Soldier's Guide to Italy" and "Italian Words and Phrases". So, I think it is safe to assume where we're headed. The Army is anything but subtle. When I heard last week the Italians surrendered, I had lost all hope of being assigned to Italy. But now my prayers have been answered. I just know I'll find my father there.

I also hope to see Bill in Italy as I understand his unit has been transferred there as well. His letters plead for me to return home. I want to make him happy but at the same time, I need to do this for my father. It's quite a dilemma.

There are things I will miss about Morocco. The beaches, of course, but also the fact that we haven't had to deal with combat wounded. I know that will change in Italy since the Germans are still offering heavy resistance there. Since we arrived in Morocco just weeks before the allies defeated Hitler's Afrika Corps, most of our cases have been training injuries, malaria, and (dare I say it?) venereal disease. I will not miss Morocco's gigantic bedbugs, which crawl all over our mosquito nets, the beggars in the streets, the stench, nor the occasional drunken bed checks by a certain colonel whom I will not name. Fortunately, he is staying behind and the nurses of the 17th can look forward to sleeping unmolested.

Write soon, Tom. I do cherish your letters. You are a dear friend.

Yours, Claire

November 15, 1943

Dear Claire,

You're quite welcome for the little things I've done to help you along your way, but I think it's I who should be thanking you. Your letters brighten my day. It's an honor you're willing to share your experiences with me. Truthfully, I don't fully agree with your path and I'm afraid for you, but I trust you. The US Army is lucky to have you and don't let anyone convince you otherwise. You've always had what it took to be an amazing nurse. You just needed to see it in yourself.

By the time you receive this, you'll likely be in Italy. I hope you're able to see Bill and take care of what you need to take care of. I understand he wants you to go home. Claire, I implore you to do what you want to do, not what Bill wants you to do. He may be your fiancé, but you need to follow your head,

175

not necessarily your heart. Lois Beck wrote to me to tell me how much progress you have made. She's proud of you. Your unit needs you there.

Enough of the lectures. You've accused me in the past of sounding like your father and apparently, I'm guilty as charged. I wish I had news of him. The Tribune reporter left the unit when it disbanded and isn't able to give us any additional information.

I saw Barbara Ann at St. Ignatius last week and she asked if it was okay if she sent you a case full of makeup. I told her it was likely you'd prefer Chapstick and American candy, but she accused me of not understanding women at all. So, I fully expect you'll receive a package of eye shadow and cold cream. Maybe you can trade them for some extra mosquito repellant.

Claire, you said in your letter that I'd be proud of you if I knew how well you were doing. I want you to know I am proud of you. I always have been.

Take care of yourself, look after your head and your heart, and write to me often.

Tom

December 8, 1943

Dear Tom,

Today I received four letters from you and I'm doing everything I can not to open them all at once. We've been in Italy for over a month and today was our first mail call. I don't know when we'll receive mail again—it seems we get a month's worth of mail all at once, so I'm trying to spread out the joy and open one letter a day.

Along with your letter, I received several from friends at home, but only one from Bill. He knows I'm in Italy and said he'll "see what he can do" about getting leave to see me, but is still insisting I request a transfer home. I keep repeating your words about following my head, not my heart. I won't make any decisions at all until I learn about my father, so for now it is easy and I don't have to follow either. I just wait. But trust me, I'm not just sitting around waiting.

We arrived at Paestum and have since moved north toward Naples. Our 700 bed hospital currently has over 1000 patients. We evacuate as many stable patients as we can to Naples but two leave and three more replace them. Bonnie and Marie are in the surgery ward and those doctors are working around the clock. I alternate between the receiving tent and the medical wards, where we see soldiers with malaria, VD, upper respiratory infections, and the ever-popular trench foot. Many of my patients are headed back to the front once they are better. Marie's post op recovery patients are in much higher spirits  because for many of them, their wounds mean they are headed home.

Bonnie, Marie, and I share a tent. It seems like we're more mud than human anymore. Everything is mud soaked. We do our laundry in our helmets and use the helmets to hold our bath water. Bonnie said she's going into town tomorrow to find us a laundry woman. Clean clothes would be a miracle. You certainly were right about the package of makeup Barbara Ann sent me. I traded it all away to the Italians—but not for Chapstick and repellant. I have a nice little stash of wine and nut candy and we all ate fresh fruit for a week (although I did keep one tube of lipstick).

The infantry divisions frequently invite our nurses to dances they've set up. As much as I only have eyes for Bill, I certainly can't say no to brightening an evening in the lives of these brave soldiers. They're so grateful just to talk to American girls. We met a unit with a number of boys from Minnesota and they kept me out until two in the morning just talking about the Minneapolis Millers and the Saint Paul Saints. I think I now know more about baseball than my father.

One of my biggest frustrations is that I know we are only about 25 miles from Salerno, where my father was last seen. In fact, we drove directly though Salerno on our route to Naples and I was tempted to jump right off the truck. Because of what Marie's cousin said about my father heading in the direction of San Giordino, I strongly believe if I could get there, I could find some answers. But nurses aren't allowed to leave the unit unchaperoned and with no legitimate reason to travel to San

Giordino and no transportation, I'm stuck. I continue to hang on to hope, but it's getting more and more difficult as each day passes.

We heard yesterday we're each getting a five day leave to the Isle of Capri. The girls are all so excited. We're going to get to sleep in a hotel (clean sheets!). Just to have the time away to breathe will make such a difference.

Tomorrow, I'll let myself read letter #2. Keep writing. I hope to see ten letters in my next batch!

Yours, Claire

*****

"Thank God for these new uniforms," Marie called from the bedroom, "I was sure I'd be growing a snout and oinking if they didn't come soon. No amount of laundering could have gotten the old ones clean! And hell, this olive drab will hide the mud better than the navy ones did."

"Forget the uniforms. I'm never, ever, ever leaving this bathtub," Claire called back and submerged her head, allowing the warm water to encompass her, opening her eyes beneath the water to reveal the bright white ceiling hazed in a foggy dream sequence. She emerged to Marie still talking.

"Son of a bitch! You should check out these sheets! They're linen, Claire. You gotta come see this!"

Claire smiled. She'd given up scolding Marie for her sailor language. Other women would appear gauche, but it worked for Marie. Claire reluctantly rose from the white clawed tub. The sparkling bathroom, its white fixtures and tiled walls made her feel human again. She silently vowed to never again take such luxury for granted.

Early that morning, Claire, Marie, Bonnie and a third of the nurses of the 17th Evacuation Hospital departed Naples on the two-hour ferry shuttle to the Isle of Capri. The ferry weaved through the harbor graveyard of sunken ships, the isle jutting from the sea on the horizon. The ferry docked on the bottom of the high cliff walls of the island which was being used by the US Air Force as a rest area. After ascending a steep stairway, cheery enlisted men in jeeps delivered the giddy nurses to the Paradiso Hotel.

Claire wrapped a towel as big as a bed sheet around her body and joined Marie at the window. The crystal blue Mediterranean loomed in front of them, Naples on the distant horizon.

"Your hair is never going to dry. We're supposed to meet Bonnie and Ellen downstairs. Bonnie met a group of airmen in the lobby who want to take us sightseeing after lunch."

"Order me whatever you're having, and I'll be down in twenty minutes. I can just pin it up wet and hope it doesn't dry too frizzy. However it looks, it was worth it. Look, squeaky clean." Claire's hair whistled through her fingers and Marie leaned into the mirror to apply a third layer of lipstick.

"I'm going to swing by that lobby balcony before going to the dining room. Hurry up. I saw the menu and you're not gonna want to miss those appetizers."

Claire put on the olive drab skirt and white blouse of the new uniforms that arrived the day before. She had been measured nearly two months before and the skirt hung low on her hips. She had to have lost more than ten pounds. She was thinner but seemed bigger, stronger than she ever had. Her soft arms were muscular from lifting stretchers and carrying 170-pound men to surgical tables and recovery rooms. The edges of her blonde hair were jagged, from Bonnie's apologetic haircutting skills. Her cheeks were bright red and freckled from sun and wind burn. Claire was glad Barbara Ann couldn't see her. She'd have a fit at the condition of her fair skin. The tub of cold cream she had sent had been traded for  two bottles of wine and a tray of olives. Claire had gotten the better end of that bargain. She sighed and picked up a brush. If she pinned her hair up enough, she could hide it under her hat and maybe it would be wavy, not frizzy, when it dried. A knock on the door caused her to jump, poking her head with the pin.

"Five more minutes! I'm on my way!" she called to Marie.

Typical of all the New Yorkers Claire had met in the past seven months, Marie was one of the most impatient people she knew. Seconds later, another rap came from the door. Claire plopped the pin on the dresser, her wet hair tumbling to her shoulders as she opened the door.

Broad olive green shoulders filled the doorway. Claire froze as she stared at the man in front of her, recognition slowly creeping though her as she took in the once thick, wavy black hair now shaved to the scalp. His dark eyes met her own as she whispered,

"Bill." She flew into his arms, laughing. "How's this happening? How did you know where to find me? I can't believe it."

He came into the room and held her out at arm length and studied her.

"Oh Bill, I look terrible. My hair's wet, I'm not wearing makeup. I wish I had known you were coming."

"Well, that would have ruined the surprise, wouldn't it? I made some inquiries about when your leave would be and found out all the nurses were coming here. It wasn't too difficult to arrange my leave at the same time. But I only have 24 hours. I wanted to surprise you."

She stood on her toes, and he leaned down to accept her kiss.

"Well, it worked. I can't believe you're here. We have so much to talk about."

"All that can wait. You go ahead and get yourself pretty. We can talk later."

He left as quickly as he arrived, and Claire shakily finished getting ready, grateful for the small amount of makeup she still had. She met him in the lobby and giddily introduced him to the girls as a waiter added another place setting to the table. She watched him during lunch, her hand in his under the table, as Bonnie and Marie peppered him with questions, and teased them about their engagement.

Bonnie mouthed to her silently, "He's gorgeous," making Claire blush.

His sculpted face quickened Claire's heartbeat. The way his large hand cradled her own gave her hope. He was here. No matter that he didn't understand her joining the ANC, no matter that she didn't request the transfer when he told her to, he was here. He was here and holding her hand.

Three men from Bill's platoon joined them, much to the dismay of Bonnie's prearranged dates, as they strolled to the piazza in the center of the island. Army and Navy uniforms crowded the streets, mingling with the natives selling their wares. The little shops were mostly empty but a small ragtag band set up in the piazza played vague versions of American tunes, adding to the festivity of the soldiers basking in their R & R. Bill walked close to her and Claire touched him every chance she could, to point out a shop or a stunning view, making sure he was really there.

"Let's take a boat ride to the Blue Grotto. I've heard we shouldn't miss it," Bonnie suggested.

"I think Bill and I will pass," Claire spoke before Bill could. "We have some catching up to do."

The others left them at the lobby of the hotel and Claire, brushing off the awkward feeling of illicitly having an unchaperoned man in her room, led Bill upstairs. She took off her green jacket and necktie and laid them across the bed.

"I wanted to see the Blue Grotto," Bill sulked. "I don't know when I'll get another chance."

"Let's go just the two of us later. I want to be alone with you. We need to talk."

"There's nothing to talk about. I've thought about it and can accept what you did. I think it's nuts, but there's nothing you can do to change it. I just wished you had consulted me first. But then again, you wouldn't be here now if you had."

He reached for her and she lifted her lips and met his. His kiss had always sent butterflies through her stomach. His tongue teased her own as he pulled her into him. She could feel the muscles of his chest, his arms thicker in the year since she had seen him. His hand stroked her back as they kissed. His hands slipped to her waist, pulled her blouse out of her skirt, and he began to unbutton her shirt.

"Bill, no," she whispered.

"Come on, Claire."

His tongue caressed her and his hand cupped her breast.

"Bill, no. We agreed to wait."

"I haven't seen you for over a year. We're engaged. I could be killed over here at any time. What's there to wait for?" As he spoke, he drew open the last button on her shirt, revealing her white bra.

"God you're beautiful," he murmured as he pulled her closer to him.

"I don't want it to be this way. I want us to be married first."

"Damn it, Claire, this is the least you could do."

Claire gasped and pushed Bill away. Tears blinded her vision as she attempted to rebutton her blouse. Bill sighed loudly.

"Look, it makes me crazy to think of you surrounded every day by horny soldiers. And I'm lonely out here and all I do is long for you." Bill's voice verged on anger. He then sighed and wiped her tears with a handkerchief from his pocket.

"Claire, marry me. Marry me tonight. My unit chaplain is on the island, and I know he'd do it for us. We can make it all more formal and have that big party you want when we get home. But let's get married and get it done with. I want you to be my wife."

Her tears began to fall.

"I can't marry you now. If I get married, I have to leave my unit. I need to find my father."

"Good Lord.. It's been three months with no word from him."

"I can't, Bill. I have to do this."

"I've never known you to be like this. I've been patient imagining my girl pawed over by hundreds of soldiers, imagining you shot and killed while on this crazy adventure of yours, and now you're choosing a muddy tent over me?"

"I'm not choosing anything over you. I want you. I want to be your wife. But I need you to wait for me. That's all I'm asking. Wait. When you left Minnesota, that's what you asked of me and now I'm asking the same."

"Are you going to marry me or not?"

"Yes, I'm going to marry you."

Bills' shoulders relaxed. "That's my girl."

"But not here and not now," she whispered.

Bill stepped back and snatched his jacket from the overstuffed chair.

"I want the ring back. My ring shouldn't be on the finger of a girl whose priorities lie elsewhere."

"No Bill, please don't do this. I love you. I want to marry you."

"Then think about that every day while you look at your bare hand. When you're ready to marry me, I'll put the ring back on your finger in front of a chaplain."

Bill grabbed her left hand and pulled the ring from it. Claire's tears dropped onto the crisp linen sheets as the door slammed behind him.

*****

December 14, 1943

Dear Bill,

Please reconsider. I want to marry you. I love you. I just need more time. I've made a commitment to this hospital, and I can't leave until I find the truth about my father. Please Bill, I need you. You're all I have.

Claire

From her cot, Claire glanced up from sealing her letter to see Marie pulling on her boots.

"Are you headed to the mess? Will you drop this at the mail truck on your way?"

"Is it for Bill?"

"Yes."

"Ok then, give it to me."

Claire handed Marie the envelope.

Marie marched across the tent and tossed the letter in the paper trash bag.

"That, Claire, is where letters to and from that jerk belong."

"Marie!"

The tent door flapped behind her as Marie stomped out.

December 23, 1943

Dear Claire,

I am sorry to hear about what happened with Bill. I feel honored you're able to confide in me. I know about heartbreak firsthand. I have a confession you likely already know through the Green Meadow rumor mill. All those months I told you Ginny was visiting family in Des Moines, I wasn't being entirely truthful. Ginny left me nearly a year ago. I wish I could tell you it was mutual, and we fought the good fight but just couldn't overcome our differences. But in fact, she left me for another man. Every day I look in the mirror knowing I wasn't enough for her. Claire, I can only hope Bill is the man you imagine him to be. If he is, he'll come crawling back to you, and be able to fully see the amazing woman asking him to stand by her side. If not, like me, he's a fool.

Tom

December 23, 1943

Dear Claire,

I received a letter from Bill today. He said you turned down his request to marry him and come home to Minnesota. He asked that I write and talk some sense into you. While I applaud your decision not to marry him in some mud-filled hole in Italy, you do need to come home. Your presence overseas is not going to bring your father back. Having you home safe in Minnesota is what your father would want. You need to continue with your own life. As soon as you get here, we can start planning for your wedding. Perhaps we can have a double wedding when both Bill and Albert return.

Speaking of weddings, I believe Tom Parker will be having one of his own soon. As I told you before, his wife moved back to Des Moines. The divorce must be official, because he's picking up Ava Sorenson from work nearly every day and word has it around the hospital that she and her daughter spent Thanksgiving with his mother in Green Meadow. If that isn't serious, I don't know what is.

The snow is a foot deep here as usual. Merry Christmas to you, Claire. I hope, if you heed my advice, we will spend 1944 planning our weddings together.

Barbara Ann


MISS CLAIRE WEBER
17TH EVACUATION HOSPITAL APO 42
THE SECRETARY OF WAR DESIRES ME TO INFORM YOUR FATHER MAJOR ROBERT J WEBER'S STATUS HAS BEEN CHANGED FROM ABSENT WITHOUT LEAVE TO DESERTER STATUS SINCE FIFTEENTH NOVEMBER IF FURTHER DETAILS OR INFORMATION ARE RECEIVED YOU WILL BE PROMPTLY NOTIFIED.
UL10  THE ADJUNCT GENERAL


"Quit whatever brooding you're doing and let's go. We only have a few hours to get back before the night shift."

Claire looked up from her letter writing as Marie poked her head through the tent flaps.

"What're you talking about?"

"You'll see. Grab your helmet and your photographs and come on."

Confused, Claire tucked her photograph album under her arm and followed Marie out of the tent, trudging after her through the thick mud, past the medical complex and behind a supply tent on the far end of the camp. Marie stopped at a mud-splattered jeep and got in, jingling the keys in front of her.

"What are you doing? How did you get permission to use this jeep? You didn't steal it, did you?"

"Now what kind of question is that? Of course I didn't steal it. I overheard Corporal Brody saying he was making a delivery to Salerno and I generously offered to make it for him. By the way, you owe me a fifth of whiskey. On our way back from a quick delivery, we might accidentally get lost in San Giordino."

"San Giordino! Really? Oh my God!" Claire leapt into the jeep next to her. "Does Major Beck know?"

"You ask too many questions. Tuck your hair under that helmet and let's get outta here."

The jeep rattled up the battered mountain roads from Salerno to San Giordino. In Salerno, Claire slumped discreetly in the front seat, hoping no one would question her presence while Marie flirted with the clerk accepting the delivery of penicillin and syringes, innocently weaseling directions from him to the town that might lead Claire to her father.

Italian farmers plodded down the muddy mountain paths, gaping at the American girls as they rattled past. A freckle-faced goatherd's thin flock scattered into a military-dug trench as Marie jolted the jeep around a tight corner, nearly bowling them over. The ten kilometers took forty-five minutes to navigate, and Claire glanced at her watch nervously, wondering how long they would have to investigate and still get back in time for their shifts. She didn't care what happened to her, but she wouldn't allow Marie to get in trouble.

The occasional smattering of farmhouses erupted into a village of white and grey buildings, fruit vendors, and children playing in the mud-packed streets as they approached the town of San Giordino. A brown, stone medieval church stood in the center of town, its bronze door gleaming in the afternoon sun. The stares of the town people made Claire jittery, and Marie pulled up in front of the ancient, regal church.

"Next to my mother, the Catholic priests are always the best source of information in Brooklyn. Let's see what he can do for us here," Marie said.

Claire pulled three pictures of her father from her photo book and followed Marie through the bronze door. Four black-clad women on their knees peered at them suspiciously from the pews. A frocked priest entered the chapel from a concealed doorway near the altar and nodded to them, as if he had anticipated their arrival. The girls met him halfway down the stone-tiled aisle.

"Do you speak English?" Marie asked.

"No," replied the priest, "little."

Claire handed the priest the pictures.

"My Papa," she said, pointing at her father's smiling face in front of their Green Meadow Christmas tree. "My Papa, Robert Weber. Have you seen him? In September?"

The priest sorted through the three pictures, studying them closely. He looked into Claire's face and then back at the photographs. He handed them back to her without a word then turned and walked back down the aisle into the vestibule.

"Well, now what?" she asked Marie. "Are we supposed to follow him?"

"Let's give him a minute."

Marie shifted uncomfortably at the four women's stares, their black eyes still boring into Claire and Marie's olive-clad backs. Claire surveyed the small medieval church. The glass in the arched east window was cracked, leaving a heavy, jagged bolt pointing at the marble altar. The dark wooden pews were well loved, the smell of the polishing oils wafting in the air.

The priest reappeared after several minutes with a wrinkled paper in his hand. He handed it to Claire. A map to what appeared to be a representation of a farmhouse was sketched on the paper. Claire's stomach flipped.

"My Papa?" she asked, feeling tears of hope crest.

"No," the priest shook his head sadly, "Senora Isabella Giannelli."

He tapped the farmhouse with his finger. He bowed to them slightly and retreated into the vestibule.

"Why didn't you ask him who this woman is?" Claire asked.

"How would I do that?"

"Don't you speak Italian?"

"Just swear words and prayers," Marie cackled, "But don't worry, if Isabella Giannelli doesn't speak English, we might very well need both."

Dark shutters lined the burnt orange brick house at the peak of a hill. The view over the mountains was breathtaking, but Claire couldn't focus on anything other than her frenzied eagerness to get to this woman. Fear and hope spun simultaneously through her. When the house was in sight, Marie slowed to manage a black mud pit, and Claire fought the urge to leap out of the jeep and race ahead to the farmhouse.

A dark-haired woman with an infant in her arms stepped out of the door onto the neatly swept stone-lined entryway. A boy around ten or eleven years old stepped in front of her, as if shielding her from them.

Claire and Marie stepped out of the jeep.

"Senora Isabella Giannelli?"

The woman nodded cautiously, clutching the infant closer to her chest. The boy stood straighter, making an obvious effort to make himself larger.

"Parla inglese?" Marie asked.

Senora Giannelli shook her head. Claire stepped forward, her pictures extended toward the cautious woman.

"I am Claire Weber," she spoke slowly. "My Papa is Robert Weber. Do you know him?"

Senora Giannelli's face changed as Claire said her father's name. Fear turned to recognition and then to something Claire couldn't identify. The boy gasped and ran into the house.

"Roberto," the woman said indicating her baby.

Claire's heart fell.

"No, not the baby. My Papa. Robert Weber."

Frustration flashed across the woman's face. Shuffling the baby to one arm, she made a sweeping gesture across her stomach.

"Bambino no come. Medico Robert Weber here. Bambino yes."

Understanding flooded through Claire.

"My father delivered her baby!" Claire squealed. "Where is he? Where is he now?"

The woman looked flustered.

"Dove?" interjected Marie, pointing to the photograph in Claire's hand.

Senora Giannelli took a step back and shook her head sadly.

"Tedeschi," she whispered. She reached out and patted the photograph compassionately. "Catturato dai tedeschi."

She backed into the house and shut the door, leaving Claire and Marie standing on the brick porch.

"Catturato dai tedeschi? What the hell is catturato dai tedeschi?"

The jeep flew down the black roads, mud coating the girls and everything they passed until they reached the base of the mountain. Claire jumped out of the slowing jeep, no longer concerned about being seen. She grabbed the arm of the nearest corpsmen.

"I need to see a translator. Find me someone who speaks Italian."

The pock-faced corpsman yelled to a group of uniforms unloading a supply truck.

"Hey Tony! It's your lucky day! This dame wants to talk to you."

The smiling olive-skinned Tony ran over and grinned at Claire.

"What can I do you for, Ma'am?"

"Catturato dai tedeschi. What does it mean?"

"Catturato dai tedeschi?" The young man's smile disappeared. "Where did you hear that?"

"Tell me what it means!"

He spoke quietly.

"Captured by the Germans, Ma'am. It means captured by the Germans."

# Min-He
## West of Shanghai, China
## Spring 1944 - March 1945

Days blurred into weeks. Twenty men a day, six days a week. Medical exams with Dr. Kono every Monday. Sometimes he would rape her, sometimes he would leave her alone. Still, she always looked forward to Mondays: only nine men to contend with on Mondays. Officers regularly spent the night, demanding vile and strange sex acts. Min-He learned to comply, to never resist. Her defiance was futile and just led to bruised cheekbones and blackened eyes.

The worst times were when the mobile units descended upon them, passing through to ensuing battles. Hundreds of men lined up at the nine doors, the thirty-minute time allotment thrown to the wind.

"Get them in, get them out," Mother told the panic-stricken girls. The little Chinese maid brought the girls rice balls to eat in their rooms, as a break in the unending line was an impossibility. Fifty, sixty, seventy men in one day. Min-He reached for her rice ball to eat while the men pumped away, one blending into the next. On the day after their departure, Mother closed the house down, her only humane gesture, allowing the girls a day to heal. On that day, even Fujiko and Hinata were quietly civil, all of them sisters in their agony.

Despite everything, what Min-He dreaded most were the nights Umeko was visited by Colonel Ushida. She would lie awake and listen to Umeko's muffled cries, her screams of pain and desperation. Min-He longed to protect Umeko, to save her from the horror behind her harrowing cries.

For months Min-He's attempts to discuss the Colonel were met with a brushing away by Umeko's hand or a quick change of the subject. After one Monday's medical exam, in which a clearly hungover and disinterested Dr. Kono glanced briefly at her chronically swollen genitals and sent her on her way with another tube of the same useless cream, Min-He and

Umeko sat playing Hanafuda cards in Umeko's room. She had recently acquired a child size card table and two petite backless stools.

"The table is lovely, Umeko."

The tiny table's dark mahogany finish was inlaid with cherry geometric triangles. Despite knowing exactly where she got it, Min-He asked anyway.

"Colonel Ishida brought it for me. It is beautiful, isn't it?" Umeko sighed. "He probably stole it from a Chinese family he killed, but I'm happy to have it." Umeko's casual nonchalance never failed to shock Min-He. She cleared her throat and brushed off the comment.

"Tell me about Colonel Ishida."

Umeko was quiet as she looked at her cards. She discarded a Matsu Crane card and laid it on the table.

"He ordered me."

"He ordered you to do what?"

"No, he ordered me. He placed an order for me. Not for me specifically, but for someone like me. He likes girls. Little girls. I was ten years old when a man came to my mother and told her the army needed children to work in a uniform factory. He said I'd be sewing buttons on jackets. He gave my mother 1000 yen. 1000 yen! We were starving. We had started eating the sap from pine bark from the woods near our house. My little brothers and sister were getting so thin. My mother cried but she sent me. She sold me."

Umeko eyes glazed over but she continued.

"I'm not angry with her. I would've done the same. She had to choose her four children over her one child. What choice did she have? The day I left, she cried and cried. She knew. She knew exactly what she was sending me into. I didn't know. I thought I was going to be sewing buttons. Can you imagine? What a stupid, ignorant child. But she knew.

"When I got here, Mother and Father took me to the waiting room, and they went into the dining room. I could hear them yelling. Father told her they couldn't keep me, that he wouldn't have a child work for them. I thought, 'What's wrong with a child sewing on buttons?' Can you believe it? I still didn't know. Then Colonel Ishida came in the front door. They were still yelling in the dining room and he walked over to me, kissed my cheek, and told me I was perfect. He stood and listened to them fight. He heard every word. He turned and walked out the door. They didn't even know he'd been there. A few minutes later, two policemen came and took Father away. He came back three days later with a broken arm."

Umeko stopped and stared at the door, as if seeing Father walk through, broken and bloody. Min-He laid down her cards and willed her to continue, barely breathing.

"That night, Colonel Ishida came to my room for the first time. I was eleven years old. He did terrible things, things you can't imagine, his sword...." Her voice trailed off. "He told me I would work for Mother and Father but three nights a week I would be his. Three nights a week I would be his special little girl.

"He brings me gifts, you see. All kinds of gifts: dolls, candy, games, storybooks, this little table. All gifts for little girls. And in exchange, I let him do terrible things. He gets every piece of me, and I get dolls and candy and to live. I get to live, Mio. That's the gift he keeps reminding me of."

They sat in silence for several minutes, Min-He not knowing what to say other than,

"I'm sorry."

"No! Let's not be sad. Our lives aren't long enough to spend them feeling sorry for ourselves. Let's play." She picked up her cards and began to sort. Min-He passed her a Momiji Normal card and played along quietly, unable to get Umeko's image out of her head: "his sword".

*****

Takao came into her life on a rainy Thursday afternoon. He was customer number 7 in a line of young privates who smelled worse than usual, tracking mud onto her freshly cleaned tatami mats. She preferred the privates, however. Most were quick and easy to get over with, many of them barely meeting her eyes. Some were so embarrassed they took off their shirts before they entered her room so she wouldn't be able to see their names. Others wanted to linger, to talk, to remind themselves of what it was like to flirt with a girl, even if that girl wasn't allowed to be coy and say no like the girls back home.

192

Many of the boys came back to her over and over and she got to know them, listening to their stories of family, and pets, and girlfriends, and home. Some didn't even want sex. They spent their quiet thirty minutes lying with her on her mattress, wanting to be held and wanting simply to talk. She realized their lives were not that unlike hers: they weren't their own. The Japanese army was cruel; regular beatings were normal, discipline was strict, and most weren't allowed to return home until the war was over. Vacations or furloughs were not part of the life of a private in the Japanese army. They, too, were trapped.

The last boy she saw before Takao came into her life had cried through his thick glasses, missing his mother. She patted his back and stroked his hair until he clumsily ejaculated and knocked over her lamp as he went out the door, apologizing. She was bent over, retrieving the toppled lamp when Takao entered the room.

"That's exactly the view I am paying for."

Min-He jumped, startled, and turned to see the man who had entered her room without knocking. She had never seen him before. After eight months, she had at least seen, if not repeatedly had sex with, most of the men who were permanently stationed at the base.

"You should knock before entering a woman's room," she scolded.

"I didn't know I needed to." He was a head taller than she and not any older. Stubble was forming on his cheeks and when he smiled, which he did just then, she noticed one of his front teeth was slightly chipped. The front of his uniform read "Hayashi".

"Well, Private Hayashi," she snapped, "Give me your ticket. We have thirty minutes."

He pulled the ticket from his front pocket and walked over to her shelf, where he placed it next to her jade dog. He picked up the figurine and turned it over in his hands.

"My sister has a dog like this at home. It must be fate."

"What do you mean 'fate'?"

"I saw your name on the wooden paddles at the front desk and I chose you because of your name. My father planted a row of cherry blossom trees in our yard the day before I was drafted. And now the dog."

"Mio's not my real name," she grumbled, then bit her lip. Mother repeatedly reminded them of the consequences if they spoke of home, spoke Korean, or revealed they were anything other than what they were now. She watched his face for a flash of anger but saw instead a shadow of sadness.

"Of course it's not. What's your real name?"

She ignored his question. Something about him was unsettling. His almond eyes hadn't left her face since he arrived.

"Come, your thirty minutes is passing by."

She was anxious to get done with him, to stop the nervousness fleeting through her.

"I'm not in any hurry," he said as his eyes scanned the room, her little dog still in his hands. "May I have this?" he asked.

"Of course not, you idiot" she snapped. "You should be giving me things."

She snatched her dog out of his hands and placed it back on her shelf. She looked back at him and glared at the smirk on his face. Her face flushed, realizing he was teasing her. For a moment, she saw her brother Hyo in his smile. She looked away.

"Let's get you taken care of."

She handed him a condom from the box on her shelf and sat down on her mattress, lifting her skirt, and opening her legs, beckoning him to join her. That usually moved the process along. He didn't move, just watched her, his face indecipherable.

"Sit with me," she said in her well-practiced purr, "I can help get you started."

He laughed.

"I don't need any help getting started. I'm just not sure I want to lie with you."

Min-He sighed. She had had this conversation before. A virgin, a homosexual, an impotent, a devout Catholic, ridiculed by their buddies until they finally agreed to come to the Pi House, where they could pretend to get laid. Or, on the opposite extreme, the narcissist who wanted her to beg for it. She hadn't gotten any of those vibes from this Private Hayashi, but sometimes there were surprises.

"I've never been to a prostitute before," he stated. Usually that statement, which she heard often, was accompanied by sheepishness, shyness, or guilt, but she was getting none of that from him. It was just a statement.

"We had a Pi house where I received my training, but I always managed to avoid it when the guys headed that direction. My girlfriend wouldn't have been too happy."

So, it was guilt then. She could work with guilt. Keep him talking about the girlfriend and the thirty minutes would be over before he realized they hadn't had sex. Her body could get a much-needed rest.

"Well, we can just talk then. What's her name?"

"Azami. She married my brother shortly after I was shipped to China."

So much for the guilt theory. She began to apologize, hoping to move him to tell a sob story for the remainder of his time, when he interrupted and asked,

"Why does a girl decide to become a prostitute for the Japanese army?"

Min-He's eyes narrowed, and her temper flared in a way she hadn't realized still existed.

"Well, Private Hayashi, I was told by a lieutenant colonel last week that I'm a soldier in the Japanese army. I'm one of the emperor's children and am no less important to him than the highest general in the army. So perhaps I do it for national pride. Or maybe I just like to fuck thousands of men."

She jumped up, pulled her skirt back over her thighs, snatched his ticket off her shelf and handed it back to him. She flung open the door. The soldier waiting in line outside leapt back in surprise.

"Goodbye, Private Hayashi. Trade your ticket in at the front desk for another girl. Fujiko and Hinata are delightful and will be sure to meet your every need." He stood, staring at her, his mouth half open.

"Go," she growled between her teeth. He walked past her and as he left, she saw that same smirk and slammed the door behind him.

She kicked the side of the mattress. How dare he assume she had decided to be a prostitute? Is that what he thought? That she CHOSE to be there? That they were all like those two Japanese witches who were there to profit? And who was he to ask her that question? And that smirk! Her palms stung as she dug her fingernails into them. She sat on the edge of her mattress, put her head in her hands, and waited for Mother. As soon as Private Hayashi returned the ticket, Mother would come in raging as she always did when a girl refused a man. The last time Min-He turned a man away, he had been so violently drunk he vomited all over her. Mother heard about it and beat her with a wooden ladle until it broke over her back.

Hoping to delay the inevitable, she invited in the jumpy soldier waiting in line. By dinner, Mother still hadn't come. All through dinner she watched Mother, but Min-He barely seemed to be on her radar. By the time the officer who spent the night left at 5:00AM, she knew the young man had not traded in his ticket. For a moment before she remembered she hated him, she was grateful.

The next day, as her fifth client of the day opened the door to leave, she saw Takao standing at the front of her line. He walked to the door, shut it, and knocked. Trying to suppress a laugh, she opened the door.

"I knocked this time. May I come in?" He handed her two tickets. She recognized the wrinkled blue ticket from the previous day.

"I suppose I owe you." She stepped aside and allowed him to enter.

"Why do you owe me?" he asked surprised.

"You didn't turn your ticket back in."

He looked confused.

"Why would that make you owe me?"

"It doesn't matter," she said, knowing she almost revealed too much. "Why are you back?"

"I have something for you." He reached into his pocket and pulled out a white porcelain arched Siamese cat. "To keep your dog company. And because I'm supposed to bring you things."

Min-He blushed.

"That... came out wrong. I'm sorry."

"No, I'm sorry. I offended you yesterday and didn't intend to. I'm here to make a peace offering and start over."

"Why? Why not just go to someone else? Why do you care if you make peace with me? You don't even know me."

"The cherry blossom tree, remember?" His face revealed his chipped-toothed smile, and she couldn't help but return it.

"Well, I suppose the four yen you've spent between yesterday and today can at least buy an acceptance of your peace offering."

He grinned at her sheepishly and pulled another ticket out of his pocket.

"Seven yen actually. I paid the man behind me in line three yen for his ticket."

She led him to her bed where she wished their hour would never come to an end. He talked of home, a village outside of Tokyo, where he and his father ran a drapery shop. He talked of endless marching and brutal discipline in the army, and long, lonely nights. She told him about her home by the sea and explained to him the truth of why a girl becomes a prostitute for the Japanese army. When the hour was long over, and the door rattled with the nagging of the next impatient soldier, the young man she now knew as Takao cupped her face in his hands and kissed her with a tenderness she had never known.

Min-He barely noticed as the spring days grew longer and the Chinese summer settled upon them. She thought only of Takao's next visit. Thirty precious, fleeting minutes. Thirty minutes where she was no longer a whore, a slave to a foreign army, but a teenager in love. She loved to touch his face, hold him close. He brought her gifts of candy, soap, and blankets. At first, he visited daily but she grew concerned when his visits became more sporadic: five times a week, three times a week. When seven days passed without a visit, she panicked. She asked every private who visited her, had he seen him, had he gone off to battle, where was he? On the eighth day when Takao finally appeared, she questioned him, terrified of the answer. He blushed and hung his head.

"I didn't have the money to buy the tickets to see you. I've spent my salary, my poker winnings, I've even taken other soldier's latrine duty to get the money to buy tickets. I don't know what else to do."

Waves of relief flooded her. He hadn't been avoiding her. They just needed to get creative. A plan developed. The room next to her, the one which was meant to be Soon-Yee's, had remained empty since her arrival. Takao would come in with a large group of customers and wait for Father and Mother to be distracted at the reception desk. He'd then sneak around and blend in with the lines of waiting soldiers. Leaning against the wooden door, smoking a cigarette, he'd slip into the empty room in the chaos of a thirty-minute shift change. There he'd wait, until Min-He knocked on the wall, signaling she had ended early. He often bribed his friends by taking their latrine or kitchen duties: two friends would buy tickets, take fifteen minutes each with Min-He, leaving him the remaining thirty minutes with her.

They talked, and laughed, and made love. He was gentle and careful with her. She felt nothing physically, not knowing it was possible to for a woman to feel physical pleasure, but she loved pleasing him, wanting him more and more so she could be part of him, so he could possess her. She thought less and less of home and even less of escape. Everything but him was just a deafening buzz around her. She wanted him completely.

"Someday," she said one afternoon as Takao slid back on his wrinkled sand jodhpurs, "we'll have to invent a story to tell our children about how we met."

She brushed her hair with the soft horsehair brush he had brought for her. Her black tresses had grown to her shoulders, the schoolgirl bob nearly vanished. Takao didn't respond. Min-He stopped brushing and turned to him. The silence was an impervious fog. Takao's almond eyes darted away.

"Min-He," he said. Her heart quivered at the sound of her Korean name. "I don't expect there to be a someday."

"What do you mean?"

"I don't expect to survive the war."

He spoke with such simplicity, so consummately, she wondered if she misunderstood his words.

"I don't understand."

"Min-He, I'm a Japanese soldier. I've been lucky these past months to be stationed here, to have avoided the front. That won't last forever. I love you, but we have to live for now. I knew it was fate I met you, just as I know it's my fate to be killed in battle." He kissed her lightly on the top of the head. She buried her face in his jacket, the brass flowered button embedding into her cheek.

"Don't say that, never say that. You're all I have to live for. You're all I have to hope for."

He knelt beside her and removed the brush from her hand, kissed her palm and placed it on his cheek.

"It's ok. It will be ok. Shh...let's talk no more of it, let's talk no more."

She felt relief at his soothing tone, sure he didn't mean what he said. It wasn't until after he left, she realized his words were no comfort at all.

*****

A unit of kamikaze soldiers came through camp as the late fall wind began to redden the cheeks of the line of soldiers awaiting their services. Mother closed the house for the day to everyone but the kamikaze unit. Mother spoke to the girls with awe in her voice. No tickets were to be taken. The kamikazes could come and go for free the entire day or night. They could do what they wanted, when they wanted, and with whom they wanted it. The kamikazes were somber and hard. They were rough, brutal in their sex acts, not unlike the officers except they came in drunk, rowdy, and cold. They refused to wear condoms, unconcerned with STDs.

After an exhausting hour with a kamikaze with the bare fuzz of a late adolescent mustache, Min-He asked as he rolled off her mattress,

"Why? Why would you choose to take your life?"

"I'm happy to give my life so my mother doesn't fall into the hands of the enemy."

"I doubt your mother could imagine a fate worse than the death of her son."

"As a third son, I know my brothers and their wives will care for her. My mission will ensure her safety. I will bring her honor. I'm proud to serve my emperor. My death will decimate the American ships trying to destroy our empire and will bring a victory to Japan. My death will be a beautiful and honorable death."

He wrapped his white scarf around his neck. He tapped the rising sun flag emblazoned on his right sleeve with his left hand and his shout echoed off the wooden walls,

"Long live the emperor!"

As the next Kamikaze stormed into the room and rolled her onto her stomach, Min-He thought of Soon-Yee. She died trying to escape the same Japanese empire these men were killing themselves to protect. Min-He loved a man, an enemy to her family, who was expecting to die for the same empire that forced her into the hell she was living. As the kamikaze bit into the back of her shoulder, she muffled her cry into the mattress and wondered if her own survival was worth it.

*****

Umeko poked at the cabbage on her plate. Dark shadows lurked below her eyes and her typically flushed cheeks were sallow. Min-He kicked her gently under the dinner table to get her attention. Min-He had come late to dinner, relishing a few minutes with Takao, who had snuck in when the last NCO left for the evening. He had evening guard duty at the base so could only stay long enough for a kiss.

Mother gave her a scowl when she slid into the dining room ten minutes late and she sat down to her now cold plate. Looking at Umeko, Min-He was immediately concerned. She had paid little attention to the girl lately. Between long lines of clients and Takao, Min-He had barely noticed the drastic change in Umeko's appearance. She gulped down her stale cabbage, took Umeko by the arm and led her back to her room.

"Are you sick? What's going on?"

"I'm fine. What do you care anyway?"

Min-He winced at the words, knowing she deserved them.

"Umeko, I'm so sorry. I haven't been there for you. I've been with Takao so much. He's the only thing keeping me going in this place."

"Well, what's keeping me going? Nothing, that's what. Go back to your own room." The little girl began to cry, hiding her face in her hands. Her emaciated body trembled with sobs.

"I'm so sorry, Umeko, please tell me what's going on. If you're sick, I'll get Mother and she can call Dr. Kono. Please."

Min-He curled next to the sobbing girl on her bed and pulled her into her arms. Umeko stiffened at her touch. Then, when Min-He refused to back away, melted into her, succumbing to the tears.

"It's the Colonel," she whispered. "He's coming more often now, nearly every day. Before, when it was just a few times a week, I could do it. But now, I can't do it anymore, Mio. I'm not going to make it."

Guilt flooded Min-He. Umeko's cries had become such a normal part of her existence, Min-He sometimes slept right through them. She hadn't noticed the increase in frequency. Shame pierced through her.

"If I could have even just one night away from him, I feel like I could pull myself together again. I've tried to ask Mother and the doctor, but they said there's nothing they can do. He's the Colonel. He gets what he wants."

Min-He's anger squashed the guilt and shame in her chest. She would not let this bastard destroy her Umeko.

A knock on her own door broke her concentration. It was her first officer of the night. She called out the window,

"Go in. I'll be right over."

She turned back to Umeko who was wiping her nose on the sleeve of her robe.

"I'm going to take care of this, Umeko. I'll think of something."

She left Umeko sitting on her bed, shaking her head in doubt.

After the second officer of the evening departed whistling a Japanese gunka war song that grated through her, Min-He stationed herself at her window, waiting for her next client to arrive. She watched as the snow melted, sloshing off the tin roof into a dreary March slush. When Min-He saw the officer approaching, she exhaled in relief. It was Major Watanabe, a relatively amiable soldier who occasionally brought her tins of fruit-flavored Sakuma Drops and flasks of warm sake. She stuck her finger down her throat as he knocked. She vomited, making sure her retching was loud and especially awful. She bent over and pulled open the door, clutching her stomach.

"Oh, Major Watanabe. Please come in. I'm not feeling very well tonight, but I don't want that to prevent us from being together."

She opened the door widely, so he could see her pile of vomit on the tatami mat.

"I'll just get that cleaned up."

"No," he said, taking a step back. "You're sick. I'll just come back tomorrow."

"Oh no, please, it'll be fine." She turned her back on him and made herself retch again.

"No, no, it's ok." He began to back away.

"But Major Watanabe," she said, her eyes welling with tears, "if you return your ticket, I'll get in trouble with Mother and Father. You must come see me."

"I won't return my ticket tonight. Perhaps we can work something out another night where you can make it up to me." He smiled crookedly.

She gave him her best seductive smile.

"Of course. Thank you. I owe you." She bowed to him as he left.

It worked. She sat in front of the bamboo-framed mirror a thickskulled lieutenant had brought as a gift some months ago. Dipping heavily into the makeup pots, she transformed her face into the image of a porcelain china doll: round cheeks, long, dark lashes, fuchsia lips. She gathered her hair into two long pigtails and studied her image. She was a schoolgirl who had stolen her mother's cosmetic case. At eighteen, she didn't look ten, but maybe she could pass for thirteen. Was it enough? She bit her swollen pink lip. It would have to be.

She planted herself by the window and waited. She counted on the Colonel coming later than 11:00. Since he usually stayed the whole night, he rarely came immediately after Umeko's 10:00 client. Min-He watched Umeko's 10:00 leave. As Min-He eyed her own client approaching, she stepped outside and banged on Umeko's door. Umeko opened it at the same time Min-He's lieutenant arrived.

"I am so sorry, Lieutenant Enoki," she gushed. "Tonight, I'm ill and am likely contagious so Umeko is more than happy to serve you. I hope you find that acceptable. She told me how much she enjoys your company, so I do hope you find pleasure in her."

Umeko gasped as Min-He bulldozed the flustered lieutenant through Umeko's door.

"What are you doing?" Umeko whispered frantically. "The Colonel will be here any minute."

"Trust me."

Min-He leaned against the frame of her doorway and waited. Despite the chill of the March air, her makeup drooped with sweat, and she dabbed her forehead with the inside of her blouse collar. White oil tinged the pink cotton. Minutes later, the colonel turned the corner. As he approached Umeko's door, he eyed Min-He suspiciously.

"Hello, Colonel Ishida. May I have a moment of your time?"

He seemed taken aback by her brazenness but said nothing. Ignoring the churning of panic in her chest, Min-He continued.

"Colonel, I've noticed how much time you spend with Umeko and I have to say my jealousy has gotten the best of me." She poked out her lower lip. "I did something very bad tonight and I hope you won't be too angry with me."

She bent her head, looking down at the ground then raised her eyes to him and gazed at him through her painted eyelashes.

His mouth turned up slightly, seemingly humored.

"What was this bad thing you did?"

"I've been so jealous Umeko gets you to herself that I tricked her and Lieutenant Enoki. I told them I was sick and, without telling Umeko, I told him he'd be seeing her tonight. She begged me not to do it, but it was too late. Please don't be angry with me."

She started to sniffle. The Colonel paused. Min-He was sure he could hear her heart beating and see the beads of sweat forming on her upper lip. She clasped her hands together to hide their trembling.

"Come child, let's talk about it inside."

He pushed past her, through her door. She gulped a breath of air. It worked. For tonight, Umeko was safe. And for tonight, Min-He would endure her hell.

As the door rattled shut behind Min-He, the Colonel seized a fistful of one of her ponytails and hurled her onto the mattress. The right side of her head exploded with pain. She reached to her ear and was surprised to find the ponytail still intact, sure he had ripped it from her head. The Colonel hovered above her, in full uniform.

"Undress," he ordered. Her hands shook as she unbuttoned her pink blouse. She raised her skirts to her hips.

"All of it off."

She pushed the skirt over her knees and removed her panties. She lay before him stark naked, a rabbit in his trap. He removed his belt and dangled it above her breasts.

"Not quite a little girl," he commented, frowning. "All the same..." he murmured beneath his breath.

Min-He could barely hear him. She watched the black belt sway back and forth above her. Without warning, he flung the belt back like a whip and it lashed across her bare breasts. She yelped and curled into the fetal position, her hands across her searing breasts. She could hear him remove his clothes, pants hitting the floor, jacket rustling.

"Turn around," he ordered.

She unfurled herself and turned from her side to lie facing him. He was naked, a long scar like a sash across his stomach, his arms taut at his side, his right hand still holding the belt. His penis lay flaccid between his legs. Min-He knew this was a bad sign. A powerful man who was unable to perform was a dangerous man. He lifted his right hand and she saw it was not his belt he was holding, but a silver sword. Her breathing stopped as he began to trace her body with the tip of the blade. It moved, lightly touching her, up her leg, across her stomach, mimicking the pattern of the scar on his chest, then moving across her chest. He lingered on her breasts, tracing the red welt that had risen across both breasts. He moved the sword up her neck and flicked her hair. He laughed at himself, a hollow chuckle of self-pleasure. Bile rose in Min-He's mouth. She needed to get him in her bed to end this. She began to speak.

"Would you like to lie..."

"Shut up. You do not speak."

He spoke through his teeth. His face reddened, wrinkles forming around his pursed lips. He took the sword to the welt on her breast and flicked his hand. Blood trickled from her nipple. She cried out. He smiled. The sword swiped down to her stomach, back and forth across her belly, in the exact shape of the scar across the Colonel's chest. Eight, ten, twenty times. Her body tense, she waited for the cut. Instead, after an eon of minutes, he moved the sword down. He traced her pubic hair then moved lower. He tapped the sword at her inner thigh, forcing her legs open with the threat.

"Please," she whispered, "please no".

"I said shut up," he said, still smiling.

Min-He began to cry, silent tears ran down her face. She fought them, knowing the pleasure they would bring him, but they were out of her control. Tears turned to screams as he cut her. Tiny sharp nicks across her labia. Each cut brought him more and more pleasure. When she opened her eyes she could see his penis, now erect, looming over her. Blood spots filled the sheet beneath her. His eyes glistened at the blood. He moved the sword back down her legs.

He loomed above her, moving his sword to every spot of her body. Fifteen, twenty minutes passed with the sword just tracing, the tip barely touching, then unexpectedly, another cut. Her breasts, her arms, her anus, her back. Two hours passed before he finally mounted her. She screamed with the pain from the cuts. It was over in seconds. He pulled out and slapped her face. She didn't move.

As he dressed, he eyed her, his mouth forming a poisonous grin. Lifting the sword, he carved a thin slice across her stomach, mirroring his own. He turned to leave, and Min-He's pain merged into anger then satisfaction. He was leaving now. Leaving, and she had protected Umeko. Whatever her pain, Umeko had endured so much more. She had protected her from one night of his hell.

The door slammed behind him and Min-He had just begun to breathe again when she heard a shout from next door. She sat upright in bed. No. No. She heard his laughter, his sinister hollow laughter, and leaned over her bed and vomited.

She curled up into a ball and wept, more sorrowful than the day she arrived, the worst moment of her life. He had left her room and still gone to Umeko. It had all been for nothing. All the pain, for nothing. Umeko would still suffer at his hands tonight. They had lost. Hope was lost.

# Marianne
## Munich, Germany
## October 1944

Eric returned to Munich just as the autumn leaves were beginning to fall. The air raid sirens, now a regular feature of their daily life, had quieted upon morning and the family came up from a sleepless night in the shelter and found Eric sitting in the living room reading the paper completely unfazed by the allied bombing, as if he had never left. The girls ran to their father, squealing in delight. Hans gave him his loudest 'Heil Hitler' and was rewarded with a hearty pat on the shoulder. Marianne stood back and watched, unsure how she felt. She hadn't seen her husband in fifteen months. He was thinner, his face drawn, the skin beneath his eyes puffy and sagging. She barely knew him.

Eric sent the kids to the front room to pilfer his suitcase for treasure and approached Marianne. He took her hands in his and pulled her close.

"Oh, my Marianne, I've missed you. I believe you are more beautiful than the day I left."

She tried to feel warmth and compassion but felt only emptiness. She hadn't missed him at all.

"Oh Eric," she sighed, having nothing else to say.

That night, their lovemaking was sterile. Marianne thought of all the other women she knew he'd been with, thought of Andreas and Franz, thought of what her father had told her years ago about her cousin's dead child.

As Eric lay snoring afterwards, she curled to the farthest end of the bed and remembered her false promise to Andreas.

*****

"I need you to help me with something."

The children were at school. Martha had left hot coffee and rolls before she left for the market to prepare for a special homecoming dinner. Eric planned to go into the SS office that morning, barely 24 hours since coming home after being gone over a year. The day before, they discussed his taking a few days of vacation to spend with the children, but Eric waved the idea aside. Family bonding could wait until they had won the war.

Marianne raised her eyebrows but said nothing about what was obvious to so many around her: this war was a long way from being won. Every evening for the past five months, she had secretly turned the dial on their radio from the marked spot assigned to the Party-approved radio station. At the lowest audible volume, she moved the dial to the BBC and listened with her ear to the radio to the war report from the allies. They were in direct contrast to the Reich's own reports. Listening to illegal radio stations could send her to a KZ and she carefully turned the dial back to its marked spot after each broadcast.

Eric didn't turn down the volume on the radio.

"What?" he asked.

Marianne walked over and flipped the radio off.

"I was listening to that!"

"I'm sure they can fill you in at the office this afternoon. I need to ask you something."

She took a deep breath. She would keep this promise.

"A friend of someone I know was sent to a Konzentrationslager three months ago. Can you find out about him?"

Eric stared at her.

"Who do you know that was sent to a KZ?"

"Eric, we know lots of people who have been sent to KZs. The Cohen's from the butchery, Bella and Horst Freimann who gave us dance lessons before our wedding. Don't act like I don't know that people are being sent away."

"No need to get all excited, Marianne," Eric sighed. "Who are you asking me about?"

She spoke carefully.

"I did some business with a man who ran an art gallery in Schwabing. I bought a couple of pieces of artwork from him. His friend, Franz Uhler, was sent to a KZ."

"What did he do?"

"He was an artist."

"No, Marianne, what did he do to get sent a KZ?"

"I believe he's a homosexual."

"Why do you care about what happens to a homosexual? You shouldn't be getting involved with people like that, Marianne. There are plenty of reputable art dealers in this city who aren't abhorrent."

He flipped the radio back on and leaned back in his chair. Marianne reached over to the radio and snapped it back off. He looked up at her in surprise. Her hands were shaking. She couldn't tell if it was anger or fear. She pushed forward.

"I didn't ask you to advise me on where to buy art. I asked you if you could help me. I've been alone here for months, Eric. All I have are the children who are never around, Martha, who hates me, and a bunch of women from Frauenschaft who only talk about cooking and how perfect their ten children are. I had a few friendly conversations about art with this man and I'd like to know what happened to him."

He stared at her for several moments without speaking. She met his eyes and waited, her stomach in knots. But there was more.

"And there's something else too."

"Really? Searching for your schwul friend isn't enough?"

"I need you to find out what happened to my cousin Louisa's daughter Brigitte."

"Brigitte died in a mental institution, Marianne. That was years ago."

"No, I want to know what really happened. Louisa got a telegram saying Brigitte died from pneumonia. Is that true?"

"Marianne, how am I supposed to know if she died from pneumonia or not? Am I a physician? Was I there? That was in Vienna, Marianne. We live in Munich."

She hated how he kept repeating her name, as if he were talking to an insolent child.

"What do you think happened to her, Eric?" She emphasized his name. "What most likely happened to her?"

He let out an audible sigh.

"Marianne, the fact you even know to ask, tells me you already know the answer."

"So, it's true then?"

"I'm truly sorry for Louisa's loss. However, for the Reich to prosper, we need only the healthiest and strongest to propagate. Marianne, I don't know what has gotten into you. I think it's sweet you care for the mentally challenged and the homosexuals. You always had a soft heart. However, like feeding those prisoners, asking these questions are only going to get you in trouble."

Eric got up from the table and turned to leave. He stopped before reaching the door.

"I'll find out about your homosexual friend, Marianne, as a favor to you because you're my wife. But this needs to be the end of the questions. You need to turn your attention to our children and the running of this home."

*****

Martha proudly delivered the steaming pot of pork and tomato stew to the table. Martha beamed at Eric and Marianne rolled her eyes. One-pot casseroles were considered superior by the Führer for their economy. But when Eric was gone, Martha refused to make them, calling them peasant crap. Now that he was back, she glowingly put them on the table like a good German housekeeper.

Eric smiled at her briefly then reverted to a scowl when he turned to Marianne. An hour before, they had argued.

"This is my family homecoming dinner. Why does your father have to be here?"

"Because he's part of your family. If I had known you hadn't wanted him here, I wouldn't have invited him. But it's too late now. I can't very well uninvite him."

So, Eric scowled through dinner. Marianne encouraged the children to talk about school. Hans spoke extensively about the Hitler Youth and his aspirations to join the army. Christa chatted about her role in the school's winter pageant. Erika, however, had her own role to play.

"I have news."

Marianne's heart sank. Looking at her fifteen-year-old daughter's face, she knew.

"Well don't keep us in suspense, darling. What's your news?" Eric smiled at her.

"I'm getting married!"

Marianne breathed again. Getting married she could live with. She could delay a wedding—force her to wait a year and Erika would forget about whoever she was in love with today.

"And I'm going to have a baby."

Eric's face lit up.

"Congratulations, my darling! It will be wonderful to have a baby in the family again! Who's the lucky man? A soldier for the Führer, I imagine?"

"Oh yes!"

Marianne stared blankly at her daughter as she began to rattle on about the father of her child. Klaus Adler was at the front. They would marry as soon as he returned. The family had never met him. He was on leave in Munich when she met him three months before. She had known him two weeks before he was shipped to Russia. Maybe her father could find him there? Klaus didn't yet know about the baby, but Erika was sure they would marry when she told him. Marianne was incredulous at her naivety. They would never see this boy again.

Martin began a soft chuckle in the middle of Erika's speech. Marianne glared at her father, forbidding him to comment. He took another bite of spaetzle and shook his head. But Martin stayed quiet until the children were excused from the table.

"Well, from my own experience, I must tell you that grandparenting is a joy. Congratulations to you both."

"Thank you, Martin," Eric said, oblivious to the blatant sarcasm.

"And I'm sure this young man will return to Erika, thrilled to become a father to the child of a girl he knew for a week."

"Every German child is a blessing, Martin. Whether or not this boy returns is irrelevant. Marianne will help Erika raise the child."

"I didn't hear you ask Marianne how she feels about that."

"Father, leave it," Marianne whispered.

Martin ignored her and continued,

"Erika said this boy shipped out to Russian front. That doesn't sound so good for him."

"Whatever sacrifices the father of our grandchild makes are for the good of Germany." Eric's voice was beginning to rise.

"Ah, yes, for the good of Germany. And what about your son? He seems awfully intent on joining the army. Eric, are you planning to sacrifice your only son to the Führer?"

Eric's glare bore into Martin.

"Hans is a bright, capable young man who can take care of himself in any situation. I don't think it will be any kind of sacrifice to have him serve our Führer."

Marianne, sensing the danger this conversation was heading into, quickly changed the subject.

"How did you find the office today, Eric? Is it much changed since you left?"

Eric squinted at Martin, but conceded the peace to his wife.

"Not really. I ran into Standartenführer Scarf today. He said he saw you at the clinic a couple of months ago. He asked me to greet you both."

Marianne winced at the man's name and his newly promoted title.

"I thought you hated Scharf."

"I did, a long time ago. But he was sent to Kiev to inspect my unit last month and we saw eye to eye on a few things. He's been promoted and is clearing the way for my promotion as well. I may as well announce this now. I am being promoted to Obersturmbannführer at the end of the month. That is largely due to Standartenführer Scharf's approval of my unit's operations."

"Congratulations, my dear, that's wonderful."

Marianne felt confused. Pride and panic rose in her at the same time. Why couldn't she just be happy for her husband?

"Oh yes, Eric, congratulations. Tell me, of what operations did Standartenführer Scharf so overwhelmingly approve?"

"You know I can't talk about that, Martin. It's classified information."

Martin smiled at him. "Of course it is."

Eric ignored him and turned his attention to Marianne.

"I'll be returning to Kiev in November and would like to take Hans with me. He won't serve in my unit as it's a specialized operations unit, but he can serve under a friend of mine in a festung unit in the area. It will allow him to serve but will keep him off the front until the end of the war."

Marianne sat frozen, unable to fully comprehend what her husband was saying. Martin interjected, breaking the silence.

"Hang onto Hans for a few more months, my dear, and this will all be over. He won't need to fight."

"After the war, it will be far better for Hans to have served in the military. Honorable service will open many doors for him in the Reich."

Martin laughed.

"Oh, Eric, as usual, you are inexplicably single minded. It will be far better for Hans to have NOT served in the military after this war comes to its inevitable conclusion."

Marianne was stunned. She knew her father was reckless, she knew his opinions, but to imply the war might be lost was treasonous. Eric stood up and threw his bowl at Martin, hitting him square in his head.

"You are defeatist swine. If you weren't my wife's father, I'd arrest you on the spot and send your treasonous ass to a concentration camp where you belong. Get out of my house. You are to have no more contact with my wife and children!"

Martin rose and spoke softly, his eye beginning to swell from the impact of the bowl. Brown stew dripped from the front of his shirt.

"I'll stay out of your home, Obersturmbannführer Hofmann. But you need to open your eyes. A year from now, I won't be the one worrying about living the rest of my life behind bars."

Marianne watched as Eric's eyes flickered. Something in Martin's words hit home. Then just as quickly, his eyes flashed back to anger. The front door slammed behind Martin, and Eric turned on Marianne.

"Your father is no longer welcome here. If he steps with 500 meters of this home, I'll have his ass hauled to Dachau. And I expect you to behave as the wife of an SS Obersturmbannführer. You will no longer gallivant around this city associating with lowlife scum. I expect you to restrict your days to kinder, kuche, and kirsche. You will give your full attention to the children, the kitchen, or the church. I don't know what nonsense was happening while I was away, but it will not continue."

"I don't know what you are talking about, Eric. I haven't been gallivanting..."

"Shut up, Marianne. Don't you think it was humiliating to find out from my inferiors that you've been working at an art gallery for a couple of homosexuals? That you have been skipping Frauenshaft meetings, sneaking around the city, and neglecting our children to do all of this behind my back? And then Scharf tells me the same day he saw you at your father's clinic, one of the criminals disappeared and you were seen at his gallery. You were also seen leaving the Bahnhof that same night with Christa. I lied to him, Marianne, and told him I had sent you to Nuremburg that day to get a gift for Hans. Thank God they didn't have the sense to put it all together before then and follow you to the train station. Where did you go that day, Marianne?"

"Christa and I went to Nuremburg. She wanted to see the castle."

"Funny. That's exactly what she said when I asked her. Nice work, Marianne. Teaching her to lie with that sweet, straight face. Maybe she can work for the Gestapo someday."

"We're not lying," she said weakly.

"Enough. In fact, I don't want to know the truth. Knowing the truth will likely put me in a KZ, which is where you're headed if this bullshit doesn't stop. Scharf gave me your file so it wouldn't get into the wrong hands. But that's the last I'm doing for you. I'm done protecting you, Marianne."

He threw the chair aside and stormed past Marianne to the dining room doorway. He whipped back around to her.

"And one more thing. You don't have to worry about your faggot friend anymore. He was shot at Buchenwald trying to escape."

*****

214

Marianne was finished crying. She had cried for a full day in her room after hearing the news about Franz. Eric scoffed at her for being emotional over someone so insignificant. He sarcastically offered to buy her a kitten to replace the lost friendship. She hurled a vase at his laughing back. She missed but was satisfied when Eric sliced his bare foot on the remaining shards later that evening.

Eric and Hans spent much of the next month together. Hans stopped attending high school and left for the SS headquarters with Eric every morning. Many nights they came in after midnight or not at all. Marianne imagined them in brothels and at strip shows and was surprised to find herself feeling indifferent. A year ago, when Eric told her about the Lebensborn program, it had nearly driven her insane. Today, she didn't care who he bedded.

She met her father for lunch at the café in Schwabing where she first introduced him to Andreas. Eric had only said Martin couldn't come to the house. He didn't say she couldn't see him outside of the house. Still, Marianne found herself looking over her shoulder. After lunch, she asked her father to drop her at the corner near the house, fearing his being any closer would set off Eric. On the drive home, she told Martin about Franz. He wasn't surprised but was deeply saddened.

"Have you heard anything about Andreas? Do you think he's safe?" she asked him.

"I've heard nothing. I've asked no questions of my contact. It's safer not to know."

Marianne sighed. Exactly what Eric said.

"Maybe he's lying to me about Franz. He could have said that to hurt me."

"Maybe." Martin looked doubtful.

"Eric said the SS had a file on me. Scharf gave it to him so he could protect me. Maybe it has information about Franz and Andreas. Do you think it's in his office?"

"Stay out of it, Marianne. Nothing good can come of finding it. Even if you find out what you want to know, there's nothing you can do to change it."

He pulled the car to the corner, and she leaned over and kissed her father's cheek.

"Marianne, be careful."

She nodded and shut the car door.

*****

Eric never locked his office. In their seventeen years of marriage, he hadn't needed to. Marianne had never taken an interest in his day-to-day work. In the fifteen months he was gone, she had entered the office only once, to use the hefty metal stapler for one of Erika's volunteer pamphlet distribution drives.

The girls ate breakfast and left with Martha for school. Eric and Hans departed in the Mercedes, both men impressive and intimidating in their uniforms. Hans was anxious to trade the tan shirt and youth-designated armband of his Hitler Youth uniform for the black boots of the Wehrmacht army. Eric was taking Hans on a tour of the SS facility and KZ at Dachau. Any other day Marianne would have objected to Han's exposure to a prison, but today she was just relieved they were getting out of the house.

Despite knowing the house was empty, Marianne crept silently up the stairs. She gently pushed open the door of Eric's office. His heavy oak desk sat in the middle of the room framed with bookshelves lined with military history and strategy texts, a battered copy of Mein Kampf given to them on their wedding day, and dozens of old law school textbooks interspersed with the works of Plato, Nietzsche, and Heidegger. She walked slowly and carefully to the desk and slid open the right-side drawer, bulging to the brim with files. The desk drawer clicked audibly as it opened and every muscle in her body froze. She took a deep breath and reminded herself that no one was home. She had a cover story prepared: she was simply looking for the receipts from last year's Frauenschaft orphanage fundraiser. But she knew Eric was unlikely to buy it. Martha certainly would not.

She thumbed through the files – personnel files of soldiers, supply lists, travel documents; but nothing with her name or any documentation of Andreas or Franz. She eased the drawer shut, cringing at each click, and moved swiftly to the left side drawer. Stacks of memos, a weapons inventory--- she smiled at a few of Christa's drawings interspersed with a map of Western Russia. But nothing she was looking for.

She leaned back in Eric's mammoth ebony leather chair and surveyed the room. Despite her disappointment, she felt a brief glimmer of relief. Her father was right. Even if she found information about Andreas and Franz, what was she going to do with it? She rose from the chair, pushed it in, and tripped over Eric's briefcase.

The briefcase. She stared at it like a snake in the laundry, afraid to touch it, afraid to leave it alone. She heaved the briefcase onto the desk. She reopened the desk drawers and felt around the rims and edges for a sign of a key. Nothing. She scanned the desk and overturned the pen holder, toppled the marble paperweights, and rifled through the wooden document box Hans had made for him at youth camp. Her frustration was turning to anger.

The possibility Eric took the key with him discouraged her and she slumped back into the leather chair and glared at the photograph of Hitler staring back from the desktop. It was in the gold frame she had given Eric two Christmases ago. It once held a photograph of her. In an irritated fit, she took her thumb and forefinger and flicked the frame off the desk. It landed with a clatter on the carpeted floor. She leaned over the desk to determine the damage and was irritated it hadn't broken. A flash of silver gleamed next to the grim-faced Führer. The key. Marianne smiled.

Marianne flipped open the latch. Inside the grey silk interior lay three folders, all labeled with initials she didn't understand. She leafed through them, finding hand-sketched maps and more mundane military reports. Nothing here. She began to close the briefcase, when her eye caught the corner of a pale yellow folder peeking out of the lining of the briefcase cover. She glanced at the door, paranoid, and slipped the yellow folder out of the lining. The folder was dated January 1943, shortly before Eric arrived home from his first long tour, over a year and a half ago. It clearly had nothing to do with Andreas and Franz. CONFIDENTIAL was stamped forebodingly on the front. She glanced at the door again, opened the yellow folder, and began to read.

EINZATZGRUPPEN C DIVISION 1  OCTOBER 1942
MAJOR ERIC HOFMANN'S REPORT TO SUPERIORS ON PROGRESS OF EINSAZTGRUPPEN C DIVISION 1
CONFIDENTIAL REICH BUSINESS
COMPLETE LIST OF EXECUTIONS CARRIED OUT BY EINSAZTGRUPPEN C DIVISION 1 THROUGH 1 DECEMBER 1941

ON MY INSTRUCTIONS AND ORDERS THE FOLLOWING LIQUIDATIONS WERE CONDUCTED BY LITHUANIAN PARTISANS:

4.8.41 DOVNIK  416 JEWS, 47 JEWESSES    463
6.8.41 DOVNIK  JEWS    2,514

FOLLOWING THE FORMATION OF A RAIDING SQUAD UNDER THE COMMAND OF MYSELF SS-HAUPTSTURMFUHRER HOFMANN AND 10-12 RELIABLE MEN FROM THE EINSATZKOMMANDO C DIVISION 1, THE FOLLOWING LIQUIDATIONS WERE CONDUCTED IN COOPERATION WITH LITHUANIAN PARTISANS:

18.8.41 DOVNIK  689 JEWS, 402 JEWESSES, 1 POLE (F.), 711 JEWISH INTELLECTUALS FROM GHETTO IN REPRISAL FOR SABOTAGE   1,812
19.8.41 SEPULKA 298 JEWS, 255 JEWESSES, 1 POLITRUK, 88 JEWISH CHILDREN, 1 RUSSIAN COMMUNIST   645
22.8.41 ALTOYA   MENTALLY SICK: 269 MEN, 227 WOMEN, 48 CHILDREN 544
23.8.41 OBEDONSK 1,312 JEWS, 4,602 JEWESSES, 1,609 JEWISH CHILDREN 7,523
24.8.41 KRETIK 466 JEWS, 440 JEWESSES, 1,020 JEWISH CHILDREN 1,926
25.8.41 ZADAYAK  112 JEWS, 627 JEWESSES, 421 JEWISH CHILDREN 1,160
25.8.41 SEPIRA  230 JEWS, 275 JEWESSES, 159 JEWISH CHILDREN 664
26.8.41 TOKSKA 767 JEWS, 1,113 JEWESSES, 1 LITH. COMM., 687 JEWISH CHILDREN, RUSS. COMM. (F.)    2,569
28.8.41 KRAWLAK  402 JEWS, 738 JEWESSES, 209 JEWISH CHILDREN 1349
26.8.41 JONIKVA  ALL JEWS, JEWESSES, AND JEWISH CHILDREN 1,911
27.8.41 DAHGA   ALL JEWS, JEWESSES, AND JEWISH CHILDREN 1,078
27.8.41 VINIAK   212 JEWS, 4 RUSSIAN POW'S 216
27.8.41 KEPOLNIA  47 JEWS, 165 JEWESSES, 143 JEWISH CHILDREN  355
28.8.41 UBITA    76 JEWS, 192 JEWESSES, 134 JEWISH CHILDREN 402
28.8.41 ROKAWKSA 710 JEWS, 767 JEWESSES, 599 JEWISH CHILDREN 2,076
29.8.41 SISRUMSKI   20 JEWS, 567 JEWESSES, 197 JEWISH CHILDREN 784
29.8.41 ULEANDA  582 JEWS, 1,731 JEWESSES, 1,469 JEWISH CHILDREN 3,782
31.8.41 TUSAKA   233 JEWS    233

4.9.41 GHETTO 1   315 JEWS, 712 JEWESSES, 818 JEWISH CHILDREN (REPRISAL AFTER GERMAN POLICE OFFICER SHOT IN GHETTO) 1,845
9.9.41 GHETTO 1      2,007 JEWS, 2,920 JEWESSES, 4,273 JEWISH CHILDREN (MOPPING UP GHETTO OF SUPERFLUOUS JEWS)   9,200
11.9.41 LOZIAKNA  485 JEWS, 511 JEWESSES, 539 JEWISH CHILDREN  1,535
12.9.41 WOZKAS  36 JEWS, 48 JEWESSES, 31 JEWISH CHILDREN  115
14.9.41 GHETTO 2  1,159 JEWS, 1,600 JEWESSES, 175 JEWISH CHILDREN (RESETTLERS FROM BERLIN, MUNICH AND FRANKFURT AM MAIN   2,934
15.9.41 GHETTO 2 693 JEWS, 1,155 JEWESSES, 152 JEWISH CHILDREN (RESETTLERS FROM VIENNA AND BRESLAU)   2,000

EK 1 DETACHMENT IN DOSELBERG IN THE PERIOD 13.9-21.9.41: 9,012 JEWS, JEWESSES AND JEWISH CHILDREN, 573 ACTIVE COMM.   9,585
25.9.41 MADYNPOL 1,763 JEWS, 1,812 JEWESSES, 1,404 JEWISH CHILDREN, 109 MENTALLY SICK, 1 GERMAN SUBJECT (F.), MARRIED TO A JEW, 1 RUSSIAN (F.) 5,090

The pages blurred in front of Marianne's eyes. Dozens of identical lists followed, chronicling inexplicably, in exact specifications, her husband's atrocities. Beneath the stack of papers lay a handful of photographs. Black and grey testaments to the horror of the reports: lines of naked men, women and children clutching each other, dazed and afraid; a smiling, uniformed SS officer holding a gun to the head of a terror-stricken teenage boy; laughing, celebrating SS officers and their Lithuanian collaborators toasting the camera while hovering over a pit filled with the bodies of countless innocents. A sole picture of Eric placed him in front of a pit of fire, a smudged cloth held over his mouth, bodies dangling from the flames. Her hands began to shake uncontrollably, creasing the crisp, white paper. Andreas's words rang in her ears:

"You said he cleaned up after the Wehrmacht army leaves. What does he clean up?"

'Political clean up' she had wanted to say, wanting to defend him, to make excuses. The horror revealed on these pages was not political clean up. Her head churned with the evidence of the 'clean up' her husband participated in. How many thousands, how many hundreds of thousands had he murdered? And children. The numbers swam in her head. The folder collapsed onto the floor and Marianne sprinted into the hall, barely reaching the bathroom, before she vomited.

She curled by the toilet, heaving, and sobbing. Franz dead. Little Brigitte dead. Anna Gruber from art school, the Cohens, the Freimanns, all the people from the neighborhood resettled. Resettled. Another code word like 'liquidate'. Father knew. He tried to tell her. Andreas and Franz knew, they questioned her and she defended her husband. She defended a murderer. Maybe everyone knew and she was the fool, the stupid one, so faithful and loyal she'd follow like a starving puppy. Anger began to boil. Marianne rose from her heap on the floor and returned to the cold office. She laid out every incriminating sheet of paper from the yellow file into a collage on her husband's desk. Installing herself into the mammoth black leather chair, she waited.

# Rachel
## Warsaw, Poland
## September 1942 – January 1943

The apartment was empty when she got home. Strange. Her mother rarely left the apartment since Dora and Mira were deported. Her father's hat lay on top of the dresser. Rachel put a pot of water on the burner and began to slice greenish potatoes, peeling off the black bits, trying to salvage every edible bite. An hour passed. She placed four cracked plates on the table and watched the door. She began tidying the house, for lack of anything better to do. A noise at the door lifted her spirits. It opened. Aron.

"Where are Mama and Dad?" Aron asked.

"Dad's not home yet. Mama wasn't here when I got here."

Aron looked around, noting nothing unusual about the apartment. He slipped off his shirt, stained black from the construction work detail he had joined in the past two weeks. Rachel tossed him a clean shirt from the top of the small dresser.

A timid knock came from the door. Aron opened it. Shmuel Edelman, a bulky man with a black mustache who lived across the hall, filled the doorway.

Aron stepped back and the large man entered the room. He spoke softly.

"My wife was coming home from the nightshift this morning when she saw two Ukrainian guards leaving the building with your mother. Your mother kept telling them her husband had papers. They took her anyway. Angelina heard your father come home shortly afterward. She came here and told him. She begged your father not to go, but he was headed to the Umschlagplatz. He said he was going to get her or go with her."

"That makes no sense, Shmuel." Rachel said. "Why would they take her? She had paperwork. Wives of documented workers are exempt from deportation."

"That's what she kept telling them, but they wouldn't listen. Things have changed. I think they'll take anyone for any reason, papers or no papers."

The man bowed his head sadly and left the apartment.

"Do something Aron. Let's go to them!"

"I can't, Rachel. There's nothing we can do."

"You can try. Go to Marek. Ask him. You know people. Get them back!"

Aron shook his head, staring at the floor.

"My work detail was at the cemetery today. I was walking home and saw the trains leave. I walked by the Umschlagplatz and it was empty. It was empty for the first time in weeks. I thought 'maybe this is a sign the deportations have stopped. Maybe it's done'. I felt grateful, Rachel, grateful we were all safe. Oh my God, our parents were on those trains."

He squatted down, his head in his hands. She ran to him. They were alone.

*****

Marek watched from the basement window as two thousand Jewish policemen and their families were rounded up and marched to the Umschlagplatz. Again, the Nazis had gone back on their word that the policemen were protected and exempt from deportation. They decreed that only a small fraction of the original Jewish policemen were now needed to police the dwindling population of the ghetto and these same men who had done much of the Nazi's dirty work under duress, bribery, or desperation were now being sent to their own slaughter. Rachel studied Marek's face from the table where she peeled photographs from identity cards. She didn't know how to read him. Was it smugness, or sadness, or something else?

"Bastards," he mumbled.

"Which ones?" she asked.

He looked over at her in surprise. She rarely spoke to him. She felt awkward in front of this enigmatic man. They were alone. The others had scattered at word of the round up, hoping to free some of their compatriots from the lines. Bribery still had its place in this world. Marek had stayed behind, the only one of them without authentic work documents. Although he had his forgeries, he rarely ventured out, willing only to take the risk when absolutely necessary.

"What?" he asked.

"Which ones are you referring to as bastards, the policemen or the Nazis?"

"Both," he said.

"Some of them are. Others are saints. Most were just doing what it took to keep them and their families alive."

"That's very noble of you," he sneered.

"Your hate for the Germans doesn't have to make you an asshole to everyone else. Some of us are on your side, you know."

"Not enough of them. Most of them are just sheep. Every day I watch them herded to the trains. Where's their fight? Why are they sitting back and allowing themselves to be taken? They need to fight."

"Not everyone can be a fighter, Marek. Maybe they believe that by going they can save their families. Maybe they think there really is a labor camp in the East and they can stay alive. Maybe they have been starved and diseased and beaten down for so long that there's no fight left. Each one of them has fought in their own way, even if it's not your way."

"You're quite the angel of sympathetic causes."

"I just know where to direct my anger, and it's not toward my own people."

Marek looked back towards the window, the lines of black boots and battered brown shoes trudging past.

"I'm sorry about your parents. I want you to know that if the train hadn't already left, I would have culled every last favor I had to free them. I really would have."

"Thank you. I know Aron means a lot to you."

"No, not just for Aron. You've proven yourself. We would never have gotten those two traitors if you hadn't been there. Stefania's gorgeous of course, but we didn't have a good second girl to get it done. Zivia just doesn't have the assets for that kind of job."

"I'm glad my assets could be of service."

"No, I didn't mean it like that. There are other attractive girls we could have used, but it was more about you, not your looks. People are drawn to you. I'm trying to thank you."

"I'd say 'you're welcome' but I didn't do it for you. I did it for all of us. All of us left here and all of us taken on those trains to Lord knows where and Lord knows what. I'm in this until the end."

"People keep saying you're so much like Aron. But I don't think so."

"What makes you say that?"

Rachel started to feel defensive again. Something about this man lured her in and repelled her at the same time.

"Aron's more like me." Marek continued. "We're fighting this war out of hate. Hate for the Nazis, hate for the collaborators, hate towards everything that's destroyed our lives. You aren't like that. It's like you're fighting this war FOR something. You still have a soul. I don't understand it, but I envy it."

"Stefania told me what happened to your family in Lodz."

"Stefania needs to learn to keep her mouth shut."

His face clouded over, and he turned his back to her. She hesitated, wanting to reach out to him, but she remained frozen, staring at his stiffened back. The last of the long lines of boots passed their window and she gazed at the now empty street.

The door sprung open and Zivia burst in, excitement brewing on her face.

"We need more money. If I can get them the cash in the next hour, Aron found a connection to get ten of them out. We need five thousand zlotys."

Marek grabbed a crowbar out of a dresser drawer, pushed the dresser several feet to the right, and pried up a floorboard underneath it. Reaching in, he brought out a stack of cash. Counting it quickly, he handed Zivia two large stacks, keeping a third stack in his hand.

"Here's eight thousand. See if you can get their families too."

Zivia nodded and fled the room. Marek pushed the dresser back in place and replaced the crowbar. He stood quietly for a moment, staring at the wall behind her. He walked back over to the table and tossed the rest of the stack of cash on the table.

"Go see if you can get some more work permits."

Rachel picked up the cash and before she left, she turned back to him.

"You're wrong, Marek."

He looked at her questioningly.

She smiled. "You do still have a soul."

*****

That night, Soviet planes bombed Warsaw. Prayers echoed across the ghetto for the Soviet's victory and for the bombs to hit anywhere but the within the ghetto walls. Five days after the roundup of the Jewish police force, the Nazis enacted new, smaller ghetto boundaries. Aron and Rachel moved into an apartment on Gesia Street with Vera. As they left their old apartment, Rachel cried. How much she had lost in that apartment: her husband, her parents, her aunt and nieces, and, her heart twisted in pain, her son. She left a note on the table with her name and new address. A Polish family would be moving into the apartment. Maybe they would save or remember her new address and if Irena or Adam ever returned here, maybe they could tell them where to find her. She had to hope.

Almost daily, one of the men remaining at the ZTOS offices invited Rachel to live with them. Few single women were left in the ghetto and most of them moved in with one or more of the remaining men. There were no moral judgments passed: one did what they could to survive, and loneliness was as painful as hunger. But Rachel refused all offers. She had Aron and was one of the lucky few to still have a family member in the ghetto.

Rachel longed for the touch of a man and looked enviously on the love between Vera and Aron and of Zivia and Artur. But the thought of betraying the memory of Josef pushed those feelings aside. Marek kept his distance from her since their conversation the day the policemen were taken. He was polite but seemed to make an effort not to be alone with her.

Her feelings for him embarrassed her and she shied away when he was around. Occasionally their eyes would accidentally meet, and Rachel would blush and turn away. She had no right to these feelings.

In November, another major manhunt ensued, this time emptying the ghetto of all the tailors and shoemakers. Rachel rushed to get Artur another work permit as his original document listed him as a shoemaker. This roundup left the ghetto with only 40,000 inhabitants: one-tenth of its original population. The streets were quiet. The remaining 40,000 ghetto residents either worked at Nazi-approved jobs or hid. The homeless had been swept up, the food kitchens closed, and children were a rare sight, seen only at a glance, fleeing into brick entryways and behind a flash of curtains.

Marek began talks with a young man who had risen to prominence amongst the ghetto resistance. Mordecai Anielewicz began consolidating the unstructured, individual resistance groups and was elected leader of the newly named ZOB, Zydowska Organizacja Bojowa, the Jewish Fighting Organization. Marek pledged his allegiance and his small group's loyalty to the ZOB. Rachel saw him less and less as he divided his time between his own apartment and the meeting places of the leaders of the ZOB. His new inspiration lifted his mood, he growled less and occasionally she'd hear him laugh with the others. With her, he continued his subtle avoidance.

The nightly bombings ceased in November and December. The ghetto continued its eerie quiet. As the New Year's Day of 1943 rolled in, there were whispers of hope. Perhaps the deportations were over. Perhaps the remaining 40,000 would be allowed to be the Nazi labor force until the end of the war.

Rachel settled into a comfortable routine. She went to the ZTOS each day and made efforts to collect and copy as many labor documents as she could. Some days she'd get two or three. Sometimes, to Marek's obvious disdain, she'd go several days without any. The others continued to stockpile food, ration cards, and a small number of weapons. Marek repeatedly stomped on any sentiment of hope that the Nazis would leave them alone. On January 18, Zivia brought news that he was right.

They looked up at a knock on the door as they finished a breakfast of fish balls made from sztynki, tiny decaying fish Vera purchased easily and cheaply from makeshift wagons all over the ghetto. Aron put his finger to his lips, quieting Vera and Rachel. He crossed the room and checked the peephole crudely carved into the solid wooden door. Aron opened the door to Zivia, her face flushed with agitation.

"The deportations are beginning again," she heaved, breathless. "The Nazis are ordering everyone to report to their apartment courtyards to have their papers examined. You must get to Marek's immediately. Go through the sewers and side streets. It's not safe on the main streets."

Rachel felt the words like a hammer to her chest.

"Marek wants us all at his apartment in ten minutes."

Aron snatched their work permits off the counter as Vera handed him his tattered coat. Without a glance backwards, they left the small apartment and swiftly descended the stairs. The slam of a door echoed behind them. Shmuel Edelman appeared at the top of the stairs.

"Oh God," murmured Aron. "Wait. Shmuel! The Nazis have entered the ghetto. The deportations are beginning again."

Shmuel stared at them blank-faced for a moment then turned back his heels and fled to his apartment.

"We need to warn them all. Vera, you take floor 1 and 2, Rachel, take 3 and 4, I'll go up to 5. Meet back here in 3 minutes. Hurry!"

Rachel scurried back up a flight of stairs and began banging on apartment doors.

"The deportations are starting. Get to a hiding place. Don't report to the courtyard. Hide!"

Some doors opened in tiny cracks as she raced down the hall. Behind others she heard only scurrying and panicked voices. She swept the third and fourth floors and met Vera back in the stairwell. Aron was close behind her.

Reaching the door of the apartment building, Aron leaned out slightly for a view of the street. Only a scattered few people were on the streets, each looking confused as to why the streets were so eerily empty on a workday morning. Aron called out a soft warning to two men walking by their building. Both turned around and scuttled back the opposite direction in panic. Aron couldn't risk calling across the street to the others. He signaled to the girls and, keeping close the building, they fled to the manhole cover at the end of the block and descended into the dank sewer.

The stench was overwhelming. Rachel lowered into the sewer too quickly and fell forward, catching herself with her hands. Standing back up, her hands were layered in the foul waste coating the floor and ceiling. She knew about the sewer routes. Both Aron and Vera travelled them extensively, smuggling in food and weapons, travelling after curfew, and they were Aron's route in and out of the ghetto. But this was Rachel's first time in the sewers. Bile formed in the back of her throat, and she covered her mouth with her sleeve.

"Breathe through your mouth." Aron advised. "It helps. After a while you don't even smell it."

She highly doubted that but followed his direction. Aron led the way, winding Vera and Rachel through brick-lined passageways of varying height and width. Rachel prayed she wouldn't have to find her own way back. The enveloping blackness was only interrupted by fragments of light from manholes and cracks in the ceiling. Aron stopped at a manhole, identical to the fifteen other manholes they had passed, and using a long wooden stick that had purposely been left against the sewer wall, he propped open the cover a few inches. He boosted Vera up and she peered out the cover. Flashing an "Ok" signal, she cleared the cover and pulled herself out. Aron boosted Rachel up. The streets were nearly empty, but Rachel could hear shouts from the next block.

"Hurry!" she implored.

Aron jumped and pulled himself out of the manhole. He replaced the cover and led them running to Marek's apartment building.

Aron knocked on the door agitatedly and they heard a scurried rustling inside. The peephole darkened and the door opened. Marek stood before them, his right arm hidden. He ushered them quickly in. When he shut the door behind him, Rachel glimpsed the rifle in Marek's hand. Without a greeting, Marek began,

"The Nazi's have divided into three groups. One in the shop district, one in the brushmaker's ghetto and one here in the Central District. They're ordering everyone to their apartment courtyards. Many have been able to hide, but a line's being formed of those they captured. Mordecai sent us orders."

Stefania handed Aron a handgun.

"There are only a few bullets, so be sure you don't miss."

"What about me?" Rachel asked.

Aron looked at her.

"You and Vera go into the bunker. We'll leave you a rifle. If the bastards come, shoot and run. Try to get back to the sewers."

"No. I want to fight."

Marek met Aron's eyes and he shrugged.

"We can use all the help we can get," Marek said flatly.

"No. You're staying here," Aron said.

Rachel took one of the two remaining handguns off the table.

"I'm going."

"Ok then, it's settled," Marek ended the discussion. "Here's the plan..."

An underground bunker was connected by a tunnel to the two apartment buildings to the east of them. They walked through the tunnels, knocking at each bunker door to gain passage. Rachel watched the faces of the people hiding in the bunkers as they passed through. Would these people still be alive in two hours? Would she? She wondered what they thought of the armed little group, Marek followed by Aron, Pinkus, Stefania, Zivia, Artur, and Rachel. Despite heads held high and proud as they paraded past, she wondered if they could see the fear in her eyes.

Through the second bunker, they slipped out the hidden entrance into a barren apartment. Exiting the apartment, they stood immediately inside the entrance of the building and waited. Within minutes, exactly as Marek said, the long line of unfortunate captured began to pass. She remembered the day, months ago, when she had been part of one of these lines of death. What she was about to do now would have been incomprehensible then. When about half the line passed and Rachel estimated silently that about 500 people had shuffled by, Marek whispered,

"Now."

The seven soldiers slipped out the door and blended themselves into the line. She sidled up next to a man with a grizzly beard and matched his pace to keep up with the line. She looked around nervously to see if anyone had seen. None of the Ukrainian guards in her sight gave any indication they noticed the new line inhabitants. Who would sneak themselves INTO such a line? The expression on the grizzled man's face asked the same question. She winked at him. He stood up straighter and a slight smile formed on his face. He knew.

Rachel watched her brother whisper to the people surrounding him. Marek and Stephania were behind her, and she knew they were doing the same. She whispered to the now smiling man,

"When the battle starts, fight or run. Pass it on."

He nodded and whispered to the woman behind him. Rachel slowed down, letting people pass her, whispering the same message to as many people as she could. A man in a dark green coat appeared at her side. She began whispering the message to him and he spoke to her at the same time, nearly echoing her words. She looked at his face, startled. It was Marek. Despite the twist in her stomach, she nearly laughed out loud.

"I guess I'm not moving backwards fast enough," he murmured, and she swore she caught a glint in his eyes. He sidestepped to the left and disappeared into the crowd.

The line was moving slowly but was steadily getting closer to the Umschlagplatz. Rachel fought the panic stirring in her belly. What if something happened and the signal wasn't given in time? What if no one fought but her own small group of rebels? She began to feel dizzy with doubt when she heard a ruckus at the front of the crowd. She stood on her toes to see over the heads in front of her. Then she heard the whistled signal and repeated the cry to the others. She pulled the handgun out of jacket and yelled, strength coming from her where she thought there was none,

"Fight or run!"

The column began to disperse. About half the people in her sight began to flee, headed into buildings, onto side streets and around corners. Shots were fired towards them, but the firing guards soon found themselves dodging bullets. Hand to hand fighting filled the street as bands of five or six men attacked one guard after another. Rachel fled to a building entranceway and saw a Jewish boy, no older than thirteen, attack a Lithuanian guard. Rachel reached for her handgun, remembering Marek's warning that the handguns were useless unless you were close. In a full sprint, Rachel ran toward the boy and the guard. As the guard lifted his weapon to the boy's chest, Rachel pulled the trigger. A splash of blood spattered from the Lithuanian's head. The blood-soaked boy froze, staring at Rachel in disbelief.

"Run!" she yelled.

Without looking back, the boy fled. The grizzled man from the line appeared at her side. He brushed past her to the body of the guard she shot and picked up the guard's gun and bayonet. He acknowledged her with a nod and disappeared into the chaos.

A grenade exploded where the front of the line had been just minutes before. Rachel ran towards the explosion, keeping as close as she could to the walls of the buildings lining the streets. She slid into an apartment hallway as two Nazi soldiers turned the corner in front of her. She held her gun close to her, ready for them if they entered the building. One of the Nazis called across the street to a charging colleague,

"Turn back around. The goddamned Jews have weapons!"

She felt a burst of pride as she watched the three frightened Nazis sprint in the opposite direction of the fighting. She slipped out the door and continued towards the smoke-filled square. Someone ran up behind her and she turned quickly, gun raised.

"Careful there!" It was Marek. "Do you have bullets left?" he panted.

"I've only fired one."

"Did you hit him?"

She nodded.

"Good girl. I'm out of bullets so give me your gun. Head back to the apartment. Stay close to the buildings. Have you seen anyone else?" She shook her head as she handed him the gun. "If you see anyone, tell them to rendezvous back at the apartment. The Nazis are fleeing. They had no idea this was coming. We're really doing it." He checked the gun then reached out and unexpectedly touched her cheek. "Stay safe."

Rachel stood shocked at the tender gesture as she watched him run toward the fray. She put her hand to her cheek and raced back to the apartment.

*****

"I can't believe we're still alive. Those bastards never saw it coming. And they ran. The cowards ran!" Aron was shaking in excitement.

Aron and Marek had arrived together at the apartment minutes before. Stefania and Zivia had shown up thirty minutes earlier. Vera, who had nervously guarded the apartment in their absence, took their weapons, and brought them weak coffee. Pinkus burst through the door.

"There's more fighting at Mila and Zamenhof Street. We have snipers from an apartment mowing them down! Every time one falls, someone swoops in from one of the buildings and takes their guns. Damn Nazis getting their own weapons used against them. What's more beautiful than that?"

Pinkus surveyed the room. Vera took his gun and handed him a cup of coffee and a thin blanket. Like the others, he had come in too excited to feel the cold but would soon enough.

"Artur isn't back yet?"

"No. We've only been back a few minutes. He should be here shortly," said Aron.

"I saw him after that girl threw the grenade. He'd taken cover in a shop and was joining a group of Mordecai's men headed toward the action at Mila."

"Do you think we should head over to Mila?" Aron asked Marek.

"No. Our ammunition's depleted and we can't risk being on the streets unarmed right now. One of those fleeing Nazis might decide to take some farewell shots. Rachel, that's why I sent you back. You couldn't be on the streets unarmed."

"I know. I wasn't offended. I wish I'd been able to get more of them."

"Something tells me you'll have plenty more opportunities. After nightfall, Rachel and I will head over to Mila Street to see if we can get more bullets and guns. We'll talk about tomorrow's plan with Mordecai. No one else leaves here tonight. We need you all alive."

"Why Rachel?" Aron asked defensively. Rachel couldn't tell if he was offended not to be asked himself or simply being protective.

"Rachel's proved herself today. She needs to know where to go if our group gets disbanded. It's time for her to meet Mordecai."

Aron tentatively nodded his approval. The early evening hours dragged on. Occasional shots were heard in the distance, but the streets were unsettlingly quiet. Marek paced the apartment anxiously, waiting for darkness to fall. Zivia perked up at every sound in the hallway, watching the door vigilantly.

"He probably had to spend the afternoon at the Mila Street bunker. I'm sure Artur knows it's not safe to leave. Marek and Rachel will find him tonight and get word to us," Stefania comforted.

Zivia nodded.

"Yes, that must be it. Mordecai would want his best fighters to stay there. Rachel, you'll get word to me, right?"

"Of course. As soon as we can."

Zivia went back to checking the guns, one eye still on the door.

"Rachel, it's time to go."

Marek led her through a weave of side streets and alleyways. Aron's thin black coat didn't keep out the chill but concealed her in the darkness. They stayed far from the ghetto borders, knowing guards would most likely be near the walls. Only a handful of shadowy figures shared the streets with them. No policemen or guards were in sight. Marek moved quickly, nearing the pace of a jog, when Rachel tripped and fell onto her hands. She turned to see what she had fallen over. It was the body of a young Jewish man, a bullet hole in his head. Marek reached down, took her hand, and pulled her to her feet.

"Ok?" he whispered.

"Yes."

They continued onwards, Marek not letting go of her hand. Her heart began to pound, and her face felt hot, even in the bitter wind. She felt a flash of guilt— she had just fallen over the body of a boy who had given his life fighting, and here she was blushing like a schoolgirl with a crush. She resolved to put all that out of her mind. But she kept her hand in his and allowed herself the comfort of the heat of his grip.

Marek gave a series of short and long knocks and an eye appeared in the crack of the door. It was opened by a lanky boy of fourteen.

"Tomas."

"Marek."

Her hand still wrapped in his, Marek led Rachel in. Walls had been removed to combine apartments, creating one large room filled with several dozen men and women, many clearly still teenagers. Five men sat at a table in front of a large map of the ghetto. Red and black marks dotted the map. One of the men, barely out of his teens, stood and walked over to greet them. His quiet manner exuded confidence, and Rachel knew by the looks of reverence as he passed, this was Mordecai. His face was kind, but his dark eyes were deadly serious.

"Mordecai, this is Rachel Zylberman. She's Aron Kaplan's sister. She's been working with my crew these past months."

"Were you out with us today, Rachel?"

"Yes, I killed one of them. He was attacking a young boy. I shot him from behind." She blushed at her obvious eagerness to impress him.

He nodded approvingly.

"I know your brother. He's a fine fighter. I'm pleased to have his sister in our midst."

"Have you seen Artur?" Marek interrupted. Mordecai's face darkened.

"Artur fell on the flight from Nalewki Street to Mila. He and Pawel Litewka turned a corner right into a band of Lithuanian guards. They got two or three of them but not before Artur fell. Pawel was shot but made it back. Artur was a good man. Tell Zivia he died a soldier."

Rachel's eyes filled for the gentle Artur. Zivia would be destroyed. Rachel couldn't bear to return to her with such news.

Marek's face glassed over, and he was silent for a moment. Rachel leaned into him. He squeezed her hand and exhaled.

"What's our next move?"

Mordecai gestured to the map on the table, and they stepped forward to examine it. Mordecai walked them through the blue and reds lines of streets, indicating where he thought the Germans might regroup.

One of the older men at the table stared overtly at Rachel's hand, still held tight in Marek's. He raised his eyebrows at Marek questioningly. Marek's grip tightened on Rachel's hand, and he pulled her closer. She realized Marek was publicly laying claim to her. It occurred to her to be offended, but she wanted nothing more than to belong to him. Her heart beat faster. Looking at the map, Mordecai's words faded as she focused only on Marek, the sound of his voice, the nod of his head, the heat of her hand in his. She left him only when a young woman with a wild head of frizzy hair entered the room and Mordecai called to her,

"Tatiana, show Rachel around."

Marek nodded his consent, and she followed the wild-haired girl through a maze of underground bunkers, filled with fighters, mostly young men, mostly her age or younger, none much older than 30. Tatiana led her directly beneath the apartment where a bunker was under construction. The large windowless area was freezing. A team of men and women worked on wiring lights and men hauled in furniture from the apartments above. Tatiana pointed out the entrances and exits to the sewers. Many were loosely blocked off with bricks, to hide them from the Nazis. Metal ladders led to exits to the apartment buildings and onto the streets.

When Tatiana led Rachel back to the main room, Marek was waiting for her by the door.

"It's too dangerous to return tonight. We risk not only running into Nazis but also getting shot by some of our overzealous own who might shoot at anything that moves. There's an empty room in the apartment upstairs where we can stay until morning."

"What about Zivia?"

"Eight hours won't change the news we have to give."

Rachel followed him up a stairwell, into a small, peeling apartment. Three men sat on mattresses playing cards. They nodded at the men as they passed, headed towards the closed door of the only other room. One man whispered something to the other two and they all laughed. Rachel blushed but pretended she didn't understand the nature of what was said. Marek closed the door behind them. A mattress with two thin blankets rested on the floor. A wood stove cozied up to the mattress, spitting bits of flame onto the blanket, creating small, black rimmed holes in the fabric. Rachel pulled the mattress back a foot and brushed the ash onto the floor. She surveyed the mattress, her back to Marek. She was afraid to turn around, afraid of what might, or might not, happen next.

"I can sleep on the floor," Marek said softly.

Without hesitation, she shook her head.

"I don't want you to sleep on the floor," she whispered.

He moved to her, his warm breath on the back of her neck. She turned to face him, her eyes meeting his. His lips fluttered over hers. Despite the cold, she felt the perspiration pool in the small of her back. Her heart quickened. He lowered her onto the mattress and slid off her coat, warming her with his body. He pulled off his shirt and slowly unbuttoned her blouse, his mouth never leaving hers. His body was lean, sinewy, and solid. She traced the scar on his shoulder with her lips, remembering Stefania's story. The madness around them dissolved as she escaped into Marek, each kiss, each caress, erasing a thousand sorrows.

Marek stroked her hair absently as she nestled next to him, shivering in the cold. He pulled his coat onto the mattress and covered her with it. She kissed his chest and laid her head against it, listening to his heartbeat.

"Move into my apartment with me," he whispered. She laughed softly.

"I'm not sure my father would approve of a proposal like that," she teased. She thought of her sensitive, religious father and how tentative he had been of Josef's proposal.

Marek propped himself onto his elbow.

"I'm serious, Rachel. I don't know how much longer we have, but I want to be with you. I've lost everything I've loved in my life. I no longer have time for courtship and games. I want you. Nothing else matters."

Her mouth covered his as she murmured her assent. For this brief moment, it was all that mattered.

# Claire
## Anzio, Italy
## January 1944 – March 1944

January 19, 1944
United States War Department Adjunct General

Dear Sirs:
Through three telegrams I have been informed that my father, Major Robert Weber of the US Army 173rd Field Hospital has been declared MIA, AWOL, and lastly, given Deserter status. In the course of my occupation as a nurse with the 17th Evacuation Hospital in Italy, I have come across information which reliably indicates my father has not deserted his unit, but has, in fact, been taken as a POW by the German army. I have attached the names and location information of a woman and a priest who can verify the truth of this statement as well as provide details the Army needs to change his status to POW and begin searching for my father. I request your investigation be reopened. Please contact me immediately with any further information.

2nd Lt. Claire Weber
17th Evacuation Hospital Europe

January 20, 1944

Dear Bill,
It's been over a month without a word from you. Bonnie has been corresponding with Carl Nordhagen from your unit. He said you will write to me only if you can mail the letter home to Minnesota. I love you, Bill. Please reconsider.

Yours, Claire

January 30, 1944

Dear Tom,

It's been a while since I've heard from you. I hope you received the information I sent about my visit to San Giordino. I'm anxious to hear if you've been able to make progress from the States with this information.

I've heard nothing from Bill. Every day I wonder if I'm making the right decision. Last week I was walking to Nurse Beck's tent to tell her I was leaving when Marie interceded and dragged me back to the tent. A couple of whiskeys later and I reconsidered. After a difficult night, Bill's ripped up picture is now safely glued back together and in its frame.

You may not hear from me for a while. Tomorrow morning we're shipping out to Anzio. Two other hospital units have already set up there and I understand the fighting is fierce. This will be the first time our unit is assigned directly to the front. I'm hoping we can break through soon and our boys can take Rome swiftly with minimal casualties. Honestly though, I'm terrified. I'll write soon but I don't know what the mail delivery will be like once we're there. I'm trying to stay brave.

Yours, Claire

"What the hell are they doing here?"

"Get hold of the first vehicle you can and get the hell out of here!"

Voices from dusty hiding places shouted from the side of the road as the trucks carrying the nurses of the 17th Evacuation Hospital jostled over rocks and bombed out potholes. A sea of tents filled the sandy marsh in front of them. Red crosses on white circles marked the hospital tents. Four women in men's trousers and field jackets ran to meet the truck.

"Welcome! Thank God you're here. We need all the help we can get," one of the women said. Dirty brown hair stuck out under her steel helmet. Claire jumped off the truck and followed the woman.

"How long have you been here?" Claire yelled above the screeching of a missile in the distance.

"Nearly two weeks. We set up the first hospital tents and have slowly been getting supplies. We got our first wave of casualties two days ago. I'll show you where to put your things. Then you need to start setting up so you can relieve some of our load. Our nurses haven't slept longer than 15 minutes in two days."

The steel-helmeted nurse continued to talk as she led the new nurses through a barrage of two-man tents.

"Colonel Blesse is huddling all the hospital units together hoping the Germans can identify us more easily as a hospital and we can avoid their bombs. But we're not holding our breath. Those krauts just disregard our medical crosses and aren't holding back their artillery."

As if to prove her point another screeching whistle sounded over their heads. Bonnie clasped her hands over her ears.

"We like to call that one the Anzio Express. Mostly you'll hear it at night. The krauts fire from the mountains and shell all night long. Here are your hospital's quarters. Two to a tent. Consider getting one of the men to help you dig a foxhole. Some of the officers are building them in their tents. Colonel Blesse says it's not necessary, but it sure makes us feel better to have somewhere to hide when the shelling gets bad. Blackouts are every night as soon as dusk hits, so if you're planning on writing home, do it during the day. Not that you'll have any time."

The harried nurse left them standing in front of the small tent. Marie and Claire paired off and Bonnie and Ellen took the tent next door. Two green cots with bedrolls encompassed most of the tent. Marie brushed some of the beach sand out the door and surveyed their paltry accommodations.

"Well, at least it's not mud."

The Anzio Express screeched overhead.

Claire sat on her cot, nearly tipping it as she plunked down. At least it wasn't mud.

*****

Claire walked the blood-stained aisle between the endless rows of cots, each nearly stacked upon the next. Bloody, battered men moaned from beneath their bandages, eyes glassed over. All the nurses in the world couldn't heal their wounds.

A slight boy, barely old enough to be out of high school, raised his hand to Claire as she passed. His head was wrapped in a blood-encrusted bandage, still stained from its last wearer. Bandages were in short supply and the last supply ship had sunk before reaching the beachhead. Claire glanced at his chart before she leaned over to hear him. Shrapnel had pierced his throat and while the surgeon had performed a miracle, his voice would never be right.

"Please nurse," he rasped, "Please send me back."

"Private Hanson, the doctors said you're eligible for medical discharge. Once the paperwork's processed, you'll go home. It shouldn't be more than a few days before we can get you on a transport to Naples."

Wild fear struck the boy's eyes.

"A few days?" he croaked. "I need to get outta here now." He pushed her aside and rose from the bed, knocking over his IV tubes. He ripped the tubing from his chest.

"Private Hanson, lay back down! Corpsman!"

A passing corpsman ran to her side and eased the now weak Private Hanson back into his bed.

"You need to stay put, Private," the corpsman ordered, "You keep pulling that shit, you won't make it out of the hospital alive."

The young private began to weep.

"I know I won't. You have to get me out of here. You have to send me back to my foxhole."

The corpsman looked sympathetic. Claire was flabbergasted. The boy's next words chilled her.

"Send me back to my foxhole. I'm safer there than in this hospital. Anywhere is safer than this half acre of hell."

February 5, 1944

Dear Tom,

It is day five in Anzio. The soldiers here call the hospital beachhead the "Half Acre of Hell". If hell is anything like this, I plan on repenting all my sins immediately and will consider going into a convent. We're overwhelmed with wounded. Our 700 bed hospital is serving over 1200 battle casualties. To expand, we simply added more tents. Not more staff or more supplies, just more tents.

The problem isn't only the capacity, it's the constant shelling. Shells are flying day and night. The krauts have absolutely no regard for the fact that we're a hospital and should be off limits. Our hospital complex is spread over half an acre of beachhead with the mountains on one side and the harbor on the other, with no place to hide. The nurses are supposed to work 12 hour shifts, but the 12 hours turn into 18 or 20 because there's no one to replace us.

I'm losing the light and need to sleep a few hours before my next shift. I'm so tired. I'm putting this in the mail, but don't know if or when you'll get it.

Yours, Claire


Claire and Marie trudged back towards their tent, exhaustion etched into their faces, their bodies slumped.

"I'm half-starved but I think I'll fall asleep with my face in the spaghetti if I go to the mess tent."

"I bet the cook's supply tent has some C-rations we could shovel down before bed. Maybe we can get an extra hour of sleep."

They detoured around the back of the mess tent. The Anzio Express whistled from the mountains. After two weeks, its screech had become part of the background noise blending into a permanent, dull roar.

Claire and Marie approached the supply tent, too tired to engage in conversation. They slipped through the tent and rifled through the boxes.

"Ah ha!" Marie cried and lifted a bag of meat and potato hash.

As Marie called out, a shelving unit at the back of the tent collapsed and a female voice yelped. Marie and Claire jumped over and pulled the shelves off a hollow-eyed nurse from the 125th Claire had seen but never spoken to.

"What are you doing here?" Marie asked.

"I could ask you the same question."

"We're just avoiding the mess hall. Let me help you up." The nurse reached up and Marie pulled her to her feet.

A shiny glint fell from her lap and rattled to the floor of the tent. The three women stared at a syringe, filled halfway with blood, its metal tip exposed.

"Why do you have that in the cook's tent?" Claire asked, confused.

The nurse began to weep.

"Please don't tell on me. Don't say you've seen me. I just can't bear it anymore. I'll do anything to get out of here."

"What do you mean?"

"Hepatitis," Marie said flatly. "Someone from the 125th told me yesterday that some nurses were injecting themselves with hepatitis-tainted blood in order to be sent home."

"Please don't tell. Please," the nurse wept.

"Get out of here. You should be ashamed of yourself."

The nurse reached down, pocketed the syringe, and fled past them.

"We shouldn't tell," Claire sighed. "She's going to have to live with herself. Maybe that's punishment enough."

"That and hepatitis. What a coward," Marie snorted.

As Marie and Claire rearranged the boxes from the fallen shelves, Claire wondered what it would take for her to be that desperate. She shook the thought from her head but her dreams that night were haunted with telegrams and hepatitis needles.

*****

Claire stretched out her legs under the makeshift table of eight stacked helmets and a travel case. The cards she dealt were sticky and damp, coated with spilled whiskey, red wine, and the ever-present layer of sand. Claire, exhausted after a 15 hour night shift, but too wired to sleep, had shuffled her way to Ellen and Bonnie's tent with two bottles of acrid red wine. Axis Sally's melodious voice floated from the radio. The Nazi propagandist could drive an allied soldier to drink, with her smug remarks about inept American soldiers and attempts to lure the nurses with promises of handsome blonde men who knew how to take care of a woman. Ellen greeted Claire with a gallon of Anzio moonshine: part canned grapefruit juice, part medical alcohol.

"Ahh... the Anzio cocktail," Claire took a cup from Ellen, and settled next to Bonnie on the thin cot.

"When's Marie getting back?" Bonnie asked.

"She's making a delivery to the 95th. They were low on gauze and towels. She better not have been suckered into pulling another shift."

Ellen downed a quick shot of the rancid liquid and sorted through her cards.

"When has Marie ever said no?"

Claire folded her lousy hand.

"Speaking of saying no, any news from Bill?" Ellen asked.

Claire looked down and shook her head. Bonnie, next to her on the cot, elbowed her.

"Nothing from Bill, but before we got here, Claire was getting quite a stash of letters from one Major Tom Parker."

Ellen squealed.

"Tom Parker? Who's this Tom Parker? You turn down one man and have another on the hook in days!"

"It's not like that!" Claire bristled defensively. "Tom's an old family friend. He helped me out when I needed him and now we're good friends."

"Well, considering Bill's keeping his distance and this old family friend holds no interest, maybe you should write to my Bert's friend, Charles. He saw you in Capri and asked to meet you, but then saw you with Bill and gave it up."

"Well, he'll have to remain given up. Ellen, I'm with Bill. We just had a misunderstanding. I'm still marrying him."

Bonnie showed her cards and the other women groaned. Bonnie always won. The roar of planes close overhead drowned out their chatter.

"Damn, they're close," Bonnie said.

Claire laughed at her swearing. Genteel Bonnie was sounding more like Marie every day. Gunfire rattled and the ground beneath the tent shook. Simultaneously, all three women grabbed their steel helmets and the card table toppled. Claire felt guilty ignoring the strictly enforced regulation that steel helmets be worn at all times, under a penalty of twenty-five dollars an infraction. She still hadn't gotten used to the weight on her head and the near impossibility the helmets brought to sleeping. She moved in closer to Bonnie and Ellen and began dealing a second hand on the cot when the tent flap flew open, and George Hadley rushed in. George, a corpsman in their unit, had a permanent smile blending together the freckles on his red cheeks. His smile was gone.

"We need to get to the hospital, stat. The 95th Evac's been bombed. The bombs landed right on their hospital. I don't know how many were killed but they're rushing the wounded to post op right now and they need all personnel."

As fast as he came in, he rushed out and they heard him delivering the same news to the neighboring tent. Claire gasped.

"Oh my God. Marie. Marie went to the 95th."

The women froze and stared at each other. Then, without a word, they abandoned their card game and sprinted toward the hospital.

February 15, 1944

Dear Tom,

I'm sending this letter home with a nurse who's been diagnosed with hepatitis and is returning to the states. Most of the other nurses here are jealous. Can you imagine being jealous of contracting hepatitis? If you can, you'll then have a clear idea of how we're feeling. I'm writing though tears so please forgive the water stains.

This past week has shown me very clearly why they call this place the Half Acre of Hell. The hospitals have been bombed three times. In the first bombing, I lost my dear friend Marie Salazar. She was making a delivery to the 95th when it was bombed. Twenty-six people were killed, including everyone in the postop ward, many of whom were patients wounded in the earlier fighting.

Three days later, the 33rd was bombed, killing two nurses and an enlisted man. Yesterday was the worst shelling yet. Last night the red alert sounded, and we ran to the air raid shelters. Hundreds of German planes dropped antipersonnel bombs that unleashed jagged fragments of metal into anyone near the explosion. They also bombed the nurses' tents. The body count from last night hasn't been announced yet but we lost at least two more nurses, a doctor, and dozens more are wounded.

Everything that moves here is a target. The krauts set themselves up in the mountains and we're under constant surveillance. We call the road leading to the harbor 'Purple Heart Alley'. Morale is beyond low. The krauts drop leaflets mocking us and Axis Sally fills our radio airways with propaganda about how much better things are on the other side. Every night is like a hellfire 4th of July with flares, tracers, and planes falling from the sky in flames. Our tents are full of holes from bomb fragments. Many of our meals are eaten under our tables. I'm writing this from the foxhole dug in my tent. Some nights we simply put our cots in the foxholes. Our steel helmets leave our heads only to bathe or do our laundry.

But, Tom, despite all of this, despite the shelling, the horrific conditions, the constant fear of injury or death, I won't leave. The boys fighting for us must put up with all of this and so much more. I will not abandon them. I'll complain and vent to you in this letter, but I'll smile at them to help keep them strong. I'll be here as long as I'm needed.

Yours, Claire


Claire gently placed Marie's belongings into a footlocker she delivered to the mail truck. A dozen times she started a letter to Marie's parents and brothers, but each time, she ripped it up. Words couldn't adequately describe the loss she felt, what Marie had meant to her. In the end, she closed the footlocker and vowed to tell them in person what she could not put on paper. Alone, she looked around at the nearly empty tent, curled into a ball and sobbed.

January 2, 1944

Dear Claire,

Please excuse the delay in writing to you. The loss of my husband was a shock. One is told to expect the worst when a loved one goes to war, but I never thought I would lose my John. My own misplaced confidence has left my wounds unprepared to heal.

Three weeks ago, I received my husband's belongings and I was just able to bear opening them this afternoon. Enclosed in the package was the final letter John wrote to me, left unmailed in his footlocker. I suspect he planned to mail it upon his arrival in Naples.

In that letter, John wrote he had, just that very night, allowed Major Weber to leave the unit to assist a pregnant woman in a nearby town. John was fitful as he feared Robert would not return in time to depart the next morning. Knowing your father as I did, I too would be inclined to believe he would stay as long as it took. It was also in violation of the regulations and John was quite anxious about it.

What this means to you, dear Claire, is that I hold in my hand clear evidence your father did not desert his unit. As soon as I finish writing this letter to you, I will write letters to every commanding general in the US Army. I will scream it from the rooftops if I must in order to clear Robert's name.

I pray every day Robert will be found safe. No matter what the outcome, you can be proud in knowing your father is an honorable man.

Fondly, Mildred Keller

Claire sat with the letter in her lap and wept. Alone in her tent, she had no one to tell this bittersweet news. Her father's name would be cleared. A small victory. But he was still gone. And she was still alone.

*****

Claire changed the bottle of plasma for the handsome soldier and replaced the stained cloth over his head with a fresh one.

"They'll be taking you into surgery soon."

She gave him a comforting smile. A bloody bandage covered the stump of his leg. The odor of antiseptic interspersed with smoke from the shelling outside overpowered the tent. Litter after litter of wounded men rested in pre-op, each man lying in wait for his turn on the surgical table. Claire started to describe the wounds she saw in last week's letter to Tom, but never finished. The grotesque mangling of human bodies that passed through the flaps of these tents every day defied description. Bloody rags covered gaping wounds. Filthy, mud and sand coated clothing was cut from the men's bodies. Every day, every cot was filled with freshly wounded men. The emotional wounds were raw, as the wounded soldiers mourned for the friends they watched die. Their guilt at having been so lucky to end up on a surgical table rather than in a body bag nearly destroyed them.

Major Beck passed from cot to cot, comforting each man, checking their dressings, whispering encouraging words. Claire changed the bandage of the amputee and met her in the aisle.

"I heard two new doctors just arrived on LCIs."

"Assigned to our unit?" Claire asked, surprised. They had been short staffed since the death of Marie and Dr. Coons nearly a month before. But she hadn't heard they were getting new staff.

"No, I don't think so. They're assigned as floaters, I believe. But we're lucky to have them. I heard they brought more supplies and, if you can believe it, more penicillin. Will you go find them and ask where their shipment was taken? I don't think we have a single clean towel left in pre-op." Lois sighed and looked over at the pile of what were now rags, mostly stained, thinning cloths washed then reused, never getting clean enough. "I think the new doctors are in triage or reception."

Claire left the tent into the sun of the beach. The spring air of mid-March brought hope of the warm, dry weather the army would need to be successful in its takeover of Rome. Claire approached the reception tent, surveying the pile of mud-caked clothing by the entrance, a constant reminder of the sheer number of patients entering the hospital every day.

"Where are the new doctors?" she asked a thin nurse with black circles under her eyes.

A sign hung on the walls of the reception tent: 'When did you last eat?' meant to remind the wounded soldiers to take care of their basic needs. Claire considered the irony when looking at the pale, thin visage of the nurses who posted the sign. The pale nurse pointed to the rear of the tent as she scooted past Claire to a newly arriving litter carried by two soldiers.

Claire spotted the doctor leaning over a patient. Reception was a good introduction to new medical personnel. Seeing this area first would give him an idea of what he was facing. She shifted through the litters of patients, stopping twice in the fifty feet to assist with a dropped head cloth and to change a bandage so fully soaked it was seeping into the wound. The new doctor was standing at the foot of a cot, a chart in his hand.

"Excuse me, Doctor? Our head nurse sent me to inquire about the location of the new supplies..."

The doctor turned around. Claire's words stopped with the impact of familiarity. His blue eyes met hers and the all too familiar wrinkle formed on his cheek. He spoke first, practically a whisper.

"Claire."

"What.. I don't ...what...?"

She couldn't form a sentence. He opened his mouth to speak when the tired nurse called from the entrance of the tent.

"Dr. Parker! We need you here immediately! Corporal Oliver, please escort Dr. Parker to Operating Tent 1."

Tom's eyes left hers and he sped past her to the patient being transported to the OR. Claire stared at his back as he rushed out of the tent. She stood frozen until her hazy thoughts were interrupted by a sullen soldier with a three-inch gash in his forehead.

"Nurse, could I get some water?"

Claire didn't lay eyes on Tom until much later that evening. She found the supply of new syringes, plasma, penicillin, and linens being unloaded from trucks that arrived unscathed from the harbor and directed their placement to the pre-op ward. The next ten hours, occupied by a never-ending transfer of patients from reception to pre-op after a particular nasty air strike, passed with Claire on autopilot, seemingly engaged with her patients, but her mind captured by the moment she saw Tom Parker standing in front of her.

At 0800, the next shift of nurses arrived, most of them working for hours before the start of their actual shift. Starving, Claire headed for the mess tent. Over the past two months, what was once the nurse's mess had merged into a medical mess tent serving any medical personnel who entered its flaps. The strict line between nurses, paramedics, and doctors had dissolved into the sand and mud that was Anzio.

As she got her tray of salty chipped beef and green beans, she saw Tom sitting at a table on the far left of the tent, surrounded by a gaggle of nurses. She didn't want to be part of any "getting to know you" session. As she sat alone at an empty table, Tom suddenly looked up and his eyes found her. He smiled. He said something to the nurses surrounding him, picked up his tray and walked to her table. Claire's stomach fluttered unexpectedly.

"What on earth are you doing here?" she asked.

"I asked for a transfer. I was tired of sitting in Minneapolis helping others get ready to go to war. I needed to be doing more."

"But Anzio? Surely you didn't ask to be transferred to Anzio?"

"Well, your letters made it sound irresistible."

Claire began to laugh. There was so much she wanted to ask him, so much she wanted to say. His laughter subsided.

"Claire, I..."

"Now you don't get this new doc all to yourself, Miss Claire!" Bonnie's voice cooed behind them. Bonnie and Ellen circled the table and sat across from them.

"Bonnie, I'd like to introduce you to Dr. Tom Parker."

"Tom Parker! The infamous Tom Parker?"

"Oh, I'm infamous, am I?"

Claire turned scarlet. While usually endearing, Bonnie's southern flirtatious charm was not exactly welcome today.

"Well, she writes more letters to you than her fiancé and family combined, and she refuses to tell us anything about you!

Family friend, my eye. You are the keenest family friend I've ever seen."

"Bonnie!" Ellen giggled.

"Sorry, doctor. We don't stand on ceremony at Anzio. If you've got something to say, you better say it now before Anzio Annie gets you."

"Anzio Annie?"

"Just another one of the krauts' guns. You'll get to know them all within a week."

A voice piped up from the crowd starting to form around the table. They were soon joined by a group of nurses and corpsmen.

"I hear you came directly from the states. All we get here are two-week-old Stars and Stripes newspapers. Tell us what's going on. What're the Yankees looking like this season?"

The rest of the meal, Tom's attention was stolen by a crowd of news-starved nurses and corpsmen. Claire was quiet, taking it all in, the heat of Tom next to her present in her mind. She understood the desire of all these people to connect with him. But she felt jealous. She wanted him to herself.

"Claire!" Ellen's shriek startled everyone at the table and there was a hush. "I'm such an idiot. With all this Tom Parker business, I forgot to tell you. Mail call came today, and I picked up yours. You have two letters and a package on your cot. One letter and the package are from your friend Barbara Ann. I hope she sent some of that pressed powder. We could trade it for some more olives. But the other letter is from one Mr. Bill Vincent."

Ellen beamed at her news. The others at the table, uninterested in the contents of Claire's mail, resumed their buzzing around Tom. Claire met Tom's eyes and saw something there she didn't understand. But a letter from Bill!

"Tom," she interrupted the bees, "if you'll excuse me. I'm exhausted and need to get some sleep before an early morning shift. I'd like to catch up with you later."

"Good night, Claire," he whispered so only she could hear. She rose from the table, looking back at him for a brief second to see him re-engaging with his new fan club, and she headed to her letter.

March 15, 1944

Dear Claire,

I've received your letters and have had a long time to think. This war has made me realize what's important. I don't care you joined the army without consulting me. I forgive you. I love you. I want to marry you. I'm willing to wait. I know within a year we'll be home and can put all this mess behind us and we can marry and start our family.

Your ring is enclosed. I'm entrusting the US Army mail with this ring, which is a huge risk, but I don't want you to be without it for one more day. Put it on your finger and think of me every day and the future we'll have together. I love you, Claire.

Bill

She turned the open envelope over in her hand and the diamond ring fell into her palm.

"Oh my goodness! Your ring!" Bonnie flung herself through the tent flaps. "It's about time that boy came to his senses."

Claire turned the ring over in her fingers. "Congratulations, honey. You must be excited."

Claire smiled and nodded, waiting to feel the relief. "I'm excited, Bonnie. I'm just a little overwhelmed, I think. This is very good news."

"Could you be overwhelmed because of one Dr. Tom Parker?"

"Bonnie! That's out of line. I love Bill. Tom and I are friends."

Bonnie sniffed but made her way to Claire's cot to inspect the contents of Barbara Ann's package. Claire laid the letter on her cot, placing the ring on top of it.

"Max Factor rouge! Thank goodness," Bonnie smiled, "We've been needing to replenish our whiskey stash!"

A male voice outside their tent cleared his throat loudly. "Uh. Claire?"

Bonnie sang out, "Come in."

Tom opened the flap and stepped into the battered tent. "I'm sorry. I just realized I don't know how to knock on the flap of a tent."

Claire laughed.

"The things you learn in Anzio!"

Bonnie stood up. "I best get back to my own tent now and get caught up on some sleep. I bet you two need to catch up on some Minnesota news. You can talk about corn fields or blizzards or what not. I'll be next door if you need me."

Bonnie caught Claire's eye and winked. Claire glared at her. Bonnie flounced out of the tent, and they were alone.

Claire motioned, with a pang in her chest, to the second cot, which had sat empty this past month. Tom sat down on it and asked,

"Marie's?"

Claire nodded.

"I'm sorry."

"I know," she whispered, then smiled. Marie would love the scandal of Tom Parker sitting in her cot. "I just can't believe you're here. Tell me the whole story."

"It's not much of a story really. Every day, I examined boys fifteen years younger than me who were about to risk their lives. I felt ashamed. I asked to be sent overseas. The Army was only too happy to oblige."

"But Anzio? I hardly think the army would send a doctor to his first combat hospital in Anzio. Did you request to come here?"

Tom's eyes left Claire and travelled to the letter sitting beside her on the cot. His gaze focused on the ring.

"So, I take it your letter from Bill was good news?"

"I haven't heard from him in three months. He sent back my ring.

"Congratulations, Claire. That's what you wanted."

She hesitated for a moment.

"Yes, it is. Thank you."

They settled into a moment of awkward silence.

"So, tell me about your girl. Barbara Ann prides herself on her gossiping abilities. I hear you've been seeing Ava Sorenson. It must be serious?"

"Yes, see...when I return from the war," Tom stammered, "Well, she and I have an understanding."

"That certainly sounds serious." Claire's voice teased, but she felt irritable. "What's the understanding?"

A loud whistle sounded overhead and the gunfire perpetually roaring in the distance was drowned by ear-blistering explosions.

"Get into the hole, quick!" Claire yelled.

Tom followed her into the dirt trench, dug deep into the floor of the tent. The ground shook. Tom covered Claire's body with his own as the shelling reverberated around them. Her heart pounded and she convinced herself it was fear but was acutely aware of his body enveloping her own. They lay together until the guns could again be heard in the distance and the screech of the German planes faded.

As they crawled out of the hole, Ellen and corpsman Bert Conner, who never said no to a card game with Ellen, flew into the tent.

"Are you all ok?"

"Jesus, they were close. I read your letters, but I didn't realize... Jesus."

Tom's face was bright red, and his shoulders shook.

"You better head back to your tent. If they can't find you, they'll think you got hit and will start a search. "

"Yes, well, ok," Sweat dripped from Tom's forehead, creating lines in his dirt encrusted face.

"We'll catch up later," Claire said.

Bert escorted Tom out of the tent. "Those krauts sure know how to welcome our new doctors, huh?"

"That's the truth."

Claire sat on her cot and reached over and picked up Bill's ring that had fallen to the floor. She slipped it onto her finger and stared at it. She guessed she and Bill had an understanding too.

# Min-He
## West of Shanghai, China
## March 1945 – March 1946

Min-He was still awake, lying on the floor in a pool of her own vomit and blood when Umeko flew through the door at 5:00 AM. Min-He heard her gasp and minutes later Mother and Father surrounded her. Father carried her into the main house to the medical room. She moved in and out of consciousness on the metal table as Umeko paced, alternating crying and yelling. Doctor Kono sauntered in lazily an hour later and gave her a shot. Min-He woke in her room when the sun was in the middle of the sky, with Takao by her side.

"What are you doing here?" she gurgled. Her body felt numb and her tongue was thick. She ran her hand over the stitches in her stomach and between her legs.

"I came to see you and there was a sign on your board stating you were "indisposed" for three days. I paid to see Umeko and she told me what happened. Oh Min-He, why? How could you? Umeko knows what she's doing with him, but you just invited in an angry wild boar."

Min-He couldn't believe what she was hearing. He was blaming her? Surely, she misunderstood him. If she had any energy left, she would rebuke him. Instead, she croaked,

"Bucket" and vomited into the wash bucket he rushed to hand her.

"Stay with me tonight," she whimpered. He hesitated and she watched his face change from worry to...something she couldn't identify but filled her with dread.

"I can't. I... just can't. I actually came today to tell you something. Oh Min-He, how can I tell you this now, but how can I not?" He hung his head and stared at the matted floor. "I'm shipping out tomorrow. My unit is leaving for Okinawa. We've heard rumors the Americans are dominating and reinforcements are needed. Min-He, I think Japan will hang its head in defeat. But all troops have been ordered to the front, ordered to fight until the end. The rumors say that in Okinawa we'll be given grenades to blow ourselves up if we aren't killed in battle so we can't be taken prisoner by the Americans. I came to say goodbye. But how can I leave you like this?"

"Don't go. Hide. Run. You can't go to the front. Please."

"It's my fate, Min-He. I must go. If I run and hide, my family will be humiliated. How can you ask that of me? This way I fight and I die and my family can honor me as a hero."

"You don't know you're going to die. You aren't going to die. I need you to come back to me. To save me. You can't die."

"Umeko will take care of you. I've made arrangements with the man you call Father to take care of you. I've paid him everything I have to make sure you get out of this. I've written my family of this promise, and they will hold him to his honor if you don't make it home safely."

He pulled her into his arms.

"I love you, Min-He. Never forget me." Takao brushed his eyes with his arm and then he was gone. Min-He wept bitterly.

Umeko came to her with bowls of cabbage during dinnertime. Umeko sat in sullen quiet, making no attempt to comfort her. This was so unlike her, Min-He found herself comforting Umeko, ensuring her things would be okay. After an hour of mostly silence, Umeko left at the rap of an officer's knock at her door.

Min-He walked slowly to the kitchen to return the bowls, the stitches grinding into each other with each step. Father was seated in the reading room. He smiled at her gently as she passed and when she walked back through the sitting room, he brushed past her, placing in her hands three gold, foil-wrapped chocolates, a rare treasure. Later that evening when she heard Umeko leave for the toilet room, she slipped into her room and left the three chocolates on Umeko's shelf. She knew the Colonel would return that night. Min-He returned to her room and cried herself to sleep.

She was shaken awake by Umeko, her face bloodless and streaked with tears like cat scratches.

"Mio, what have I done? Come next door. Please help me."

Umeko grasped her hand and pulled her out of bed. When Min-He entered Umeko's room, she reached for a light but Umeko pulled her back. It took a few seconds to focus her eyes in the moonlit room. When Min-He finally saw what lay in front of her, she gasped in horror.

The Colonel was lying face down in Umeko's bed. The handle of his dagger protruded from the back of his neck. Blood pooled around his head and shoulders.

"What am I going to do? He fell asleep like he always does when he's through. He was just lying there like nothing was wrong. I kept staring at him, Mio. I stared at him, and I hated him and I wished he was dead. He hadn't put his pants back on and I saw his knife and I just…. I can't believe it, Mio. What am I going to do? We have to hide him. We must get him out of here. They will shoot me, Mio. They'll kill me for this. You have to help me." Umeko was rambling and her voice was getting high pitched and louder.

"Shh. You have to be quiet or someone will come."

Fear rose in Min-He's throat. Umeko was right. They would kill her. The Japanese army would shoot her straight through the head and make them all watch as an example to the rest of them. It was likely Min-He would be killed along with her for even being here right now. Umeko's sobs became more and more hysterical.

"Stop it. We don't have time for you to lose control."

Min-He thought over the options. They could run away but they wouldn't get far. As soon as the body was discovered, a hunt would be on and there was no doubt they would be found. They needed to hide the body. While Umeko took deep gulping breaths, Min-He walked over to the Colonel and studied him. He was not a tall man (or hadn't been a tall man, she thought to herself), but he was thick and muscular. She wondered if a tiny girl and an invalid could move his body. There wasn't any choice. They needed time to think up a plan, but the sun would be up soon and there would be no moving him then. They had no time.

"We need to move him to my room. No one will be in my room for two more days and that will give us time to figure out what we're going to do."

Min-He knew it was the most half-baked idea imaginable but there were no other options. If they left him there, the first enlisted man to visit Umeko would be face to face with the dead colonel. She reached down and gripped the handle of the dagger. With more confidence than she felt, she gave a firm yank and pulled the dagger out of his neck and dropped it next to him on the bed.

"You need to help me."

The girls wrapped his body in the sheet. Umeko grabbed a crimson blanket she had been given as a gift by an enamored lieutenant and placed it over the bloody roll.

"We're going to drag him."

Min-He looked outside the door; there was no one in sight. Each girl grasped a wrapped leg, pulled him out the door and dragged him the six feet into Min-He's room. They lugged Min-He's mattress into Umeko's room and replaced it with Umeko's own bloody mattress. Min-He winced, her stomach stitches ripping. Umeko shuffled back and forth across the drag marks in the dirt outside until they could only see her footprints, not the imprint of a murdered colonel's body. Looking over Umeko's room, Min-He was surprised how normal it looked, no blood on the floor or walls. It was like it never happened. They sat together in silence, each wrapped in their own thoughts, until the sun came up.

They forced themselves to go to the breakfast room. Things had to appear normal. Hours passed and they still had no plan. They thought of burying the body that night but had no shovel and nowhere to bury it. They could move him to the bathhouse and hope when he was found the blame would be shifted somewhere else, but there was no explaining away the bloody mattress which was sure to be found in the ensuing search. Min-He knew their only option was to run. That night, after all the officers had left or were in for the night, they would leave. The fence behind the bathhouse was concealed enough they could climb it without being spotted. The Colonel's body would be found the morning and the blame would be placed on Min-He. They would head toward Shanghai. As she leaned over her plate, she could feel her stitches shift. She knew she wasn't in any condition to be running. But there were no other options. She smiled tenderly at Umeko.

"Don't worry. I have a plan."

The little girl's face changed to relief, trusting in her Mio. The morning passed quietly. Sounds of laughing and impatient men in line for the other girls filled Min-He's room and made her tense as she worried someone would disregard the "No Entry" sign on her door, open it, and discover the Colonel. She had placed one of her blankets over the roll and the other over the bloody mattress. She filled her yellow rucksack with a few items in preparation for leaving: some clothes, her cosmetics, and finally the porcelain dog and cat. She clutched the little Siamese cat in her hand. She ached at the loss of Takao. Her own despair had been overtaken by Umeko's plight. Nothing like covering up a murder to take your mind off lost love, she mused. She kissed the figurine and placed it in her sack.

She was applying the doctor's white sticky cream to her remaining stomach stitches when she heard them: doors slamming open and shouts of anger and fright from the girls and soldiers in the rooms. One door after another was pulled open and the occupants startled out of their embraces. Min-He stopped breathing as she heard them coming from the rooms on her left, one door then the next. She knew it was over.

Sunlight flooded her room, and the bulk of a Japanese soldier filled the door frame. His eyes met her face then traveled to the roll of blankets on the floor. He shouted out words Min-He barely registered and three more soldiers ran into the small room. Min-He huddled in the corner. The soldiers crouched together on the floor and unwrapped the Colonel's body. She watched as his body rolled face up out of the sheets, onto the floor, stiff and solid. His face had turned a pasty greenish white. She couldn't take her eyes off it. A kempei's black boots entered the room. Min-He didn't look up, focused instead on the black boots stepping toward her, stepping over the Colonel, and her cheek stung with a sudden slap. The black- booted kempei grabbed her by the arm and pulled her into the courtyard. All the girls stood in front of their doors and dozens of soldiers were gathered in the courtyard, all staring. It was deathly quiet.

Min-He turned to Umeko's door. Umeko stood there, white as death. Umeko started towards her, and Min-He shook her head frantically. No. They would not both die for this.

Umeko took a step back, her face scrunched up uncertainly. The soldier yanked Min-He forward and dragged her around the side by the bathroom and past the main building. More soldiers joined them, and she saw the gleam of excitement in their eyes. They would likely be richly rewarded for such a find, she thought sourly.

As they passed the front door of the main building, she saw a flash from the corner of her eye. She turned her head and saw Father running toward her at a full sprint. Without slowing, his body hit her full on, slamming her to the ground. Before she knew what was happening, he was flailing wildly, punching her in the arms and around the shoulders. His fists were coming at her frantically, but she felt little pain as their impact was surprisingly light. As the soldiers pulled him off her, he managed to lean over her ear and whispered,

"Say nothing. Not a word."

Stunned, she watched as Father ran ahead of them, through the gate, and toward the military encampment.

She walked out of the front gate for the first time in nearly two years. They passed rows of tin-roofed barracks with soldiers milling about, all stopping to stare at the girl being pushed forward by the kempei. The kempei led her through the black door of a brick building, down a flight of stairs, the air growing wetter and colder with each step. At the end of a long hallway, he threw her into a dank room with a tiny, barred window at the top. The walls were streaked with dark smudges, what she could only imagine to be blood, or feces, or both. The room reeked of urine. The door clanked shut behind the kempei and she was left alone. She scrunched on the icy floor in the corner, opposite the only other object in the room, a dilapidated wooden bucket. Water dripped from the ceiling onto the floor. She crawled across the floor to position the bucket under the drip. Listening to the plop of the water hitting the wooden base of the bucket, she waited.

Hours passed before the door slammed open. In the doorway stood a short, balding police officer she had never seen before. The water on the tops of his black boots glistened. She got to her feet.

"You have been condemned to die for the murder of Colonel Ishida," the kempei stated, nearly emotionlessly. He stared at her, clearly expecting her protest, her cries of innocence, or begs for mercy. She remembered Father's whispered words and said nothing. She mustered every ounce of energy and courage in her body, and instead of cowering, she forced herself to stand up straighter, and lifted her jaw. He would not see her cry or beg. The kempei's forehead creased and his face grew red. He pulled back his fist and punched her full force in the jaw. She fell to the ground, her mouth filling with blood. The door smacked shut, echoing in the empty room. She spit out one of her bottom teeth onto the filthy floor.

Hours passed as she waited for the men to return to take her to her death. The room echoed with the dripping water into the bucket. No one came. She dozed against the wall and was surprised to wake and find the sun beginning to rise. Shadows flashed and pairs of tattered brown boots tromped by the sliver of window above her. Shouts reverberated in the distance from soldiers going about the business of the day. Her final day. Her stomach rumbled, nearly 24 hours since she last ate.

As the day progressed, she imagined her death. Shooting? Beheading? Hanging? She couldn't imagine any other options. Her hunger came and went, intermingling with the gnawing fear in the pit of her stomach. She had thought very little about the afterlife in her nineteen years. She wasn't sure she believed in the Christian heaven, and she already knew hell. Night fell and still no one came. Panic rose and she banged on the door for help, for food, but still, no one came. Sleep relieved her in brief respites throughout the night, but panic and hysteria threatened to steal her courage.

Finally, hours after the sun had risen on the third day, the door flew open. Relief flooded her. Even if it meant death, at least the uncertainty was over. The respite from fear was brief. As she was escorted up the stairs, into the blinding sunlight, she found herself wishing to be back in the cell. She did not want to die.

The kempei walked, bayonet to Min-He's back, past the rows of barracks to a wooded area outside the base gate where a massive congregation of soldiers had gathered.

"Move aside!" the kempei shouted.

The soldiers separated in a great wave, like the Red Sea her father had described in his Sunday bible stories. Her father.

Min-He's eyes stung. What would the Japanese tell her family about her death? Or would she simply not return, her family forever wondering what had happened to their daughter, wondering if she was still alive?

As they reached the front of the parted crowd, she saw Mother and Father standing beside the eight other girls. She looked away at Fujika and Hinata's smirks and scanned to find Umeko. She saw only the top of her head as Umeko stared at the dirt, her shoulders shaking. The other girls' faces were pale. Ayame stroked Kiku's hair as the glaze-eyed girl shifted anxiously from foot to foot. The kempei herded Min-He with his bayonet towards them. Then, shockingly, with a shove into her back, she was pushed into Mother.

She turned and watched the kempei march away. This made no sense. Why was he leaving? Was he setting her free? Umeko leaned against Father, her face ashen. Mother grabbed Min-He's arm, nails digging into her loose flesh. Min-He opened her mouth to speak when she saw the reason the crowd had gathered. In front of them was a long trench. On his knees at the mouth of the trench, his hands roped behind his back, knelt Takao. Her breath left her body.

"What's happening?" she shrieked.

"Shut up!" Mother dug her nails in deeper.

A Japanese major, a long sword in his right hand, approached Takao. A hush fell over the crowd of soldiers. Takao's eyes met Min-He's. He gave her a weak smile. She couldn't wrap her mind around it. What had Takao done? Why was he tied? The soldier with the sword stopped beside Takao and turned to face the crowd.

"In the name of our honorable emperor, Private Takao Hayashi has been condemned to die the dishonorable death of a traitor for the murder of Colonel Ishida."

As the sword rose above the executioner's head, Min-He fell to her knees. Her scream and the executioner's sword pierced the air simultaneously. She watched in horror as Takao's head toppled to the side and his lifeless body was kicked mercilessly into the trench. Everything went black.

She awoke alone in her room. A soldier's moans of pleasure reverberated from Umeko's room. Two cold rice balls sat on a plate by her door. Her starvation outweighed the lack of desire to ever move again, and she shoved them down tastelessly, not wanting to feel any satisfaction. Blood stained the front of her blouse and skirt. Her jaw throbbed and her tongue sought the empty space in her mouth where her bottom tooth had been. She gathered some clothes from her packed bag that still sat on the mattress soiled with the colonel's blood and limped from the room to bathe. The soldiers waiting in line in front of the eight other doors pointed and whispered.

Min-He left her bloodied clothes in a pile near the tub. She sat in the cold bathwater and watched as the stitches in her stomach and leg came unraveled in the bloody water. She welcomed the pain. Takao's loss was like a machete through her own throat. The light he brought into her dark cell had been extinguished. She grieved the loss of his laughter, his sarcastic charm, the way her head fit into his shoulder as he lay next to her. Takao's death was the abolishment of hope. Her hope to escape this hell, her hope to return to a normal life, shattered.

Leaving the bathhouse, she walked purposefully around the main house and found Father sitting at the front desk, counting blue tickets from the week. He raised his eyebrows at her appearance. She opened her mouth to speak but he held up his hand to silence her and gestured for her to follow him. Father led her into the medical room and pulled the door shut behind them.

"What did you do?" she demanded.

"I saved your life."

"I didn't want saving," she lied.

"I didn't do it for you. I did it for Umeko. I know it wasn't you who killed that monster. I didn't know what they'd force you to say. I won't have that child's blood on my hands."

"And what of Takao's blood? You let an innocent man go to his death."

"He chose that death. I merely told him what the soldiers had found. He chose to confess to the crime. For him, this is how he could save you. This was his seppuku, his honor suicide."

"But he died a dishonorable death. His family will think him a murderer."

Father smirked bitterly.

"The Japanese army will never admit the disgrace of a mere private killing a decorated officer. That would not be good for morale or public opinion. You'll find the stories reaching home bear little resemblance to the truth, Mio. Both Takao's family and the family of Colonel Ishida will hear of honorable deaths fighting for the glory of the emperor." He looked at her stricken face and touched her gently on the shoulder.

"He wanted this, Mio. He loved you."

*****

Her body healed as the crisp breezes of spring melted into the clammy heat of summer. The soldiers came and went, days blending into one another, each one blurring into the next. Min-He and Umeko spoke little of the events of that day, the only reminder were the brown stains on Umeko's mattress that still remained in Min-He's room. Umeko had tried to take the mattress back, but Min-He insisted it stay with her, the blood a daily reminder of Takao's sacrifice.

As the sluggish July sun bore down upon them, the Japanese soldiers changed. The officers were colder, more distant, and angrier. The enlisted men were clingy. They were worn, sad, often weepy. While some became more physically intense, using her body as a pounding board, others sat and cried, talking of home, of shame, of defeat. The girls could smell the change in the air. In the distance, they could feel the echoes and trembling of air raids over what Min-He imagined was Shanghai, sometimes even hearing the planes buzz overhead. In early July, Amaye and Kiku were taken by an officer out of the gates and never returned. Father said they were shipped out with a unit departing for Peking. Two days later, Botan, Ren and Ran came to say goodbye, told they were leaving with a unit to Manchuria.

"Our uncle is in Manchuria. Maybe I can find him there," whispered an excited Ren. Botan snorted. Min-He smiled at Ren and nodded, not having the heart to tell her what she remembered from her school geography lessons about the massive size and scope of Manchuria. She hugged her goodbye, and they exchanged Korean addresses for the days when they would all be home again. Umeko claimed not to know her address but hugged them all with intensity.

It came as no surprise to any of them when, as August came, Umeko and Min-He spent most of their days playing cards, strolling around the complex, entertaining only a handful of men a day. Fujiko and Hinata kept their distance, giving them nasty looks as they passed their open doors. Then one day, no soldiers came. A second day passed with not a single soldier taking a ticket at the pi house. On the third day, Mother called the four remaining girls to the sitting room. Her hair was in disarray, her eyes wild. Sweat dripped from her brow. Father hunkered by her side, staring at the floor. Mother spoke directly.

"Hiroshima and Nagasaki have been bombed. Three days ago, the emperor declared surrender. The war is over. Father and I are leaving here tonight with the last of the troops. Fujiko and Hinata may accompany us and the remaining troops. However, you Korean girls are staying behind. I would not advise staying here, as the Chinese are said to be killing anyone is Japanese or who collaborated with the Japanese."

Fujiko and Hinata scurried out of the room to gather their belongings. Mother stared at Min-He and Umeko for a moment then turned without another word and walked out. Father spoke.

"Shanghai is a few days walk to the east. Follow the main roads and the river. I know a woman there who can help you."

He handed Min-He a wrinkled sheet of paper with a name and address and a small bundle wrapped with string.

"Give this to Madam Chang." Along with the bundle, he handed them each a small pile of Japanese military cash and two hundred yen.

"Take care of yourselves girls. I don't know what's going to happen to us now." His eyes teared up and Min-He was shocked to feel a lump in her throat. He reached out, caressed each of their cheeks, then turned and left the room abruptly.

Min-He and Umeko stared at each other. It was over. They were free to leave. A panicked urgency overtook Min-He.

"We need to go now."

Umeko followed numbly as Min-He sprinted to her room and began packing. In minutes, all her meager belongings were in the yellow rucksack the old Chinese maid had given her on that first day almost exactly two years before. The last thing she placed in the rucksack was Takao's porcelain cat. With one last look at the bloody mattress, she slammed the door behind her.

Min-He and Umeko arrived in Shanghai dirty, wet, and starving eight days later. The food they had taken from the kitchen had run out the day before. Their hopes to take food from farmers' fields had been dashed. Thousands of refugees filled the streets and fields, all headed somewhere other than where they were. All were hungry and poor. The girls quickly found their Japanese military money was worthless and the street price in yen for bread or rice was far more than they were willing to part with. They spoke to nearly no one, remembering what Mother said about the Chinese killing Japanese collaborators. They tried to blend in but kept a distance from the others on the crowded roads. Both girls only spoke only a few words of Chinese and understood very little of what was being said around them.

Shanghai was filled with Chinese, Japanese, Koreans, and people of a hundred other nationalities. Walking though the crowded, trash-filled streets, Min-He heard Korean being spoken by a group of young men lurking at the entrance to an alleyway. She raced to the men, leaving Umeko scrambling behind her.

"Please... you are Korean? Please help us. We're also Korean. Can you help get us home?"

A thin man with a shadow of a mustache sneered at her. "I know who you are. Pi. Fucking the Japanese isn't going to get you a welcome mat at home, you little whore. But I'll give you a yen for a suck." The boys howled with laughter. Umeko pulled her away, Min-He's eyes filled with tears.

"But... they're Koreans. They were brought over here to fight for the Japanese too. I don't understand." Umeko put her arm around her as they walked. Min-He was surprised at how much taller Umeko had gotten. At fifteen now, she was no longer a little girl.

"Come," Umeko whispered, "Let's find Father's friend."

Hours of walking the jagged, winding streets of Shanghai eventually led them to a red roofed rowhouse at the end of a laundry-lined alley. Umeko knocked and a short, squat Chinese woman answered the door.

"Please, we were sent here by..." Min-He realized she didn't even know his name. "By a man we called Father. He was our...guardian."

"You are ufaro?" the woman asked, referring to the Japanese name for whore.

Min-He looked down in shame. Umeko stepped up, "Yes."

Umeko handed the woman the bundle. The Chinese woman unwrapped the package and studied the brief letter from Father included in the contents. Min-He caught only a glimpse of the sparkly stones that lay beneath the letter.

"I am Madam Chang."

The woman stepped back and indicated they should enter. She led them through a sitting room where two Chinese girls perched on a long, red couch. The girls stared at Umeko and Min-He and giggled.

"I'll provide you with room and board. We no longer regularly serve the Japanese forces, but the Americans landed a couple days ago and will provide us with a nice customer base. You'll receive 25% of everything you earn."

Madam Chang continued to rattle on about rules and regulations, but Min-He's head roared and she heard nothing. They were in a pi house. Father had sent them to another brothel to work. She stopped.

"No. No, I will not work here." She glared at Madam Chang.

Surprised, Madam Chang said, "Suit yourself. I thought you were here looking for work and a place to stay. Feel free to leave anytime." The woman turned and sauntered back to the sitting room.

Umeko grabbed Min-He's arm.

"We have no other choices. Where are we going to stay? What are we going to eat? We don't speak Chinese, we know no one here, the Koreans aren't going to help us. Until we can afford a ticket home, we need to do this. At least we're here by choice." Min-He had never seen Umeko look so intent. Without waiting for Min-He's consent, Umeko crossed into the sitting room and said,

"We will stay."

Within a week, the first major units of Americans entered Shanghai and the Japanese surrendered the city. The Americans were frightening: large and unencumbered with booming voices and laughter that bounced off the walls. Min-He could understand nothing of what they said and tried to avoid all eye contact with them. The Americans refused to wear condoms and Madam Chang refused to require them to. Within a month, both Min-He and Umeko were infected with venereal disease. Unconcerned, Mother brought in the first doctor they'd seen since arriving. He gave them a stinging white powder and a shot and sent them immediately back to work.

Madam Chang generously brought in an American officer to help Min-He and Umeko fill out paperwork to be repatriated to Korea. They were told it would be months before a ship was available. In the late afternoons, Min-He walked the Bund of Shanghai, searching for a way to get a ticket to Korea. Hundreds of American and Japanese ships left the port those weeks, ships filled with repatriating Japanese. Every attempt to find a ship to Korea was futile: all ships were full. The weeks turned colder, the war was over, but Min-He was still trapped. Her shame grew as each day passed, knowing that selling herself was no longer being forced upon her but was her choice. There were not enough tears to cleanse that wound.

As the last snows began to melt, a ginger-haired American soldier tracking yellow mud appeared at Madam Chang's door with a letter. Space had opened on a carrier ship and Min-He and Umeko were scheduled to leave for Inchon, Korea the next morning. Min-He clutched the letter and flew into Umeko's room. She was underneath a Chinese businessman. Min-He flung through the paper door, ignoring the disgruntled man's protests.

"We're leaving! We're going home, we're free!"

She waved the letter in front of Umeko's nose. Umeko glared at Min-He. She said in Korean,

"I'm not finished here. This client pays well. I'll come see you when I'm done."

Min-He left the room to the sounds of Umeko comforting the startled businessman and ran down the hall to her room. She packed, for the final time, her yellow rucksack. An American customer came to her door, and she shooed him away. Madam Chang could kick her out tonight for all she cared. She and Umeko could sleep on the docks and await their boat. She would never, ever again touch a man unless it was her choice. Her choice. The words were delicious.

She waited in her room for Umeko, who never came. She joined Madam Chang and the other girls for their evening meal and Umeko sat quietly beside her, saying little. After dinner, she smiled at Min-He's stories of home and begged off to bed early, saying she needed rest for the trip home.

Morning came and Min-He was up with the sun. She tapped on Umeko's door and slid it open. Umeko was lying on her mattress, sleep clearly not yet reaching her red eyes.

"Do want me to help you pack?" Min-He joked. Umeko's belongings were as meager as her own.

Umeko patted the bed next to her and sat up.

"Mio, I'm not going." Min-He stared at her, not comprehending. "I have nothing to return to. You have your family, friends, a home. I have a mother with too many children who sent me to this. I can never return to Korea, Mio. Never. I can't read or write. What am I going to do? Marry an old man who'll treat me like his whore? I may as well stay and be paid for that."

"But Umeko, we're free. We don't have to have this life. Come home with me. My family will welcome you as their own. Please."

"Your family will never welcome me. They'll see me as what I am. You, they may be willing to forgive, but I will only be a daily reminder of what they sold their daughter into. No, Mio, I'm staying. This is my home now. These Americans are kind to me. You see the gifts they bring me?" She gestured to her shelves, indicating the bottles of perfume, soaps, and candy. "Maybe I'll work here for a few years, then one of them will marry me and take me away to America. I can meet Betty Grable." She picked up one of her Hollywood magazines and sighed at Min-He's tears.

"Oh, Mio. Don't be angry with me. We're different. This is not who you are. But it's all I know."

Min-He walked alone to the shipyard and found the ship listed in the letter. A medical officer examined her and permitted her to board. Alone, she leaned across the railing, remembering Soon-Yee's chatter on a similar railing two and a half years before; remembering Takao, his warm embrace, his final smile; remembering Umeko, her childlike innocence, her fateful choice. As the ship pulled out of the port into the Huangpu River, Min-He turned from the railing, and vowed never to look back. She turned her face towards the sun and began her journey home.

# Marianne
## Munich, Germany
## October 1944 – October 1945

Eric and Hans arrived home for lunch as expected. Martha had returned from the market earlier that morning, gaped quizzically at Marianne stationed firmly in Eric's office, and was ordered to "Get out and go home."

One look at Marianne's face convinced her not to argue. Marianne heard Hans dash straight into his room, oblivious to her presence in his father's office. Eric strolled in minutes later. He froze in the doorway at the sight of his wife parked at his desk, a spillage of documents before her.

"What is this?" he asked, shaken at the sight of his wife in his chair.

Marianne did not speak. She simply stared at her husband. Eric marched over to his desk and began to shuffle though the papers spread out before him. Recognition flashed through his eyes, followed by confusion, anger, and, for a brief second, fear. Marianne watched as each emotion replaced the next in the empty blue pools she thought she knew so well. Anger settled back in.

"Where'd you get these? This is classified military information. You opened my briefcase. You could be arrested for possessing these."

"So, arrest me then, Eric." She spat out his name. "Or perhaps you could give me the same treatment as these enemies of the Reich."

She thrust forward one of the grey photographs from the file: an image of a mother, leaning over and clutching her child in the protective grasp of her arms, her body shielding him from the Stormtrooper's rifle aimed at their backs.

"They're Russian Jews, Marianne. Vermin. We were ordered to clean up after the Wehrmacht army. This is the ugly part of a united, powerful Germany."

"This is a defenseless woman and a child. A child, Eric. What kind of monster are you? How could you do this?"

271

"Do you really think we can just leave the children alone? They will grow up and seek vengeance for their fathers' deaths. Germany and Grossdeutchland must be free of Jews and unfortunately that involves activities that are difficult. However, as Hitler's soldiers, we must do our duty to the Fatherland. They're not the same as our children, Marianne. They're like rats, breeding and infesting."

"You murdered these people. These are not soldiers. This..." her finger tapped the photo of the mother clinging to her child, "This is not war. These are women, children, old men. You murdered these people."

Bile began to reform in her throat. She fought the urge to vomit.

"It is not murder. It is necessary. You must think of our children and their futures. They're going to be part of the perfect society, but we need to purify and cleanse to achieve an Aryan civilization for our children."

"I am thinking of our children. I want you out. Pack your things and get out."

"That's your treasonous father talking. I told you to stay away from him."

"This is not my father. This is all me. The man I married would never do this. To murder women and children? How can you look at yourself in the mirror? How can you look at our children? I want you out. I never want to see you again."

Eric began collecting the papers from his desk. He circled around the desk and grabbed the briefcase from the floor and stacked the documents in it. Slamming it shut, he bent over, inches from her face.

"I'm going to assume this is the result of your nerves getting the best of you with our daughter's pregnancy and your son's pending departure. I'm going to call Dr. Hauser and make you an appointment. I'll give you the space you need to pull yourself together, so I'll leave in the morning. Hans is coming with me. When I return, I expect you will be back to being my wife." He walked across the room and turned in the doorway to face her.

"And Marianne, if you ever open my briefcase again, I will shoot you myself."

Eric and Hans left the next morning. Marianne begged Hans to reconsider, to finish high school before going into the army. Eric ignored her and Hans just gave her glaring looks, shunning her interference. She hugged her son, who stoically refused to return her embrace, cold and embarrassed at her affection. The girls cried when they left, not understanding why their father and brother were leaving weeks earlier than originally planned. Marianne sat at the kitchen table and cried with them.

Erika stroked her on the back and buried her blonde hair into her mother's shoulder.

"I know how much you'll miss them," Erika comforted.

Marianne just nodded, letting her daughter misunderstand. Images of Hans behind the rifle pointing at that woman and child poured though her. Her only son was in the clutches of the devil, being delivered to hell itself. She knew he would become his father. Hans was lost to her. When he returned, if he returned, what kind of monster will he have become?

She reached for her two daughters. As she held them close to her, stroking their innocent, tear-stained faces, she silently promised to save them. She would not lose them too.

The doctor's office called that morning. Eric had done what he said and made her an appointment. Rather than give an explanation of a cancellation to the nosy receptionist, she kept the appointment. And now, hearing the doctor's words, she was rooted in shock.

"Congratulations, Frau Hofmann. You'll be getting your Mother's medal after all!"

The doctor beamed.

"Oh no, Dr. Hauser. I only have three. Erika's baby will make four, but that won't count toward my Mother's medal."

When he laughed and explained it to her, she smiled politely and pretended to be excited. Eight years of trying and the first and only time she had been with her husband without desperately desiring to get pregnant, she conceived. The doctor's words echoed in her ears. A year ago, she would have been beyond blissful. Today, fear and dread filled her. How could she bring another child into this world? How could she raise this baby alone? What would Eric do when he returned if he knew she was pregnant? He would never let her leave.

She took the bus to Schwabing and paused at the FeldherrnHalle. Each passerby stopped and saluted. "Heil Hitler" echoed through the air. Chills ran through her. For the first time in months, she circled the hall and walked the stone streets to the gallery. 'Vogel's Gallery' had been painted over in dull, white paint but could still be made out behind the new lettering 'Schultz's Books'. She stared at the window display, now filled with military guides and cookbooks. Images of Andreas and Franz made her weak. She leaned against the window, feeling faint.

"Are you ok, madam? May I help you?" The bookkeeper stepped out of his shop. She looked at him, an elderly man with spectacles. She emphatically shook her head. She didn't need any help.

After the third month of her silence, the wives stopped calling. She was done. When women of the Frauenschaft called to check on her, she knew they were looking for gossip fodder. The day Eric left for Russia was the day she stopped attending their meetings, ending the charade of the good German wife. She took great pleasure in setting fire to her Frauenschaft membership card. Martha watched her suspiciously, but Marianne kept her employed, her fear of betrayal outweighing her dislike for the woman. She grew larger every day, all the while watching Erika's stomach expand. Erika's soldier never wrote. Erika held out hope where Marianne knew there was none. She held her daughter at night, as the tears were boundless.

The air raids grew worse. Four, sometimes, five nights a week, Marianne and her girls cowered in their shelter and prayed. Martin pleaded with them to move to the countryside, away from the bombings, but Marianne refused. This war had taken her family, she would not let it take her home. They huddled at night over the BBC and listened to their country collapse.

The day Erika went into labor, Eric came home. Martin had refused to take Erika to a hospital and risk being trapped there in an air raid surrounded by disease and infection. So, Erika's baby would be born at home. When a loud rap sounded at the door, Marianne, thinking it to be the nurse's aide she called, opened the door. A red jagged scar slashed across his left cheek. She stared at it then met his eyes. She began to shut the door, but his foot stopped it. Erika's cries from upstairs echoed in the background. Eric's eyes flew to the stairs.

"Erika," he said.

Marianne didn't resist when he shoved the door open and pushed past her. He brushed against her stomach and froze. His eyes fell to her bulging belly. He reached his hand out to touch it. The baby shifted under his calloused palm.

"I didn't know."

Marianne shook her head and swatted his hand from her stomach. It was then she noticed his uniform. Not the uniform of an SS Obersturmbannführer, but that of a Wehrmacht corporal. Gone was the crisp SS uniform guarded by the Totenkopf skull and menacing black boots. Instead, Eric stood before her in a tattered grey-green wool jacket and leaking brown boots.

"Your uniform..." she stuttered in confusion.

"Things are not safe for SS officers, Marianne. The Russians are coming from the East and the Americans from the West. Our German officers are being shot or arrested. The only way for me to make safe passage home was in this disguise."

"Where is Hans?"

He didn't respond and his eyes shifted to the floor. Marianne felt her legs weaken. Her heart began to race.

"Eric. Where is my son?"

"I don't know," he whispered. "His detachment left Budapest in February. I arranged for him to be shipped home, but he refused. He said I wasn't going to take away his right to fight for the Führer. I was so proud of him, Marianne. I tried to find out what happened to his unit, but we lost all communication. You don't know what it's like out there. No one knows what's going on. Soldiers are deserting, entire companies are disintegrating. We're lost, Marianne. Germany is lost."

"I don't care about Germany. You were supposed to take care of our son."

Tears began to form in Eric's eyes which only amplified Marianne's heartache. She fought to reconcile the anguished man who stood before her with the monster she knew he had become.

Erika's cries echoed down the stairway. Fear struck Eric's face. Marianne felt the strange need to comfort him.

"Erika's ok. My father is with her."

"He is forbidden to be in this house!"

"You aren't exactly in the position to make that decision now, are you, Eric?"

His face reddened and his shoulders slumped. Marianne felt no sense of victory.

"Can I see her?"

"You can see her, but you can't stay."

"No, it won't be safe for anyone. I'm leaving tomorrow. I had to come here first. Marianne, I need your help to destroy everything in my office. Even the most benign files need to be destroyed. Anything can serve as evidence. You must help me, for all our protection."

"So, you didn't come all this way to see us."

"No, I came all this way to protect you. If the Americans get those files, even you will be arrested."

"But I didn't do anything."

"It doesn't matter, Marianne. You're the wife of a high-ranking officer. And you knew. That alone will make you guilty."

"But I didn't know. Not until last summer. I didn't know."

"Don't be naïve. Where do you think it all came from: the furs, the jewels, the stockings, the food? By accepting all of that, you're guilty too."

"I am not. I would never do what you did. You're despicable, Eric."

"And you reaped the benefits of it. Look at this place. Don't fool yourself."

Erika's screams sent him scrambling up the stairs, leaving Marianne in the foyer. She looked around at her home, the home where her children were raised, and realized he was right. She couldn't stay in this house built by the blood of thousands. She climbed the stairs to welcome her grandchild into a world she no longer knew.

Louisa Maria Adler was born in the bomb shelter that evening. Shortly before she began to crown, Martin and Eric carried the howling Erika down two flights of stairs to escape the whistling in the skies. By candlelight, the infant girl, with the surname of the father she would never know, came into the world with the screech of a fighter pilot. Eric hovered over his grandchild and whispered things Marianne had no desire to hear. The sweet cooings of a grandfather to his first grandchild had no room in her heart in this black bomb shelter of Germany. At first light, Marianne carried little Louisa up to the waiting bassinette that had once held her mother and went to Eric's office to begin the culmination of their former life. Minutes later, he followed.

"Everything's boxed?" he asked, surprised.

"Yes. I needed it out of my sight. Turns out, it will make our job much easier."

"Martha's lighting a fire in the yard. We can burn it."

"An act you're quite familiar with, I gather."

He changed the subject.

"Why didn't you write me about the baby?"

"What would it change? Would it have undone everything? I wanted this baby for so long, but not now. Not after all this."

"We can start a new life, Marianne. I'm leaving for Italy tonight. I have a visa for South America. I have money there, waiting for us. In a few months when the baby's born, when things have settled here, you can join me, and we can have a fresh start. I have documents for you, Christa, and Erika. And Hans when he returns. Once I'm there, I'll make arrangements and send documents for Louisa and for our baby. These documents will give you new names and will allow you to disappear.

"I've arranged a place for you to hide in Weisbaden. You can go there and no one will know who you are. Your husband, a corporal in the Wehrmacht Army, was killed in France, and your home in Munich was bombed. So, you and the children can go there with no suspicions at all. You should see it out there, Marianne, so many people are homeless and wandering everywhere. The bombings, the destruction..." He faded off for a moment, then refocused his attention onto Marianne. "Then you can join me in Argentina, and it can be a whole new life for us. A whole new life for this baby."

She looked at the hope in his eyes, the delusional desire for everything to be as it once was. She, Hans, the girls, and the new baby were all enveloped in the fantasy of his new life. She gave him a weak smile, and for reasons she couldn't put a name to, she nodded at him.

They spent the morning hauling boxes into the fire, transforming Eric's guilt into embers carried away with the wind. When Eric left that afternoon, he handed her an envelope of new identity papers. As he walked away toward the bus station in his ratty corporal's uniform, Marianne made one last trip to the backyard bonfire. She threw the envelope in. Along with the evidence of Eric's guilt, she watched her escape route become devoured by the flames.

Her son, Andreas Franz Hofmann, was born in Stadelheim prison on a warm early June day. In April, the Americans had come to Munich. She and the children had moved into her father's compact apartment over the clinic shortly after Eric had left, abandoning their beautiful home. She was arrested when Martha told the Americans, in exchange for a ham and a basket of rolls, that Marianne helped her husband burn SS documents. When the American officer came for her, she went willingly, despite the sobs of her daughters and the protests of her father. Days later, with a group of thirty citizens from the town Dachau, she was brought to the concentration camp.

The American major with angry grey eyes assembled them beneath a gateway that read,

'Arbeit Macht Frei'.

"You are here to witness what has been done by your countrymen, in your town, under your noses. You must see for yourself the atrocities of what has been done here. You must look within yourself to recognize your own guilt." The angry American colonel condemned them.

Marianne walked through the typhus-ridden camp, bore witness to the amassment of bodies in the crematorium, the mounds of decaying corpses in the boxcars. She listened as the citizens of Dachau covered their eyes and pleaded with the Americans.

"We didn't know. How could this have happened? We sent shipments of food to this camp. How could they have starved? We knew the camp was here, but we didn't know this."

The Americans forced the Germans, at gunpoint, to look, to not close their eyes at the sight of maggot-ridden flesh and diseased piles of emaciated bodies.

But Marianne said nothing. She looked, she listened, and she said nothing. Hans and Eric had spent time here. Weeks before they left in August, Eric had taken Hans to tour the camp. They knew. They were responsible. Her son, her flesh and blood, fought for this. She was guilty. She would accept whatever the Americans brought her way. She would not look away.

After Andreas was born, Marianne tearfully gave him up to her father. She held him for mere minutes before he was pulled from her arms by the female guard in attendance at his birth. A week after Andreas's birth, Marianne learned she was to be transferred. With a line of other blue prison-garb clad women, she trudged to the yard to await the transfer truck. Dozens of male prisoners roamed the yard, some in small packs, some alone and heavily guarded. Whistles and hoots followed the women to the gate. Some of the women giggled and waved, ignoring the admonition of the guards. Marianne averted her eyes from the other prisoners until the crow-faced woman next to her nudged her stomach with her elbow.

"Somebody has an admirer," she cackled.

Marianne turned towards the woman's gesture. Across the yard, the former Standartenführer Scharf stood, his stare boring into her. He was alone except for a single, armed guard standing five feet away from him, scrutinizing his every move. An SS Standartenführer was a prize for the allied victors. Scharf raised his arm, as if to greet her. She took a half step out of line, gathered the bile forming in her throat, and spit. She met his eyes, raised her chin and, slowly, deliberately, turned her back to him. As she exited the gate in her line, she did not look back.

Marianne was taken to Aichach Prison with other SS wives who were rounded up in the weeks and months after the war's end. They proclaimed their innocence and insisted upon the innocence of their husbands. Marianne said nothing. She listened to the stories of the female SS guards in the prison with them. The stories of the Bitch of Buchenwald, Ilse Koch, wife of the commandant of Buchenwald consumed her with disgust. They regaled stories of Ilse's collection of lampshades, book covers, and gloves made of human skins and her affinity for shrunken human skulls. Marianne turned away from their gleeful gossip and huddled by herself, refusing to engage with other "innocent" women.

The only time she spoke was to the American interrogators. She told them everything, again and again. To each new colonel or lieutenant who brought her into the bright white room with the cushioned brown chairs, she repeated her story. She recalled in detail the Einsatzgruppen documents. She could recite them verbatim, the names, locations, and events documented in the papers from her husband's office. She admitted burning the documents with her husband. She gave them every piece of information they wanted but one: the location of Eric. She hated him. He was guilty of monstrous crimes. She told them every detail of his corporal's uniform and his leaving and giving her false documents that she burned. But she could not bring herself to utter the word "Argentina." She had given her son to this war; she could not give it her son's father.

Two months after the birth of Andreas, she was inexplicably released. A guard informed her to pack her belongings and she assumed another prison transfer. Instead, her father greeted her at the gate of the prison. The August sun burned down on them as she raced into the arms of the beaming Christa and Erika and held her infant son again.

She cradled Andreas as they drove back toward Munich, towards the city she wondered if she would ever recognize again. She listened as Christa chattered on about the Americans in Munich and her new school. Marianne exhaled for the first time in months.

"I was surprised when they told me I was going home. It was unexpected. When I was told you were at the front gate, I thought it was trick. I had no idea my sentence had been commuted."

Martin looked at her sideways.

"Your sentence wasn't commuted. The charges against you were dropped."

"I don't understand. I'm guilty. I pled guilty."

"That plea was withdrawn. Evidence made its way to the courts which convinced them to drop the charges against you."

"What evidence?"

"Not all Nazi documents were destroyed, Marianne. In fact, much to their dismay, those bastards left an enormous amount of evidence behind. Let's just say that on a tip, the prosecutors were led to some documents the Nazis gathered against you located inside the SS headquarters. Your criminal charges with the Nazis of 'aiding enemies of the Reich', in fact, brought about your early release."

Marianne watched the countryside go by, reflecting on the twists fate brought her way.

They laid the babies down in matching bassinettes and she sat with her daughters and Martin in the kitchen of his apartment. He poured her a cup of coffee.

"Have you heard anything from Andreas?" Marianne asked her father.

"No. Nothing. My contact in Würzburg has disappeared. I don't know if the Nazis got him or if he was able to get away. Maybe he's just laying low. Either way, I don't know how to contact him to find out who Andreas became after he left him. I assume you've heard nothing from Eric."

"Of course not. He's smarter than to try to contact me in prison."

Martin never asked what she told the Americans; she knew he didn't want to know.

"I don't think you can stay here, Marianne."

She looked at him, surprised.

"We'll try to find our own place as soon as we can."

Martin shook his head.

"No Marianne, of course you can stay in this apartment as long as you want. I meant stay here, in Munich, maybe even in Germany. If they don't already know, people are going to find out who Eric was and what he did. They're already talking about public trials for the war criminals. Eric's name is going to come up. People around here, the very people who spat at the Jews and rallied around Hitler, are pretending they knew nothing. They're pretending they were innocent bystanders. Some were. But if they were all innocent bystanders, these atrocities would never have happened. And now they're looking for a scapegoat, someone to blame. Someone to point the finger at and say 'THEY, THEY are the ones responsible for what happened to the Jews, the homosexuals, the disabled.' If they have someone to blame, the finger is no longer pointed at themselves. I'm afraid you and the children are going to be amongst those scapegoats."

"Where would we go?"

They were silent for a moment then Martin started to laugh.

"Well, I think we can rule out Argentina."

Marianne raised her cup in agreement.

"No, certainly not Argentina."

*****

Summer chilled into fall and Christa returned to school. Erika replaced Martin's pretty receptionist when Karin's fiancé returned from the war and she headed north to get married. Marianne spent her days with the babies, pushing a double pram through the streets of Munich. She frequently walked past the old gallery, hoping one day she would show up and Andreas would be hanging a new painting in the window. The bookstore had gone out of business and the windows were boarded with graffiti-laden planks.

On a brisk October day, she returned to the apartment, babies bundled up like babushkas in their pram. A wheel had come loose on the walk home and she yanked the stroller in the door and flew three feet backward from the jolt. She heard laughter behind her.

"Do you need a little help there?"

She swung around and flew into Andreas's arms.

"Oh, thank God! You're safe! You're home!"

He helped her pull in the damaged stroller and inspected the contents.

"Twins? You have twins?"

"No. The boy is mine and the girl is my daughter Erika's."

They each took a baby into their laps and settled on the sofa. Marianne clutched his hand.

"Tell me everything."

Andreas told her how he went to Würzburg the day they parted and was given a new identity and the name of a safe house near Hamburg. He travelled north, convinced every conductor was ready to arrest him, and was offered a job on a farm.

"You, a farmhand?" She laughed. "You've never worked a day in your life!"

He told her stories of pretending to know how to milk a cow and stealing naps behind haystacks. When the owner of the farm was drafted and he feared his identity would be questioned if he was unemployed, Andreas took a job in a shipyard warehouse in Hamburg.

He was drafted from the warehouse in November when all men who were remotely fit to fight were taken. At that desperate point in the war, even a missing arm didn't exempt him. He served in the army as a private under his assumed name until March, when he was able to escape. He slept in barns and in mountain shelters, hiding with other army deserters in the forest until the war was over.

"When I finally returned to Munich, each day I searched the lists of survivors to see Franz's name. I haven't found him, Marianne."

Marianne broke his gaze for the first time. She told him everything: about her husband, about Hans, and finally, heartbreakingly, about Franz. His eyes glazed over, and he nodded.

"I knew. I always knew. But I hoped."

"I know," she said simply. "I know."

They sat quietly together for a long time, each lost in their own thoughts.

"And now," Marianne said finally, "you'll stay here with us. You're my family now, Andreas."

"No, I haven't come here to stay. Quite the opposite. I've come to take you."

"What do you mean?"

"Marianne, my brother in the United States asked me to come there. He's able to get me a visa as I had my application in even prior to the war and have no Nazi party affiliations. I can take my spouse and children with me. Marry me, Marianne. Marry me and come start a new life with me."

He laughed at her startled expression.

"I know I'm not exactly the marrying type," he said. "But we can work that out when we get to the states. We can have one of those amiable divorces and live happily ever after. But for now, marry me and let me help you have a new life as you helped me. You and the girls and the babies can come as my family. When we get settled, we can get a visa for your father. You were never a Nazi party member officially and when you take my name, the details of the past will get lost in the paperwork. This is a chance for a new beginning."

She paused, her mind racing. "But I'm already married."

"You can file for divorce. If he never returned, Eric can more than likely be declared dead." Andreas watched her wince. "I'm sorry."

"What if Hans were to return and we weren't here?"

"Your father will be here for months, maybe even a year or two, before he'll be able to secure a visa. Hans would know to look here for him. Marianne," Andreas said gently, "You can't hold on to false hopes. If he doesn't return by the time Martin's ready to join us...."

She nodded.

"Like, you, Andreas, I know. I know, but I hope."

"What do you say, Marianne? Will you marry me?"

She smiled. "Yes, Andreas. I will marry you."

"I do love you, Marianne, and I wish I could offer you this for real."

"I know who you are, and I love you too. I'll settle for a short and happy marriage and an even happier divorce."

The door rattled open, and Erika and Christa rushed through followed by Martin. He was all smiles.

"So, you found our house guest!" Martin exclaimed. A flash of recognition spread across Christa's face.

"Andreas!" She rushed to him, as if she had known him a lifetime. His face lit up.

"Come sit down everyone," Marianne gestured. The girls perched on the couch as Martin settled in the corner to listen. "There is much to tell..."

# Rachel
## Warsaw, Poland
## January – May 1943

Rachel and Marek returned to his apartment shortly before first light. The streets home were empty, but they knew the battle would soon fill the streets again, and this time the Nazis would know what to expect. Rachel's glow turned to sorrow at Zivia's hopeful face when they returned to the apartment. Marek took Zivia aside and Stefania held her as he told them Artur's fate. Rachel joined Aron at the stove, taking the cup of ersatz coffee he handed her.

"I'm sorry about Artur, Aron. I know he was your friend."

"He was a good man. I expected we would all have met that same fate yesterday. To be alive another day is a miracle."

"A miracle? I thought you didn't believe in God."

"I don't know what I believe in anymore," Aron sighed. "I have Vera and I have you. And I have the strength to fight. For now, that must be enough." Rachel nodded. He continued.

"And I see you now have Marek."

"How do you see that?" She blushed.

"I can tell. You looked this way the day you agreed to marry Josef. I'll never forget it. Dad said you shined."

She thought of Josef and how his hands shook as he proposed that spring day five years ago. It seemed like another lifetime.

"I didn't say that to make you sad. You can't feel guilty about Josef. You loved him. You still love him. You should honor him by remembering him with happiness. But you have to survive here, and part of survival is reaching out to each other. Part of survival is finding someone to live for."

She watched Marek in the corner on his knees, whispering to Zivia in soft, comforting words.

"Vera and I will be lonely in the house without you," Aron teased.

She took a long drink of the tepid ersatz.
"It's time for me to move on."

*****

Mordecai had been able to supply Marek with only one new gun. The next three days were spent in the lower bunker, waiting for news, and making plans to acquire more supplies. Aron and Marek came and went, reporting back on each new development. The resistance kept the Nazis fleeing with rooftop and window snipers and an occasional grenade. Regardless, the Nazis rounded up nearly 5000 Jews from the ghetto, jammed them into trains, and deported them from the Umschlagplatz. On Sunday, January 21, the Nazis killed nearly 1000 Warsaw Jews in the streets in retaliation for the resistance. Then, suddenly, the deportations and manhunts came to an end and the ghetto was quiet again.

The Polish resistance outside the walls, encouraged by the will and fight of the Jews, increased their supply of guns to the ghetto, now knowing they would be put to use. Mordecai and the other leaders of subgroups of Jewish resistance banded together to become unified in their renewed efforts to prepare to fight again. They knew the silence was a temporary reprieve, and they had every intention of being ready to fight again.

Rachel stopped going to work altogether. The work permit meant nothing anymore and there was other work to be done. Bunkers were built in nearly every building across the ghetto. Rooftop escape routes and underground paths were developed. Several weeks' supply of food, water, medicine, and necessary provisions filled the newly created bunkers. The flow of weapons and supplies from the Polish resistance multiplied and the sewers created a virtual railway of goods into the ghetto. The icy days turned to a cool, breezy spring as February melted into March.

Rachel removed her shoes, covered in filth from her trip through the sewer. She had been away three days, exiting the sewer on the Polish side, and staying in the lavish home of a Polish physician who smuggled medicine out of a hospital. Marek met her at the door, taking the small package from the waistband of her pants. He squeezed her hand but barely looked her in the eye. Something was wrong.

She surveyed the room. A blanket covered a jagged pile that Rachel knew to be guns. The ZOB had designated Marek and Rachel's apartment as one of several places within the ghetto where weapons were stockpiled. Pinkus sat at a makeshift plywood table covered with glass bottles. He dipped rags in a wooden bucket and stuffed them into the bottles. Zivia stacked the completed bottles in a pile in the corner. Stefania lay quietly on a cot against the wall, a cloth covering her face. In the back room, Vera and Aron sat on the bed. Even from across the room, Rachel could see Vera was crying. Vera got up and left the room, her eyes red and puffy.

"Rachel," Aron called.

She passed Vera, who wouldn't meet her eyes, walked into the bedroom, and shut the door. Aron gestured to the straw mattress. She shook her head. She didn't want to sit. Being told to sit meant bad news. She wasn't going to sit.

"Rachel, I'm leaving the ghetto. The leaders have decided some of us need to leave to ensure the group is divided up. Soon, they're going to fight. But if it doesn't end well, some of us will still..." he stammered over the words.

"You mean in case the rest of us die, at least some will still be alive."

"There's information we hold, and if all of those people die, then the information goes with it."

"What kind of information?"

"Information that can save lives. Names, addresses, locations of people in hiding, locations of people who can provide valuable resources. Marek was only able to secure a false Polish identity for one man. I look Aryan enough to pass."

"If you're caught, they'll kill you."

"I think my chances are the same if I stay or go."

"No. Your chances are better if you go. Aron, you go, and you run. Get as far away from here as you can. Don't look back. I know you plan to fight from the outside, but I don't want you to fight. I want you to hide."

"You know I can't do that, Rachel."

"Aron, you must. You must stay alive to find Adam. When this is all over you need to find him."

He smiled at her, "When this is all over, I will find you and together we'll bring Adam home."

His eyes began to well up. She touched his cheek and whispered,

"I love you, Brother."

"I love you too. I will find you when this is over. Make me proud."

They embraced and after a few moments, wiped their tears and returned to the others, where Aron said his goodbyes. Vera wept grievously and Rachel held her as Marek accompanied Aron into the quiet street. Rachel and Vera watched from the window as Marek handed Aron a stack of papers he shoved in his jacket pocket. The men embraced. Marek returned to the apartment minutes later and pulled Rachel into his arms. She buried her face into his shoulder, but not before she saw his cat eyes were as red as her own.

The remaining Jews in the ghetto prepared for the end. Bunkers were built to hide, and rooftop passageways were built to attack and flee. Every Jew in the ghetto now had two addresses: one where they lived and one where they would hide when the time came. March eased into April and they had one date on their minds. They knew the Nazis, predictable and consistent in their terror. April 19, Passover, the eve of Hitler's birthday, was in their sights.

*****

The sound of voices in the distance brought them to the window.

"The bastards are singing."

Rachel stood behind Marek and watched the long line of uniformed soldiers, marching in unison, row after row though the main gate. Amid the line were black tanks, Nazi soldiers sprouting out of the top like weeds in a metal garden.

"It is time."

Hours before, they gathered their weapons and went to their designated posts, awaiting the arrival of the enemy. Every window on their upper floor was filled with a fighter and a gun, a pile of grenades, and a collection of handmade bombs. Hunkering down on the rooftops lay snipers, positioning themselves to fight. The ghetto was silent except for the chanting of German voices in unison and the clunking of their boot steps. The fighters waited, hearts racing, barely breathing.

An ear-splitting explosion filled the air with thick, grey smoke. A remote bomb detonated at the hands of what Rachel knew to be Mordecai's crew. The battle had begun. The Germans on the ground were barraged by bullets from windows and rooftops. Rachel saw a grenade fly past her window and land on a tank below. The German driver leapt from the tank and Rachel set him in the sights of her rifle as he hit the ground. She fired and hit him squarely in the chest. He fell back into the flaming heap of metal. She diverted her attention to the Nazis fleeing on the ground and began firing. Inches in front of her face, the glass shattered, and she threw herself against the wall next to the window. A bullet hole sat in the opposite wall, inches from where her face had just been. She peered back out and watched two Nazis run into the front door of their building.

"Marek! Two just got in!"

"Don't worry,' he called across to her, "They'll get them."

She nodded, knowing they had a small brigade arming the stairwell, waiting in silence for this opportunity. Second later, shots echoed through the hallway. She heard Stefania's bird-like hoot. The Nazis were down.

The Germans fled en masse back toward the entrance and around the corner. Soon there were no more in their line of sight. Gunshots and explosions still echoed across the ghetto.

"Let's go!"

Rachel followed Marek up the stairwell to the rooftop pathways they created on each building, linking one to the next. From the rooftop, she could see the locations within the ghetto where the fighting was still taking place. They ran, crouched as low as possible, over the rooftops toward the gunfire. Marek stopped to talk to a soot-covered teenager Rachel recognized from Mordecai's crew.

"They came in at three locations: the main ghetto, the brushmaker's ghetto, and the shop-keeper's ghetto. We have news the fighting is continuing in all areas and the Germans are falling back. Word's coming down to hold your post and fire at anything in a Nazi uniform."

"Get word to Mordecai to send a messenger over to..."

Marek's words were interrupted as the young man's head flung backward and he collapsed into a heap. Rachel and Marek fell flat-bellied onto the rooftop. Marek began shooting into the small band of soldiers below who had fired the fatal shot. Rachel lay flat and averted her eyes from the hole in the boy's forehead. Marek fired at the backs of the fleeing soldiers, hitting one in the leg. The Nazis turned the corner before he could get another shot in.

"God damn it. Come on."

She looked at the young man, memorizing his face.

"I'm so sorry," she whispered. She grabbed the rifle lying next to him and, crouching as low as she could to the roof, trailed Marek back to their apartment windows.

By nightfall, the ghetto was still. The Germans had fled and groups of Jews gathered in the streets. The dead Nazis were stripped of their weapons and uniforms. Marek kissed her before he left for Mila Street to assess the situation for tomorrow. She didn't sleep until hours later when she heard the door unlock and he lay down beside her. She curled into his lean body and lost herself in his embrace.

Waves of black smoke billowed from the brushmaker's ghetto the next day. Hundreds of Nazis entered the ghetto with torches, setting fire to buildings and shooting or rounding up the hundreds of people forced from the flames. Nazis laughed as they used the Jews who hung from the windows to escape the flames as target practice. Dozens of fighters from the outer ghetto sections fled through back alleys and underground passageways through the thick smoke into the central ghetto. As the days passed, countless new faces filled the bunkers of the main ghetto.

Rachel sat on the lower bunk of a wooden-slatted makeshift bunkbed and folded her hand of cards in concession to Vera. Marek came into the room, his face black with soot. She smiled at him and wiped his face with her sleeve as he bent down to kiss her.

"Some fighters have come in from the city. One of them was living in the safe house where I sent Aron."

She and Vera jumped from the cot and followed Marek through the bunker. Hundreds of people, wearing little but their undergarments, lay in varying states of rest, playing cards, reading, or just fanning themselves, trying to breathe in the thick stifling air of the bunker. A handful of illicit radios spewed static as their owners turned the dials in search of reception. In a corner of a third room, they approached four men Rachel didn't recognize.

"Is one of you Iztak?"

"I'm Iztak," said a bespectacled man with thick black hair and a matching moustache.

"I understand you were at the K house with Aron Kaplan. What do you know of his where-abouts?"

Iztak frowned and shook his head.

"I was at the K house with Aron for a couple days when we were warned our location had been compromised. We split up and arranged to meet at an alternate location. But Aron never showed. The house was stormed shortly after we left. I know Aron wouldn't have stayed, but he never arrived at the safe house. I heard a dozen Jews were rounded up and taken to Pawiak Prison and shot that day. I believe Aron was with them. Otherwise, I don't know why he wouldn't have returned." He looked at their shattered faces. "I'm sorry."

Vera began to cry. Marek reached for Rachel, but she pulled away and crossed the stale bunker. She climbed the metal ladder into the rubble of the former apartment building. It wasn't safe in the open during the day, but here, at least, she could breathe. She heard her name called from the bottom of ladder but ignored it as she gulped the fresh air at the top. She ascended into the sunlight beaming through the shattered walls of the first floor apartment, weaved her way through the rubble and curled into a corner. She sat quietly, waiting for the tears to come. Marek found her curled behind a pile of bricks. He stroked her matted hair and she reached for him. In the rubble, they made love desperately, looking for impossible solace in each other's arms.

Days were spent in the bunker as the Nazis stormed the ghetto, torching, bombing, and gassing the remaining buildings. They left the bunker each night to fight, spending their remaining ammunition and throwing their last grenades. News came from the outside that the Poles, sensing the impending doom of the ghetto, refused to supply the Jewish fighters with more weapons. Weapons were now scarce and ammunition nearly depleted. The few handguns that remained were useless except at close range. Rachel and Marek kept handguns tucked into their pants. Marek checked with her frequently to make sure it was still there. Marek called it their last resort. She didn't need to ask what he meant.

Rachel took her daily turn at guard duty, watching the entrances to their bunker for signs of Nazi recognition. Several times though out the weeks they moved from bunker to bunker as Nazis discovered their hiding places. Escape routes were utilized through the sewers and underground passageways to the relative safety of yet another airless bunker.

Marek spearheaded an effort to organize an escape route out of the ghetto through the sewers. But communication with the outside was scarce and difficult. The sewers were a maze that could only be managed with a guide, and once out of the sewers, the escapees would need a place to hide. Word was out that the Nazis were flooding or gassing part of the sewer lines and were stationing guards under the main streets to capture any attempting escapees. Daily battle victories were growing fewer, with more news of Jewish fighters captured than news of Nazis killed. Each day they survived was their only victory.

Rachel thought of Adam, and it seemed like he belonged to her a hundred years ago. The faces of her parents and Josef blended into the dust of each bunker they fled. She escaped into the arms of Marek each night, their lovemaking hidden under a thin blanket on a cot, their sighs blending into sounds of other desperate couples, each finding comfort in the heat of another.

It was early in the morning. Rachel curled more closely into Marek, the rough stubble of his cheek brushing against her neck. She tried to block out the sounds of the fifty odd others sharing the airless space. Her eyes shot open at a sound that didn't belong in the morning rustling. Marek sat straight up, nearly knocking her off the canvas cot. A whistle.

"Damn it, damn it," Marek murmured. The bunker had been compromised. They slipped on their pants and shirts in seconds, their speed becoming almost routine. She slipped her handgun into the front of her pants. They raced through the crowded bunker.

"The north exit has been blocked!"

They heard the cry and turned with the crowd toward another exit. Panic brewed in the enclosed space. A line of bodies formed around the east exit, a metal ladder leading into the rubble of an alleyway. Two dozen people disappeared into the hole above until shots were heard and the exit sealed shut. A thick bearded man called down from the top of the ladder.

"We've been found."

Marek grabbed Rachel's hand and pulled her through the crowd.

"To the sewer exit," he yelled out as a swarm of people began to follow.

They arrived at the exit to find a small group of people already peeling back the bricks blocking the sewer exit. Rachel's hands shredded as she pulled at the bricks, desperate to uncover the opening to the sewer. They had bricked off the exit to hide the bunker from Nazi guards navigating and searching the sewer system. Now those bricks were the obstacle to their survival. A victory cry from Pinkus led to the kicking in of the remainder of the wall and the bricks fell, forming a gap into the sewer. Marek led the group of twenty through the hole.

"Where's everyone else?" Rachel asked as she helped the last woman standing on the other side through the gap.

"Gas," she said.

Rachel grabbed Marek's hand, refusing to acknowledge the horror, as they set off through the sewer. She shook away the images of the dozens of people who hours before she had laughed with, played cards with, now lying dead from gas piped into the bunker. Pinkus and Zivia were there, but she hadn't seen Vera or Stefania in the chaos. The thought of their bodies lying swollen from the gas terrified her. She pushed the thought from her head as she fled through the sewer.

The maze of the sewer encompassed them. At each turn, small groups of two or three of the refugees set off in different directions as the sewer branched out. Pinkus and Zivia split off with a group of ten with Marek's consent. Smaller groups were more manageable and likely to survive. As she watched them flee down a dark corridor, Rachel knew she'd never see them again.

The sewage was knee deep; each turn down a different tunnel became more and more difficult to manage. After an hour of twist and turns, the remaining group reached a brick wall. A small tunnel veering to the left would require crawling on hands and knees. The other option was turning back.

"What do we do?" demanded a thick-bearded fighter.

"We head back. Find another route," said a woman carrying an infant, sleeping in her arms.

"No, the crawl space might lead outside the ghetto," Marek said.

"How do you know? How does anyone know? We are lost."

The six others milled around anxiously.

"What do you think, Rachel?" Marek looked at her to make the decision.

"We know what is back where we came. I say we go forward."

"I'm not. I'm heading back." The others nodded in agreement with the woman with the baby.

"Then you go." Marek said. "We're going forward."

He looked at her with such confidence Rachel felt a pang of panic. What if she was wrong? The others disappeared into the dark, leaving Marek and Rachel staring at the crawl space.

"Maybe we should go with them. Lord knows where this will bring us."

He pulled her to him, the stench of the sewer momentarily suppressed as she buried her face in his neck.

"If you think we go on, then we go on."

Echoes of gunfire broke their embrace. German voices mixed in the distance with screams of the Jewish fighters. The high-pitched wail of the infant was silenced with a gunshot. Rachel hit the ground and crawled through the tiny space with Marek at her heels.

"Hurry, Rachel!"

Sewage splashed into her mouth, and she vomited into the spillage as she forged herself ahead. Echoing German shouts came from the entrance behind them. Gunshots blared off the walls. Marek yelped behind her. She stopped and turned around in the tiny space.

"Keep going!"

"You've been hit!"

"It will be worse than just my foot if you don't keep moving!"

They crawled through two hundred meters of raw sewage until the narrow tunnel spilled into a passageway that allowed them to stand. She helped Marek to his feet, and he leaned on her as they hobbled far enough through the new passageway that they no longer heard the German shouts from the entrance of the tunnel. They came to rest in an area where the sewage was only a few centimeters deep and Rachel could inspect Marek foot. His leg was bleeding profusely where the bullet had pierced above the ankle. Even in the dim light, Rachel could see his face growing pale. She ripped off her wet, filthy shirt and wrapped it around his ankle. Her camisole clung to her, and Marek smiled.

"You look beautiful."

"You're crazy."

"They know we're here."

"Yes."

"I can't run with this ankle."

"I know."

He took her face into his hands and kissed her.

"I love you, Rachel."

"I love you, too."

Marek reached in front of her pants and pulled out the handgun and placed it in her hands.

"How many bullets do you have?"

"Two," she whispered.

"I have one." He took out his own gun and inspected it.

"They won't take us alive."

"No," she whispered, "I don't want to give them the satisfaction."

"Maybe there's a small chance."

"There isn't," she replied.

Their eyes locked. Rachel had never felt so sure in her life.

"I love you," Marek whispered.

In the distance, the echo of Nazi footsteps bounced off the brick walls. Marek held his gun in front of him.

"Are you sure?"

"I am sure."

She curled next to him in the sewage and Marek pulled her into his lap. Rachel thought of Adam and smiled. Her son was safe, she was sure of it, and that was all that mattered. Adam would survive. She leaned into Marek and kissed him, her lips lingering on his. He smiled as they parted and raised his gun to his temple. She held her own gun to her head.

"I love you," she said. Rachel pulled the trigger.

## July 1946

He watched the children race through the yard. There was no mistaking him. His tiny frame weaved through the other children in pursuit of the ball and after he threw it, he collapsed in an exhausted heap on the playground.

"That's him," the nun said, pointing her finger at the boy.

"I know."

"We call him Tomasz."

He crossed the yard toward the boy, and as he got closer, the boy became aware of the lean, blonde man.

"Hello."

He sat down next to the boy. The boy gazed up at him. The man breathed in sharply at the boy's deep, expressive eyes. His father's eyes.

"Hello, Tomasz."

"Do I know you?" The boy spoke with no note of suspicion, only curiosity.

"You did once."

The boy tilted his head to the side and the man smiled.

"Are you my father?" the boy asked.

"I am not."

The boy's face fell, and the man covered the boy's dirty hand with his own.

"But I knew your father. And I knew your mother. Your mother was my sister."

The boy looked back up at him, his eyes wide.

"I'm your uncle. My name is Aron. I've been looking for you for a long time."

"Well, I've been here," the boy gestured to the convent orphanage and Aron laughed at the obviousness of a five-year-old.

"Do you like it here?"

"I don't know. I like the other kids and Sister Noemi is very nice. But Mother Edzia is not. She smacks my hand if I take too much food at dinner."

Aron tried to match the boy's seriousness and struggled not to smile. The boy rose and stood in front of him. Aron's heart pounded as he looked at him and saw Rachel. He longed to pull him into his arms but was afraid to frighten him. The boy startled Aron with his question.

"Yuri's mother came to get him last year. Have you come to get me?"

Aron's eyes filled.

"What would you think if I said that I did?"

The boy stood quietly for a moment and reached out and touched Aron's cheek.

"Your face looks like me."

"It does," Aron whispered.

The boy sat back down, his knees touching Aron's. Aron reached out and took the boy's hands in his own.

"Tomasz, I've come to bring you home."

The little boy crawled into his uncle's lap. Aron breathed him in and allowed the tears to fall.

# Claire
## Anzio, Italy
## April 1944

April 10, 1944

Dear Barbara Ann,

I'm sure you've heard the news from Bill that the wedding is back on. As soon as we're both home, we'll be married. He mailed back my ring and I, of course, accepted. He would still like me to go home. Now that my father's name is cleared and his status is again changed to MIA, Bill feels I've done all I can here. I said I'd consider going home after Anzio. I can't abandon my unit here.

You won't believe this, but Tom Parker is here. In Italy! He's been temporarily assigned as a floating physician within the units until they settle on a permanent assignment. I was shocked when he showed up. What's the likelihood two people from Green Meadow will run into each other in Anzio? Honestly, though, we've seen very little of each other. It seems we're always working opposite shifts. Occasionally I'll see him in the mess hall and we'll eat a meal in a group but that's the extent of our time together. He splits his shifts between the 95th and my unit, so we rarely work together.

We still remain very busy, and I am, to say the least, tired, but I'm grateful for every moment I can help our boys. The shells continue to fly day and night. They've dug the hospitals nearly three feet into the ground and we feel much safer knowing we have that bit of protection.

However, I won't be here much longer. My unit ships back to Naples next week. We lost three nurses in the past two weeks: two from hepatitis and one who found herself in an awkward situation, if you know what I mean. All three were shipped home, leaving us short-staffed. Rather than replace the nurses, they're replacing our entire unit. I'm reluctant to admit this and feel guilty saying it, but I'm grateful my time at Anzio has come to an end. These three months have been the most challenging of my life. I'll let you know as much as I can about where we end up. For now, we're headed to Naples for a short rest period and then the unit will be given its next location. Tom won't be accompanying my unit, so he will remain in Anzio.

Please continue to write often. Mail call, however infrequent, is always a thrill. I so look forward to your letters and packages.

Yours, Claire

As Claire carried the envelope to the mail truck on her way to the triage tent, she watched a couple of recovering patients throw a baseball. She thought of the impromptu baseball game the men played a few weeks ago. The late March sun had brought warmth to a surprisingly quiet, still day. Several of the doctors, corpsmen and ambulatory patients assembled a pickup game and played for much of the afternoon. They drew a huge crowd of fans, including the nurses who wheeled patients out to watch. Axis Sally, the Nazi radio announcer, commented on it in her broadcast. It was unsettling to know they were being watched. Shortly after the broadcast, the shells began to fall again. The brief respite was over. Axis Sally now called Anzio 'the largest self-supporting prisoner of war camp in the world.' Last week German aircraft littered the beach with leaflets, urging Allied soldiers to surrender. 'The beachhead,' the leaflets read, 'has become a death's head.'

Claire couldn't begin to count the number of young men she watched die in her three months at Anzio. Healthy, vibrant young men, with families who loved them, with so much to live for, struck down by the vengeance of war. The ones who survived to be sent back to their foxholes or home to their families, had death lingering behind their eyes, and could never again be whole. Anzio had stolen a piece of them. As Claire cringed at the whistling of the Anzio Express from the mountains, she knew that she too, would never be the same.

*****

"Claire!"

"You can't just barge in here, Tom. What if I was dressing?" she snapped, but her stomach fluttered.

"Look, Claire! Letters..." he gasped for breath. "I was at mail call and I heard your name but you weren't there so I got them for you. Letters. A letter from your father. A letter from Robert."

Claire leapt from the cot. She grabbed the two letters from his grasp, one with her father's name written in a hand she didn't recognize, and one from the US War Department. She ripped her father's letter open and sank to the ground. Tom knelt behind her, and they poured themselves into the words.

January 30, 1944

Dear sweet Claire,

You must have been frantic with worry these past months. I'm sure by now you've received notification from the War Department that I've been found. I know what those telegrams look like, and I want to fill in every detail I can for you. Forgive the strange handwriting. A British nurse is transcribing this letter for me.

In mid-September my unit was preparing to move with the 15th Army from Salerno to Naples. John Keller and I were having a drink in his tent after a long shift and Lt. Edmond Romo, the unit translator, came in. He informed John that an Italian boy had shown up at the hospital, pleading for a doctor to help his mother who was struggling to give birth. The boy refused to leave. After much discussion with John, I convinced him to allow me to help the woman, on the condition I return to the unit "hell or high water" by 0800 the next morning. Because it was in violation of regulations, the translator arranged to have the boy and his horse meet me a kilometer up the mountain. I packed my medical kit in my duffel bag to be discreet and exited the camp through the forest on the mountain to rendezvous with the child.

The boy took me to his home where I delivered breech twins in less than three hours under the eye of an inexperienced young midwife. Regretfully, we lost one of the twins. The other, a scrawny but healthy boy, survived. I was humbled that the mother named him Roberto. She was so thankful and warm, despite the loss of her other child.

Shortly after midnight, I woke her eldest son from his sleep and asked him to return me to Salerno. Halfway down the mountain, we were descended upon by a band of the Wehrmacht army. The boy fled into the woods. I only hope he made it safely home.

I was taken by gunpoint to their unit, which consisted of only a few dozen German soldiers, as apparently they engaged in a losing battle with the Americans and Brits only days before. I was certain they would kill me. All I could think about was you. Every two or three days the unit moved from point to point, and I was transported with them, tied at the wrists and ankles. No one spoke to me for days. I heard the soldiers arguing amongst themselves and I could only assume they were discussing me. On the sixth or seventh day, a foul-breathed barbarian named Schroeder came into the tent where I was held and threw my medical kit at me. In rough English, he asked if I was a doctor. I told him nothing. He informed me I'd be attending to his men's medical needs or he would kill me. If any of them died on my watch, I, too, would die.

I demanded to be sent to a POW camp under the authority of the Geneva Convention. I don't want to upset you, Claire, but he managed to show me how little interest he had in hearing my demands. For the next four months, I travelled with this German unit, tending war injuries and common ailments. Each night, I wondered if it would be my last. I was kept in a tent with rudimentary medical supplies. At least three times I attempted to escape but each time was recaptured. On my third attempt, I was severely beaten in both knees after being apprehended. Let's just say I'm glad my high school track and field days are over.

I'm quite sure my presence was not known by any Nazi authorities. I was never interrogated and never contacted by the Red Cross or other personnel. I strongly believe this group of soldiers decided to keep me hidden, not only to have immediate access to a physician, but also to use me as a safety net. And that's precisely what happened.

The unit received orders to evacuate. The Germans had me tied and gagged in the back of a truck as we headed west to a new location. A British Infantry unit began firing upon us from a forested area. I could hear Schroeder, clearly trapped, yelling to them,

"British doctor! We have a British doctor here."

Schroeder crawled into the back of the truck and I was terrified, but also had a flicker of hope. That's my last memory until I woke on an RAF hospital ship nearly a week later. According to information I've since received, the Germans attempted to trade me for their own freedom. The only result I know of that outcome is I am alive and in Allied custody, and an RAF airman walked by my bed the morning after I regained consciousness and whispered,

"No worries, Yank. We got those bloody bastards for you."

When I awoke in the hospital, I was under heavy military guard. The British Army had no idea who I was, since I had been stripped by the Germans of all my identification and my uniform. The soldiers who took me into custody told the medical personnel that I had been delivered to them with a severe head wound. My best guess is that Schroeder knocked me out before attempting to trade me. These past three days since I have awoken, I've undergone hours of interrogation by both the Americans and the British to confirm my story and my identity. A letter a general in Washington received from Mildred Keller went a long way to clearing my name. My grief over the loss of John Keller is profound.

With all my heart, Claire, when I look back at the entire experience, the only regret I have is the suffering you must have endured. I never lost sight of the fact that had I not left camp that night, a mother and her child would be dead.

I've enclosed an address where I can be contacted. At this point, I don't know if I will receive a medical discharge. I'm not requesting one. I love you more than anything in this world, and I'm sorry for the hell you had to go through these months at home, worrying about me. I'm hoping for a few weeks of R & R and to be able to return to Minnesota to see you. I love you.

Dad

MISS CLAIRE WEBER
17TH EVACUATION HOSPITAL APO 42
THE SECRETARY OF WAR DESIRES ME TO INFORM YOUR
FATHER MAJOR ROBERT J WEBER HAS RETURNED TO US
CUSTODY SINCE JANUARY 23 IN ITALY IF FURTHER
DETAILS OR INFORMATION ARE RECEIVED YOU WILL BE
PROMPTLY NOTIFIED.
UL10  THE ADJUNCT GENERAL

Claire handed Tom the telegram from the War Department as he finished her father's letter.

"He's been found for over two months and I'm only hearing now?" Claire was incredulous. Her father was alive. He was safe.

"I can only assume the rerouting of his letter from Minnesota caused the delay. He had no idea you were anywhere but home. His letter and the War Department's must have landed in the same shipment."

Tom sat on her cot next to her. "What now, Claire?"

"I need to write to him. I need to tell him everything."

"I mean, what after that? You came here to find your father. He's been found and is safe. What now?"

Claire hesitated before speaking. She glanced at the photograph of Bill she displayed on her table after receiving her ring.

"I guess I'll marry Bill and go home to my father."

She looked at Tom's face and saw a glimpse of anger she didn't understand.

"Is that who you've become, Claire?"

"That's who I always was, Tom."

"I thought you were more than that. What about your unit? What about Marie? What about...," his voice trailed off.

"I don't know. I promised Bill. And my father will want me home."

"Your father will want you happy."

Claire sighed. "What do you know about my happiness, Tom? Bill could make me happy. Maybe you came here to babysit me, but I don't need your protection or your fatherly advice. Ava Sorenson is waiting at home to marry you. I don't see you encouraging her to leave her fiancé and focus on her job. You have Ava. I have Bill and my father."

"You think I came here to babysit you?"

She looked up at his incredulous expression and struggled for words. His eyes seemed so wounded and raw, she wanted to reach out and pull him to her.

They spoke at the same time.

"Tom..."

"Claire..."

They laughed awkwardly.

"Claire," Tom continued, "I need to tell you..."

The high-pitched squeal of the air raid siren blasted through camp.

"Sounds like Anzio Annie knows my unit is leaving tomorrow and is bidding us her farewells."

"Damn it!" Tom cursed, "Get to the shelter, Claire. I need to get to the hospital to assist in surgery in case we lose power again."

He ran out of the tent and Claire fled to the shelter to huddle in its darkness one last time, her mind struggling to make sense of the question Tom posed. What now?

*****

Claire pushed down the photograph album on top of the duffel bag and with a tug, it zipped. Except for the green trousers and jacket she had on, everything she possessed was in that bag. Two new nurses would move into this tent in the next few days, and it would be as if she and Marie had never been here. Three months of her life in this hole-peppered tent. Marie's last night of sleep was on this cot. Bonnie and Ellen's voices chirped outside. Claire tossed her bag over her shoulder and joined them.

As the truck filled with the nurses of the 17th evacuation hospital jostled toward the beach and the waiting LCI landing crafts that would transport them out of Anzio, Claire looked back at the Half Acre of Hell and saw Tom standing where they had just departed, too late to say goodbye. She raised her hand to wave, but he didn't see her. Their truck sidled over to allow another to pass, this one filled with new, eager-faced nurses fresh from North Africa, on their way to the beachhead. Their replacements.

"Good luck, girls," Claire whispered and waved to them as they passed. They would need it.

*****

"Oh, this is heaven, simply heaven!" Ellen sighed.

Bonnie, Claire, and Ellen simultaneously flopped backwards onto their beds. Real beds. With real sheets. Who cared that the sheets were stained and the ceiling cracked and the walls paper-thin? Their new assignment in a hospital that was an actual building with nurse's quarters that were not tents was a luxury beyond any scope of their imagination. After two days of settling in, they had just completed their first hospital shift, a miraculously short 8 hour shift as opposed to the 15-16 hour stints they had become used to.

"Don't get comfortable, girls."

The door opened and Mary Sue Beall, a nurse in her early 30s from Columbus, Ohio, plopped down on the fourth bed in the spacious room.

"I just overheard Major Beck telling one of the corpsmen it looks like we'll only be here two or three weeks."

"I don't care," Bonnie sighed. "I'll take however long they give us of this paradise!"

On move-in day, the three friends watched Mary Sue unpack her bag and settle into the fourth bed. Mary Sue was perfectly pleasant. But they knew that bed should have belonged to Marie. Claire placed a photograph of Marie on the dresser, her smile glowing from the balcony that first day in Capri, what seemed a lifetime ago.

"How do you think our leaves will be assigned?" Claire asked.

"Probably in shifts of twenty nurses again. I hear we're getting four days in Capri."

"I wouldn't mind getting one of the last shifts. I think if I went into that Capri hotel again right now, my system would shut down and I'd fall right into a coma of shock with that much luxury so soon after Anzio!"

The girls laughed and a knock sounded on the door. A voice called from outside the door.

"Lieutenant Weber. You have a visitor in the lobby."

A visitor? A tingle ran up Claire's spine. Tom.

The girls whistled as she checked her hair in the mirror. They knew the visitor was a man, as a woman would have come directly to their room. She was grateful to have washed her hair last night. For the first time in three months she could actually style her hair, as the steel helmets were now stored under their beds. There was no makeup to be found, as all had been traded in Anzio. She pinched her cheeks, ignored her friends' giggles, and dashed down the stairs to the lobby.

Standing by the front door, nervously shifting from foot to foot, stood Bill. Claire froze. Disappointment rushed through her, but she angrily shook it away. Guilt flooded her as she realized she hadn't once thought of Bill since leaving Anzio. Between the excitement of moving and settling in to new surroundings, she hadn't thought to try to locate him.

"All I get is a blank stare?"

"Bill!" Claire mustered up excitement and ran the final few feet. She hugged him quickly.

"Why are you here? How'd you find me?"

"You're my fiancé, Claire, I keep track of the goings-on of your unit. I'm stationed about twenty miles from here. A supply convoy was coming this way for a delivery, and I hitched a ride."

He took her left hand. "Where's your ring?"

Claire looked down at her finger. The day after he returned the ring, Claire took it off, as it had become too large for her. He'd given it to a farm-fed Minnesota girl and returned it nearly two years later to a battlefield nurse, stripped of nearly fifteen pounds. Other girls wrapped string around their rings, making the holes smaller to continue to wear them. Claire placed hers in her cosmetics case.

"I just got off a shift. I hadn't put it back on yet. I can't wear it in the hospital."

"Hmm…" Bill raised his eyebrows and she looked away, afraid he would see her lie. "Let's go for a walk."

Mount Vesuvius hovered in the distance, still spewing smoke from the eruption a few weeks earlier that had been all the talk when they arrived. The smell of sulfur permeated the city. Black-haired children, wearing little more than rags, surrounded them, begging for chocolate and coins. Bill shooed them away and offered his arm to Claire as they walked to the wreckage-laden harbor.

"Have you spoken to your head nurse about returning to the States?"

"No," she whispered.

"I think you should. I expect we'll be taking Rome any day now and we'll be wrapping up the Italian campaign. I know new hospital units with new nursing enlistees are arriving every day. You could easily be replaced. Your father will be relieved to have you home."

Claire could feel her heart beating within her chest and her breath fell short. She looked down at her hand, wrapped in Bill's and felt numb. She stopped and gazed out onto the harbor, the isle of Capri in the distance. Smiling soldiers waved to them from a boat on its way to three days of salvation in Capri.

"Bill, I can't marry you."

He sighed exaggeratedly. "Claire, you said you were going to give this some serious thought. I know you feel some kind of inexplicable loyalty to your unit, but there are wounded soldiers at home that would benefit from your care as much as they would here."

"No, Bill," she whispered.

He turned his back to her. "I told you in my letter I'm willing to wait. And I will. But when we get back to the States, it's going to be your turn to start making some sacrifices. When your tour is over, I need you home. I need you to be there for me, not every Tom, Dick, and Sammy Soldier who needs you. I'm going to be your husband, Claire. I need you to focus on me for once."

"You don't understand."

"I understand perfectly. You chose your father over me and now you're choosing this job over me. But I love you, and I'm willing to forgive that."

"No, Bill. I don't want your forgiveness. I don't want to marry you. Not now, and not back home. I care about you, but I can never marry you."

"There's someone else," he accused.

Claire recognized the look in his eyes as the same look of fury he had shown in Capri. She felt nothing.

"This is not about anyone else."

"That's not exactly a denial, is it? Which soldier have you been fucking? Or have there been many? Maybe you've been nursing a lot more than their wounds."

"I'll mail back your ring."

"Keep it. I don't want it. I don't know who you are anymore, Claire."

He left her standing at the harbor. She didn't cry until she arrived back to the dormitory and lay in her bed, Bonnie stroking her hair.

"I loved him once, Bonnie, I really did. He said such hateful things."

"I know honey, I know. There are thousands of men out there right now who'd give their left leg for a chance with you."

"I don't want any of them."

Ellen opened the door and stood for a moment, taking in the scene.

"Claire, there's someone here to see you."

"He's horrible. It's over. Tell him to leave," Claire sobbed.

"Well, I didn't think you felt that strongly about me," Tom's voice echoed behind Ellen, and he passed her into the room.

"Thanks, Ellen. Hi, Bonnie," he nodded to them. "May I have a couple minutes with Claire?"

"You aren't supposed to be in here," Mary Sue scolded.

"Shut up, Mary Sue," Ellen snapped as she herded her out of the room and shut the door behind them.

"You've been crying?"

He looked at Claire closely for the first time since entering the room.

"No," she sniffed. "Well, yes. What are you doing here? How are you not in Anzio?"

"I'm returning in about three hours. I promised to be back before my next shift. Colonel Blesse agreed to let me go as they were short a doctor on a medical ship transfer to Naples. There was so much I wanted to say before you left, but I never had the chance. I never had the guts. I haven't slept in three days since you left. I needed to see you."

Claire stared at him wide eyed. He shuffled his feet nervously.

"God, I feel like I'm sixteen years old. Claire, you can't marry Bill."

"I'm not."

Tom opened his mouth to argue with her, then the realization of what she said crossed his face.

"What?"

"I'm not marrying Bill. He was here a few minutes ago. I thought you were him at the door. I ended it with him. I don't love him."

"You don't?"

"I was just used to the idea of loving him. It turns out coming here made me figure out what I wanted, and it wasn't Bill."

"You wanted to stay in the Army."

"No. Well, yes. I finally feel like I'm somebody, like I'm doing something real with my life. But that's not what I mean."

"What do you mean?"

Claire shook her head and hot tears rolled onto her olive skirt. She couldn't risk the humiliation. Tom sat down next to her and took her hand.

"I don't have a lot of time but if I don't say what I came here to say, I'll regret it forever. Although, it's even more likely I'm going to regret it forever after I say it. But I can't let one more day go by. I requested my assignment to Anzio. I wanted to be near you, Claire. When you came to me last year to tell me you were joining the Army and leaving Minnesota, it ripped me apart. I wanted more than anything to stop you. But I couldn't. I just wanted you to be happy. Every letter I received from you was like a hole in my heart. Every profession of your love for Bill was like a gunshot wound. Claire, I love you. I've loved you since those dinners in Minneapolis where we argued for hours. In Minnesota, I fought it. My marriage was falling apart, you were with Bill. I thought it was a fleeting attraction. But with every letter, I loved you more."

He was quiet for a moment, his hand still gripping hers. "I'm sorry to throw this at you, Claire. I didn't know if I'd get another chance. I needed you to know before you married Bill, before I died in an Anzio firestorm. I think of you every day. When I got to Anzio, I thought maybe things with you and Bill had ended. I thought I had a chance. Then I saw his ring. After that, I tried to stay away. It hurt. I'm such a fool."

Claire opened her mouth to speak but couldn't find the words. The air in the room felt light, she couldn't catch her breath. After a long silence, Tom rose from the bed. Sweat dripped off his brow and he wiped it with the back of his hand. He turned toward the door. Claire jumped up,

"Tom, wait."

She stepped forward and took his hands.

"I didn't speak before because I don't have words to express how I'm feeling. What I discovered I wanted when I came here was you. I love you, Tom. I think I've always loved you."

Tom bent down and kissed her tear-stained cheek and his lips found hers. When they parted, she pulled away.

"But, Tom, what about Ava? What about your understanding?"

"Ava and I did have an understanding when I left. She understood that I loved you."

He kissed her again and whispered,

"Marry me, Claire".

She buried her face in his shoulder and shook her head.

"I won't leave the Army, Tom. I may never leave the Army."

He smiled. "I would never ask you to."

"Yes, Tom, I'll marry you."

He leaned down to her then stopped suddenly.

"I don't have a ring for you."

She laughed. "I don't need a ring. What would I do with a ring? I have everything I need."

A knock startled them from their embrace. Bonnie poked her head in the door and Tom and Claire stepped apart.

"I'm sorry. I don't know what I'm interrupting, but Claire, Major Beck wants all the nurses back to the hospital. The 57th has been overloaded with two ships from Anzio and casualties from Salerno are pouring in at the same time. All nurses need to report to triage. Sorry, Dr. Parker."

Tom pulled Claire back to him.
"Here we go," she whispered.
"Yes, my love, here we go."
With a final, lingering kiss, they raced out the door.

# Katelyn
## Minneapolis, Minnesota
## September 2014

Katelyn tossed Jake a beer and sat down beside him under the umbrella. Smoked poured off the grill across the lawn as her grandfathers argued about the state of the burgers.

"Should I go help them?" Jake asked.

"Not if you value your sanity," Katelyn laughed. "They take their grilling seriously. They'll rattle on about it for hours, even in the middle of winter when neither of them has been near a grill in months. And just wait for the Thanksgiving dinner conversation. We no longer let either of them carve the turkey."

"So does that mean I'm invited to Thanksgiving?"

"We'll see how you go over with my family first. Let's give it a few hours," she teased.

Jake opened his beer and took a drink, studying the two men at the grill.

"So, the one in the blue shirt, his father was a Nazi? I can't believe it."

"Yes. That's my dad's dad, Grandpa Andy. His mother and stepfather didn't even tell him about his real father until he was a teenager. They moved from Germany to Minnesota after the war and never told him anything about their past. After he found out, he was ashamed of it for years. But Grandpa Andy never even knew his father. Rumor has it, he escaped to South America before Grandpa Andy was born.

"Grandpa Adam, the one waving the tongs, is my mom's father. His parents were killed by the Nazis. When my dad proposed to my mom, Grandpa Andy was terrified of how her family would react to her marrying the grandson of a Nazi, but my Grandpa Adam took him aside and they had a long talk. Since then, they're inseparable and like nothing better than getting together to debate chicken rub versus barbeque sauce."

"So, the grandson of a Nazi married a Jewish girl? There's something beautiful about that."

Jake raised his beer and they clicked their bottles together.

Busy setting paper plates on the picnic table, Katelyn's mother turned at the sound of the glass clinking. She paused to readjust the clip in her sleek, black hair and smiled at the couple. It was Katelyn's smile. Jake studied her.

"OK, let me figure this out. Your Mom is both Jewish and Korean, so Adam must have married Min-He's daughter. How on Earth did they all end up in Minnesota?"

"After Aron found Adam, they stayed in refugee camps until they got a visa to America. Min-He married an American soldier during the Korean War and moved to Minnesota with him. Their daughter Hannah met Adam in New York, where she was studying violin, and he was her instructor. They married, had my mom, and moved back here to be closer to my Great-Grandma Minnie. They both played for years in the Minnesota Orchestra."

"And what about your dad's parents?"

"After the war, Claire and Tom stayed in Europe and worked in hospitals with refugees and concentration camp survivors. They moved home to Minneapolis when she became pregnant with my grandma, Marie. When Marianne and Andreas left Germany, they moved to Minnesota where his brother lived. They raised my Grandpa Andy and the other children here. Twenty years later, Andy married Marie and they had my dad."

"So, those four women in the war, your great-grandmothers, all their histories come together with you."

"It's a lot of pressure, isn't it?" Katelyn laughed.

As Jake leaned in to kiss her cheek, the screen door of the house flung open, and Katelyn's father walked down the short steps propping open the door. He reached out his hand as a white-haired woman with a cane slowly descended the steps.

The old woman eased into a lawn chair, her thin hair flowing across her shoulders, her dark eyes meeting Katelyn's from across the patio. She raised a paper-thin hand in greeting.

"There she is," Katelyn said, "Come meet her. She's remarkable."

Jake rose and followed her to the elderly woman's chair. As Katelyn bent down to kiss her great-grandmother, the woman's straight white strands were a stark contrast to Katelyn's pitch-black hair that once so nearly matched Min-He's own. Min-He placed her hand on Katelyn's cheek, seeing nothing else around her but her great-granddaughter, her legacy.

"Nana, I'd like you to meet Jake." Katelyn said. She bent in closer and loudly whispered, "He's the one I was telling you about."

Min-He gestured for Jake to sit next to her. Katelyn playfully rolled her eyes as Min-He began to regale him with stories detailing the perfection of her only great-grandchild.

Katelyn scanned the backyard. Grandpa Andy and Grandpa Adam at the grill, Katelyn's father poking at the fire pit, her mother shooing flies off the potato salad and gossiping with Grandma Hannah while preparing Min-He a plate. She was proud of her family. Proud of this legacy given to her by the strength and courage of her great-grandmother's lives that intertwined and intersected, culminating with her. She smiled at Jake, rapt in attention to Great-Grandma Min-He, and she couldn't wait to continue the story.

**Kelly Comiskey**

Kelly Comiskey's career as a writer began as a child but she decided to write her first novel after reading too many books she wished she had written. She is an avid reader, with a special affection for historical fiction and young adult dystopian novels. With a passion for genealogy and travel, she never passes up the chance to combine the two. Her interest in World War II and the Holocaust and her travels to memorials in Poland, the Czech Republic, and Germany inspired her novel, Unwavering Branches. Kelly lives in Des Moines, Iowa with her husband and two sons.

www.ingramcontent.com/pod-product-compliance
Lightning Source LLC
Chambersburg PA
CBHW022021310726
48972CB00006B/1756